Soul Catcher

By Allan Dennis Rivard de Lacoursiere

Dedicated to my Little Junebug.
I see the girl you were, the woman you are, and the mother you will become.... Have a little faith and be true to yourself. I'm always just two steps behind....

SOUL CATCHER

By
Allan Lacoursiere

Copyright © 2011
ISBN 978-09868847-0-2

Prologue

Legends. Legends speak of many things. By the time a moment becomes legend it is coached in hyperbole and turns of phrases that have long since lost their significance to the current generation.

One such legend from the Judeo-Christian tradition speaks of a war in heaven - a war between two hosts of angels. The Choirs of Heaven led by the Archangel Michael battled the Legions of Hsatan for supremacy of everything, and when the war had ended the Fallen Ones were cast from Heaven.

Medieval legends tell of the one hundred and forty-four choirs of Heaven- it seldom speaks of the one hundred and forty-four races of daemons in the battles of Hell. Nor does any text still extant speak fully of the dominions of the four horsemen of the Apocalypse, the commanders of the four battles.

History seldom speaks of the defeated.

Only fragments… and some merely phrases mentioned in other scraps of parchment like the crumbs of a once sumptuous feast. Here is all we now know:

Numerous texts, often mistaken for fiction by mainstream scholars, speak of the accursed one: the many flavours of the lycanthrope, bitten by a tormentor daemon to become the prey for others of its kind. Amongst these came the Vampyre, infected by the bite of a seducer daemon, those who rise with the night to spread their pestilence amongst mortals.

Even with daemons there are the accursed amongst the cursed. The Succubus, the progeny of an angel who joined the Fallen One's armies for love – cursed by Hsatan or perhaps God to forever consume the souls of their beloved - are amongst these.

Where there is competition, there is strife. This is as true in the world of Daemons as it is in the world of Mankind. The Vampyre lives of the blood of his victims- the blood where the ancients believed a part of the soul resides. The Vampyria - imperfect hunters. Another, darker harvester of souls haunts the night. Even the Vampyre must fear her bite. In an eternal cycle – when the Succubus numbers rise the Vampyres fall, and when they dwindle, the Vampyre rules the night.

To live in safety the Vampyre must strike the daemonness in numbers. They must find her when she is weakest, at the moment she takes corporeal form, before she has fed. Year by year the flights of Vampyres have hunted throughout the ages, until now only one of their ancient enemies survives.

Soul Catcher

Jean Claude stared at the words he had just typed, and then ripped the page from the typewriter and tore it in two. Again. He must start again……

Chapter 1

The alley was cold and damp. She woke to a world of pain. Six assassins had found her moments after her rebirth, when she was the most vulnerable. Blood seeped from a dozen places where shattered bones pierced her skin, and her breath came in a hissing rattle as she clung to consciousness. The pain of a fractured skull muddled her thoughts, and while instinct spoke of a need, the nature of that need eluded her awareness. A life that had spanned thousands of years was scarce heart beats from its end.

Jean-Claude Beaucour looked up from his thoughts. He often lost himself in reminiscence and musings, wandering away from his current surroundings to some twisted corner of his mind, where a troubling bit of research or random theory lay in wait for him. Much of his waking world lay deep within his mind, where few men could travel, and fewer would care to. Esoteric philosophies held little interest to the popular culture, obsessed as it was with frenetic music, sex, and other forms of immediate gratification. Still, for a rare few, it held the same excitement as a rock concert – and to fewer still, all the drama of a life and death struggle.

It was a bad place to lose track of his surroundings. This neighbourhood made him feel uncomfortable this late at night – like a courtesan, it changed its face so suddenly after dark. A transplant from Quebec, he volunteered at a youth centre in the Bronx twice a week. It was a street scene straight out of a movie – buried in a sea of litter and graffiti, broken bottles and broken lives on every corner, and dealers of flesh and drugs hiding in its dark niches. The street lamps, both of them, had been broken for so long he no longer remembered them casting any light, and the darkness hid a multiple of sins. And not everything in the night was human.

Thin to the point of gauntness, his sweater-vests and bowties often left him a target of the older kids. Violence was against his beliefs. A monk did not go around beating on children, even if they were bigger than him and tended to carry razor blades and knives. Jean Claude was anxious to reach the relative safety of his car.

His car was a yellow Pinto whose colour was lost beneath a storm of rust. He never worried about parking it on the street – the kids said it was too much of a piece of shit to steal. But it was reliable. It started on the first turn of its ignition every time, carrying him across New York City to this impoverished neighbourhood twice a week, and every day to the elementary school where he taught a kindergarten class.

Half-way across the street he spotted the crumpled form in the mouth of the alleyway. Even from here he could see it was a young girl. Moving into a jog, he rushed to her side, oblivious to the dangers that may still lurk in the alley. Dropping heavily to the sidewalk, he felt for a pulse. It was there. Very weak and faint. He made a hasty decision, knowing that by the time an ambulance made it to this neighbourhood – a neighbourhood dangerous even to EMS personnel – it would no longer matter.

She felt him there. Instinctively she began to feed on a soul as meek as she was weak.   He was no Caesar or Mahatma Gandhi, but she clung to him, knowing he was her only hope for survival.

Jean-Claude felt the world jump as he stood with the girl in his arms. `Merd! Is she the one the Church is searching for?' He thought he recognized the sensation - or was it just age and a fear-laced moment? Yes, he knew the sensation. Head spinning, world whirling by like water circling a drain, vision blurred into a confused kaleidoscope. Two things in life made him feel this way, a life and death struggle, and the terror of coming face to face with a demon. In his work as one of the Church's few recognized exorcists he often dealt with matters that were not written in History books and that were ignored by science - matters as real and tragic as any natural disaster.

Fighting his dizziness, he crossed to his car, unlocking the passenger door and placing her gently inside. He was born and raised in Montreal, where despite the claims of the owners' manual, a general belief was held that a car came equipped with only two pedals – the gas and the clutch. The third pedal was for the *Anglais*, who knew nothing of driving. He had no time for such thoughts as he used his emergency break to drift around a corner ahead of a light. Driving in a city full of English required all his concentration. He began the sixteen block Baja to the hospital that, had the girl been awake, would have stopped her heart.

His car squealed to a halt in front of the hospital emergency doors. Excited cries in French rose above the chaos, drawing eyes towards him. Jumping out of the car, the doors left open and keys still in the ignition, he grabbed the injured girl and raced inside. Just another Saturday night in the Bronx.

She was so cold. So very cold. She could feel his warmth from a very great distance and desperately drew it into her. Again she fed.

When the triage nurse saw the man in the bloody shirt run through the doors with a broken girl in his arms, she reacted immediately. A team lifted the patient onto a gurney, a doctor materializing from nowhere to yell instructions that seemed to be all stats and CCs, a dizzying maze of medical jargon and initials that enveloped the two and quickly separating them. As the girl, a stranger, disappeared into the depth of the emergency room, an admitting nurse corralled Jean-Claude and drew him to the counter.

"Are you hurt?"

"Quoi?" He muttered, looking up. "No."

"What is the girl's name?" The nurse asked, drawing his focus back to the here and now.

"I do not know," Jean Claude replied, distracted. "A white

girl in a neighbourhood predominantly Hispanic and Black – a runaway perhaps?"

"What happened to the girl? A car accident?" The nurse asked. The man was rambling, and had a slight accent of some sort. "How was the girl hurt?"

"I don't know," Jean-Claude's breathing became erratic, and he reached inside his pocket for his puffer. "I found her outside Saint Vincent's Youth Centre. Perhaps she was mugged? Or beaten by the pimp?"

"So, no insurance then?" The nurse checked the box for `no known medical history' and for `no insurance'.

"I will pay for her bills, no?" Jean-Claude insisted. "Do I need to pay now? A cheque, maybe cash?"

"No, not now," the nurse replied gently. "Let me take your contact information. You do realize that we are talking about thousands of dollars?" There were many would-be benefactors who did not realize how expensive a hospital stay could be.

"It is nothing" Jean-Claude shrugged it off. "I have money, what is the English expression? I am comfortable."

The nurse's questions faded into the background. Is this girl the one? No, it was too early. Definitely a demon kit, though, there could be no denying that. But if she was not the one, who had tried to kill her at the moment of her incarnation? Was the Brotherhood dealing with another group of renegades? The last group of vigilantes they had had to deal with was back in the seventies, in a place called Jonestown, and that had ended in the deaths of nine hundred and eighteen people, many of them innocents caught up in something they could not understand. God, it could not be. Not now. Not with so much on his plate already.

Every violent injury automatically triggered a call to the police. It was not only the law, but hospital policy. Shortly after he had filled out the admittance forms, and had just turned to await the results of the emergency surgery, two police officers came to talk to Jean-Claude. Led by the admitting officer, an officer stationed in the emergency ward for just such circumstances, the two confronted him by a coffee machine, where he was standing to avoid the overcrowded waiting room. Sick people made him nervous.

"Mister?"

"Beaucour."

"I understand you brought in the Jane Doe?" The officer asked brusquely. "May I ask what you were doing in that neighbourhood? I mean a white guy in that district at that time of night, it doesn't look good."

"I vol-volunteer at the Saint V-v-vincent Youth Centre," he stammered through another asthma attack. He reached for his puffer.

"Hey!" The officer grabbed his hand, holding it away from what he thought was a weapon.

Slapping his hand away, the admitting nurse beat him to it. "It's his inhaler. Can't you see the man has asthma?"

She was a short woman. Built low and solid, she displayed that New York toughness that would make a junk yard dog back down. In this neighbourhood, in this hospital, she needed to be that tough. He was a New York street cop, but he was no match for her.

"Sorry, for Christ - sorry." The officer backed down. The man in front of him really was too scrawny to have beaten someone like this. "So, tell me, how did you find the girl?"

"She was lying on the sidewalk by my car," Jean-Claude explained. "It is, how do you say, kitty-corner from the youth centre."

"The one several blocks from here? And you park your car there?" The officer asked, incredulously. He knew the street. The kids in that neighbourhood would strip a skateboard if it slowed down enough. He was beginning to doubt the man's story.

"It is, what do the kids say?" Jean-Claude admitted. "A piece of shit."

"Is that your car out front?" The other officer asked.

"Merd!" Jean-Claude swore. "I apologize. In the excitement I forgot to move it!"

"If you give me the keys," the second officer continued, "I will park it for you."

The officer was calculating, weighing the opportunity to search the vehicle against a complaint for illegal search and seizure. He would risk it. Jean-Claude looked for his keys, and, realizing he must have forgotten them in the ignition, shrugged in apology. He was just happy the officer was so helpful and not looking to issue a citation. He had enough of them to deal with.

"And so you took it upon yourself to bring her to the hospital?"

"The ambulances," Jean-Claude shrugged. "They will not come so fast to that neighbourhood."

"And what do you think she was doing there?" He asked, trying to trip the foreign prick up.

"White girl in that neighbourhood," Jean-Claude shrugged again. "Maybe a crack whore? We see that at the centre from time to time. Runaways."

The other officer returned and whispered, "blood all over the front passenger seat, otherwise clean as a whistle. Too clean."

"My partner says there's blood all over the seat in your car," the first officer offered as idle conversation. "Blood can be difficult to clean."

"Perhaps Jamal's father can clean it," Jean-Claude mused. He really wasn't too interested. He really wasn't too interested. It couldn't be helped after all. All he really wanted now was for these two to go away to give him time to think. He could not know if she was the girl they were searching for until he could determine whether she possessed the Wiccan sacred item given to her centuries ago. What was a few blood stains compared to the end of a search that had spanned two centuries?

"Who's Jamal?"

"From the centre," Jean-Claude supplied. "I taught him basketball, and he got a scholarship to college. His father is so happy he cleans my car twice a month."

"I see," the officer wrote down Jean-Claude's vitals, and concluded the interview. "Okay, Mr. Beaucour, we'll be in touch."

"Merci."

Why the hell did he ask for mercy? The cop wondered as he walked away. These foreigners should really learn to speak English if they were going to live here, especially if they planned to start lying to a cop. And he was pretty sure the man was lying about something.

Jean-Claude wandered over to the admitting nurse, bringing her a coffee to thank her for helping out. How was he to find out the one thing he must at all costs know? It was so hard to think here. After having had his soul leeched twice, the assault of noise and motion now raping his senses left him feeling dizzy and nauseous. Jean-Claude realized that if he did not seek April's help immediately his own health would be at risk, but he suspected he was the girl's only friend in this world.

"It has been a long time," he said with a weary sigh. "This is not a good thing, no?"

"No." The nurse replied. "She's in the best hands in the city. They may not make the money those big shots do at the other hospitals, but no-one treats more trauma injuries. If she has any kind of a chance, Doctor Gilmore is it."

"That is good," Jean-Claude nodded. "I would like to ask her for her name."

Two hours later he was dosing by the coffee machine when a doctor in bloody scrubs came up to the admitting nurse. Pointing him out, she led the doctor across the emergency room.

"Mr. Beaucour?"

"Oui."

"I'm Doctor Gilmore. I'm the surgeon. Your friend is out

of surgery and is in stable condition for now. She's a very sick little girl, and is going to need a lot of care." The doctor paused, holding out a crystal figurine of a raven. "This is all we found on her. Do you have any idea who she might be?"

The Crystal Raven, the most ancient Wiccan relic still in existence, given by the Church to its Succubus ally during the Long Night of the Vampire. Jean-Claude recognized the object, but said nothing of it. "No, I'm afraid not. Perhaps we might call her Crystal Raven until she can tell us her name, no?"

"It's better than Jane Doe," the surgeon smiled.

"May I see her?"

The doctor frowned. "We'll be settling her into a room soon; you can go up then. She has a lot of broken bones, and required surgery. There's not a lot to see past the casts and the bandages."

"I understand," Jean-Claude nodded. "I will just let her know she is not alone. Sometimes, this is important, no?"

"Yes."

It was another ninety minutes of quiet worry before they had the girl settled into a room. Secrecy and concern saw Jean-Claude arrange to move her into a private room, giving a credit card as security – and even leaving this much of a record kicked up his ulcer. Tomorrow he would come and pay her medical expenses, already approaching ten thousand dollars, but he would pay that in cash if he could. Health Care bills here in the US often caused more trauma than the initial illness, and he understood little of the mystical working of his HMO, although his union did provide an acolyte who was steeped in this occult science. As a citizen of Quebec, he was still covered under the province's Health Care system. Between the two he could afford any type emergency. But which one would cover the exorcism he may still yet need?

The Brotherhood abhorred paperwork. There were no official records of the organization – no membership lists or organizational charts, no budgets or operational orders.

Knowledge of their existence was on a need to know basis, and that knowledge was kept strictly to an oral tradition since its founding. Even their archives, seven sets, kept in seven different locations - each moved periodically- contained not the slightest hint of their existence. Situations like this, in this age of instant communication, were becoming increasingly difficult to contain. What to do about this girl?

His first sight of her stopped him cold. This little stranger lying in a hospital bed, only one blue eye and a hand not covered in bandages and casts - he could feel her tugging at the edges of his soul. Was she the succubus they were searching for or some other kind of demon sent to eliminate him? The consequences of the decision of a long ago pope were a gathering storm on the near horizon, time was running short, and if this was the savior they were all waiting for the Church and all humanity faced dark days ahead.

She sensed him then as he took up her one unbroken hand. A gentle wave of concern washed over her, and she fed on it as if it were the water of life. She was weak and vulnerable, and had never felt so frightened in all her long existence. Yet she clung to life, clung to the hope – to this slim anchor her unknown rescuer offered. She did not remember her name, or anything of her past, but as she slipped into a peaceful sleep she knew this man was her future.

It had been a long day. As he sat at her bedside, holding her hand gently in his own, he fell into a dreamless sleep. Throughout the night he could feel the connection between them. Despite all his training, exhaustion and worry were leaving him easy prey – trust and demons was a volatile mix that led to the eternal fires of damnation. How many times had he preached this same thing to new recruits to the Brotherhood? Practice was a hardship in a seductive world where dreams and reality collided, and a soul was a mere concept in a dusty metaphysics book in an equally dry classroom. Yet, even knowing all this, he could not bring himself to pull away from the girl and her palpable need for human contact.

The hospital staff left the pair alone, too harried and overworked to bother with one more old man sleeping where he did not belong. Most had found worse in a patient's room, and one overwrought parent keeping vigil at the bedside of a daughter no-one expected to survive earned more pity than anything else. Finally, a nurse, coming on to do her rounds, woke him from his sleep and chased him from the room. It was fifteen minutes before he was due to begin teaching his class, and, realizing he could not make his shift, Jean-Claude went off to find a telephone and phone in. Someone would need to cover his class for today – and probably longer.

After he had called in to arrange for some time off, Jean-Claude made his way out of the hospital and headed towards his home for a shower and a change of clothes. Amazingly, he had survived the night, and he was not sure if that meant any more than that the demon's host was too damaged to finish him off. At his apartment he made a quick, second call to his lawyer – a man still in Quebec, but who was licensed to practice in New York as well. Jean-Claude started the process to have himself declared her guardian until her parents were found. There would be none. And they could not have a demon child loose in the foster system. That was one disaster he did not wish to contemplate, at least not before breakfast.

On the way back to the hospital he stopped at a diner for breakfast. April Moonshadow, a neighbour, and mother of a young girl about the same age as Crystal, was its owner/operator. A Wiccan steeped in the true traditions of the Covens, she too was an initiate of the Brotherhood – one they had come to rely on to heal the unseen damage inflicted during their operations. She fixed him a plate of bacon and eggs, then poured herself a cup of coffee and joined him. A strict vegetarian, she had inherited the business from her parents, and had not bothered to change the menu, or to try attract a different clientele. The diner with its working class patrons, and the memories of her mother and father that lingered in every corner and niche, suited her fine just the way it always had been.

"You were not home last night?" She questioned archly. "A girl?"

"Oui." Jean-Claude replied between bites. "She is in the hospital."

April raised an eyebrow. 'And you should be too,' she thought, reading the signs in his eyes and the gray pallor of his skin. She fished out a crystal from a black velvet bag she wore around her neck.

"A runaway…?" Jean-Claude explained, accepting the crystal with a crooked grin. The energy it contained would help revive him quicker than a day long dance with caffeine. "I found her in the alley by the centre, badly beaten."

"I see," April replied. "How old is this waif?"

"About as old as Gwen, no?" Jean-Claude speculated. "Much trouble in her future, I think."

"Much." April replied with a smile.

"I will need to bring girl things to her," Jean-Claude frowned at April over his coffee.

"I see." April nodded. "I can help with that. Do you know her size?"

"About Gwen's size," Jean-Claude shrugged.

"What hospital is she at?" April laughed. "I'll come see for myself."

Much relieved, Jean-Claude finished his breakfast before making his way back to the hospital. Women's undergarments were more of a mystery to him than the obscurest denizen of the Stygian depth, and he would rather face a trio of vampyre assassins naked than the women's hygiene section of the local drug store. One never knew where his work with the Brotherhood would lead him, and somehow he suspected this waif would carry him to places he'd never pictured himself visiting in this lifetime. What was a monk to do with a child, any child, let alone a three thousand year old woman in a girl's body?

He arrived at her hospital room to find Doctor Gilmore just finishing his rounds. He was asked to step out for a moment, left alone with his worries while the nurse and doctor finished up their examination. And then the doctor joined him.

"Your friend has made a remarkable rally over night," the doctor enthused.

"This is good?" Jean-Claude replied, asking. "How long does she need to be in the hospital?"

"At least six weeks," the doctor warned. "She is still a very hurt little girl."

"I see," he nodded in agreement. "My friend will come and bring some things. What will she need?"

"I'll make you a list," the nurse offered.

Jean-Claude sat through the day at the girl's bedside, reading an ancient tome in some long dead language. His reading suffered from his preoccupation with the girl and what her presence here might mean, unable to keep his mind from picking at a scab made up of possibilities and fear. So much rested on his finding the one demon before another found him that he could no longer trust anything, even his own instincts that had kept him alive through four decades of hunting and studying her kind. Was she the one? Or had the demon lords who began all this placed her here as part of some wider scheme not even he could see through? From time to time he spoke to her, hoping for some sign as he spun a tale from one of her possible lifetimes, his face set in a mask of worry and confusion that made him look all the more older.

April and Gwen found them like this when they arrived early that evening. As like as two peas in a pod, both sported long blonde hair, straight and not dyed, laughing blue eyes and gentle, ready smiles. They were earthy and unpretentious, and enjoyed an easy-going, practical nature. While Gwen took his place holding the girl's hand, and introducing herself with an ease and glibness that one would think they were meeting under normal circumstances, the two adults stepped back to talk.

"She'll be one size smaller than Gwen on the pants," April suggested. "It's hard to see with the top through all that plaster. A nightgown might be easier to manage."

"The nurse," Jean-Claude offered, "She made a list."

April studied the list. She frowned. "Most of this can wait for a while. How long is she going to be here?"

"Six weeks," Jean-Claude shrugged.

"That will run quite a pretty penny," April warned.

"There is money."

"When the majority of these casts come off," April offered, frowning at the drugs listed on the girl's chart, "she would be better off at home with us."

April was a holistic healer, and she did not agree with modern medicine's dependence on chemicals. She reached into her purse and withdrew a black silk pouch, undoing its drawstring with long, slender fingers. She upended the bag and an amulet made from a blood-red crystal slid out. Prepared in a blessing ceremony, it held the natural healing patterns of the earth. She carefully placed it around the girl's neck with the help of her daughter. The three of them said a quick prayer.

"What is she?" Gwen asked suddenly.

"A very sick little girl," Jean-Claude replied with a gentle smile.

"I know you know what I mean," Gwen pouted. Why did the always treat her like a child? She was sixteen, not a little baby anymore. Nor was she without talents of her own. She could see Crystal's aura was ancient, shot through with black veins that pulsed in time to her own heart beat. She was something, right? Wasn't what all that training was about, because Gwen could see people's true selves?

"You will be staying at the hospital again?" April asked, changing the subject.

"Oui." Jean-Claude asked. "Did you bring it?"

April handed him a rosary with a large wooded crucifix that came down to a sharp point at the bottom. The prayer beads were made of several rare woods and semi-precious stones all linked together with pure silver settings. It was gaudy and bulky, and incredibly ancient. Anyone looking in would see a very religious man praying for his injured daughter. Things were not always what they seemed, and while he was indeed praying, he was also keeping a vigil.

Chapter 2

The hour was growing late. Jean-Claude's eyes were gritty from staring at pages filled with archaic Latin, Hebrew and Sumerian, searching for some clue that may never have been written, and if written, long since destroyed in some ancient natural disaster or war. Demons could be as much trickster as seductress. Not all traps were baited with honey, and hope could be as much a betrayer as your basest desire. Looking at the shattered girl who was lying less than a foot away, Jean-Claude wondered if he could trust the fallibility of his own emotions with so much at stake. Was it his own heart telling him to love her, the pheromone storm she instinctively released whenever she felt threatened, or the connection that now lay between her souls?

The decision was his to make and the weight of its consequences bore down on his thoughts like the gravitational pull of a black hole. If only his soul was all that was at stake it would be so much easier.

Even in the metaphysical world that so few stilled believed in everything was not black and white. Not all angels were good, nor were all demons evil. It was a puzzle he could not solve without more information, and perhaps more wisdom than he possessed. He had been up all day and most of the night, pouring over a large volume as he sat at the girl's bedside, and had still not found the passage he wanted. Jean-Claude remembered coming across the paragraph ten or fifteen years ago when he had first read this text in a fevered rush during a hurried trip to confront another crisis. A fragment, a vague recollection as were so many of his memories these days. This demon business was a young man's game and he had left his prime a good decade ago, back in those foggy days before he woke each morning groggy with stiff joints, and found his bed each night with a tension headache and eye strain. Now, without rereading that passage, he could not make the decision whether to let her live or send her back to Hell from where she had come.

Decades of studying bleary tomes like this had ruined his eyes, and he now wore a thick pair of glasses for more than just reading. They had a frustrating habit of sliding down the bridge of his nose. Just now, as he stumbled upon a familiar paragraph, they slipped down and blocked his view. Annoyed, he lifted his hand to fix them and found the girl would not release it. It would be a hard decision, one he did not know if he was emotionally equipped to make.

Pushing up his glasses with a shoulder, he returned to his reading. His eyes quickly scanned the page and found the familiar words. He read:

In that time before time, in the dawn of creation when only the Heavens and the choirs of angels existed, the Dark One arose. With him came creation's first love story, a tragedy that unfolded during the height of the celestial war. He was a powerful dark angel, strong and proud, and dedicated to the path of Hsatan; she was a minor singer in the middle choir – torn between her love and her morality.

Choosing love, she condemned her immortal soul for all eternity. Cursed for this betrayal, Hrathgar became her first victim, his soul consumed during the act of love, and their children - all daughters – became a race of demons destined for a life of heartache and torment.

He paused in his reading to rest his eyes. Dozens of origin myths and no clear truth, this was the crux of his dilemma, a Sword of Damocles hanging over his head with moral pitfalls on every side, and more than one interested party looking to trip him up – including several factions within his own

Brotherhood . Femme Fatale or tragic victim, a black widow spider always luring her victims to their doom, or praying mantis condemned to consume her mate in a never ending pattern of love and death. Without knowledge of her true origin there could be no understanding the demon's motivations or her character – and that character would play a crucial role in the days to come.

He returned to his reading:

Heaven hosts twelve choirs of angels with twelve varieties in each choir. Thus twelve times twelve is the number of the angels. One hundred and forty-four varieties of angels reside in heaven, each charged with the care of a portion of heaven.....

Twelve are the number of the battles of hell. Twelve times twelve are the kinds of demons to torment the sons of Eve. One hundred and forty-four are the temptations to mortal sin.

Fragments! Jean-Claude cursed. Nothing but fragments of lost texts! How was he to complete his research without the proper resources? Frustrated to the point of breaking, he picked up his reading further down the page:

Amongst the legions of hell power comes through the harvesting souls, but to protect future creations God limited their ability to take corporeal form to twenty years out of every century. To satiate their unholy hunger during those long years of exile the daemon hosts began to prey on their own. Different species specialized, developing skills to stalk and feed on lesser species. For the Succubus a race of demihumans – the undead known as Vampyres, who feed on portions of mortal souls, called by some pranic energy – provided what they needed to survive. The compulsion to eat is an undeniable impulse – and the vampyre offer the succubi the only opportunity to feed without the soul-crushing tragedy of their natural habits....

"But what is her name?" Jean-Claude complained out loud. "I still do not know who she is, just like you, ma petite!"

"Still talking to your self, I see," an urbane voice asked from the shadows.

Her world was a place of muted pain and distant aches. She swam through a haze of drugged induced euphoria, and still she felt her panic nibbling at the edge of her muddled thoughts. She could not remember where she was, knowing only it was some place she both feared and wanted to be. She could feel him, somewhere beyond the darkness. Slowly she opened her eyes, but only one seemed to be working.

Through the murk she sensed two figures - one she longed for, the second she feared without knowing why.

"Hello, Vlad," Jean-Claude greeted the newcomer.

The third player in this drama strutted into the scene, but was he the jester here to provide comic relief, or the harbinger of doom here to mark this piece a tragedy? A double-edged Puck who could cut both ways?

"It has been a long time, Jean-Claude," Vlad nodded politely. "So, the girl lives..."

"Yes, despite the best efforts of you and your assassins." Jean-Claude shrugged, not budging from his station.

"You know we must finish what we started," Vlad warned.

"And you know I can not allow you to continue in this foolishness," Jean-Claude replied easily. "We must maintain balance in all things if we are to continue."

"I do not care for esoteric debates," Vlad sneered, momentarily losing his composure. "I apologize. We must agree to disagree.""

"If we must."

"She is pretty," Vlad said, looking beyond the casts and bandages – or perhaps commenting on them. "I had forgotten how alluring this one was. She has fed well on the best of your people."

"And on many of yours. It is the nature of the beast, no?" Jean-Claude replied. "All part of His plan."

"And it is your turn now?" Vlad asked sarcastically.

"I think not," Jean-Claude replied calmly. "I am a simple scholar, and times are not what they were."

"Yes," Vlad said, turning. "She is merely a girl."

When the other figure had faded into the darkness, Jean-Claude moved to take up Crystal's hand. "No, mon ami, not merely a girl. And without the clue you just gave me, I would never have been sure who she really is."

Crystal sighed and fell back into a deep sleep, buffered by the warm link of his presence. Fragments of images from her past life floated by in a chaotic kaleidoscope, the name Vlad shaking loose a memory that spun itself into a dream....

She did not dream it, but she knew the back story as only a dreamer could. For centuries it was known and hidden from the general populace, remembered only in that instinctual ancestral dread and the fairy tales that persisted everywhere. Tasked to keep these secrets and to protect mankind and nature from the predations of Hell's minions, an ancient order of men and women hid in the shadows of the Church. Long since folded into its structure, in the thirteen hundreds, in an area known as Transylvania, open warfare broke out between the Church and three European clans of vampyres.

She sat on a dapple grey gelding, overlooking a surreal battle field. For three years the sun had failed to pierce the roiling cloud cover, bathing everything in a perpetual twilight. Taking advantage of this unnatural gloom, the local vampyres had waged a campaign that left behind a charred and bloodied countryside. Thousands had died before the Brotherhood and its allies had turned the tides of battle.

At her side sat a man who was the champion of the church, a local prince known infamously to history as Vlad the Impaler. He sat a large black horse on the crest of a hill, studying a misty valley below. In his burnished chain mail and black cloak lined with the finest English linen dyed a deep red, he cut a chilling figure. Hooded eyes stared out of a face few would call handsome, narrow, with a hawk-like nose – redeemed only by a strong chin and full lips.

She waited on his pleasure, knowing only that she had never been so in love.

"My namesake is close," Vlad announced. "What do you think, my love?"

"Yes, very close." Crystal replied, fingering the crystal raven that

hung around her neck. A love gift, she would cherish it forever.

Her dream eye shifted, and she travelled down to the valley below. In a natural cave wedged deep in the surrounding limestone an ancient vampyre sat on a throne created by a natural rock formation. Centuries of use had worn it smooth. Before him, a dozen vampyres of various ages stood awaiting his pleasure. One young soldier with classic Romanesque features hung back in the shadows, working hard to avoid notice. Luminescent lichen gave the chamber its only light, though none was needed, and lit columns of stone decorated with skulls and rusting weapons from centuries of battles won by their clan. None had stood stronger, and only the curse of sunlight had kept them from ruling all of Europe.

"This battle is lost," the ancient one grated. "It is time to get whoever we can away from here. The clan must survive."

"My lord, if we can but –." One of the others interjected.

"It is lost!" The ancient one snapped. "And I'll tell you what has defeated us. It is that harpy of a lap dog that rides at his side!"

"And what shall we do?" Vlad the Blackheart asked, speaking for the first time. He was the youngest on the clan council, and preferred to listen more than he spoke, biding his time. One day, he knew in his heart, he would rise to rule this clan as it always should have been ruled, and its triumph would be his triumph. Even in this bitter defeat he could taste his ultimate victory.

"Our time has ended," the ancient one hissed. "But yours has just begun. You will take the best of what is left and find a new land. You will make overtures to all the other clans, and together you must find all of her kind and destroy them!"

The Vampyre King reached into a satchel at the side of his throne and removed an ancient papyrus scroll. "Here is all you need to accomplish this deed. Go now, we will make our stand here to buy you the time you need."

Vlad turned, disappearing down a dark corridor. Already he could hear the sounds of battle as the human hunters fought their way into the sanctuary. He vowed as he moved to join the others now fleeing to have his revenge, not only on these humans, but on their immortal allies....

Crystal whimpered in her sleep, and Jean-Claude left off

his reading to gently stroke the side of her face until she settled. He would wait until the day shift started before heading home for a shower and a nap. In a few short hours he and the Moonshadows would return to be on hand when the doctors brought Crystal out of her coma. Until he brought her safe home Jean-Claude would continue to spend his nights at her bedside, his days sleeping and doing research. He would not think about the cruel decision he still had to make, not now, not when her prognosis was so improved the doctors were starting to think they were witnessing a miracle. And definitely not while Vlad showed so much interest in her, even if it still might only be an elaborate ruse to put Jean-Claude off the scent of his real target.

Subterfuge in this three-sided war was a headache that could not only blind, but kill. Jean-Claude often found himself wondering which side he was struggling for when everyone had some objective buried in each and every encounter. And within the three alliances there were multiple factions, each grasping for the merest gossamer strand of advantage or power, the whole fracturing into a corrupted prism of sullied light. At the end of each day Jean-Claude was greeted by a migraine, his emotions blasted from his soul, leaving a dry husk barely able to function as a human. And this particular crisis was just beginning.

A four o'clock low front brought Hurricane Gwen gusting into the building with banging doors, rattling windows, and a panicked herd of schizophrenic elephants stampeding up the stairs. In a few minutes she would storm into his apartment with a non-stop prattle about her day that he would not miss for all the rare manuscripts in the world. But four o'clock came earlier every day. Still groggy, Jean-Claude rose to dress, fitting his glasses on his ears first because without them he could not see beyond the end of his nose. Since she was but a localized rain shower in his kindergarten class, Jean-Claude had taken care of Gwen until her mother got back from the diner at seven. Had it really been twelve years ago? Either she was growing up too fast, or he was rapidly aging – and he wasn't sure which of the two he liked less.

Often April would bring dinner home with her, and the three of them would have a quiet meal together – each replacing a missing family unit in the others' lives. Soon there would be another face around the table, and Jean-Claude could not help wondering what kind of havoc two opposite storm fronts would carry into his life. Contrary to his and April's expectations, who anticipated a rough adjustment period, Gwen was in her words 'stoked' about the prospect. The diminutive Frenchman was curious as to whether her definition of stoked included screaming jags over misappropriated articles of clothing, fits of jealousy, and dark pouty bids for their divided attention?

Nothing legal had yet been ventured and the authorities were barely involved in the case – unsure whether she was a runaway or a missing child whose family was unaware of her injuries. Jean-Claude and April knew differently.

"Did you know that Bobbie-Lynn dyed her hair this atrocious green?" Gwen burst out the second she entered the room.

"Is this good or bad?" Jean-Claude asked.

"Bad, of course," Gwen sighed, exasperated. "You know that Amy wants to dye her hair this wicked green for the Harvest dance."

"Mon Dieu!" Jean-Claude teased. "How could I forget?"

"Oh!" Gwen huffed.

"You will come see Crystal tonight, no?" He probed.

"Of course!"

"And so," Jean-Claude replied pointedly, "you will now complete your homework."

"I don't have any," Gwen protested, huffing as he raised his eyebrows pointedly at her. "Well, almost none. Only a little math."

"Bon." Jean-Claude concluded. "You will be done in no time. And you can finish telling me about Lynn-Bobbie's purple hair as you work."

"It's Bobby-Lynn," Gwen taunted, taking out her homework, "and it's green, you silly little man."

"And green is an improvement over purple, silly little girl?" Jean-Claude teased.

It was good to fall into a familiar routine, something comforting to counter the weight of the stress and worry on his mind. Continuing their banter while she through teenage legerdemain attempted to make twenty math problems appear to be a mere five, and take as long to unravel as three times as many, they passed an enjoyable afternoon together. She was one of the things in his world that made this all worth it, the fights with the Vatican over budgets, the dark, musty under-cellars and sewers, the constant threat from supernatural and natural sources, and the struggle to keep his world a secret from the authorities. No matter where their difficulties took them, Gwen always brought a ray of sunshine and innocence with her, and for that he would love her forever.

At six, early tonight because of their appointment at the hospital, April arrived with three lasagna dinners from her restaurant. One of Gwen's favourite meals, she had saved these servings especially for tonight – pampering her daughter in anticipation of future haunting by green-eyed monsters as two girls battled for their attention and affection.

"Tonight!" Gwen announced with an excited squeal. "We get to find out Crystal's real name. I don't think I can eat a bite, I'm so excited!"

Still protesting her lack of appetite, the vivacious teen ate her serving and portions of both her mother's and Jean-Claude's. With loud lamentations of their inability to afford to feed her, had she truly been hungry, the monk teased and cajoled his two favourite women out to the car. Mother and daughter belted up in anticipation of Jean-Claude's soul-rending odyssey to the hospital, traumatizing both car and passengers as he took the vehicle through a walk way

25

between buildings at sixty, around a corner, and up a series of alleys. He drifted into a parking spot like some character in a movie, and brought the car to a complete stop in one breath.

"I find a good short-cut this time, no?"

"No!" Both women exploded.

After parking, Jean-Claude muttered a familiar litany of complaints against the injustice of their criticism of his driving that carried him and the two women up to a waiting room just down the hall from Crystal's room. The duty nurse explained to them the vagaries of hospital time that left them waiting despite being twenty minutes late themselves. A trap for teenage ennui, the waiting room contained no interesting magazines– nothing about any of the latest rock stars or Hollywood romances – and Gwen was growing bored and anxious to meet the new girl. Or for something to do! Anything! Desperately bored teen here, people, she thought.

At least she knew enough to be properly bored, not like the old farts she had drag along with her. Her mother was studying a treatise on crystals, and Jean-Claude read from some achingly boring ancient tome – but they did really lame stuff like that all the time. It was not like they understood a teenage girl's need for constant stimuli, or how quickly her brain could atrophy from lack of it. It was right up there with lack of oxygen as the number one cause of brain death amongst the young, and she could feel herself rapidly age with each and every tick of the clock on the wall. An old-school, non-digital clock at that!

"You old farts suck," Gwen complained. "Here we are, stuck waiting until some glacier melts or something, and all you to can do is read."

"We did suggest you bring a book," her mother reminded her.

"Who wants to read? Reading is all you two ever do!" She sighed and rolled her eyes.

"And what would you have us do?" Her mother asked speculatively. "Should we sigh and flounce?"

She mimicked her daughter with a twinkle of humour in her eye, sighing and throwing herself about her chair like a rag doll.

"Oh April," Gwen groaned, "you're such a dweeb!"

"She may be right," Jean-Claude observed, setting aside his book. "She does do it with far more panache."

He made his own attempt at mimicking Gwen, and soon had both his companions laughing.

"But certainly I did it with far more panache, no?" He protested just as the doctor walked in.

"I have to agree with the two young ladies," he teased. "Definitely not even close to anything I've ever seen my daughters do."

"Oh well," Jean-Claude shrugged admitting defeat. "There goes my dream of winning an Oscar."

"How is Crystal?" April asked

"She is awake and responsive," the doctor warned, "but does not seem to have recovered all of her memory. She was unable to tell us her name, and still does not know where she is. She does pick up clues from those around her, but we watch for that in cases like this."

"Can we see her?" Gwen asked with her best seductive eyes that never fooled anyone, but were often too cute to say no to.

"Yes," the doctor conceded, "a very short visit. She is still a very sick girl, although I am very pleased with her progress."

The two women gave Jean-Claude a few moments alone with the girl. He moved to her bedside, gently taking her hand in his own as she turned her good eye towards him and smiled weakly. She did not know why, but the man made her feel safe and happy.

"Bonjour," Jean-Claude greeted. "My name is Jean-Claude."

"I-I am," she paused, confused. "Sorry. I don't remember."

"No worries, no?" He replied gently. "May we call you Crystal until you find your name again?"

"Why?"

"It is a pretty name, no – and you are a pretty girl," he could see her blush beneath the gauze. "And because this crystal raven is all we found with you."

"I," Crystal replied, letting him place it in her good hand. "I was afraid I had lost it."

She paused, squeezing his fingers to prevent him from taking his hand away. She could feel the warmth and energy flow between them, felt her hunger rising in response to his presence.

"There are a couple of people I would like you to meet," he soothed. "This is okay, no?"

He rose and signaled for April and Gwen to join him. Gwen brushed past the adults, taking possession of the chair at the bedside and the girl's hand in the same motion.

"Hello," Gwen gushed. "I'm Gwen. You're going to live with us when they let you out of here, and we'll be best friends, and share clothes – and. Oh, you can go to the same school, and maybe we'll be in the same class...."

Crystal did not know what to make of the chattering wren, although she did feel strangely content in her company. There was an instinctive bond between the two, as if they had known each other in past lives – and known each other well. She smiled, exhausted, and closed her eyes. She retained her grip on the other girl's hand, letting Gwen's words wash over her as she slid back towards sleep. She was very tired and very happy, and felt safe for the first time since she woke up in the alley to the pain and the fire.

She cringed in her dreams. Gwen immediately leaned over her, raising a hand towards her brow, but hesitated to touch the bandages.

"It's okay Crystal," Gwen breathed. "Mom and Jean-Claude won't let anything happen to you."

Chapter 3

The daily plunge into the cesspool of human misery, the vicious divorces, the hurt and confused children, and the unrelieved cruelty had long since bleached the idealism from his bones. He had been a sitting judge in New York Family Court for almost thirty years. Many times over the last ten Judge Michael McConnelly had thought about retiring, but never more so than today. And then the `Baby Jade' case – as the media had dubbed the scandal currently rocking the court – had thundered onto his docket.

A colleague had mistakenly ordered the girl returned to her parents – the son of a long time friend and supporter, and his socialite wife. Now she lay in a hospital bed, a withered shell destined to spend her remaining days on this mortal coil as a vegetable – if she lived out the week. Not the `nanny abuse' case it appeared on the surface, the stench of patronage had the press pounced onto the story like a hound on a blood trail. The nanny, an illegal Philippine woman disappeared by the INS before the investigation could generate charges, had been telling the truth all along – the father was the abuser. Why hadn't Jensen just recused himself? That stupid bastard!

It was a cluster-fuck. A tangled skein of shadowy dealing and ' old boy' network back-slapping, it had exploded in his hands. McConnelly shoved the paperwork from the case aside, disgusted with the futility of it all. He sat in his large office, one of the few perks of having survived on the bench for almost three decades and rising to the rank of supervising judge, staring at his pride wall. Dozens of pictures of him and various minor celebrities from the city, plaques and certificates – a fractured monument to his failure to make any real difference in the broken lives he ground through the grist mill of justice. Were all those years of campaigning worth this? Another day of sending neglected children and crack-babies into an over-burdened foster care service. Another day of wasted live, of saving no one, of accomplishing nothing. God pray it was his last.

He was just reaching for the imported bottle of Irish whiskey that he kept in the top drawer of his desk when the telephone rang. It was his private line.

"Hello?" He answered, a little annoyed despite welcoming the interruption.

The Bishop was on the other line. The two men went back nearly six decades to those shadowy days when they were both boys in a mostly Catholic neighbourhood. Childhood pals, they had kept in touch over the years and spoke together at least once a week, usually on Saturday nights.

"Your Grace," Judge McConnelly replied. It wasn't Saturday night, and he knew at once this was not a social call.

"Sorry to disturb you at work, Michael," Bishop O'Malley replied. "I have a bit of a situation here, and the Church needs your assistance.

"You know you can always count on me, Brian," the judge replied. "How much a plate is this one?"

"I'm afraid I need your professional services, Michael," the bishop returned. "If it wasn't so important to the Church, you know I would never ask."

Besides the many nuisance suits any property owner faced in a large city – falls on stairs, or slips on icy sidewalks – the only legal issue the church face these days was the thorny issue with sexual abuse amongst priests. Michael frowned. He really did not want to get involved in anything this controversial, not on top of what was already staring up at him from his plate like cold, runny eggs and shrivelled day-old bacon.

"I'm just a family court judge," he hedged.

"I would never ask you to do anything unethical, Michael," the bishop reassured his friend. "It's not in either one of our job descriptions. There was a little girl beaten half to death, the one found by the school teacher. Did you read about it?"

"I seem to remember something about it," the judge admitted.

"The girl has special needs," Bishop O'Malley continued cautiously. "Special protection only the Church could provide. As long as she remains on sacred ground those who put her in the hospital cannot hurt her again."

McConnelly was dumbfounded, and remained silent. The bishop was the most rational man he knew, and now like an extinct volcano gone insane was spewing up some superstitious gibberish about what? Demon possession?

"The school teacher is applying to foster the girl," the bishop explained. "He's an agent of the Church who specializes in protecting and teaching children the Church has an interest in."

"And how is the church involved?" The judge asked, curious, to say the least.

"The only item found on the girl was a very ancient and holy church relic," the bishop explained. "With her recovery, there is some talk of a modern miracle. It is very important that the Church be seen taking care of its own, especially a child in light of recent scandals. Rest assured, the background check will be impeccable."

"I'll see what I can do, Brian," the judge explained, unable to banish the phrase 'her recovery' from his thoughts, as if the girl were someone the church had lost years ago. "And I admit you are a hell of a character witness. Pardon the language. There's just no guarantee I will hear the case. And Brian, I will do nothing to see that I do. The court has enough of its own scandals right now."

"The case will be on your docket," the bishop assured him. "There will be too much political heat on this one not to go to their most senior judge. All I ask, Michael, is that you see that all the *i*'s are dotted and the *t*'s are crossed. The process must seem as transparent as possible. The case has too much notoriety already."

For a long time after Bishop O'Malley had hung up the phone, Judge McConnelly sat holding the receiver and looking at the picture of the two of them taken nearly sixty years ago. Who was this school teacher that he could have a bishop call in favours for him? Or was it the girl? He reached for the bottle of whiskey and the shot glass, now needing that drink more than ever.

Charles Evans was an up and coming junior partner in one of Wall Street's largest law firm. Complete with conservative cut Armani suit, white shirt and dark tie topped off with highly polished wing tips and tasteful accessories, he stuck out at the social services agency like a peacock in a trailer park hen house. But when the founding partner asks you to personally walk through the application to foster a child, you didn't send one of your associates. He had even filled out the form himself, or at least his secretary had under his direction. Charles doubted the big man did anything so menial himself, not even researching the motions he argued in court.

"I have an appointment with your manager," he informed one of the receptionists, handing her his card. "Charles Evans."

Bored, she looked up at the slick dressed lawyer, and unimpressed, continued to chew her gum like cud. "Have a seat."

Charles took one look at the sorry state of the chair in question. "No thank you. I prefer to stand. Will he be long?"

"You'll have to wait your turn," she replied without looking up.

He looked over at the eleven or twelve people who were waiting, and frowned down at his watch. He calculated how long he expected to be here and pulled out his cell phone. Roger, the founding partner, had told him to call if he ran into any snags. Charles was a competent courthouse brawler, and very able in his familiar world of court rooms and board rooms, but he had no experience with this kind of indifferent bureaucratic malaise. And so he made the call.

Where it went to from there, and to whom, he would never know. Roger Whittingham was a powerful man in the city, and his contacts reached deep into city hall - deep enough to reach this department's immediate supervisors. In less than ten minutes he was escorted into the office of a short, balding man with a harried expression and a bad taste in his mouth.

"I don't like being pushed," he complained by way of greeting.

"I apologize," Charles said diplomatically, thinking this man was a bureaucratic tin-pot dictator who would never make it in the real world. He disliked him immediately. "We did have an appointment. I am also due in court at four."

"How can my department help you?" The bureaucrat minion replied with as much grace as he could manage. It wasn't every day he got his butt chewed off by someone so far up the food chain.

"Our client is applying to foster one Jane Doe, herein referred to as Crystal Raven," Charles explained, handing over a neat file folder. "You will find the application in order. There is also all the required background checks from both the New York City Police and the Quebec Provincial Police. You will find the requisite number of references from impeccable members of the community."

"He will have to go through the proper channels," the bureaucrat complained. "We cannot give a child to just anyone, at least not without a hearing."

"A hearing has been set for two weeks from tomorrow in front of Judge McConnelly. That should give you enough time to complete your investigation. After all, the man is a teacher with almost seventeen years experience educating children."

Crystal came awake to find herself lying in a fuzzy white world, sunlight splitting through the window onto the only splash of colour in her room. Someone had set a vase of blue roses on her bedside table. She lay back against the pillow, trying to track her reality and absorb her surroundings. She wondered what had awoken her, and studied her immediate environment until she noticed the strange man standing in her room. Instinctively, she did not like him. Did he not realize that a man should not be unattended in a lady's room? Her eyes red as blood, Crystal hissed her annoyance, and then wondered where her chaperon had taken herself. Suddenly she felt like ripping the arms from the odious creature, watching and hating him as he studied the chart at the end of her bed and frowned down at her, judging, and finding her wanting. Where had those violent thoughts come from?

"Good morning, young lady," he greeted her in a condescending manner that grated on her nerves and made her withdraw. "Can you tell me who you are?"

"Crystal," she muttered darkly. Who was he to question her? Where were her guards, and why did she think there should be guards to keep rabble like him from reaching her?

"And do you have a last name?" He frowned, eyeing the name on her chart. "Jane Doe, a.k.a Crystal Raven."

"Raven."

His frown deepened. Someone with this level of memory loss should remain in-house – even if he knew the facilities were so swamped with juvenile delinquents that children with real problems often got lost in the cracks. Mostly, he hated being railroaded by someone with money and connections, someone who thought they could circumvent the system for their own benefit.

"Can you tell me where you're from?" He paused, glancing at his case notes.

She looked confused. She reached up towards her head with an arm encased in a cast, and it did not reach.

"From here," she ventured.

"And where is here, exactly?"

"Uhm, aha," Crystal stopped paying attention to this annoying little man, and turned to look out the window.

Surely she must have servants who would chase this thing out of her presence. Where were they?

The nurse came bustling in to get her patient ready for lunch. Right behind them walked Gwen, off early from school, and anxious to help Crystal with her first solid meal. Finding the officious bureaucrat in the room, the nurse frowned.

"I'm afraid you ladies will have to go until I'm finished my interview," he suggested mildly.

"You will have to wait until after lunch," the nurse returned brusquely. "This is a hospital. We do not change our schedule for anyone. Patients come first."

At first it seemed as if he was going to protest, but the sight of two rather large orderlies wheeling the lunch trays down the hall changed his mind.

"What about her?" He asked defensively.

"The patient does not have the use of either arm," the nurse pointed out as if she were speaking to an idiot. "She's here to help Crystal eat. What, you never heard of a Candy Striper before?"

Crystal was so glad that the creepy little man had gone away that her eyes had teared up. He made her feel exhausted. She smiled for Gwen, a weak little thing that never reached her eyes.

"Hey girlfriend!" Gwen greeted. "Man, was that guy ever a butthead."

Crystal smiled. She had never heard that expression before – at least she didn't remember it.

"Okay girls," the nurse took charge. "Let's raise your bed and sit you up."

Together Nurse Henderson and Gwen settled the table in front of Crystal, and propped her up with pillows, mindful of her broken hip and fractured ribs. Crystal reached out for the controls with a hand encased in a cast, fascinated by the whirring sound that made the top half of her bed rise up and down until the nurse moved it out of her reach. Just as they finished their preparations an orderly came in with a tray of pureed foods. Gwen made a face and giggled. Carrots, potatoes and an entrée of pepper-steak, all mashed up into coloured pastes. It did not look very appetizing, but Crystal let Gwen spoon it into her mouth, accompanied by a storm of chatter about the doings at school. She did not know any of these people, and things like I-pods and cell phones made no sense to her – still the company felt comfortable and familiar.

"This kind of looks gross," Gwen giggled. "How does it taste?"

"Good." Crystal replied. She really wasn't that hungry, and if any cook of hers ever brought her something that looked like this, she would probably have had their head taken off, or at least dismissed him from her service. As she recalled, killing a servant was no longer an acceptable method of dismissal. She was confused and frustrated – none of her memories seemed to fit this time and place. There was something important she was forgetting, and it was picking at the edge of her consciousness like flies at a festering wound.

"It kind of looks like a guy's thing," Gwen confided, followed by a giggle that threatened to consume her.

"Gwen," Crystal complained, almost choking as she laughed. "I have to eat that!"

"Sorry," Gwen gulped contritely, and then broke into a big grin. "Honest."

Giggling and whispering, the two girls passed a happy hour together. Sometimes it felt good to be a girl again and let the sounds of giggles wash away your worries and cares. And then Crystal's energy melted into a pool of foggy half-dreams, and Gwen sat quietly at her side, holding her hand. She wondered what it felt like to be beaten so badly you needed to eat mush. And the agony must be unbearable – even if the drugs kept you knocked out most of the time. Gwen had a very high empathy rating for a girl her age, and although the older women in her mother's Wiccan Coven found this fascinating, mostly it meant she cried a lot. She felt like a wimp, and wished she could be as tough as the girl lying in the bed.

She looked up through a curtain of tears to see that same man standing at the door. "She's sleeping now. The drugs make her do that a lot."

"I see," he harrumphed. "Perhaps I could best utilize my time speaking with her doctor."

"Whatever," Gwen muttered.

Scott Peterson was Children's Aid's top investigator. A bulldog, he zealously weeded out unfit prospective Foster parents and uncovered the most careful abuser. Too many years of watching a system fail children as it bent over backwards to keep families together – not always for the sake of the children, but to stretch dwindling resources to their limit – had left him with a misanthropic view of his fellow man. He set off to find the doctor in charge of this case, immediately suspicious of a Catholic who had pulled so many strings to get his corrupt hands on a young girl. After all, the Church had a problem with these things at the moment – no matter what the conviction statistics said to the contrary.

He found Doctor Gilmore in an office off the Emergency ward. It was not often an admitting surgeon from the Emergency department held onto a case, and that should have tipped Peterson off. The two men sat across a small industrial desk, two professionals approaching the impending interview determined to treat the other with respect despite their prejudices.

"The girl, Crystal Raven," he began with very little preamble, "what is her status?"

"She has a lot of broken bones and trauma that will take some time to heal," the doctor replied, "but she is recovering remarkably well. The support of Mr. Beaucour and the Moonshadows is helping immensely."

"This Mr. Beaucour," Peterson all but sneered saying the name, "what is his angle here?"

"What do you mean?" The doctor hedged, not sure where

this was going.

"I mean, why is he so involved?" Peterson pressed. "What is his connection with this girl?"

"Mr. Beaucour is a very gentle and caring man," Doctor Gilmore replied, a definite chill in his voice. "He teaches kindergarten at St. Michaels, where my niece is amongst his students. He volunteers at the St. Vincent's Youth Centre in one of this city's poorest neighbourhoods – and I understand he is one of the centre's biggest contributors."

"Crystal is lucky to have him involved in her life. In fact, she has a life because of his quick thinking and compassion. Some people, Mr. Peterson, are naturally charitable towards their fellow man."

"And how about her memory lapses, how will that play into this?" Peterson pressed stubbornly. "Would she not be better off with professionals?"

"No," the doctor disagreed firmly. "She would be better off in a loving home, where she can live as normal a life as possible. And until we find her real family, these people are the closest thing she has."

A Children's Aid investigator not only had to be as hard-nosed as any big city cop, what with the assaults, the risks of being shot, and children being used as hostages, but had to rely on the same investigative instincts as any seasoned detective. Something wasn't right here. The whole scenario stank, right from this `saintly' foreign prick finding a half-dead girl to the phalanx of heavy hitters lining up behind him. Peterson was being stonewalled, and there had to be a reason. And he would find it. No-one hid anything from `Bull-dog Petey'.

Peterson was still at the hospital chasing phantoms when Jean-Claude arrived around dinner time to begin his nightly vigil. The CA investigator hated leaving a job half completed, and this hasty investigation had an unfinished feeling to it that was beginning to intrude on his sleep. April and Gwen, the Moonshadows according to the investigator's notes, sat with his target as he quietly fed Crystal a colourless meal of pureed pork, mashed potatoes and corn. Watching unobserved, Peterson noticed that the girl could not keep her one hand off of the small man. He wondered what was going on there, always looking for small signs that may or may not mean anything. They seemed too familiar – too intimate. Was this what he was looking for?

Jean-Claude moved Crystal's hand from his inner leg and leaned over to spoon in some mashed potatoes.

"So, ma enfant," he asked pleasantly. "How have you been today? The doctor has reduced the pain medication, eh?"

"Achy," Crystal admitted. She gave him a seductive smile, or as seductive as her bandages and ravaged face would allow. "And hungry, and tired and bored."

"We can bring you some magazines," Gwen offered. "Oh, and I can lend you this book. I just finished and it's awesome."

Jean-Claude helped Crystal hold up the book with a page open.

"What language is this?" Crystal asked.

"English, you silly goose," Gwen teased.

"I," Crystal hesitated, "I don't think I read this language."

"Try this one," April offered her a book in Modern French.

"It's a bit familiar," Crystal squinted down at the page, moving it from side to side. "I don't recognize it."

"Try this one," Jean-Claude suggested, setting the plate aside and opening his Demonology, a book written in ancient Latin.

Crystal smiled up at him and edged closer. She had an insatiable need to be touching him. She sat looking at the lurid pictures and reading the captions beneath them.

"I can read this one," Crystal replied happily. Anything that had to do with Jean-Claude made her happy. Some might think he was frumpy and old, still, as Gwen often said, referring to some vague boy or another, Jean-Claude was the bomb.

"I will find you something a little more appropriate, no?" Jean-Claude replied.

"What language is that?" Gwen asked suspiciously.

"Latin."

Gwen pouted. She really wanted to share her favourite series of books – they told the romantic story of a Wiccan girl– and maybe together find some real life romance with some cute boys. Mostly, she desperately wanted to avoid having to read one of Jean-Claude's achingly parched demonologies with her new best friend. Where was the joy in that? Didn't she read enough dead languages in school already?

"I know," Gwen offered. "I can teach you how to read English."

Crystal hesitated until Jean-Claude said, "this would be a wonderful thing, no?"

"Yes," Crystal smiled. "It would be fun..."

She drifted off to sleep in mid-sentence, so suddenly that for a heartbeat Gwen thought she had died. Each time Crystal woke up she remained awake for a little longer, although the pain and the medication left her drained and disoriented, and she had a disturbing habit of passing out in mid-sentence like this. Her visitors watched her sleep for a few minutes, and then April and Gwen left for home. Jean-Claude settled into a corner with his book and his rosary, his every action under the close scrutiny of Peterson. Why was he allowed to stay past visiting hours? What was going on around here?

The next morning Scott Peterson took a trip out to the precinct that was in the same district as the hospital. He had been told that the two officers who had taken the initial statements would be there, and would be coming off shift at seven AM. Here, at least, he was hoping to find a couple of allies. There was something just too good to be true about this Beaucour character, and Peterson was too old and too jaded to believe in fairy tales. He knew most cops tended to think the same way he did – he had worked with enough of them over the years, especially out in the Projects, where removing a child from an unfit home could be hairy. And this child was the victim of a crime, and the first place any good investigator looked was close to home.

He arrived at the station about a quarter to seven. The same chaotic swirl of arresting officers, perps in hand-cuffs and complaining citizens that clung to every station in New York like a miasma ambushed him just inside the door. His work often took Peterson into police stations, even this one, and he knew where he needed to go. The desk sergeant even saw him enough to greet him by name – if not his first, at least his last.

Detectives Jablonski and Kraus were about as opposite physically as two human beings could be. The former was stout, dark, and hairy – it grew from his nose and his ears, and there was even a tuff sticking out of his shirt where the buttons failed to cover his ample belly. Kraus was tall and slim, with that German blue-eye, blond-hair good looks, trim and athletic with a storm trooper's ramrod posture. And yet the shorter, pugnacious man was the more intimidating of the two.

"You want to see us, Peterson?" Jablonski asked through the stub of a cigar. His shift was over, and the pre-shift wind down rituals had begun.

"You two did the initial on that Jane Doe a couple of days ago – the beating victim?" He asked in his forthright manner. New Yorkers did not like to dick around, and he was as New York as they came when he needed to be.

"Yeah," Jablonski nodded. "I remember, the one that weird little foreigner found."

"That's the one. Just wondering what was your impression of this guy?" Peterson asked pointedly.

"Definitely did not have anything to do with the beating," Kraus confirmed, hedging. "The doctors and forensic confirmed the beating involved more than one person – maybe as many as five."

"But?" Peterson had definitely heard a ' but', and he

thrived on such verbal lags in this business. Often what was not said told him more.

"Well," Jablonski admitted. "The guy seems a bit fruity. Those sweater vests and bowties. I never trust a guy in a sweater vest."

"Can't judge a book by its cover," Kraus warned. "Even Brooks who does the police league stuff says he's a great guy and a good basketball coach. Took one of his teams to All City."

"Yeah," Jablonski grumbled. "He's so wimpy it's hard to believe."

"You get a funny vive off of him too?" Peterson pressed.

"Well, no," Kraus supplied. "He just doesn't like him. Not manly enough for him. No hair in his ears, or on his butt, eh Jabby? Why are you asking anyway?"

"He's applied to foster the girl," Peterson replied. "Under the circumstances I find it suspicious. Especially in light of his recent behaviour."

"Like what?" Jablonski asked sharply.

"Well," Peterson pretended to hedge. Sometimes he could get more done by dropping the right word into a special ear. "He is spending every night in her room despite the hospital's 'visiting hours' policy. And it is kind of strange that he's only there at night, when so few people are around."

Having accomplished what he came for, Peterson made his goodbyes and headed back out to his car. He still wanted to talk to a couple of his subject's colleagues at the school where he worked, and to check out exactly what this Beaucour did at the youth centre. Nobody was this squeaky clean, and he was determined to uncover this man's secrets. Normally, with the youth centre so close, he would have started there. Unfortunately, it did not open until after school, and no-one was likely to be there until at least noon, nor did Peterson see any point in wasting daylight hours with so little time to complete his mission. This left him facing a drive across the city, and he began to appreciate the effort Jean-Claude put in to volunteer in this neighbourhood – which only convinced him all the more that the man had darker motives.

The school was one of those aging yellow brick affairs built during the twenties and thirties by the Carnegie Foundation, but the community had taken time to restore the lot during one of those playground renewal programs. Now a neat patch of grass covered the back lot, and a play set with slide and swings had been assembled. Still too small for any sports, it was safe, clean and green – absolutely kept that way by a lot of parent volunteers, some of whom Peterson could see working on a flower plot in the back.

Sometimes the unofficial line was more conducive to his investigations, so Peterson decided to chat up the three individuals he saw working in the back. Gossip could be vicious, and for all its darker motivations, it often held a grain of truth that hid a buried mountain.

"Hello," he greeted in his friendliest voice. "I thought this was St. Michaels Elementary School. Do I have the right place?"

"Yes," the first woman answered. They were all in their late twenties, early thirties. "This is St Michaels."

"What are you doing here?" It was obviously some form of community garden, and not planted with flowers after all.

"Oh," a second woman responded. "This is part of our breakfast program. Not all are families our well off, and growing some of the food lets us offer the children better meals."

"Impressive," Peterson nodded. "And who came up with this?"

"Jean-Claude Beaucour," the first woman replied, "he's the kindergarten teacher here."

"That's amazing," Peterson replied. "I'm just here to see about him."

"Oh?"

"Yes," Peterson nodded seriously. "He's applying to foster that girl that he rescued."

"Well good for him," the first woman replied. "Although you would think he would be more comfortable with a little boy. I don't think he's ever dated a woman."

"No Claire, you're wrong," the second woman interjected. "I'm certain April and him are an item."

"No," the third woman spoke for the first time, "they certainly make a non-traditional household, but they are not a couple. My Bobby-Lynn is good friends with her Gwen, and she says while they all eat upstairs together, the women live in the apartment downstairs."

Pay dirt! No heterosexual relationships, Peterson thought as he made his goodbyes and headed inside for his interview with the principal. Definitely a warning sign. Or not, it was hard to tell with these monkish sorts and their vows of celibacy. Perhaps this was the dark secret he was looking for, and with this in mind he set off to interview the principal. He would have access to Beaucour's records at the Board of Education, and although the New York Licensing Board had a rigorous screening process, an occasional bad apple snuck through. And his instincts told him there was something not kosher about this man. No kindergarten teacher had this much pull no matter what kind of saint he seemed to be.

If he was hoping to find the answer at the school amongst his colleagues, it was a forlorn hope at best. Even the Board's records said little about the man, except that he had not missed a single day of work in ten years. There was one complaint lodged against him, but when Peterson had investigated further, he found that the individual in question had lodged a complaint against every one of his teachers. He was grasping at straws, because this irritating little nobody was proving harder to pin down than it was to punch at mist. There was something there, behind that saintly façade, and Peterson knew if he could just find the right question, the right individual, and the right moment to ask this house of cards Beaucour had built would come tumbling down around his ears.

Scott Peterson had taken down politicians and celebrities, and once one of the infamous Bartons who owned much of upstate New York. His boss had set him on this case to produce results. It looked like this would be the first time he failed....

Chapter 4

Dark shadows still clung to the hospital room when Crystal started from a restless sleep. She shivered, wondering as she did every time she woke up just where she was, and if she were safe. Why did she always feel like she was swimming through tar, only distantly aware of a thousand aches and pains? Strange lights stared at her from out of the darkness like malevolent eyes, unfamiliar sounds drifted to her from every direction, and the black shapes of unnamed devices crowded about her bed – vague memories of a torture chamber teasing her muddled thoughts. A hand touched hers, settling her post-waking fears. She knew that touch. It was warm, and gentle, and woke a hunger in her she just could not seem to feed. She sighed in confusion and turned her head towards the careworn face she knew she would find there.

"Good morning, ma petite," Jean-Claude greeted warmly.

"Morning Jean," she yawned as best she could without stretching.

"Breakfast will come soon," he commented, asking. "You are hungry today, no?"

"Yes," she replied, thinking of more than her physical hunger. She studied him critically, seeing little beauty there to explain the sexual tension he awoke in her, and still she could not keep herself from wanting to drink his soul to slake a thirst that would not die.

"I need go home soon and sleep," he yawned. "It will be a busy day. Gwen will be let out of school to come see you at lunch. You will be good, no?"

"No," Crystal grumped.

"This is no way to win hearts," Jean-Claude teased,

brushing his thumb at the corner of her frown until she smiled. "That is better, no?"

"No," Crystal teased.

The pair spent a pleasant ninety minutes chatting quietly about inconsequential matters – growing up in Montreal with four brothers, trips to the sugar bush, and a stray memory of her own from a carriage ride through a Paris, France that hadn't existed for several hundred years. Crystal found that while she learned more of the everyday things from Gwen, she gained a sense of her own past when she spoke to Jean Claude. He made her feel warm and loved and wanted, and the more time she spent with him the more she needed his presence.

In her eyes he was not bone-skinny, he was lithe; his hair was not unkempt, he wore it in a wild mane – a manly style. She could even see, if she looked at him at just the right angle, the rugged athleticism that lay buried beneath the baggy clothes he wore. And if no one else saw him in that particular light, well, as Gwen always said, it sucked to be them. What lay in her own heart was all that really mattered. No-one but she could see how he filled that emptiness that was consuming so much of her life right now, giving her a sense of self and belonging in a world that no longer made any sense. He was someone for her to hold onto, like a drowning woman to a life preserver in this sea of confusion, and although the stormy waters had washed away much of her identity, she knew in this here and now she belonged with Jean-Claude.

"I need too leave now, ma petite," Jean-Claude suggested after another story about his childhood. "April will be here to sit with you until Gwen gets out of school. That is not how we smile, no?"

"No," Crystal pouted and was rewarded with a chaste kiss on the forehead.

When officers Jablonski and Kraus came up to the room they saw Jean-Claude leaning over the girl, apparently kissing her. They met him just outside the door with a scowl.

"Mr. Beaucour?"

"Officers," Jean-Claude greeted. He vaguely remembered the larger, more aggressive of the two. It was a few seconds before the where registered in his thoughts. So much was happening these days that something as trivial as two police officers and the complications of their investigation barely registered on his consciousness. He was expecting word from his superiors in the Vatican and needed to be home to meet their envoy when he arrived. If reports could be believed, and he trusted his agents with more than his life, the vampyre numbers in New York exceeded their wildest nightmares – he desperately needed more resources, and needed them last week.

"May we speak with you?"

"Mais oui," Jean-Claude replied, gesturing towards the waiting room just down the hall. The delay annoyed him. It was a pity he could not make these two disappear the way the Brotherhood once had in the past with anyone who came too close to discovering their existence. Yes, a pity times change.

At first Jablonski thought he was calling them something nasty, and did not start to follow until his partner touched his elbow. The two joined him in a corner of the room.

"How may I assist you?" Jean-Claude asked politely.

"What are you doing here so early?" Kraus asked, gesturing back towards the girl's room.

"I have been here all night," Jean-Claude admitted with a frown. "I am just leaving now, no?"

"You have been in her room all night?" Jablonski shot back. "Alone in a young girl's room?"

"Mais oui?" Jean-Claude returned, puzzled. He was not about to explain to these two the need for his nightly vigil, or that he was there to both protect the girl from harm and the hospital staff from her. "One of us is with her almost all the time. I am the only one who can be here at night – April must be home for Gwen. A young girl cannot be home alone, no?"

"So," Kraus clarified, "one of you is always with the girl?"

"Yes," Jean-Claude confirmed. "Since the first night, oui? April will be here in an hour when the breakfast rush is over."

"And the reason for this?" Kraus asked, thinking he and his partner may have been duped.

"The nurses said it was allowed on this ward," Jean-Claude explained. They had agreed on a cover story days ago. Now was the time to put their lie to the test. Just how motivated were these two officers? "Usually with the younger ones – and the doctor thought it might be good for someone to be there when she wakes up. Maybe not so good for her to wake up alone after what has happened, no?"

"Yes," Jablonski admitted grudgingly, "I would imagine so. Someone laid one hell of a beating on the poor girl."

"Have you found something out?" Jean-Claude pressed, although he knew they would not. Could not. "Is this why you have come to see me?"

"Unfortunately no," Kraus returned diplomatically. "We had heard that she was awake and wondered if she remembered anything."

"She would welcome the visitors," Jean-Claude sighed sadly, "but I am afraid she remembers nothing. Not even her name."

"Well, thank you for your time, sir," Kraus replied before turning to retrace their steps back to the girl's room.

The officers found Crystal with a nurse who was helping her prepare to eat her breakfast. With both arms in a cast, she was totally dependant on others for her basic comforts, but the nurses in the children's ward were very gentle and put her at ease. When two strange men in uniform came in, Crystal was far from comfortable. She wished Jean-Claude or April were here. These men made her feel nervous, as if they hid a threat beneath their smiles and friendly manner. She may not remember much, but she remembered enough to know that men in uniforms always meant trouble and were to be avoided at all costs.

"Hello young lady," Kraus introduced himself and his

partner. He had a better manner with children. "I m Officer Kraus and this is Officer Jablonski. We are police officers who are trying to find the people who hurt you."

April arrived just as he finished his words. She moved quickly to Crystal's side and gave her hand a comforting squeeze. "It's okay, baby doll. They're here to help."

"Okay," she returned in a small voice, refusing to let go of April's hand.

"We were wondering if you remembered anything about the night you were attacked." Officer Kraus probed gently.

Crystal's hand tightened convulsively on April's. "It hurt. Cold."

"I imagine it did," Kraus returned gently, changing the subject. "Can you tell us your name?"

"Crystal Raven."

April shook her head 'no' to let the officers know it was not her real name.

"And can you tell us where you are from?" He pressed

"From here." She returned, bewildered.

"It's time for her breakfast," the nurse prompted.

"By all means," Kraus replied. "You've been a great help, little lady. If you remember anything, you have someone call this number on my card."

Frowning, April set the card aside on the bedside table and settled in to help Crystal with her breakfast. Assaults like this always brought too much attention for anyone's good, and while she did not condone violence, this once she would like the opportunity to kick a little vampyre ass. The truth was not something anyone was ready to learn, nor believe.

She looked down at the center of all their troubles, this battered and broken girl. Later, a nurse and April would help her change out of the hospital gown and into a flannel nightgown and housecoat set picked out by her daughter, and that she had insisted on buying to make the poor girl feel more comfortable. The bandage would be coming off of her head and eye, and the three girls planned to fix Crystal's hair in the latest style. April had even relented and let Gwen pick out some dye to streak her hair with – provided the colour was not too outlandish. Updating her hair style would certainly help her fit in better in the here and now, and whenever that ridiculous coif she wore originated, a week beneath bandages would have crushed it beyond repair.

Still, the hair was bound to raise questions- and if with nobody else, at least with her daughter. April wondered how much Gwen had already guessed. She did have that rare Wiccan talent to read auras, and she was sometimes too intuitive for her own good. Jean-Claude wished to keep Crystal's true identity hidden from all except those who he chose to watch over her. Everyone else would only be told that she was one of the Brotherhood who was injured in the line of duty, and who had to recover her memory on her own. Using her amnesia as a cover was brilliant, but still those like her would recognize her true nature, would see the girl as one of their own.

April didn't like it. She did not like it one bit.

Meanwhile, Jean-Claude escaped from the hospital and rushed off toward the school and an appointment to fill out some paperwork to cover his leave of absence. Some of Crystal's medical expenses might be covered by his benefits, according to his benefits representative, especially if the foster position came through. It all depended on the outcome of his application, and on what interpretation of the contract language one chose. To Jean-Claude it made little difference. It was just another paper trail he would prefer to avoid, and the sale of the family maple sugar farm had left him comfortably off – at least enough to cover her expenses without any extra burden.

At the school he met with the principal in his office, where his friend was full of questions about the child.

"So?" Roland asked. "How is -?"

"Crystal."

He was a tall man with a predominant Adam's apple, a

shock of black hair and brown eyes. Also from a French Canadian descent, his family fourth generation American transplants, Roland was originally from the Detroit area and had moved to New York shortly after college. Like Jean Claude he had been educated and trained in one of the Brotherhood's thirteen academies before moving onto a main stream college, and was second under Jean Claude in its administrative wing.

"She is good," Jean Claude continued. "She does not remember anything about her past."

"We expected this, eh?"

"Oui."

"That guy from the Children's Aid Society was around," Roland commented. "He was all over the school asking questions."

"That cannot be helped, I suppose," Jean-Claude sighed, exasperated. "I do not like our business being poked into."

"Who does, eh?" Roland returned.

"Well," Jean-Claude elaborated. "It will be two weeks before the hearing, and three weeks before I can take her home. She should be safe in the hospital until then."

"It is consecrated ground. And afterwards?"

"The Brotherhood is ready."

After his meeting at the school, Jean-Claude returned home for a few hours sleep. His sleep was troubled. There was still no word from his Vatican contact, and his resources were already stretched beyond the breaking point. He felt that tingling in his bones, his legs itchy and twitching the way they always got just before a violent confrontation. If this girl was who they thought she was, and if the vampyres had really managed to destroy the other eleven succubi, the Brotherhood could look forward to bloody skirmishes throughout the sewers and across the rooftops of New York. And that kind of bloodshed was not only nearly impossible to hide it could quickly lead to open warfare that he was no longer sure they could win.

God, he was going to miss the sleep. When Gwen came home from school, he would run her up to the hospital. While the three women in his life spent an afternoon 'redecorating' themselves, as he put it, Jean-Claude had several meetings, first with the hospital financial department, and then with that officious social worker from Children's Aide.

Jean-Claude's dreams were dark and unpleasant. He woke with a start to Gwen jumping on his bed. He reached sleepily for his glasses and fitted them on, frowning.

"You are too old for this, no?"

"No," Gwen giggled. "Get up and dressed. They're taking the bandages off of Crystal's face, and then we are going to do up her hair and I'm going to streak it with just the perfect colour of cherry red that will go with her eyes and..."

"And, if you will excuse yourself, mademoiselle, I will dress myself, no?"

"No," Gwen cried, dashing from the room, "but hurry."

Jean-Claude dressed and wandered out in hopes of a coffee, a dream dashed in the face of the impatience of a girl. Sighing for affect, and rolling his eyes towards heaven to tease her, he took his keys from her hand and let her lead him towards his car. For once the drive to the hospital was not too fast; instead, his short-cuts were too long and convoluted in her excitement. Jean-Claude took it all in stride. She had been in his life since she was born, and was subject to fits of enthusiasm that burnt out as quickly as they arose. He did not know how he would get through his days without her, and thanked heaven for giving him such a sweet and loving gift. He just hoped he could keep her safe in the storm that brewed on their horizon.

Parking in his customary place, Gwen was already unbuckled and out the door before the engine shut down. Chuckling, he locked up the car and followed her into the building. Ahead in the elevator, she held the door and waved impatiently for him to hurry.

"Move your bum, old man," she complained, rolling her

eyes at him. "You're slower than a turtle trying to mate with molasses."

"Why would a turtle mate with liquefied sugar?" Jean-Claude teased.

"Because it's the only thing slower than he is," Gwen harrumphed, "and both of them are quicker than you."

They arrived at Crystal's room to find April waiting outside the door while the doctor and nurse removed the bandages from her face and head. She greeted her daughter with a hug and Jean-Claude with a warm smile.

"Have you been waiting long?" He inquired.

"A few minutes," April replied. "Crystal seems excited about getting the bandages off, but she's still pretty upset about not being allowed out of bed."

"Oui," Jean-Claude sighed, exasperated. "Being immobile is difficult, no?"

"She will mend, Jean-Claude," April assured him. "Probably faster than most of us. It is only a young girl's need to be busy that is wearing her down. Why don't you let her help you with your research?"

"It is not a fit subject for a young girl," Jean-Claude returned, flustered. And because, he thought to himself, the longer she did not remember who and what she was, the easier it would be to hide. Vampyres and local authorities were not the only ones he needed to worry about – and that third party still had not made their presence known. She could easily be their agent, planted here to damage both the Brotherhood and the vampyres.

"And have you not been telling my young daughter these self-same stories for years?"

"Touché, Madame," Jean-Claude threw up his hands in mock surrender. "You win again, of course."

The nurse came to the door and beckoned them inside towards the bed, where Crystal sat looking at herself in the mirror. One eye had a purple bruise discolouring the bottom lid, the other was sunken and puffy beneath a darker bruise.

Her left cheek was scraped raw and covered with a scab, and her hair was matted from its long hibernation beneath the bandages.

"Oh!" Gwen cried as she bounced to the bedside. "You're beautiful."

"Do you really think so?" Crystal asked with a sniffle. She was really feeling horrid.

"Your eyes are so beautiful," April assured her, scooping up her chin for a better look, "and they suit your face."

"Tres belle, ma petite," Jean-Claude breathed, the remembered ruin superimposing itself on her face from the memory of that horrid night, and disappearing in a heartbeat. Only the beauty remained.

Crystal's face lit up with the compliment, and her smile was electric. Everyone immediately smiled with her – her charisma overpowering.

"See," Gwen reassured her, "you look great. And oh, you should see the sweet colour I got to streak your bangs!"

"I must go," Jean-Claude squirmed. He was uncomfortable when women began dissembling and re-assembling themselves. "I must meet with the hospital administrator. I will leave you three to your redecorating. Tabernac!"

Jean-Claude left the girls to their work and fled to the hospital business office in the wing at the opposite side of the building. While he knew updating Crystal's look was an important component of her disguise, he was glad his appointment with a Miss Henderson in the billing department gave him an excuse to escape. Girlish things made him feel uncomfortable, so Jean-Claude turned his thoughts to his accountant's recommendation to pay ahead and save on any interest payments. He could care less either way. Hopefully, they would let him pay cash to limit the paper trail that would need to be sanitized. Too many people outside the Brotherhood already knew Chrystal was still alive.

While computers made it simple to delete your electronic footprint, they also made it easier to collect and collate data.

This new breed of vampyre was extremely technologically literate, with everything from blood farms to computers at the tip of their fingertips. At this moment Jean-Claude knew they would be activating spyware that gave them access to a network with enough computing power to rival that of NSI, all focused in on any information that would lead them to the girl. When he was directed to a small office at the end of the hall, he found himself greeting a very attractive and young brunette. She wore her hair shoulder length, and tapered into her neck. Her make-up was lightly applied and barely noticeable, and she wore a professional looking blouse and pant suit combination that made her look all the more beautiful. Jean-Claude did not even notice. His mind was focused on megabytes and search engine software.

"Good afternoon, Mr. Beaucour," she greeted, rising from her desk to show just a peek of cleavage, that again went unnoticed.

"Miss Henderson, no?"

"Yes," she flashed a brilliant smile, the invisible braces barely noticeable. "Thank you for coming down so promptly."

"It is no problem," he reassured her. "It is best we get this business out of the way so we can concentrate on getting Crystal well, no?"

"That is a good attitude," she replied, smiling. "I see you have her in a private room, there are cheaper options."

"It is okay," Jean-Claude shrugged dismissively. "I have brought two cashiers' cheques for ten thousand. The initial bill is -?"

"Nine thousand, three hundred and twenty-seven dollars," she read off the computer screen, "and seventy-four cents."

"And so this will cover the next two weeks, no?" Jean-Claude insisted.

"Now that all her surgeries are over," Miss Henderson replied, scanning the chart of her proposed treatment, "it should not be as much."

"But if it goes short, no?" Jean-Claude returned. "Better safe than soreful."

"Sorry," she corrected. "The word is sorry, and you are correct. We'll refund any difference."

Jean-Claude wrapped up the paper work and gathered up his papers, frowning at them as if they were poisonous asps. These days everything was written down somewhere, stored in triplicate, or on a dozen hard drives and back-up storage units now that computers were so prevalent. Gone were the days of the quick and dirty little fire, or a quiet burglary in the dark of the night. The best you could hope for was to confuse things by changing data at as many points as possible, and one good system crash that required the use of the central back-up could undo all your work in the blink of an eye. Jean-Claude was worried about the upcoming court hearing, and although the bishop and his people had promised to have the records sealed, they would still exist on some computer file or in some musty basement. What he needed more than anything else was the services of one or two of the Brotherhood's specialists, and he doubted the Vatican would ever approve that expense.

Jean-Claude had just enough time before his next meeting to check in on Crystal and the girls and their chemistry experiments, hoping the worst of their conjurations were already complete. After this short visit he was due to meet with the hospital councillor and that odious man from the Children's Aid. Once he disposed of these matters, the four of them would gather in Crystal's room to share a meal that they were smuggling in from April's restaurant. Jean-Claude was looking forward to it. He longed for just a few quiet hours away from his worries, away from the stress of a situation that was rapidly spinning out of his control.

Jean-Claude took a stutter step as he entered the hospital room, momentarily unable to place the beautiful young lady sitting on the bed.

"Do you like?" April teased.

"Oui," Jean-Clause breathed. "I can hardly believe this is the same foundling we brought here so few short days ago."

"You like it," Crystal blushed prettily.

"Mais oui," Jean-Claude smiled, adjusting his glasses for a better look. He bent over and kissed her gently on her forehead, and she lit up until she practically glowed.

April saw the look and frowned. With any one else she would have dismissed it as a harmless crush. Jean-Claude was in for a struggle, and it was one that could be costly. Just how was she to deal with a demon with a crush?

Jean-Claude kissed all three of his girls on the forehead and made his way back to the same wing of the hospital for his second meeting of the morning. Because of Crystal's memory loss the hospital had assigned a counsellor to her case, a warm motherly woman who meant well, and someone Jean-Claude hated to lie to, unlike that man Peterson from Children's Aid. He really was an odious little man, a complication Jean-Claude did not need at this point in his life. He was oh so tempted to make a peace offering of him to Vlad, a sacrificial lamb who surely could not be missed by many. On days like this the temptations to sin were many.

The two men met in the hall outside Mrs. Washington's office.

"Mr. Beaucour," Peterson greeted stiffly.

For a man named after a saint – Jean-Claude's childhood idol – he could really set the diminutive Frenchman's teeth on edge.

"Monsieur Peterson," Jean-Claude greeted formally.

"Tell me," the other returned without preamble, "what's your interest in this girl?"

"I am like you," Jean-Claude shrugged. "I give care to the children. It is our chosen professions."

"I doubt you are anything like me."

"We have only God to thank for that," Jean-Claude muttered in reply just as a large, motherly black woman came up to them.

"Scott," she greeted. "Jean-Claude. Sorry to have kept you two waiting. I had a bit of a crisis with one of my other babies."

They were not clients to her, like with so many people in her profession, but each and every one her babies. Florence Washington, Mama Flo' to her friends and supporters, was a kind, sweet woman – but like a lioness with her cubs, she had teeth for anyone messing around with one of her children. Jean-Claude liked her for this, and an instant bond had formed between the two.

"Come in, and don't mind the mess now," she warned. "My little babies like to draw."

The walls of her office were covered in crayon masterpieces, some showing remarkable talent. When the surface of the walls were plastered – not an inch of blank space showing – she had resorted to using the skirt of her desk and the front and sides of her filing cabinet. Her office was small, almost completely taken up by the desk and the two chairs in front of it. Both men had to turn sideways to squeeze into their seats, disturbing some of Mama Flo's precious art in the process.

"Crystal Raven," Mama Flo was in charge of this meeting, and she let both men know it. She nodded approvingly as Jean-Claude smoothed down a wrinkled paper – a scribble of reds and blues that was one of her latest favourites.

"I take it she has not remembered her real name?" Mama Flo continued. "The poor child."

"Wouldn't she be better suited within the system," Scott Peterson pressed.

"Now Scott," Mama Flo scolded. "You know my babies do better in a loving home where they can get individual attention."

"But with her memory loss –."

"She will need even more attention than the overworked staff at your `baby jails' can provide. You have my report on this subject, and neither my opinion nor my recommendations will change."

Jean-Claude sat quietly through this exchange. It had very little to do with him, and would change nothing of his obligations to this girl.

"Now," Mama Flo turned to Jean-Claude, the subject dismissed. Even Peterson knew enough not to cross that line. "I feel it is important that we normalize Crystal's day to day life as much as possible. I am encouraged to see this relation-ship develop with Gwen. Her ability to form proper emotional attachments within her peer group is an encouraging sign."

"Yes," Jean-Claude replied wryly. "Crystal and Gwen are BFF, but I am sure they will outgrow it."

"Let's hope so," she smiled, and they shared a knowing look that often passed between adults with teen-aged girls in their lives.

"It's hard to gauge what emotional problems might develop," she continued, clinically, "not knowing anything about her past. But she seems to be reacting quite normally for a girl her age under these circumstances. She's even developed a bit of a crush on you."

"Mon Dieu," Jean-Claude breathed. "Will wonders never cease. I had not thought myself the crush type."

"Surely as a teacher you've encountered this before?" Peterson questioned, disbelievingly.

"With the little ones it is different," Jean-Claude shrugged. "They have crushes on everything from puppy-dogs to their teddy bears."

"Yes," Mama Flo beamed. "At that age the world is full of love. But you handle this situation much the same. It is quite natural for a girl this age to develop crushes."

"Surely all this will change quickly," Jean-Claude blushed. "When she is in school and the young ones come courting."

"And she will find a more appropriate recipient of her affection," Mama Flo soothed. She sensed this shy man was not comfortable having himself associated with any woman –

and if she knew the real source of his discomfort, he would be dragged out of here in a straight jacket. Well, it took all kinds to make a village, and a village to raise a child.

"She will be here for another few weeks," Mama Flo continued, "and if she is given into your care, as we all hope, you will find her moods and likes will change as often as the wind. Most of this will be normal, but some of it may be linked to her memory loss. You want to be alert for signs of depression or despondency- a little of which is normal for a teenage girl. Keep her talking. Keep her active and involved. And mostly, just show her that she is loved."

"With Gwen around," Jean-Claude complained good-naturedly, "it will be hard not to. God forbid she talk as much as that one or the world will know no peace."

"Gwen will be a good gauge for you," Mama Flo suggested. "She seems quite well-adjusted. I like that baby."

"Me too," Jean-Claude admitted. "But please, do not tell her that."

The fledgling family gathered in Crystal's room for the first of what they hoped would be many meals together. With the complicity of the nurses, April had smuggled in one of her famous Greek meatloaf specials, a spicy meatloaf with hard boiled eggs cooked in its centre. With a dish of roasted potatoes cooked with red peppers, French-cut beans and baby carrots, home-made buns, and corn-on-the-cob, it was a gourmand's delight.

Gwen had dyed her hair with the same crimson she had used to streak Crystal's hair, and the two sat like not quite matching bookends – one blonde, the other raven-haired. With their heads bent together, they ate and giggled at mysterious things way, way above any adult's head. Or at least beyond the understanding of any reasoning man's intellect. April looked on with a tolerant smile, occasionally sharing a look of her own with Jean-Claude. It was good to see her daughter – both of her daughters, she corrected herself – getting on so well.

They were becoming a family, no matter how odd its make-up. And it couldn't get much odder, she thought, given Crystal's background. It would be good for Gwen to have this strange little girl around, to just for the emotional growth it would bring, but the learning and wisdom that would stretch her talents as a Wiccan. She had more potential there than any other girl the Nightholm coven had come across in some decades, and still needed someone as serious as Crystal to dampen some of her rampant enthusiasm. And Crystal would need someone with her daughter's buoyancy to counter her own darkness in the days ahead.

Sometimes April wished it wasn't her daughter who had been set on this path.

"I think something was put in this food, no?" Jean-Claude complained with a mischievous twinkle in his eye. "Some new kind of spice that makes these two giggle."

And the two convulsed in another fit.

"I can't imagine what?" April played along, setting her face in serious lines. "Too much sage, perhaps?"

Jean-Claude pretended to taste his food, contorting his face into a mask of concentration. "No. The sage is just right."

"The cloves then," April guessed. "I used too few cloves."

"No," Jean-Claude paused, speculating. "Did you perhaps cook it over laughing gas?"

"Oh!" Gwen burst out between fits of laughter. "Epic failure. You two shouldn't quit your day jobs anytime soon."

"Boorish peasants, the both of them," Crystal offered. "It's the weak blood that affects their minds."

"Age," Gwen agreed, and the two convulsed into a fit of giggles.

"Hmmm," Jean-Claude offered, turning to April, "perhaps we should keep better company."

"Oh, we're definitely too cool for the likes of you," Gwen chided.

"Yes," Crystal returned. "Cold like the outer rim of the third plane of hel."

She had pronounced it with a perfect Nordic infliction, an Old Norse language that had not been spoken in centuries. A distant look flicked across Jean-Claude's eyes, but the smile did not leave his face. Her loss of memory was both good and bad – a dangerous opportunity that could mean his undoing.

Chapter 5

Three days after being liberated from her head bandages, the relief column continued through with new x-rays to replace the older ones that had mysteriously disappeared. Finding her bones knitted and neatly healed, the various casts came off and Crystal's doctors decided that she could get out of bed and move about with the help of a walker. Again the prognosis was early, but they had come to expect them with this patient. No-one was as happy as Crystal, who, like a newly arisen mummy, was ready to conquer the world – or at least a trip to the washroom by herself.

Such a small step towards true independence and still one that made her feel safer. How and why she did not feel safe here in the hospital, surrounded by people whose only concern was her welfare, she could not find the words to express? Her stability was still an issue. Frustratingly, she needed help to get up out of or into bed and someone had to be with her when she was up and about. And that tended to limit her wandering to her room and the hallway immediately outside it – an improvement, but still not true independence. And this suited Jean-Claude fine because he still had to keep her in sight.

On the afternoon of her first physiotherapy session, Jean-Claude returned to the hospital early. With the help of an orderly he escorted her down the Green Mile, a convict on her last walk from death row. Dressed in her newest night gown and housecoat, she doggedly made her way along the strange hallways. Her progress was slow, but she refused any help – even from Jean-Claude.

"Well done, ma petite," he encouraged. "You use the walker so well, soon maybe you teach me, no?"

Crystal glared at him. In her eyes he could do no wrong, but sometimes he was still an ass – no matter how salty he was. At this moment, tired, sore and frustrated, she hated the whole world.

"No." She snapped in a perfect imitation of Gwen.

"You young girls," Jean-Claude teased, "you are hard on an old man, no?"

'Not as hard as I'd like to be,' Chrystal thought as Jean-Claude found a chair just outside the physiotherapy room and waited while the orderly brought Crystal in to meet her therapist. A young woman of perhaps twenty-three, she had long brunette hair, angelic features, and warm blue eyes that always seemed to twinkle with a smile. Crystal wanted to hate her for her sweetness, but it was impossible to hate someone with that sunny a disposition. She made you want to try harder to please her, and made your inability to do so all that more frustrating. And the more frustrated she became, the more Crystal wanted to bitch slap the woman.

"Oh," Megan enthused, "I just love what you've done with your hair."

"Gwen did it," Crystal muttered. "Do you really like it?"

"Oh yes. It suits you perfectly with that dark hair of yours. And it's such a unique shade of red – almost crimson. It really makes those blue eyes of yours pop."

Megan's words touched her, and Crystal hated her all the more for making her feel good when she was frustrated and miserable, and wanted to feel shitty. Her exercises for the day involved walking between two parallel bars to strengthen her injured hip. Later, Megan explained, they would do some leg lifts, and a number of other exercises to strengthen her arms and leg where the muscle had atrophied and stiffened around her broken bones. It was hard and painful and mid way through there were tears of frustration in Crystal's eyes. Later, sounded very good to her.

"Good. You're doing really, really well," Megan encouraged. "Keep it up. Just three more now."

It was so fucking easy for her to say. She could walk. She even had a subtle and seductive sway to her hips when she moved that Crystal wished she could imitate. Not that Jean-Claude would notice. Sometimes Crystal doubted he would notice a naked woman if she jumped on him – and from a very great height at that. She doubted he saw much of the world outside his books. And she was definitely not a book. And she would make him see that if she could ever walk like a woman again, instead of a broken toy.

After two more circuits Crystal couldn't do any more. Her hip and lower back hurt beyond endurance, and she was so tired she doubted she would make it back to her room, where she planned to lay in bed and never get up. Finally, Megan relented.

"Alright," she conceded. "A very, very good effort. You did great today."

Thinking unpleasant thoughts about the woman, Crystal limped out into the hall still wiping the tears from her eyes. Seeing she had had a tough time, Jean-Claude met her with a bright smile. Wordlessly, he helped her back to her room. It took much longer to make the return trip, Crystal having to stop and rest often, refusing any kind of help – especially the suggestion of a wheel chair – her sore hip unable to support her weight for any great period of time. He hated to see her like this, felt something tugging at his heart, and knew he could do nothing to stop it if she were to regain her strength for the battles to come.

Back in the room she was angry and fretful. Jean-Claude could tell she needed a rest, but she was too upset and wound up to sleep. A demon, like a girl, was never more dangerous when she was frustrated and bitchy.

"If you settle in bed, ma petite," he urged in his gentlest voice, "I will tell you a story."

She settled into bed, nestling in against his shoulder as he sat perched on its edge, her breasts pressed against him like she remembered men loved. She wished they were bigger –

and maybe hard enough to penetrate this man's thick hide.

Jean-Claude began to weave his tale with only the slightest French Canadian accent.

"In the thirteen hundreds, before the Age they call the Age of the Great Light –"

"You mean the Age of Enlightenment?"

"No." Jean-Claude explained patiently. "This was in the middle of the Dark Ages. When a meteorite hit the earth, causing what we now call a nuclear, or a meteor winter that lasted for three years. Dust and dirt obscures the sun, and creates a perpetual twilight."

"We call them the Long Night of the Vampyre. It was well documented at the time, but it was not until the recent discovery of the meteor site that they connected the fragments of texts to a real event."

He paused and patted her arm. "In a place called Transylvania, in Modern day Romania, the darkness brought with it a host of vampyres. And a vampyre's favourite food is a young, pretty girl like you."

He tweaked her nose as if she were a small child, treating her like one of his little brats in his kindergarten class. Annoyed, she pushed her breasts harder against his side. For someone not much more than a snack, he was exceedingly hard to feed on.

Talk about random. Where had that thought come from? She meant seduce, of course. Make him fall in love with her. She was just too angry and tired to think straight, and his macabre stores were starting to get muddled in her thoughts.

"In those days, if you had a pretty daughter who was coming of age, and if you could afford it, you hired vampyre hunters to protect her. This one girl, Dionetta, was the prettiest girl in all Transylvania. She was so treasured by the people of her village that they pooled their resources together to hire the best vampyre hunter in all the land."

"His name was Vlad the Impaler."

"Wasn't he a vampyre?" Crystal interrupted.

"No," Jean-Claude replied. "There was a Count Vlad who was a vampyre, but Prince Vlad Dracula was one of Christendom's greatest heroes. His reign, however, between his war with the Vampyra and his war with the Turks, was painted in blood."

"What a waste of food," Crystal muttered.

"Que?"

"Nothing, please tell me what happened," she beamed that dimpled smile that was crafted to bend the hardest will. She must be truly exhausted. She was beginning to think like one of the vampyres in his story. The thought made her shudder.

"Vlad's pack had twelve other hunters. Always thirteen when hunting vampyres. That is important. His group included a Russian Monk, the Albino Princess – they say she got her name after escaping from a vampyre's embrace. Or so the story goes. The Mute Triplets, scions of an old Nordic family, armed with large battle axes; and the thief, master of sleight of hand – believed by many to be a wizard, but no more than a stage magician.

"That's only six," she pouted.

"Must I name them all?" Jean-Claude asked amazed.

"Yes."

His voice faded into the background as images formed in her mind. They were so sharp and clear, as if they were memories from her past and not mere figments of her imagination. The girl in the story was her. The villagers treasure was a captive, a demon of their own, and Vlad and his troop had unwittingly been her liberators. Or so her imagination fleshed out the story as his words created the skeleton. And it had to be her imagination, right? Because how could a humble man like Jean-Claude know a story from one of her past lives – if she even believed in such things. And why was she thinking she had past lives? It made her feel – broken.

"There were the two gypsy girls, skilled with the knives – one blonde as sunshine, one dark as night. And then the two soldiers, retainers from Vlad's father's court. And the brothers, two boys ten and eleven, the only survivors of a village slaughtered by vampyres. Hard as rock and pitiless these two, they tended the troops' horses and equipment."

"Only three true ways exist to kill a vampyre," Jean-Claude instructed, displaying the odd rosary that had sparked the story. "None of that Hollywood shoot them in the head nonsense."

"Really?" Crystal pressed. "And how do you kill a vampyre?"

"The surest and safest way is to impale him on a stake," he continued. "That is why so many were impaled during Vlad's reign – maybe not all vampyres, but better safe than sorry during the Long Night of the Vampyre, the three years of blood and hunger. No?"

"The second way is to behead the creature, and this must be a clean cut, like a guillotine. To do this right needs a big axe, and people, they were smaller back then."

"And the last way?" Crystal really was curious.

"A stake through the heart," Jean-Claude replied with finality. "But not just any stake. It must be a cross or a crucifix. See here?" He took up the overly large crucifix on the rosary he always carried, and she could see it looked like a dagger.

"The wood in the centre is from a crucifix – the True Rood on which our Lord and Saviour died– and sharp metal comes down to a point. That is for piercing the heart of vampyres."

`It is why they call my order The Guardians of the Cross,' he thought, but did not say aloud. He placed it around her neck. Jean-Claude did not know what affect it would have on her, but did not think it would hurt.

She remembered now. Vlad was tall and handsome, a dark brooding man with the eyes of a wolf. He and his trained killers stalked the village waiting for the vampyres. And they would come. She was too tempting to ignore. And the three she had caught and fed on that night had given her the strength to escape her captors.

Vampyres were not soulless. Just imperfect feeders that lived off of the pieces of the soul of their victims while theirs grew ancient and untouched by the vagaries of time. Aged to perfection like a fine wine or a good cheese.

She was not a vampyre. Crystal could not say what she was. Perhaps her memory, or her imagination, was failing her. She could no longer tell as her mind wandering, her thoughts fractured, each from some different lifetime unfolding like a kaleidoscope of film clips.

The visions in her head no longer matched the words of his story – the tale of that time in the village. The real story took place several years later, after Vlad had taken up his father's throne – in the days known as the Long Night of the Vampyre.

She was asleep. Jean-Claude laid her gently on the pillow and stood to stretch. April and Gwen would be here soon and he would return home for a brief nap before his nightly vigil.

..... she sat astride a grey gelding. Ahead, to her right, Prince Vlad sat on a black stallion, the black cape with its crimson lining she had presented him last evening billowing in the wind. She toyed with the talisman around her neck – a crystal raven presented to her from her beloved. She smiled at his profile, wondering why it hurt so much to look at him so.

"They are down there, my beloved," she called, confident in his presence. "I can feel them."

He looked down at the mist enshrouded valley, where somewhere lay the entrance to the vampyre lair. It would be full sun soon, when he would send his levies down to put paid to his enemy. Night was the time of these foul beasts, and although it had been three, long bloody years since the sun had shone through this perpetual gloom – in a few hours it would be true daylight once again. And in daylight his troops would conquer, and the long war with these minions of hell would at last be over.

Around him had gathered men from all over Europe. Hard men. Bitter fighters who neither asked nor gave quarter. Sent secretly by the Vatican, these warrior monks had at long last turned the tides of battle. They had brought the sun back to Europe through their blood, and once again the End Times had been postponed.

Surely, Vlad thought as he stared down into the perpetual mists, *the End Times would come as prophesized. But not until Mankind was ready to greet their Saviour and Lord. Not until God's work was done.*

He could see little, but he knew his enemy was down there – trusting implicitly in the strange talents of his beloved. She was one of the Fallen. He knew this, knew that one day she would consume his immortal soul, and still he loved her as much as one mortal man could love a woman. Not just yet, though. There was still time to be together, still time to complete his life's work. His sacrifice would not be in vain, and if he had to take his rewards here on earth, so be it. He could do even this for his God.

"It is time, my lord," the strange man in the hooded cassock intoned.

Vlad nodded. This man never showed his face, this Papal envoy who spoke only in chant, but so far his predictions had been letter perfect. It was on his word that he had let his beloved lead his levies to the lair of their enemy. This day would be theirs.

"For God and country!" Vlad cried, waving his sword above his head.

"To the Gates of Hell and beyond!" His host thundered in reply.

Crystal rode with them, in memory or in dream she could not say. Caught in the moment, she watched the chaotic flashes that were the opening moments of battle. And she fed. And grew stronger with each feeding. Her time had come.

Chapter 6

New York City. A city of skyscrapers. Reaching into the heavens in a series of Towers of Babel, teaming masses of humanity rutted and breathed and died, ate and shit and played in a chaotic tangle. Beneath this swirling infestation of life, beneath its sewers and subways, beneath the basements and countless sub-basements, where the foundations of these behemoths rested, a second city carried out a parasitic relationship with the surface world. Beyond the realm of dust and rats and cobwebs, beyond the unseen shadows, far below where the waters of a buried river flowed, lay a hidden city - home of the Children of the Night.

Few the church thought them, here where thousands lived in a world far beyond the imagination - one civilization living off the castoffs of a city of millions. Blood farms and estates, factories and schools winding deep into an unknown subterranean labyrinth, the Vampyre grew powerful in the shadows. What the farms and foragers could not provide, a complex network of privately owned donor clinics provided the blood to feed the masses. Human ingenuity and human industry added a touch of culture to these dark haunts, most mere affectations, while some endeavours, notably in the field of genetics, fed a deeper hope of the Children of the Night.

Twelve castes, twelve houses to each caste, twelve clans in each house -from the High Nobles to the Eaters of the Dead, a complex society of Vampyres lived and waited for the return of the long night. Waited for that prophesized moment, centuries in its culmination, when they would rise to the surface to claim their birthright. For they, not the meek, would inherit the earth.

From his underground kingdom, High Lord Vlad

Romanov guided his people –urging patience. Always patience. A member of the Sanguinarians –from which the top three castes took their name: the Sanguinarians, the Civatateo, and the Empusae, all drinkers of blood, who fed on the souls of living adults, he knew it was his destiny to lead his people to their former glory. Below this upper strata lived the three weaker castes, the slayers of children and virgins – the Estrie, the Jaaracacas, and the Dearg-du. The last and lowest rung that lived in the Conclave, the three castes of animal eaters, the Nosferatu, the Hupacabra, and the Loogaroo, commonly called the werewolf, provided the bulk of the labour that kept their Conclave running. All looked to him for more than just their daily blood.

Only the last three castes – the eaters of the dead – did not live here. Even amongst their own kind they were the untouchables, hunted and put down wherever they were found. But even these had their place in the Grand Scheme, and so the High Council tolerated their existence.

Delph, eldest son of High Lord Vlad Romanov, had learned this mantra of patience and caution from the moment he suckled on the blood of his first feeble victim. And all that stood in their way was one insignificant girl, a girl guarded by an individual considered weak even by his fellow humans. No match for Delph, a High Lord born a vampyre, lacking the weakness of those made vampyres of the lesser castes. This human was not even a knight of the Guardians of the Cross. An invalid! Sickly and bone-thin – not even worth draining of his blood - Delph could snap his neck with a flick of his finger.

Delph was a half-breed. His mother was a Civatateo – the prettiest, of course – married by his father to cement his position on the council. He could almost hate his father for this mixed parentage. He knew he was detested by the upper crust of his conclave, knew his tainted blood would prevent him from earning the respect of the council unless he accomplished something noble and heroic. And now presented with the perfect opportunity, Vlad, his father, had forbidden anyone from going after the girl while she was in the hospital – sanctified ground – for fear of waking the wrath of the church. But what was the church? Fat old men and molesters of children.

Vlad, his father, had forbidden anyone from going after the girl while she was in the hospital – sanctified ground – for fear of waking the wrath of the church. But what was the church? Fat old men and molesters of children.

Delph knew he could do it. Killing the girl, as weak as she was, would be child's play. And he, not his father, would usher in the perpetual twilight that would allow his people to rule the surface world.

As hero of his people, Nephafari would be his. No-one on the council would dare mention a word about co-mingling of blood. His power, and his alone, would be unlimited, and not even her family could object to his parentage. And, at long last, after centuries of careful planning, his family's honour would be restored. The name of Romanov would once again be unblemished, and he would earn his father's respect. All this with just one death.

As an adolescent amongst his people, still within his first century, Delph had often visited hospitals for a snack. The risk of detection still appealed to him and his peers, and the deception – disguising himself to blend in with the hospital staff – added a certain savour to his meal. Unexplained deaths at hospitals were routine enough to pass unnoticed, and although highly frowned upon by their elders, this current crop of youngsters found the whole experience a rush. It had become a rite of passage amongst them as ubiquitous as obtaining a drivers licence was amongst the mortals.

Arriving in the lowest levels of the staff parking lot, where a sewer grating provided access from the subterranean world, he set out to acquire a disguise. Dark-haired and fair complexion, he held that youthful all-American high school quarterback look even into his seventh decade. Startling grey eyes looked onto the world with frank intelligence and an openness that fooled many. He could play any role, but the seducer was still the mainstay of the Vampyre of his generation.

Good looks and a mesmerizing stare could be put to other uses. Even vampyres had needs beyond food. At the moment these talents helped him convince a harried young nurse that he had need of scrubs and a lab coat. Redressed, just another harried intern with too little sleep and too much work, he began to stalk along the hallways with a practiced pace. Even his pale skin fitted in with a segment of the hospital population that seldom saw the sun. This was one hospital where he and his friends had never visited, but with a clipboard in hand and a brisk stride he faded into the background and was able to stroll around and explore unhindered.

Reminiscent of his first nocturnal raid, that night when a bored and listless flight of vampyres wandered into a hospital looking for adventure and trouble, he felt safe in his disguise. All in their sixth and seventh decades, still in what passed as high school for vampyres, they had been foot loose and bored. Finding something young and tasty seemed like a kick. And infiltrating a hospital, with the threat of discovery hovering over their heads added an edge to the game.

He came to the nurses' station on the children's wing. It was a risk, but he needed directions.

"The Jane Doe that was brought in last week?" He asked without preamble. It tickled his warped sense of humour that he knew her name, but chose not to tell these pathetic mortals.

"You mean Crystal?"

"Yes," he said, hoping she was the right one, and realizing he had not done enough homework. Sometimes withholding information could cut both ways.

"Room 2130, just down the hall."

New residences came and went, that was his saving grace in this game. So much so, that another one would go unnoticed. They were always transferring in from one department and out to another during their rotation that the busy nurse would not have noticed if he had walked up to her naked.

He could sense her as soon as he entered the room. She was weak – too weak to fight off his attack. His father was wrong. Now was the time. Now the hunter would become the hunted.

Sensing danger, Crystal drifted into wakefulness. Groggy, she thought she saw Jean-Claude step out of the shadows to confront an overly good-looking intern. Her instincts screamed at her that he was a danger, but she was too sleepy to make sense of her muddled thoughts.

"You must leave this place," Jean-Claude warned. "This is not your place or your time."

"And who will stop me mortal?" Delph hissed, showing his fangs.

"That will," Jean-Claude replied calmly, pointing to the rosary that hung around Crystal's neck.

The mortal was right. Even in her weakened state with that weapon she could kill him without any effort. He could sense it now, a True weapon of the Church, one held on consecrated ground. Even one of the ancients would have difficulty overcoming that combination, and in the hands of an immortal the odds went down too drastically to overcome his sense of self-preservation.

"Does your father know you're here Delph?"

Delph hissed his frustration. This one wasn't the weak mortal he seemed – or, at least, not an ordinary mortal.

"This land is consecrated by the Church," Jean-Claude continued. "Surely you know your presence here violates the truce. Are you prepared to start a war you cannot win? Go! Leave this place now!"

Crystal awoke several hours later to find Jean-Claude sitting at her bedside, nodding over one of his books.

"Who was he?" She asked through a lazy yawn.

"Who was who, ma petite?"

"The vampyre dressed like a doctor," she stretched, arching her back as much as her injured hip would allow.

"We have been alone here all night," Jen-Claude replied, puzzled. "I think perhaps you dreamed it, no?"

"I'm pretty sure I was awake," Crystal complained. "You scared him off."

"I?" Jean-Claude questioned. "Scared off a vampyre? With my kung-fuee, eh? I think no more Vampyre stories before bed, no?"

She thought about that for a long moment. Maybe he was right. He wasn't a large man, and she had been dreaming of vampyres all night. And about Vlad. It could have been one of those bizarre dreams where she had just thought she was awake, but had been sleeping all along. That had happened to her before.

"When's breakfast?"

"Soon, ma enfant," Jean-Claude replied. "It is Saturday. Gwen will come soon, and you can go and watch the movie together in the commissary. It will be good to get out of bed for the morning, no?"

"No," she teased.

Every Saturday volunteers screened a movie on a DVD player in the cafeteria in the children's ward. Crystal was not sure what a movie was – did not remember ever seeing one – but Jean-Claude was right. It would be good bust out of this horizontal prison. And it would be good to see Gwen again. She really needed to get away and talk to someone she trusted about all these strange dreams, and about Vlad. Why did it hurt so much to think about a man who died centuries before she was born? None of it made any sense.

The cafeteria for the children's ward was a small room just down the hall from Crystal's room. The tables had been cleared to one side, and now a collection of patients ranging in age from seven to seventeen sat on the floor and in wheel chairs grouped about a television. Chrystal sat in her wheelchair with Gwen at her side, holding hands as they waited for the movie to start. They were whispering to each other as Gwen filled her in on the latest heart throb staring in this movie. Unsure of what to expect, Crystal fed off of her friend's excitement, still confused by what was going on in this room, and vaguely afraid. Too many things in her world were new and confusing, and if she did not learn to accept them, the strangeness would consume her.

A volunteer moved to the front of the room and asked for quiet. Sound and pictures came out of the box with the glass window, and suddenly Chrystal was confronted by a series of people trapped inside. At first Crystal did not understand how they had fit the people into that small box. Even though it reminded her of a puppet show she remembered once seeing, the little figures on the screen were too realistic looking to be puppets, and try as she might, she could see no strings. She mentioned as much to Gwen, who told her it was a recording – moving pictures with sound, and that no people were inside. Still, Crystal had an uncontrollable desire to wheel herself over and look behind the box.

Satisfied, she sat back and watched an amazing tale about a vampyre who was in love with a mortal girl. He was a Stregoni Benefici, agonizing over telling her his dark secret. But she too had a secret that was preventing her from giving him her heart – she was a Wiccan with the ability to see a person's past lives. It was all very romantic, and vaguely reminded Crystal of a man she knew.... In her past or from another movie she had watched?

His name eluded her at the moment, but he too had been a Stregoni Benefici – a beneficial vampyre who aided the church. She sensed that his story too had ended badly, much in the way she remembered or imagined it had ended with Vlad. The thought left her a sense of great pain, and not all the tears rolling down her cheeks at the end of the movie had been raised by its sad ending. Perhaps she would feel better if she could talk to Gwen about it, but she was not even sure how she would broach the subject, let alone articulate the deep loneliness she was feeling.

"Oh," Gwen sighed as they moved out of the room two hours later. "He is just so dreamy!"

"Delicious," Crystal agreed. "If all Nosferatu looked like him I might just give up on feeding on vampyres."

Gwen looked at her quizzically.

"The dream I want to tell you about," Crystal covered quickly. "If we can ever find somewhere to be alone."

"I know where we can go," Gwen said conspiratorially. "We'll have to sneak out."

Giggling to themselves, the two girls headed down the hall. Occasionally looking over her shoulder as she pushed Crystal along in her wheel chair, Gwen made a fast break for the elevator. On the first floor there was a small, neglected courtyard formed when a wing was added to the hospital. At one point someone had made an attempt to create a contemplation garden, but it had long ago been abandoned to the weeds.

There was something about the courtyard with its patches of sunlight and shadows that Gwen always liked. It was private and lonely, with strong undertones of peace and tranquility. There was even a small statue of Sarah Good, the only true Wiccan to be executed during the Salem witch trials. It was crafted from a single crystal, and always made Gwen feel powerful and competent when she was in its presence. Instinctively, she knew it was a place of power, a place any Wiccan was safe even in the face of the most desperate dangers. Like if her mother and Jean-Claude discovered they had snuck off on their own.

"Okay," she said as she settled Crystal's chair in a patch of sunlight. "Tell me all about this boy in your dreams."

"Not a boy, a man," Crystal protested.

"Even better."

"Jean-Claude was telling me this story about Vlad the Impaler," Crystal explained.

Gwen made a face. "Oh, that one."

"Yeah," Crystal laughed. It really was a gruesome tale. "But as he spoke, in my mind I not only saw how he looked, but how he spoke and how he moved. And when I thought about him, like I was remembering him, I felt...Heart broken."

"Maybe he was someone from your life," Gwen suggested. "Like your father or a teacher you had a crush on."

"Maybe," Crystal mumbled, not too sure. It was so hard not remembering anything of her past. It left this hollow feeling in her heart.

Gwen sensed her friend's distress, and in that moment would have recommended a past life progression. But April and Jean-Claude had forbidden it. There was something dark and haunting in Crystal's past they did not want her to know. So she said nothing.

"Was he dreamy?"

"He was tall and pretty," Crystal breathed, her eyes drifting up towards the sky as she remembered, "and brave and noble."

"Must have been a crush then. If it was your dad," Gwen teased, "that would be too weird. But I got to get me a dream like that. Do you mind if I borrow yours?"

"Don't you dare," and the two convulsed into giggles.

"Later though," Crystal continued, "I thought I woke up. There was this young doctor there arguing with Jean-Claude. Only I don't think he was a doctor, though."

"What was he?"

"A vampyre," Crystal used Jean-Claude's infliction. "Jean-Claude says I was dreaming."

"Let's hope so," Gwen said with a shudder.

Above their heads, in a deep shadow on the roof, a lone figure looked down on them. Another missed opportunity. He could not go down there. It was a Wiccan place and would not tolerate his presence....

The girls stayed for another half hour, and found two very angry parents waiting for them when they returned to the room. Neither said anything, which made their censure all the worse. It was not that they had done anything really, just went off to find a little privacy, but judging by April and Jean-Claude's reactions, maybe they had been a little thoughtless.

"Come," Jean-Claude said without a hint of anger, "you must change and get ready for the lawyer. He comes in thirty minutes."

When none of the girls moved, Jean-Claude stared at them incomprehensibly. April merely pointed to the door.

"Oui," he replied. "I will go get some coffees and juice, no?"

"That's a definite yes," Gwen replied, rolling her eyes at Crystal. Sometimes that man was as dense as a post.

The two women had brought a nice summer dress for Crystal, a patterned fabric of black and red crows that matched the streaks in her hair. They helped her out of her house coat and nightgown, and into the dress, fitting it over the cast on her hip so that its folds disguised it. Once her hair was fixed, she flounced before the full length mirror on the door to the bathroom, frowning at what she saw. The cast made her hips look fat.

"What do you think?" Crystal asked her two friends. "Will I pass a lawyer's inspection?"

"You'll steal his heart," Gwen assured her, then giggled at her mother's stern look.

"He's just here to talk to you and Jean-Claude," April explained. "To help you answer the questions in Family Court, and to help explain the process. No flirting or other foolishness. Either one of you wiggle your jiggly parts at him, and you're grounded for life."

"And if I answer correctly," Crystal asked nervously, "I get to stay with Jean-Claude?"

"There are no right or wrong answers," April soothed. "Just answer truthfully. And he will help you best say what you want to say."

Jean-Claude returned with a tray of three coffees and two fruit juices. He placed them on the small table, offering a coffee to April with a smile.

Their lawyer arrived a few minutes later. The same associate who had walked their application through Children's Aid, Charles Evans, had spent hours prepping a list of questions with one of the interns from the firm's Family Law division. He withdrew that list from his briefcase and set it on the table as he accepted a coffee from Jean-Claude. Roger Whittingham, the senior partner, would do all the actual courtroom work, so Evans wanted to make sure there would be no embarrassing surprises. He still had hopes of making full partner during the next quarterly review, and having Whittingham owe him a favour could only help his chances.

"Hello Crystal," Charles introduced himself. He was not in the habit of working with children, and was not sure how to proceed. "I am Mr. Evans, Charles, and I am one of the lawyers working on Jean-Claude's Foster application so that you can live with him."

"Why can't I just choose where I want to live?" Crystal demanded. She hadn't intended to be difficult, but her fear of losing Jean-Claude and Gwen made her angry. She hated how sulky it made her sounded. "Am I not a free person?"

"Yes, very much so." It was actually a very astute question. "But at sixteen you are still a minor and must live under the care of an adult."

He rearranged the papers, thinking maybe they could work it into their petition. Certainly, the next step, should this hearing fail, was to apply to the court to have her declared an emancipated minor. Somehow he doubted they would fail with this application. The character witnesses on Mr. Beaucour's behalf included both the Mayor and the Bishop of New York.

"Would you like to live with Mr. Beaucour?"

"Yes," Crystal replied, shaking her head fervently. "Very much so."

"And do you remember anything about your past?"

Charles asked. He wanted to get this out in the open right away.

"No," Crystal hedged. "Well, one thing. But it doesn't make much sense."

"And what is that?"

"I remember eating vampyres," Crystal returned, almost too quietly to hear.

"And how does one eat a vampyre?" Charles asked, frowning in concern.

"I don't really know," Crystal brightened. "But it was probably something from a movie I once watched, don't you think?"

"Okay," Charles nodded, relieved. "So in court, just to be clear, we will say you remember something from a movie you once watched."

Jean-Claude and April exchanged a troubled look. Their silent communication went no further, interrupted as Doctor Gilmore breezed into the room on his rounds.

"Excellent Crystal!" He greeted. "Sorry to interrupt folks, but I did not want to miss my favourite patient. Don't worry. Your memories may not make much sense as they first return, but you will puzzle them out as your mind incorporates them into your current memories. And if you are having any difficult ones, talk them out with me or your family."

"Even if they are all about vampyres?" Crystal asked meekly. She was beginning to worry that she was completely losing her mind.

"I wouldn't be surprised if many of them are," Doctor Gilmore assured her. "All things vampyre are very popular with people your age. I know both my daughters can't get enough of them. You are probably remembering things from your favourite topic."

"And this is normal?" Charles asked the doctor hopefully.

"There is no predicting which memories will return to a person first," Doctor Gilmore explained. "But the more they were associated with their everyday life, the sooner they will come back to us. At her age, it is normal to obsess about one subject. One patient with amnesia, who was a concert pianist, remembered how to play complex arias long before he remembered why he knew how to play them at all."

"And she will remember what these memories all mean?" Charles countered.

"Well," Doctor Gilmore admitted. "Some of the associations to our memories never return, even amongst those who have not suffered from amnesia. And I will be testifying to that at the hearing."

Long after the lawyer and the doctor had left, Crystal lay dozing in her bed with her new family reading in chairs around her. She still tired easily.

"Jean-Claude?" She asked sleepily.

"Oui, ma petite?"

"Are there creatures that eat vampyres?"

"Vampyres," Jean-Claude answered slowly, picking his way around the subject carefully. "Are not truly demons. They are mortals who have surrendered their humanity in exchange for a quasi-immortality. And like all mortals, they are subject to the torments of demons."

Crystal lay in her bed absorbing this. If demons ate vampyres, and her only memories were of eating and killing vampyres, was she some kind of demon then? Or had she just been obsessed with some kind of demon in her previous life? She didn't feel evil, and demons were creatures of Hell. Long after they thought her asleep, she spoke.

"Are all demons evil?"

"No. The demonologies, from both the Christian and Jewish traditions, say different. Demons are said to be good, evil or indifferent."

"Are demons real?"

"No, ma petite," Jean-Claude assured her, "they are creatures from the stories, no? Tales to entertain us on winter nights, eh?"

Again she fell silent, returning to her thoughts. Sensing that she had more to ask, Jean-Claude put down his book and waited. He searched his mind for passages from books like the Zoharistic Kabbalah, and the De Nugis Curiallium, but her next question caught him completely off-guard.

"Do you love me?"

"We all love you, dear," April answered for all of them.

"And would you still love me if I were a demon?" Crystal asked.

"With all my heart, ma petite," Jean-Claude replied. "With all my heart."

And knowing that Jean-Claude loved her, what she had been in her past no longer mattered. Even if her reality proved as lurid as the demons from his stories the man of her dreams said he would still love her. And she believed him.

With a sigh, she drifted off to sleep.

Chapter 7

A petulant dawn brought a renewal of Crystal's physiotherapy sessions, and the anticipated pain and frustration washed her morning in frowns. The sessions were hard, and facing another only reminded her about how debilitating her injuries were. She sounded childish and sulky when she wanted be hard and bitchy, and that annoyed her. Crystal could never get this wreck of a body to do anything she wanted it to do. She needed a brace of slave boys – glistening, hard-bodied young gods – to carry her around on a couch like some patricians wife from ancient Rome. Or use one of those steel-wheeled monstrosities they were always forcing on her – pushed by a salty intern.

"Come, ma petite dove," Jean-Claude cajoled. "Do you not have a smile to brighten my day?"

"I traded them all in for a frown," she muttered darkly. "You should appreciate it, it came so dearly."

"Come," he soothed, stroking her hair. "When you are finished I will show you something special, no?"

"No."

The women in his life were always saying no to him. It was a disturbing trend.

"I will kiss your pain away," he promised. "But come, be a good girl for me now, no?"

"No," she pouted, but the beginnings of a smile tugged at the corners of her mouth. She could taste his kiss already, sweet and salty and soul quenching.

April and Gwen arrived all bustle and giggles, and together they helped Crystal dress for the day. By the time they had arrived she had expended most of her grumps on Jean-Claude, and she and Gwen were once again deep in a giggling session. Something to do with a fly young man, or was that fine? Jean-Claude could never keep these things straight and only set them off again when he tried. Nor did he quite understand why his two girls lit up when the young orderly walked in, although he suspected his muscles and female hormones played a large part in creating the two flirts who left with him.

Her session with the physiotherapist was the nightmare she had envisioned. By the end her whole right side was on fire. She felt miserable and exhausted, and did not care if every pretty boy in Christendom kissed her. She was determined to be a hard-ass for the rest of her life.

Jean-Claude was waiting for her in her room. He had brought her a dozen blue roses and a crystal vase shaped like a raven.

"Oh," Gwen squealed. "They're so beautiful. I'm way jealous."

"They are beautiful," Crystal breathed, smiling despite her mood. She had never seen blue roses. At least, she thought never had. Those he had brought her before had faded to brown well before she woke up.

"Yes," Jean-Claude replied. "A pretty flower for a belle mademoiselle. And since you did so well today, I take you to see something very special, no?"

"Yes," Crystal breathed.

And even though she was exhausted from her therapy session, she sat back in the wheel chair and let him wheel her away. The chance to spend some time alone with him was too great a temptation. And he had promised her a kiss. She imagined a deep and languid one, a hot embrace with their bodies pressed tight together. She sighed wistfully in anticipation of a salty moment.

Jean-Claude wheeled her towards the nearest elevator. On the main floor he began to weave a serpentine path through departments and along strange hallways. His course was so convoluted that she doubted she could follow it with a map and compass – or even a global positioning system. It was enough that they were together, and that he was saying sweet things to her.

A massive oak grew from the floor of the building, stretching skyward, its branches disappearing somewhere above the ceiling. Startled, Crystal lost the train of their conversation as she sat staring up at the tree. Gnarled and stooped, its bark all but petrified, a thousand faces were hidden within its twisted surface. Ancient when the first block of the pyramids migrated across the desert, its majesty and power held Crystal in its sway, taunting her with its immortality.

Thunderstruck, Crystal railed against the very idea of a tree growing inside a building. She stared up in awe at its massive trunk, its twisted bark staring back at her like so many tormented souls. And then he spoke, and she only had eyes for Jean-Claude.

"It is wonderful, no?"

As Jean-Claude bent down to whisper to her, Crystal felt the moment was precipitous. She reached her arms around his neck and pulled his face to hers. Forcing her tongue between his lips, she kissed him passionately, feeling the energy and urgency of her hunger course through her body and touch her very soul.

Jean-Claude leapt back, deeply agitated. Not here! She mustn't feed! Not in this place! "Mon Deiu! You are too young. No! No! This is not right. We must go back at once."

Passing by a nearby cross-corridor, Scott Peterson caught sight of the two. In his peripheral vision he saw just enough to catch the kiss. He was too far to hear anything, and the bulk of the tree hid much of her companion. But there was no mistaking that unruly shock of grey and red hair. He had his man.

Crystal licked her lips as he pushed her back to her room, still tasting the kiss. There was nothing truly sexual in her hunger. It was something deeper. And darker. And now that the kiss had whetted her appetite, she longed to feed soul deep again. She felt electrified, energized and empowered, unable to sit still. Even the bone deep ache in her hip from this morning had disappeared. And in her ears she heard a roar, like the rush of the waters from every water falls in the world, a rush of exhilaration singing on a hurricane wind.

One look at the two as they returned early to the room, and April guessed what must have happened.

"Gwen," she instructed, "go walk in the park with Jean-Claude. You both need some sunshine and fresh air."

Gwen knew better than to cross her mother when she used that tone of voice. Meekly, she took Jean-Claude's hand and led him from the room. She did not even look up to note the look that passed between April and Jean-Claude.

When they were gone, April briskly helped Crystal into bed. She sat on the bed and placed her hand over the girl's.

"Jean-Claude is not for you, Crystal," she said gently.

"Is he yours?" Crystal asked suspiciously, feeling a wave of jealous anger rise in her breast like an apocalypse.

"No," April laughed lightly. "He is not for me either."

"Then why can he not be mine?"

April paused, stroking the girl's arm gently. Despite whatever else she was, she still was a young girl on the verge of womanhood. Her emotions ran deep and sharp.

"What happened between you is natural," she explained patiently, "but not acceptable. In this day and age a sixteen year old is not considered a woman."

Her turn of phrase struck Crystal as odd, but she pressed ahead anyway. "But in two years it would be okay? I would be an adult, like the lawyers say."

April noticed the hope and desperation in the other's voice. "Before that would destroy him. He would become a pariah, a social outcast. But there is more than that. Jean-Claude is a celibate. Do you understand what that is?"

"Is he afraid of women, then?" Crystal countered.

April laughed. A short, deep bark. "Far from it. There are

many women in his life. He has taken a vow so that he may focus on his work, work that is very important to all of us."

"A vow to whom?" Crystal asked, vowing if it were another woman she would tear her heart out.

"To God."

Crystal cringed at the name, and could not suppress the small whimper that escaped her lips. "I will give him two years to finish his work, and then he's mine!"

Under the circumstances, it was the best April could hope for. Her kind chose to feed where and when they wished, and in two years Jean-Claude would be beyond hers or anyone's reach. She bit her lip and suppressed the wave of emotion riding on that thought before turning back to Crystal.

Out in the park on the hospital grounds Jean-Claude and Gwen walked quietly along hand-in-hand. Since she was a very young girl they had often walked this way, and her hand in his always made her feel safe and content. In a strange way he had come to replace the father who had died when she was a baby.

Finally, she could contain her curiosity no longer. "So, spill. What happened?"

"Crystal," Jean-Claude exploded. "She, how do you say – slipped me the tongue!"

Gwen couldn't help herself. The giggles just exploded from her.

"It is not funny, silly girl," Jean-Claude was trying hard to maintain his sense of outrage, and failing.

"No," Gwen gulped, and once again convulsed in laughter. "It's hilarious!"

Jean-Claude gave her a small pinch in the middle of her back. Gwen yelped and jumped away.

"That's not funny, Jean-Claude!" She scolded.

"No, it's hilarious."

"Oh," Gwen glared, "you silly man."

The four gathered at the hospital again later that evening. Earlier, Jean-Claude had returned home to sleep. Even with his long habit of only sleeping three or four hours a night, lately he could not get enough rest. And since the kiss he had felt totally drained. The five hour nap did little to relieve his deep sense of lethargy. Hag-ridden, his grandmother use to call it.

As they ate another dinner from April's diner, Crystal would not meet Jean-Claude's eyes. Sensing her distress, the gentle man cupped her chin in his hand and raised her eyes to his. He said nothing, merely smiled tenderly and stroked a cheek with his finger until he received a smile in return. With that moment, much of the tension dissipated from the room. All was forgiven, on both sides.

The two Moonshadows stayed until just after dark, when Crystal succumbed to sleep despite her recent surge of energy. Alone in the darkened room, Jean-Claude studied an ancient tome. Still looking for her true name, out of desperation he had turned to the Goetic traditions. While the Lesser Key of Solomon was widely available today, he was fortunate to have access to a manuscript known as the Greater Key of Solomon. Only one copy of this demonology was thought to exist outside the Vatican vaults, although scholars suspected there was a third copy, its location unknown since some point in the Thirteen Hundreds.

Like the Lesser Key of Solomon this book contained five chapters outlining the arts, but unlike the former it contained four other parts that were of interest to his order. He knew that the line of the succubus he studies began with Lilith – the first wife of Adam – and that her sire was said to be the Archangel Samuel. Contrary to popular thought there had been only twelve succubi, who, unlike their mortal counterparts, were reincarnated along a set cycle of years. Beyond this little was known of the Daughters of Lilith, but the line of incarnations that he followed included Meridiana, the paramour of Pope Sylvester II and Dionetta, lover of Vlad the Impaler.

Demons came in three types – evil, indifferent and good.

She was one of three of the latter types. The Church owed her a great debt, but it could not help her if he could not uncover her true name. Only with the name could they complete the ritual to identify her next incarnation, and time was running out. His research was hampered by his need to keep a nightly vigil at the bedside of this girl, this demon of unknown nature and origin. It was one of those things that could not be helped despite the urgency of his work. This girl too was a demon, or had come across a demon – the crystal raven told him that much – and leaving demons to their own devices led to disaster.

His instincts told him that she was the one they, but he could not risk the fate of humanity on a hunch, nor would his superiors accept his word alone. And so tonight he concentrated on the demon Sitri – betrayer of women's secrets. He controlled our urges, according to Kabbalah and Medieval traditions to reveal out naked bodies to the opposite sex. As governor of our lusts, the Succubi and their male counterparts, the Incubus, fell under his preview. Somewhere in the writings on this Lord of Hell Jean-Claude hoped to find mention of the true names of the Twelve Cursed Daughters of the Archangel Samuel. And even with his incomplete list of her names during her carnal manifestations, such a list should lead him to her true name. Or at least one would hope.

Much knowledge had been lost during the book burnings of the Dark Ages, and coming on top of the sack of the Library of Alexandria as it did, it left his order floundering in ignorance for centuries. But this too could not be helped. Recovering that lost intelligence was a tedious and often dangerous process. Contrary to the writings of such men as Johann Weyer and Samuel Mathers, a demon could not just be summoned, and if summoned could not be controlled. Demons had to be bearded in their lair, so to speak, where one hoped to learn something while battling for your life and your immortal soul. For the most part only the demon's current incarnation was destroyed, for even demons were part of

God's ultimate plan; but occasionally, as had happened with the eleven other succubi, the demon is utterly destroyed.

A shadow passed across the periphery of his vision. He looked up to find Vlad standing in the doorway. His presence roused Crystal from a deep sleep, but did not fully wake her.

"She has fed," he commented, forgoing his usual pleasantries in his concern.

"A little, I'm afraid," Jean-Claude admitted ruefully.

"On you."

There was no real need to reply to that. Both men knew what that would mean. And both held separate concerns about the matter, for very disparate reasons.

"Your son Delph was here," Jean-Claude mentioned.

"I was not aware that you knew his name," Vlad replied flatly, his mind on other matters.

"The Goth keep track of such things, no?" Jean-Claude replied, indifferent.

If the child had fed it may already be too late. There was, however, another way to destroy her. An ancient ritual held at the eclipse of the moon, but they would need some things. The Asian clans would have to be brought into matters now, and they were extremely difficult to deal with. Meanwhile, he must keep this mortal guessing and hope he did not discover her true nature until their preparations were complete.

"Why did my son come here?"

"For the girl, one would suppose, no?" Jean-Claude replied. "He is young, and perhaps does not understand the need for circumspection in these matters."

"Patience is not the strongest suit of the young," Vlad admitted.

"He must be made to see that open warfare between our two peoples will do great harm, no?" Jean-Claude pressed.

"I will speak to my son," Vlad conceded. "Not just father to son, but as High Lord of the Council."

"And I will see that the Goths do not encroach on the lower

levels," Jean-Claude promised. "But as always, the no-man's-land between our places remains patrolled, no?"

"As always, my old friend," Vlad replied, turning to go. "Keep her safe while you can."

Once again Crystal dreamed of the dark shadowy figure that carried fear and loathing to her world. Not sure whether she was awake or asleep, she watched as the strange man spoke to Jean-Claude in a language she was now sure was ancient Latin. How was it she knew a language centuries dead, but could not read or write the language of the vernacular? Jean-Claude suggested she might have been educated in a parochial school, some of whom still taught Latin and Greek extensively. Still puzzling over this anomaly, she drifted back into deep sleep.

The next two weeks passed uneventfully. Nothing strange happened to make Crystal doubt she was anything but a normal teenage girl. Even the eerie dreams had stopped. Picturing Jean-Claude as a mighty vampyre slayer became more and more difficult as she got to know him better. His daily displays of clumsiness and slight stature put the lie to that notion rather quickly. She was growing more convinced each day that Jean-Claude's prosaic explanations were the true ones – she had in her past life been fascinated in vampyres, and had at some point studied Latin. And Doctor Gilmore's explanation that some skills sometimes returned sooner than others, and the strange phenomena that was often associated with aphasias caused by head injuries lay to rest the last of her doubts. Although the hunger she could not begin to comprehend lingered just beneath the surface of her conscious thoughts.

Since the kiss her daily physiotherapy sessions were less painful, and her hip grew stronger by leaps and bounds. Crystal no longer saw or felt the need for the walker, but suffered with its awkward bulk to placate the adults in her life. When she was alone with Gwen, however, it often lay forgotten at her bedside. The two spent progressively more time along together as Gwen began to teach her to read and write English. Together they were reading through the eight volumes Threefold Law series, and although Gwen had already read the first two novels, she said she did not mind reading them again with her best friend. The books told the tale of a teenage Wiccan girl learning to come to grips with her powers during the witch hunts of the 1600's. The story paralleled her own struggles to come to grips with a past life she no longer remembered so closely, that sharing it with her friend made her come to love her all the more.

Soon, it seemed that they had known each other forever. Crystal continued to heal at a slightly accelerated rate, and the time when April predicted she would be better off at home with them was fast approaching.

Chapter 8

Fate's kiss of doom hovered above Crystal's lips. Today strangers would set the course of her future, grinding her through a system that effectively stifled her voice and left her out of the decision. April and Gwen arrived early to help the troubled girl dress. Because of the importance of this day to their little family, April had allowed her daughter to skip school. Her mother was strict, and the unexpected vacation, a rare occasion in her young life, made it feel like a holiday to Gwen – Christmas in July, or All Hallows Eve. Ever the optimist, Gwen did not share Crystal's worries about the hearing, and would not let the other's nervousness dampen her own excitement. It was Jean-Claude, after all, and he had never failed to come through for Gwen in her entire life. Her faith in him was limitless, and besides a chronic inability to be chill, in her eyes there was nothing he could not do.

"Oh, just think," she enthused as she helped Crystal with her hair, "in a few more hours we will truly be sisters!"

"I'm not too sure," Crystal winced in memory. "That Mr. Peterson really doesn't like Jean-Claude."

"I don't think that man likes anyone, including himself. Besides, I cast the crystals last night," Gwen said unthinking, only falling silent when she caught sight of her mother's stern look.

"Oh well, if you cast the crystals," Crystal replied, "I shouldn't worry; after all, they have never failed us before.

Crystal's reply struck both girls as odd, as if she already knew Gwen's secret and had always known. Such random slips were coming more frequently, and neither girl knew what they meant, or why they caused the two adults in their lives to fall suddenly silent. April wore a frown now. She was sorely tempted to do a past lives regression with the two girls, but Jean-Claude's had made his wishes clear. Until he knew for sure what they were dealing with, he did not want his suspicions to go beyond a select few. She prayed he knew what he was doing. It could all go badly so easily – for all of them.

The three women, with Crystal sitting uneasily in her wheel chair, made their way out of the hospital. A special van sat waiting to drive them to the courthouse, all to accommodate the stupid torture device Crystal neither felt she wanted or needed. She had worn a short skirt that showed off her legs, and now no one would see them. Especially Jean-Claude. Not in this steel contraption that advertised her disability.

Inside the van Mama Flo was there to greet them with hugs all around and a kiss for her `special baby'. Once again she explained the procedure to Crystal and the Moonshadows, the role of her advocates, of the judge and of the state investigators. She went over much of what the lawyers already had – how the first portion of the hearing would cover declaring her a ward of the state before moving on to decide on Jean-Claude's custody application. Crystal cared little for the first part, and wished the woman would stop treating her as if she were mentally deficient or a child. After all these weeks, if her parents had filed a missing person's report, the police would have found it. She was obviously not missed.

The Bronx county courthouse on Sheridan Avenue was a fifty minute walk from the hospital and a twenty minute drive in traffic. Finding a parking place was a perennial problem.
The ability to use a handicap parking space should have helped – but not much. Drivers were just as likely to ignore the blue and white signs as they were the ordinance about double-parking. Crystal wished they had walked. The wait was fuelling her anxiety and she was beginning to feel the need to pee, or scream, or just run amok.

The county courthouse wore a pseudo-limestone facade

that had seen better days. The art-deco building showed its true age where smog and pigeons had caked and pitted its surface, its features and friezes now blunted by time. On the Grand Concourse in the High Bridge neighbourhood, the entrance statuary by Adolph A. Weinman and others was impressive to two young girls, but to a world traveller like April it was rather prosaic. Inside was another world altogether. The halls were dingy and crowded with a collage of humanity – juveniles and their advocates, arresting officers, parole officers and investigators from Children's Aid. The worried and stoic family members of those accused of crimes, fingering bits of paper like worry beads; the angry denials of those losing their children, or the tears of relief of those finding them returned.

The cacophony of sights and sounds assaulted Crystal's senses like the stench of an open grave as Mama Flo wheeled her inside, and she made a face as if she had just stepped into a cesspool. Even here the smell of urine and unwashed bodies clung to the air like the perfume of desperation. Any confidence she felt in her fate being decided here faded before the reality of its foetid environs. This seemed to be a place dreams went to die.

Inside Surrogate Court, room 317 was at least a little less imposing. There was Jean-Claude waiting for her with a smile, for one thing. And there was Mr. Whittingham in his power-suit, looking bluff and confident, master of all he surveyed. He inspired confidence in all around him. For an old guy, she had to admit, he looked pretty good. She had seen that look before – or at least she imagined that was how the lords and aristocrats of her past life had looked. She had to remember to stop thinking these crazy thoughts, especially while in the court room. One slip here and she could regret it for the rest of her life.

They settled her chair in behind the table of a strange man wearing a sports coat and bow tie. She sat between Mama Flo and that idiot Mr. Peterson. She really didn't like the man.

He was cold and suspicious, his eyes never staying still, as if he saw danger lurking behind every corner. It was unsettling, and made it hard to be comfortable in his presence. Crystal would much rather have sat with Gwen and April, people she knew and trusted.

The judge, when he entered the courtroom from behind the bench, was cut from another cloth altogether. He looked nothing more than Grandpa Walton - face seamed by a lifetime of laughter, a sparkle of mischief in his eye, and snow-white hair – but carried himself with the air of authority of a bishop holding court.

"All rise," the bailiff pronounced, "Superior Court, 12th Judicial District, Bronx County New York is now in session."

"Be seated," Judge McConnelly instructed. "Bailiff, call the first case."

"The case of the City of New York verses Jane Doe, a.k.a Crystal Raven. Case number 10102010."

"The first part of this hearing is to determine whether the minor – that's you Crystal- should become a ward of the state," Judge McConnelly explained. "Do you have any questions young lady?"

"Can I sit with my friends, April and Gwen?"

The members of the public tittered, and the judge smiled. "I see no reason why you can't dear. Mr. Montrose? Are you ready to proceed?"

Mr. Montrose, the lawyer for the City of New York, stood up and adjusted his bow tie, a nervous hold over from his days in the more competitive environs of Criminal court. "Yes, Your Honour."

"Mrs. Washington," the judge requested, "if you could assist Crystal over to her friends, we will get started. Mr. Montrose, you may call your first witness."

"Your Honour," Mr. Montrose stood. "The state calls Detective Aldos, Missing Persons Division of the New York City Metropolitan Police."

"Calling Detective Aldos," the bailiff responded.

Detective Aldos was a younger man. His court suit was a dark blue, which he wore with a light blue shirt and deep red tie. The colour did not quite suit his swarthy complexion, but the cut was conservative – lending him an air of authority that he thought countered his youthful looks. And he liked how the colour brought out the blue in his eyes, a throw-back to his father's Jewish ancestry. His black hair and dark complexion, courtesy of his mother's Hispanic background, made him look much younger than his thirty-two years, something he considered a handicap when testifying in court. Today, at least, he would not have to worry about the impression he would make on a jury.

"Your Honour," Mr. Whittingham stood and spoke for the first time, "in the interest of expediency, we will stipulate to Detective Aldos expertise in the field of Missing Persons."

"So noted." Judge McConnelly replied. "Mr. Montrose, you may proceed."

"Detective Aldos," Mr. Montrose continued, after nodding to the judge, "could you please explain to the court your roll in the investigation of Crystal Raven."

"Yes sir," Detective Aldos replied smoothly, turning in the witness chair to face the judge. "When the case was brought to our attention, that is forwarded from the Major Crimes Division to Missing Persons, it was assigned to me."

"The minor in question had no memory of her identity, and the detectives assigned to investigate her assault – that would be Detectives Jablonski and Kraus – asked us for an assist in trying to identify her."

"And can you tell the court your findings?" The lawyer urged.

"Well, at first, because she was found here in the city," the detective explained, "we reviewed all missing person reports in her age range and contacted several civilian agencies that specialize in missing children. When none matched her description, we expanded our search to the State of New York, and then federally. Unfortunately, we were unable to locate anyone from her family at this time. We are, of course, still looking and have forwarded a request to all law enforcement agencies."

"Your Honour," Mr. Montrose requested, "at this time the state of New York requests that the minor Crystal Raven be declared a ward of the state until such time as her parents or guardians can be located."

Judge McConnelly briefly reviewed the reports that had been included with the written petition. There was nothing in them to contradict the conclusion that the minor was without adult support at this time. "At the moment, I am inclined to grant the state's motion. I am signing an order at this time to declare the minor Crystal Raven a ward of the state of New York."

"Your Honour," Mr. Whittingham rose as he was expected. "At this time we would like to present a petition to the court to grant custody of the minor, Jane Doe, a.k.a Crystal Raven, to Jean-Claude Beaucour and April Eloise Moonshadow."

"The court will hear this motion at this time," Judge McConnelly granted. "Mr. Montrose, does the state of New York intend to intercede at this time?"

"Yes, Your Honour," Montrose replied. "The state has several questions regarding the proposed living conditions at this time. Firstly, we question the wisdom of placing a minor with severe memory loss in a private home at this time. As you are aware, Your Honour, normally under these circumstances the state would maintain custody of the minor, or at the least place her in one of our more experienced Foster homes."

"Mr. Whittingham," Judge McConnelly urged, "do you have any response to the state's concerns."

"Yes, Your Honour," Mr. Whittingham replied, looking briefly through his notes. "At this time we would call upon the testimony of two witnesses, Doctor David Gilmore – her attending physician – and Florence Washington, her councillor."

"We will hear from Doctor Gilmore first," the judge decided, "unless either of you gentlemen have any objection."

Neither lawyer did, and the bailiff called Doctor Gilmore to the stand. Dressed in a check sports coat and a lose-collar dress shirt without a tie, he looked relaxed and comfortable as he took a seat in the witness stand. He waved hello to Gwen and Crystal in the gallery, and the two girls waved enthusiastically back. The judge caught the by-play, and allowed himself a small smile.

"Doctor Gilmore," Mr. Whittingham began, "you are a resident in the Emergency Ward of Saint Barnabas Hospital in the Bronx, New York City, correct?"

"Yes, I am."

"And in that capacity, you have become the attending physician of the minor in question?"

"Yes," Doctor Gilmore took up the narrative, responding as they had discussed prior to the hearing. "She was admitted into our emergency ward about a month ago. I was the attending physician at the time, and kept the case when she was transferred to our Children's ward."

"And what is Crystal's current prognosis?" Mr. Whittingham prodded.

"Crystal has made a remarkable recovery," Doctor Gilmore enthused. "While she will continue to need some physiotherapy as her hip continues to heal, all other breaks and fractures have appeared to have healed. Of course, I would not recommend any ultimate fighting in her immediate future."

His joke elicited a chuckle from the gallery, and tended to keep his testimony light, as they had intended.

"Your witness," Mr. Whittingham replied.

They had decided to let Mr. Montrose raise the question of her mental state, and he did not disappoint.

"And what can you tell us about her memory loss, Doctor Gilmore?"

"Memory loss is sometimes associated with the type of

head trauma Crystal suffered," Doctor Gilmore admitted.

"Total memory loss?" Montrose pressed.

"While total amnesia is rare, it is not unheard of," Doctor Gilmore explained. "Patients who suffer such conditions go on to make total recoveries, and those who do not, lead perfectly normal lives. Crystal has already recovered some of her memories. I have no doubt that she will continue to make progress in this regard over the weeks to come."

"And will she not need special treatment to continue this recovery? At a state facility, perhaps?"

"No. She needs to be living in as close to her normal conditions as possible, and I doubt a state facility fits that bill." Doctor Gilmore concluded.

The doctor and Mr. Montrose bantered back and forth for several minutes, but the lawyer could not get him to back away from his position. Crystal needed to be in a stable home, attending a normal high school with friends, enjoying normal teenage interactions if she hoped to recover her memory. And if she never did, there was nothing to say she
would not be able to lead a normal, productive life. She was bright, and alert, and showed no signs of aphasia or other brain damage, and was adjusting to her world remarkably well.

Next, Mr. Whittingham called Florence Washington. Much of her initial testimony corresponded to that of Doctor Gilmore's, her report drawing the same conclusion – that the girl would be better off with Jean-Claude than in one of the state's `baby prisons'. She had testified in this court many times, and the judge was well aware of her position on the state run juvenile housing facilities.

"Now, Mrs. Washington," Mr. Whittington turned to glance again at his notes, pausing for effect. His courtroom manner changed little whether there was a jury present or not. "You helped my client arrange a school for Crystal? Can you tell the court about these arrangements?"

"Yes. Jean-Claude has chosen to send her to a private

school run by the Catholic Church. It is currently attended by his step-daughter, Gwen Moonshadow, who is the best friend of Crystal. The Academy has excellent academic standings with the state board, and has very good counselling programs that will be able to help her adjust to her new home."

"Your Honour," Mr. Whittingham announced, "at this time we would like to submit to the court Mr. Beaucour's financial papers, which include the documentation of a trust he has created in Crystal Raven's name to cover her education all the way through college – should she chose to pursue her education that far."

"Very well."

"Now, Mrs. Washington," Mr. Whittingham continued, "you have inspected the home where Mr. Beaucour intends to bring Crystal. Can you tell the court your impressions of that home?"

"Yes. Mr. Beaucour and Miss Moonshadow currently are raising another daughter, Gwen Moonshadow. While their home is not traditional – they share two apartments in the same brownstone, one above the other, there is plenty of room for their planned addition to their family."

"I also found the atmosphere to be warm and loving, with plenty of adult supervision and interaction. I have interviewed Gwen on several occasions, and found her to be a normal, well-adjusted young lady. I have also interviewed the two girls together, and am encouraged by the strength of the bond between them. As you know, when someone suffers an assault of this magnitude, there is always a concern it will affect their ability to form positive peer relationships. Their friendship gives me great hopes for Crystal."

"And the parental dynamics?"

"April and Jean-Claude have formed a very effective parental partnership," Mrs. Washington explained. "They share the discipline between them, and keep a vital channel of communication open between themselves and Gwen. Both adults spend quality time with her, separately and together. I see no difficulty for them to fit Crystal into their current family structure."

"Your witness."

Family court, especially its juvenile division, was less formal than other courts. Everyone here was well familiar with Mama Flo and her expertise in these matters, and Mr. Montrose was well prepared to accept her testimony as it stood. Besides, he still had one more rabbit up his sleeve.

Next, Mr. Whittington chose to call Crystal Raven to the stand. It was time for the court to hear from the girl herself. Crystal stepped out of her wheel chair and walked up towards the witness stand, sticking her tongue out at Jean-Claude as he gave her a dirty look for disobeying her doctor's orders. Again the judge could not help but smile as he caught the by-play and he ignored the slight titter of laughter that rose from the gallery.

Crystal took a seat and adjusted her skirt to best show off her legs. She had good legs, and if Jean-Claude was too dense to notice, she would show them off to a more appreciative audience. She looked up and smiled at Mr. Whittingham as he rose to come and question her, and he returned the smile with one that lit up his whole face. See, she thought, at least some men appreciated her for the stunning fox that she was.

"Good morning, Crystal," he greeted. "And how are you feeling today?"

"A little nervous," she confessed, fussing with her hair.

"There's no need to be nervous," he reassured her with another of his stunning smiles. For an old guy, he sure did have it going on. "We're all here to help you. Now Crystal, do you remember anything?"

"Well," she hesitated as Mr. Evans and he had instructed her, maybe a little too long in her youthful enthusiasm. "I do remember some things. About some movies and books that I read."

"But nothing about your name or your family?"

"No," Crystal paused, but because the question

momentarily threw her off balance, and not for effect. "I don't remember anything about who I was, or where and how I lived."

"That's okay, dear," he soothed. "And where would you like to live now?"

"With Jean-Claude and April if I could. Gwen and them are the only family I know now," she turned towards the judge. "I really don't want to lose another family. Not that I remember anything about my first one."

It was a good appeal, and one that was unplanned. Personal, and heartfelt.

"Mr. Montrose, do you have any questions for this witness," the judge asked as Mr. Whittingham relinquished her.

"Yes, Your Honour," he replied, rising. "A few."

He moved up to the witness stand, and stood a few steps away. "Good morning, Crystal. My name is Franklin Montrose, and I represent the state, and by extension, you, in these proceedings. I just have a few questions for you."

"Okay."

"These memories of yours," he began, "can you tell us about them? What are they about? Do you remember the movies or books they are from?"

"Well," Crystal hedged. "Not exactly. They are about vampyres, and because they don't really exist, it must be from movies and books. Right?"

"That will appear so," Mr. Montrose conceded. "Could you tell us anything else that you remember?"

"Well, I remember how to read Latin!"

"Really, Latin," Mr. Montrose walked to his table and picked up a copy of a law book that contained several Latin terms. "Would you mind demonstrating?"

"I guess not," Crystal conceded, worried.

She took up the book and studied it. She was quiet for a long time.

"Well?"

"They don't make much sense," Crystal complained. "This one says: Actio personalis moritur cum persona. It means the actions of the person dies with the person, or something like that."

"Anything else?"

"Non obstante verdicto – not withstanding the verdict." She handed him back the book. "I'm sorry, I don't know what that is supposed to mean."

"You did very well, Crystal." Mr. Montrose replied, accepting the book. "And do you remember where you learned Latin?"

"In school, I guess."

"But you do not remember where?"

"No."

"Crystal, I need to ask you something very delicate." Mr. Montrose warned. "Will that be okay?"

"I guess." Crystal wasn't sure what it was about, but she thought she would not like it.

"Did Mr. Beaucour kiss you?"

"No."

"No? Mr. Peterson saw him." Mr. Montrose insisted. "Should I call him to the stand?"

"He saw me kiss Jean-Claude. The fool refused to kiss me back! You'd think at his age he would know how to kiss a woman!" Crystal burst out in outrage, and the gallery erupted in laughter.

As the judge gaveled the court to order, Mr. Whittingham stood up. "If I may interject a question, Your Honour?"

"Very well."

"And what happened next, Crystal?"

Crystal frowned, her voice dropping. "He took me back to my room, and April and I had a long talk."

"And what decision did you and April come to?"

"That I was too young for him," she whispered, then raised her voice again. "But in two years I will kiss him again, only harder!"

Even Judge McConnelly had to laugh this time. He let the laughter of the gallery continue until he saw that Mr. Beaucour had grown red with embarrassment and had ducked his head. Once again he gaveled the court to order.

"I have another question," Crystal said in the quieting room.

"Go ahead, young lady," the judge invited.

"How do you know I am only sixteen?" She asked, and the room grew deathly still. "I mean, if I don't remember when I was born, how do you know I am not already eighteen?"

It was a very good question, one his legal team should have thought to ask. Taking advantage of the momentary confusion in the court, Mr. Whittingham added. "It could explain the lack of a missing person's report?"

"Yes," Judge McConnelly mused. "It's a very good question, Crystal. The court will take a twenty minute recess while I consider the answer."

Back in his chambers Judge McConnelly took off his robe and sank into his chair. She was right. From her looks she could be anywhere between fifteen and nineteen, and with a search of her fingerprints returning nothing, they had no way to tell. He did not normally drink during court hours, but he found himself reaching for the bottle he kept in the top drawer of his desk. What is the legal response to her question? When the state cannot prove your age, what was there to say just how old you are? It was definitely an interesting question for a classroom, not so for a courtroom.

He was interrupted in his reach for a drink by a knock on his door.

"Come?" If nothing else, he could use the distraction.

"My friend," Bishop O'Malley greeted.

"Brian," Judge McConnelly greeted. "You are a witness for the plaintive, and you should not be meeting me in my chambers."

"I am here as a friend and a spiritual advisor, Michael," the bishop replied gently. "Even in this, I would never ask you to compromise yourself."

"I know Brian, but appearances are important in the law," he explained, closing the drawer of his desk. "Tell me, what is the Church's interest in the girl?"

"Much of it is as I have explained, Brian," the bishop replied after a brief pause. "We have all been tarred with the same brush as a few bad apples, and a little good press could not hurt."

"But?"

"The item the girl was found with is not just a sacred icon," the bishop explained. "It is a promise from the Church to its holder – a promise of protection and sanctuary. Some of its history I cannot tell you...."

"Cannot, or will not?"

"It is a secret that is not mine to share, Brian. Even an institution as young as this court has its secrets. How many files have you ordered sealed over the years?"

"Touché, my friend. And now if you will excuse me, I need to read over these files before I make a decision."

"May God guide you in your deliberations."

Nothing in the police reports or the girl's medical reports gave evidence of her age. One way, or the other. Could he deny her the rights guaranteed by their society simply because she could not prove her age? And what about her medical condition? Did that prevent her from being capable of caring for herself? Not according to her doctors – she was neither a danger to herself or to others, and was expected to go on a lead a normal life. He found a compromise in the time he had allotted himself, and rose and left his chambers to return to the court.

"Please be seated," he said as he took the bench. "I have reviewed the evidence in the files presented to the court. Crystal is right. No evidence has been presented to prove, legally, that she is a minor. With this in mind I am rescinding my earlier order declaring her a ward of the state."

"Further, there was no evidence presented today that

suggests she is mentally incompetent. In fact, her medical advisors suggest there is no reason why she could not lead a normal, healthy and productive life."

"With all this in mind," the judge concluded, "I am going to declare Jane Doe, a.k.a Crystal Raven an emancipated minor with the proviso that she remain living in the household of Jean-Claude Beaucour and April Moonshadow for at least the next two years. Do the parties involve agree to this proposal?"

"I do," Crystal breathed in reply. She was happier than she had been in a long time. She was free, free to live where she wanted.

Chapter 9

Liberation lay less than a week away, and the Moonshadow women were busy organizing Jean-Claude's home, driving him from his apartment in a cloud of anxiety and dust. Idle and bored, Crystal listened to his complaints with an inattentive ear as he described walls being repainted robin-eggs blue, and the staining of hardwood floors. Her mind was on the mysteries of the world beyond the hospital walls, a world she remembered nothing about. Where would it lead her and what misadventures lurked within the great unknown? She was both anxious to escape the never-ending drudgery of hospital routine, and dreading its sudden absence.

At the hospital they had a meeting with Doctor Gilmore and Mama Flo. Mrs. Washington had some concerns with the syllabus of her new school, which included esoteric science, metaphysics, Latin, Greek, English, Math, Science and physical education. Still, the Academy was a private Catholic school whose students scored in the top ten percentile in the state in math and English, and Jean-Claude had definitely set aside enough money to allow her to attend any of the top universities in the country. Plus, the school had already assigned tutors to help her recover her lost language and math skills, and to help her catch up on the six weeks of school she had already missed.

"Well Crystal," Mama Flo opened the meeting between the four, "it looks like you will be one busy little girl over the next months. But I don't want you to neglect your social life."

"And you also have to make time for your physiotherapy session twice a week if we want that hip to fully recover." Doctor Gilmore added. "I'm going to allow you to take the physical education, but we will provide you with a note should the activity become too strenuous."

"Basketball, but no slam dunks," Jean-Claude suggested hopefully.

Crystal made a face at him and replied, "I don't weave baskets, with or without a ball."

Mama Flo laughed, and Jean-Claude shrugged as if to say, `she will learn'.

"Definitely getting involved in an organized sport would be a big positive for her social development," Mama Flo agreed. "As soon as she is physically up to it."

"And physical activity is a big plus here," Doctor Gilmore pointed out. "There is nothing like exercise to rebuild muscle and bone, as long as it is in moderation. When your hip starts to ache, it's your body's way of telling you that you are over doing it."

"Okay," Crystal agreed, maybe a little too easily for a teenager. "But darn these old basket weaving injuries, you never know when they are going to flare up."

"Like right about when it's time to take out the garbage or do the dishes, no?" Jean-Claude teased.

"Do you think Jean-Claude that eight courses might be a little too much for her first year?" Mama Flo voiced her concern. "We do want to strike a healthy balance here."

"It is a special school," Jean-Claude explained, "for the gifted, no? Already she remembers the Latin, and she will have plenty of help until she remembers more."

"What do you think dear?"

"Well," Crystal replied honestly. "I'd rather take movie watching and shopping. Gwen goes to that school, though, and we're in all the same classes."

"And that will be important socially," Mama Flo agreed, "but how about the course load?"

"We would have all the same homework," Crystal pointed out, "and we could help each other. I think I'm pretty smart."

"No-one thinks otherwise, dear," Mama Flo soothed. "But

there is more to life than books."

"Tell that to Jean-Claude," she shot back, studying Jean-Claude for signs of a reaction. She saw none, just the same inane grin all adults seemed to wear.

"Okay," Doctor Gilmore summed up, "we're just going to run a series of tests this week, and we will be releasing you on Friday I should think."

"No offence," Crystal offered, "but about bloody time. This place is boring me to death."

"Not enough boys, you see," Jean-Claude supplied, and she sent him a withering look.

Later, Gwen arrived at Crystal's room sporting a smudge of blue paint on her left cheek. Bubbling with news from the home front, she was talking a mile a minute from the first second she crossed the threshold. Laughing, Crystal held up her hand for peace, and pointed desperately at her cheek.

"What kind of make-up is that?" She gasped between gouts of laughter.

"What?" Gwen questioned, rubbing at her face.

Still laughing, Crystal brought her to the mirror and pointed again. "That blue streak! And please tell me I don't have to wear anything that silly."

"Oh this," Gwen shrugged off nonchalantly, "all great artists wear this." But she couldn't keep a straight face to save her life. "We were painting your room. Oh, it's this awesome shade of blue. And tomorrow we're painting my room the same colour. And my mom picked out this beautiful bedroom set, and Jean-Claude bought one for me too – so our rooms will match."

"Just like twins," Crystal commented, laughing at her friend's excitement.

"Exactly," Gwen responded, oblivious to her byplay. "But we mustn't wear the same clothes. That would just be weird."

"Definitely."

"Oh, and I got the world's greatest news!" Gwen was off again. "On Saturday Jean-Claude and April will let us go to the mall with Amy and Bobby-Lynn – only we're still a little mad at Bobby-Lynn, so she may not come."

"Are we?"

"Oh yes, you know she dyed her hair the same colour Amy wants to for the Harvest Dance," Gwen filled in. "It was so spiteful of her, just because that cute Goth boy, Razor, asked Amy to the dance and not her. But I guess it will be okay if she comes on Saturday."

"Oh definitely," Crystal laughed. There were some things she might not get use to in her new life.

"Oh yes, because we need four to play Diviners," Gwen explained. "Because April and Jean-Claude will allow us to have a sleep-over. Oh, we can do each other's make-up and chill. Only we can't sneak any boys over, Mom always catches us."

"Who needs boys when we can find men. But not with than particular shade of blush," Crystal teased, pointing to the smear of paint on Gwen's cheek.

"I don't share my best make-up tips with those who don't appreciate them," Gwen shot back. "I'll snap up all the prettiest men, and see if I share any."

The two girls spent the afternoon planning for Crystal's big move to the brownstone, where they would be
neighbours. Since Jean-Claude had the bigger apartment – in fact, the biggest in the building – the girls always had their sleepovers in his living room. He and her mother would go out to a movie, or just for a walk, leaving the girls alone with their own amusements, and then sit down stairs reading or talking over coffee. It was more privacy than they enjoyed at any of her friend's houses, where their parents were always looking over your shoulder, and you had to wait until everyone was asleep for any of the good conversation.

In time, April and Jean-Claude came to join them. Jean-Claude had picked up take-out from a Chinese restaurant that they all liked, and Gwen spent the entire meal moving things with strange names onto Crystal's plate, and insisting she try them. Everything was Gwen's absolute favourite, and she admitted that she had never met a Chinese dish that was not to die for. Crystal hoped she would sell her life for something a little more substantial, but admitted in turn that she really liked the egg-fried rice and the sweet-and-sour pork. Even the strange noodles tasted interesting, and when you mixed several of the dishes together, you could make a new taste sensation of your own.

After dinner the four played a game of Monopoly. Crystal was the boot, and Gwen the dog, and they played as a team against the adults. April and Jean Claude controlled Board Walk and Park Place, but the girls had managed to buy up three of the other property groupings and the railroads. When Jean-Claude managed to land on St. James place with three hotels, Crystal gave his thimble a friendly little boot with her shoe.

"Into debtor's prison with you," she teased. "You wretched little dead-beat."

"Now that is hardly Christian of you," Jean-Claude complained as he flipped over the last of his properties to mortgage it. "You should rename your hotel the Money Pit or the Last Chance Tourist Trap, no?"

"No!" The girls shot back with a giggle.

"And I'm out too," April conceded. "It looks like it's time for us to be heading home."

"Oh mom," Gwen complained, "it's only nine!"

"And we both have a big day tomorrow- work, school, and finishing up Crystal's and your rooms." April reminded her daughter. "I'm not working with a grouchy old bear who has not had enough sleep."

Once the two women had departed, Jean-Claude and Crystal quietly put away the game. When all the pieces were back in place and the lid closed on the box, he helped her into bed and tucked her in.

"Soon you will be leaving this place," he said as she lay back.

"I can't wait to see my new room," she admitted.

Jean-Claude took something out of a silk bag that sat on her bedside table. "This crystal is not just an ordinary sacred item. It is a Covenant stone. The wearer carries with her the protection of the Church. You must wear this always once you leave this place."

"Is it magic?" Crystal asked. She had had it for as long as she could remember, this crystal raven. They had given her this name because it was the only thing she had been found with.

"No," and he smiled, knowing it was his turn to use the word. "It is a promise. One that will bring you help whenever you are in trouble. I suppose that is the most powerful magic there is. Whenever you need help, bring this to a church and show it to the priest, and you will find it."

"I promise," Crystal said when she realized he was waiting for a reply. "I will wear it always."

"Never take it off once we leave this place," he reiterated.

He could be such a strange man sometimes, and so Crystal merely nodded and kept her thoughts to herself.

Next he reached up above her head and took down the bulky rosary he had placed there several nights earlier. For a long moment he studied it, rubbing the grain of the wood on its crucifix, and worrying at its beads.

"This is a rosary," he explained. "We use it to pray. Each rosary is divided into five decades, and each decade represents a mystery in the life of Jesus, our Saviour. There are four mysteries in each rosary – Joyful, Luminous, Sorrowful, and Glorious. The large beads represent the Our Father, the smaller ones the Hail Marys, and at the crucifix we normally say the Apostle's Creed."

"Look closely at this crucifix," he instructed, handing the rosary over to her.

"It is made from gopher wood," he continued. "It is edged with pure iron – no impurities, and tempered in holy water. It is shaped like a stake, as no other crucifix you see will be.

That is because it is a weapon, forged to kill demons in a time when people still believed in such things. Once you leave here you will carry it with you always."

"I can't wear that," Crystal complained. "It's...."

"Not beautiful or cool," Jean-Claude conceded. "Nevertheless you will carry it with you always. You do not have to wear it, but carry it in your purse or pocket. For luck."

"For luck?"

Chapter 10

The week wore two faces – crawling by like the slow march of years across a forgotten ruin, and expiring in the span of a heart beat. For Crystal, confined within four walls with too little activity and to many hours to fill, it passed like a dying man crawling out of the desert. For April, Gwen and Jean-Claude, each with their set of projects to complete, they blinked and it was Friday morning, and each still had a long list of unfinished tasks.

Crystal was excited about going home, but at the same time she was worried. Jean-Claude spent all his time studying ancient tomes about demons, creatures that he told her did not exist, and in the same breath insisted she carry two objects that were nothing more than talismans to protect her from these self same creatures. And then there were her dreams. Almost every night she dreamed of vampyres – dark lurid creatures who sought her death, and not the golden-eyed pretty boys of the movies. And there were visions – maybe only hallucinations, maybe memories – of stalking through dark, cobblestone alleys, or hunting through wild stretches of a forest. Hunting to feed on creatures of blood and lust, creatures who hunted others weaker than they as they themselves were prey.

And then there was the man who was not a man, a creature of light and of power who may be her father – someone she both feared and loved, and who filled her with a heavy sense of self-loathing.

These were just crazy thoughts she knew. Thoughts she could share with no one, not even Gwen. She was losing her mind, or perhaps had already lost it years ago, but did not remember her insanity. She feared it was creeping through the cracks of her amnesia, and when that dam burst she dreaded what would come rushing out from the other side. She feared mostly she would find she was some crazy homeless girl, off her meds and wandering the street, spouting gibberish about demons and vampyres that ran through a world only she could see. Someone no-one could love, and who could love no-one in return.

The long hours of inactivity in the hospital let these what-ifs run rampant through her mind, and now at long last they were coming to an end. She needed to stay busy, to be so focused on life that they had no chance to return. Mama Flo was right. There was no point in worrying about what could not be changed.

Friday evening was finally here, and Jean-Claude and the Moonshadows arrived to help Crystal pack up and to bring her home. Despite a long twelve hour shift, Doctor Gilmore was there to personally walk her through the release process. Several of her nurses were there as well, and they made up an impromptu farewell party. Left alone for much of the last few days, Crystal was happy to have the company. And despite her anxiety to escape the hospital and its restrictive routines, she would miss the people who had come to fill a world emptied by her loss of memory.

They were in reality the only people she knew in the world, as this small corner of the hospital made up the only world she knew.

"Now," Doctor Gilmore chided, "don't forget to visit us. But next time, don't feel you have to hurt yourself to do so."

"I won't," Crystal promised, wiping a tear from her eye. She reached up to accept his hug.

Once again seated in the hated wheel chair, she was ready to leave, holding one of her small suitcases in her lap like a shield against the sadness that threatened to overwhelm her. Although she would have rather walked out on her own, to please these people who had come to mean so much to her, she consented to one last ride. Besides, she did not know if she could trust her legs at the moment.

Near the doors leading out of the hospital, Mama Flo was waiting for her with a warm hug and a small bouquet of flowers. It was too much for her, and tears ran freely down her cheeks.

Outside, the early October sky slowly shaded towards night, blunting the people and objects around her with growing shadows. Through her tears she watched strange men in long, grey robes lecturing groups of youths in blacks and white silks. `Goths' Gwen whispered, giving her shoulder a quick squeeze. The contrast between the men in simple robes and the absurd costumes of their audiences – long trench coats and top hats, fishnet and silks, faces paled by white cake, lips and eyes blackened – struck Crystal as weird. Why would monks, men of the Church who had turned away from the pleasures of the flesh, be talking to such a decadent circus? And then it struck her – each of the four groups numbered thirteen exactly. Why did that number strike her as significant?

Some of the girls weren't even wearing all their underwear – no corset or petticoat – and what little they were wearing was all they had on! No-one seemed to notice, so maybe it was what passed as normal here. What would she know? She did not even remember what she had been wearing when she arrived at the hospital. She blushed at the thought that she might have been walking around in public in something that skimpy, like some shameless Parisian whore, hanging from a window with her wares on display. She was sure she would have been mortified, and doubted she had the figure to pull something like that off. Okay, so maybe she was feeling a little catty, and maybe a tad jealous.

"All girls don't dress like that!" Crystal pulled at Gwen's sleeve, pleading. "Do they?"

The girl wore only a bra fashioned from a narrow strip of black leather that met in a diamond of grey metal over her ample breasts, brass buttons protruding from the centre strategically placed over her nipples. A leather collar studded with spikes held a crimson cape that hung down to her heels. Visible in the centre of her bared midriff, a belly piercing shaped like the skull of a vampyre glared malevolently at the two girls. A long, black velour skirt hung low from her hips, slit on either side at the top of her thighs, and sheer, black nylons covered her legs. They ended in a serious set of leather boots – in the musketeer style – studded at mid-calf with two inch spikes.

"Only the Goths," then seeing Crystal's terrified look, she laughed. "Jean-Claude would lock us up in a convent if we ever tried to leave the house wearing something like that! It's hard enough getting away with a belly top with him around."

Crystal stared at the strange clothed youths as Gwen wheeled her towards the car. "They come to our house sometimes," she said in a conspiratorial whisper, "the Goths. They meet with Jean-Claude down in the basement, but no-one will tell me why."

What she did not say was that they went to the same school, that she knew who and what they were, but not why they were meeting at the brownstone more often than they had in the past.

"Ah," Crystal laughed, "a secret for us to uncover!"

"And I'll tell you another secret about that girl over there," Gwen teased.

Laughing behind their hands, the two girls settled into the back seat, leaving April and Jean-Claude to see to her luggage. Moments later, the two adults joined them in the car. An escort of vehicles might have followed, if any mortal could keep up with Jean-Claude's insane driving, as it was those watching over them could only wait at strategic points along their route and hope no immortal could match his insane speeds and wild turns either.

"You better buckle up," April warned as Jean-Claude turned over the ignition.

"And pray," Gwen added for good measure.

"My driving is not so bad," Jean-Claude complained, reversing full speed from his parking place, and throwing the car in gear without letting up on the gas.

Thrown in four different directions at the same time, the three women chorused, "oh no!"

He shot out of the parking lot without seeming to even glance at the oncoming traffic, fighting for every ounce of speed out of the old car. Using his emergency break and gear shift, he drifted around the first corner, and fishtailed his way into the first available alley. Why not use these perfectly good roads when nobody else seemed to bother with them? He always asked any new passenger who had the misfortune to ride with him. The fact that his current route was too narrow for any normal sized car did not bother him, nor did the odd garbage can that flew up over his grill. What were a few more dents to an already beat up car? It was never going to get any prettier.

"Is someone chasing us?" Crystal asked through her chattering teeth. She was not sure if it were just the rattling, or real fear that had her teeth clicking.

"No!" Gwen called through the protests of the overworked suspension. "They had a moment of insanity when they gave Jean-Claude his licence!"

"Ah-hah!" Jean-Claude cried back, "no-one drive as good as me!"

"That's because most of us have read the Driver's Handbook," April teased.

"You must learn to read between the lines," Jean-Claude replied as he brought the car to a sudden halt at the curb of their brownstone.

"Welcome home!" April offered.

"Did all of me make it?" Crystal teased, but she was half serious. She swore to herself that she would never again get into one of these metal carriages. Her life, what little she remembered, was still flashing before her eyes.

The brownstone was one of those hidden gems. Located in

a neighbourhood just on the cusp of gentrification, it had great curb appeal with its window box gardens and concrete vases on either side of his stoop that Old Mrs. Jenkins kept lovingly planted with colourful petunias. Inside, hand-restored panelling and oak balusters lined a stairwell lit by delicate crystal chandeliers. April and Gwen lived on the main floor, and the apartment Crystal would share with Jean-Claude was on the second floor, directly above.

Two dumbwaiters connected the two apartments, one in the kitchen to allow meals to be passed back and forth – April still cooked many of Jean-Claude's meals in hopes of keeping the absent-minded monk alive past a week – and a second connecting the two rooms the girls now occupied.

Originally connecting Jean-Claude's office and Gwen's room when he once cared for her over-night when her mother worked, it was just large enough for a small girl to make her way back and forth between the two apartments. Gwen had great plans for it now, but unfortunately neither girl was small enough to use it to sneak back and forth – and besides, they were getting a little too old for such things.

The apartment had a simple footprint. Directly inside the door a small entrance hall created by a book shelf and posts separated an open concept living room and kitchen. Further along the hall it led off to a full bathroom and two bedrooms. The master bedroom with its own door leading into the bathroom had been set aside for Crystal in hopes of providing her more privacy. Eight by fourteen, the room was the larger of the two, and had been furnished with a canopy bed, a dresser and a vanity with a collection of make-up pre-supplied by Gwen. Her mother and Jean-Claude were completely useless when it came to make-up, she confided to Crystal as they unpacked the three suitcases.

In the kitchen April and Jean-Claude were putting the finishing touches on a welcome home dinner. A meal that included dishes prepared by each of them – Jean-Claude had baked a touritiere (a French Canadian meat pie) and a cheese-

and-onion pie (an English dish, the second of the two main Canadian cultures). April was mixing up a dish called mishmash – a mixture of mashed potatoes, carrots and boiled onions, and Gwen was planning to toss a Waldorf salad.

"I feel bad," Crystal confessed as the two girls made their way down the hall towards the kitchen.

"Why?"

"I'm the only one who hasn't contributed anything towards supper," Crystal replied.

"Oh, no worries girlfriend," Gwen replied breezily. "You can help me put the salad together. Come on, it will be fun."

In the kitchen the two girls giggled and shoved at each other as they diced celery, julienned apples, chopped the walnuts and washed the grapes and salad. They were having far too much fun for the serious occupation of food production, offending the sensibilities of the diminutive French man, and subjecting him to the unrelenting teasing of April – who thought he took his kitchen far too seriously for someone who seldom remembered to feed himself.

"That salad has far too many giggles in it," he grumped. "We will all be acting like silly little girls if we eat that!"

"That would definitely be an improvement from a stuffy old man," Gwen teased. "Watch the pie, now Crystal. He might have slipped in a few mean pills."

"Next thing you know," Crystal added through a giggle, "we'll all be locking ourselves in a library huffing and puffing over dusty old books all day."

"Ahhh," Jean-Claude sighed wistfully, "one could only dream about such a paradise."

"Ohhh!" Gwen seethed, "you are a silly old man!"

They shared a pleasant meal in a warm, family environment that Crystal only realized she missed at that moment. April, Gwen and Jean-Claude welcomed her into their family dynamic as if she had always been a part of it, and she found she enjoyed the friendly teasing and banter that filled their time together. Gwen never did seem to shut up, but you had to love her – her constant good mood and unbounded enthusiasm for life, and the way she freely shared her joy with everyone. She would really enjoy having her for a sister, for ever long this lasted.

Later, in her own bed for the first time, she lay awake staring at the ceiling. At first the absence of the gentle susurration of the hospital night noises – the cough and moans of the sick, the beep and blips of machinery, and the soft foot steps of the nurses on their rounds that had lulled her to sleep for as long as she could remember – kept her up. Not that she remembered much. And she still worried that one day she would wake up from this wonderful dream, that her memories would come rushing back – memories of a dreadful world that would become her reality and replace this one.

As she watched the shadows from outside crawl across her wall, Crystal let her mind drift. She felt so lonely, so disconnected from the people, places and things in this world. Even her dreams seemed to belong to someone else, to another time and place than the one she found herself in. Where was her place in the world, and how was she suppose to find it?

She belonged nowhere.

Her dreams collapsed beneath the tremors of an Earthquake. Crystal woke to her second heart attack and found Gwen bouncing on the end of her bed, bursting with excitement and energy she could not contain. In a few short hours Amy and Bobby-Lynn would arrive to accompany them to the mall, and they had so much to do. Showers, and make-up, and oh, they needed to choose the perfect outfits. And if she did not wake up right this minute, there was no way they would be ready in time. Breakfast! Who had time for breakfast? Up! Up! Up!

Make-up and hair did entail a lot more than it had when she was in the hospital, after all, there would be boys at the mall, and even Crystal had to admit she wanted to make a lasting impression. She was in the mood to break a few hearts and leave behind a trail of tears, and she practiced a few seductive smiles in front of her mirror. A girl liked to know she was attractive to the opposite sex, even if she had no interest in anyone that young and immature. And maybe, just maybe, if she fixed her hair just right and was careful with her make-up, and chose just the perfect outfit that showed off her figure without descending into the realm of slutty, she could finally capture Jean-Claude's eye. One day, she would make that man love her.

At the door the adults were waiting to inspect them. Jean-Claude was easy to please. Just show him the crystal raven and that she was carrying that ludicrous crucifix, and all was right in his world. April was another matter.

"Bring jackets girls, it's getting colder. Amy, where's your jacket?" She questioned sharply. She was the shepherdess, and they were her sheep, no matter what flock they came from.

"Right here, April!" Amy held out the overly small vest she was wearing.

"There's not enough material in that to be considered a scarf," April scolded, reprovingly. "Go borrow one of Gwen's. And Bobby-Lynn, put a shirt on. The only kind of boy you'll catch in that is a pimp."

"Yes, ma'am," the girls chorused, and trooped downstairs to the Moonshadow apartment, rolling their eyes and throwing back their hair.

Bobby-Lynn came with the advertised green hair. A dark harvest green with highlighted with black under-streaks that actually suited her pale complexion. Crystal did not think the colour would have suited Amy at all, with her light blue eyes and long blonde hair. Maybe a blue to match her eyes, but definitely nothing that dark. And green! Where did the girl get off thinking green was a good colour for her? The girls wore short skirts and woolen leggings in consideration of the cooler temperatures – a compromise that allowed them to show off some leg without freezing off their appendages.

They wore white, button down shirts with the sleeves rolled up and the shirt tied into a halter just above their midriff. Amy wore a blue t-shirt beneath her blouse that still showed off her belly button, and the belly piercing that dangled half way down towards the top of her skirt. But April was right – Bobby-Lynn's blouse, on its own, did not offer enough coverage.

"Ohhh!" She complained to Gwen, "you're mom is such a prude sometimes."

"She's right though," Crystal laughed. "You are falling out of that shirt."

"If you got them," Bobby-Lynn said, sticking out her chest, "flaunt them. You get more boys that way."

"When you are as hot as we are," Amy replied, "you just need the proper application of a little hip action."

And she sashayed her hips at her three friends, who fell into a heap of giggles.

"Try not to do that at the mall," Gwen warned, "you'll get us all arrested."

"Word!" Bobby-Lynn replied, "I love a man in uniform."

"Yes," Crystal replied, "but with our luck, we'll get one who filled out his uniform with donuts."

Laughing and giggling, the four girls trooped back upstairs for a second inspection. Released from adult supervision, they thundered down the stairs and out the door towards the nearest subway. Their subway ride was a short one, just a few blocks to where they could pick up the Bartow Avenue bus out to the Bay Plaza Shopping Centre, but for Crystal it was a descent into another world. Even at their small, neighbourhood station the subway platform was jammed with people of every stripe and description. While fewer homeless people hung out down at this platform, it seemed that half the world commuted from this neighbourhood to the other boroughs in the city.

Spotting a transit cop just as they were entering their car, his belly protruding from his shirt, Crystal grabbed Amy's arm and stumbled inside on a wave of giggles. Teasing the other girl about finding her lover boy, the three girls led her to the first available empty seats.

The bus was something Crystal did not like. It made her feel like a salted ham packed away in a keg for the winter. The Mall lived up to its billing, and made the hot, smelly ride worth the effort – like being delivered to a palace in a dung cart. She couldn't believe they had not invented such a place thousands of years ago, or that she had forgotten that such wonders existed. Armed with a new credit card, and instructions to shop for school clothes – something April predicted was a disaster waiting to happen – she was ready to spend Jean-Claude into the poor house. She wanted one of everything, even the things she had no idea what they were or how to use them.

April had compiled a list. Something she was glad to have this once, otherwise she would have no idea where to start. And that was with a knapsack.

"Come on, girlfriend," Gwen cried, and the other girls chorused. "It's time to shop until we drop!"

Still Crystal hesitated.

"Don't worry," Gwen urged, pulling at her arm, "the card will tell us when we're out of money. I know, he does the same thing for me every September. I mean, if it was up to my mom I'd still have buckles on my shoes, and go to school looking like a Salem witch."

"Way too revealing," Amy teased. "I'd be able to see your ankles, young lady!"

Giggling, the four girls raced inside linked in a long chain, hand-in-hand. At the end of this conga line, Crystal struggled to read her list. Pulled into the first store by a gravity pool of teenage hormones, she soon found herself awash in sea of fabrics and colours. In a moment of honesty Gwen confessed that most of the fashions here were better suited for a night club than a high school, but didn't Crystal look dreamy in almost everything, and wasn't that colour just perfect.

Crystal hesitated as her desire warred with her common sense, teetering on the edge of an abyss of parental disapproval.

She compromised. Crystal bought one top she could wear to school, and two April would probably not let her out of her room in. The fabric of these last two was sheer, so she needed to buy a camisole to wear with each. After all, she was not about to show off her new bras to anyone – no matter how pretty they were. Besides, Crystal rationalized the first purchase not on her list, even April would understand the need to dress properly, because if a woman did not show off her assets to advantage, she would never find herself a husband.

Now that she had tops, she definitely needed jeans and skirts to match. And certainly she needed new shoes to match each skirt or pair of jeans. And a new purse, because the one she owned – as Bonny-Lynn pointed out – did not go with anything she had bought. And, as always, there were those necessary other items to accessorize every outfit, like earrings and necklaces.

She had only bought three outfits, and already she was worried that she would not have enough to buy her actual school supplies. True, she had gotten every item on sale, with the exception of that one skirt, and one pair of shoes. And she had saved Jean-Claude 'oodles of money', as Gwen had pointed out. But there was still a dozen items on her list, and they had already spent over twenty-five hundred dollars. How much was that, anyway?

Distracted, she was not paying attention to where her friends were pulling her. The collision knocked her purse from her arm, spilling the contents all over the floor.

"Hey," the boy said as he bent to help her retrieve her property. "That's a real apotropaic! Where did you get it?"

He had that dark, brooding look some girls found attractive. He wore black lipstick and a light coating of white heat to make his features paler, and his golden brown eyes were ringed by black mascara. He wore fine chain mail over a moulded leather shirt – although Crystal doubted the moulding exaggerated the muscles underneath very much.

"Jean-Claude gave it to me," Crystal muttered as she snatched it back.

"You know Jean-Claude?" He asked in a friendlier voice. Obviously well, Drake thought, if he gave her such a precious relic. That meant she had to be the girl from the newspapers.

"I live with him."

"I'm sorry," he smiled, and he looked a lot more attractive. If he were a few years older Crystal might consider him a suitable catch. "I'm Drake, First of the Eastmarch Goths."

He helped her to her feet and gathered her parcels for her. "I think we will be going to the same school. I'll catch you later."

Barely containing their excitement for the sake of appearing cool, her three girlfriends rejoined her. Drake was one of the most popular boys at their school, and it was a major coup for Crystal to have spoken to him.

"Oh," Bobby-Lynn complained. "I'm jealous. He's so dreamy."

"He's too dark and dangerous for my tastes," Gwen replied.

She was right. As Crystal watched him drift away, she could see he walked as if he carried violence in every stride. All the Goths she had seen had that look.

"Who is that dweeb?" A girl in a dress with a blue bustier and a black and blue crinoline skirt asked Drake. On her forehead she wore an elaborate Celtic design painstakingly sketched there in mascara.

"That, Meagan Dark-eyes," Drake replied with a slight smile, "is Jean-Claude's new ward."

"Her?" A second girl, her only hair a short, red and black Mohawk, retorted. "She doesn't even look like she could take out a grade schooler."

Morgana moved to join the group, the skirt from her long

black gown rustling against the tile. Her deep neckline was broken up by a large silver crucifix, her long raven bangs hiding much of her cleavage. "Looks can be deceiving. And if you need any more convincing, I believe that is Delph and his flight hiding in the upper shadows."

"Mark," Drake issued orders. "Go find Razor and his band. Meagan I think Dragrar and his are down by the food court. The rest of us will keep an eye on our guests and the girls.

"Just watch where those eyes of yours wander," Morgana teased, but there was a threat in her words.

Oblivious to the drama unfolding around them, the girls continued to shop, and then headed upstairs to watch a matinee. Shadowed by Delph and his band, who were in turn shadowed by a rival gang of Goths, the girls went to see the latest in a series of pirate movies featuring one of the latest heart throbs. Having grown use to seeing Goths wherever she went, Crystal thought no more about it than did her three friends, who went to a school heavily populated by that subculture. Inside the theatre, Drake and company sat immediately behind the four girls, and Crystal was aware of his eyes and the eyes of another girl staring at her throughout the movie. Obviously, she thought, she had come between a teenage romance amidst one of its frequent cool fronts – and she decided she had no room in her life to play in that stretch of stormy water.

Above, in the darkness of a small balcony placed there for decoration, Delph looked down at his target and hissed. There was nothing he could do while she was surrounded by the Goths, and now that she had fed little chance that anything he and his flight attempted would succeed. But nothing in his father's strictures said he could not keep a watch on her. And if an opportunity should present itself...

The four girls had literally shopped until they dropped. After the movie, they caught a cab and made their way towards home and a long evening of relaxing before the television.

Back at the brownstone they trooped up to Jean-Claude's apartment, where the two adults were awaiting the results of their shopping expedition. Excited, the four girls retreated into Crystal's room to help her try on one of her new outfits to model for April and Jean-Claude. After a thirty minute wait Crystal emerged with a blue sheer blouse worn over a black chemise, a black mini-skirt, and a pair of black high heels. She had accessorized with a pair of black nylons, a pair of her new earrings – she had had her ears pierced during their outing, and should still be wearing the studs – and the crystal raven.

"Oh sweetheart,' April scolded mildly as she emerged from her room, "as pretty as that is, you can't wear that to school. It's against the dress code. Gwen, you should know better! We're going to have to return them and find something more suitable."

"But mom!" Gwen complained. "We bought them on sale!"

"Oh you silly little girls," Jean-Claude complained. "Not to know how to shop for clothes. Now I will have to send you back to the Mall under April's supervision, no?"

But he winked at the four girls when April's back was turned.

"I don't know why you do this to me every September?" April voiced a long standing complaint. "They come back with something like this every year."

"But then how will they learn the clothes shopping?" Jean-Claude complained. "If I do not let them go and make these mistakes?"

"Come on," she said to the girls, ignoring Jean-Claude completely. `A fool and his money.... "Let's see if we have any outfits I can let you out of the house in."

Back in her room April had the girls empty all of her purchases. As the negligee came out of the bag with the rest of the bras and panties, she clucked sympathetically.

"Sweetheart, Jean-Claude will never notice that!"

And her prediction came true later that night. In the dark, without his glasses, he thought she was Gwen. And there she was, practically naked, and all he did was get up and put on a robe so he could tuck her back into the pull out couch bed she was sharing with three other girls. The damn thing was so sheer you could see her boobs, if you were not some monk, blind as a bat and as oblivious as a statue, and there wasn't enough material at the back to cover her bum.

As they entered the living room, where maybe there was enough light for him to see her, the door bell rang. Already dressed, so to speak, Jean-Claude moved out of the apartment to answer the summons. Over all, she would have to say her first attempt at seduction was a complete disaster. But one day, Jean-Claude Beaucour, you will notice I am a woman!

Down in the small entranceway that served as a lobby for the building, Jean-Claude unlocked the outside door to find Drake standing on his door step.

"Young Drake," he greeted, still groggy from having been roused from a deep sleep.

"Jean-Claude."

"It is late, no?" He inquired. "You have been out patrolling the lower levels?"

"No, Jean-Claude," Drake replied, apologizing. "We have followed your instructions and kept to the surface. I apologize for the hour, but I need to report: Delph and his flight were on the surface."

"Was there an incident?"

"No, they were at the Mall." Drake replied. "There were too many people around for us to interdict the incursion."

"Mon Dieu!" Jean-Claude muttered. "Brother Johan will come to hear your report and carry it to the Brotherhood. And I will speak with Vlad about this."

"And if talking does no good," Drake asked, hoping to be given freer rules of engagement.

"I will contact the Vatican and recommend they send us a full Choir."

A full Choir. A full Choir had not been mustered since the thirteen hundreds, since the days of Vlad the Impaler, when the Church put down an uprising of the European Vampyres. Despite all their talk to the contrary, he wondered if his Goths were ready for open warfare in the streets of New York City.

Chapter 11

Abandoned by their friends Bonny-Lynn and Amy late Sunday morning, Crystal and Gwen found themselves corralled by April for a return shopping trip to the Mall. Still in their pyjamas, they rushed to get dressed before April dragged them out of the house `as is'. Emerging from her room in the second of her three new outfits – a sheer red blouse over a black camisole, and black jeans embroidered down one side with primroses – Crystal found herself the recipient of April's critical eye.

"Honey," April reproved gently, "you're going to need socks. It's getting cold out."

"Uhm," Crystal gulped miserably. "I forgot to buy any."

"I'm on it!" Gwen announced.

And she was off, pounding stairs into splinters, slamming doors off their hinges – hurricane Gwen leaving a path of destruction in her wake. And despite all her haste, it was several minutes before she came thundering back upstairs.

"Uhm," she said in reply to her mother's look. "I couldn't remember where I put them."

"You know," April suggested mildly, "there is a simple solution to that problem."

"I know," Gwen sighed, "clean up my room."

"Did you ladies survive the earthquake?" Jean-Claude called teasingly from the living room.

"Sorry, Jean-Claude," Gwen called out, "I forgot."

"Forget and give Old Lady Jenkins another excuse to yell at me. You silly little girl," he called out.

"Oh, she would never yell at you," Gwen complained. "She's far too shy for such things –"

"Silly old man," both girls chorused back.

At the subway platform they met up with five of the women from April's coven, all dressed up for an expedition to the Mall. Gwen and Crystal rolled their eyes at each other. How were they to have fun with all their old folks tagging along? And if anyone from school saw them, Gwen was sure, she would just die.

But it wasn't all that bad. For the most part the six women left the girls to their own devices, and when they did offer advice, Crystal found it was often very helpful. And April did have good taste in clothes, despite the teasing of the girls. And she also had the sense to know the difference between the fashions for girls and that meant for women. You would never see her try to pull off an outfit like Crystal had on, no matter how good her figure. It just didn't suit. And that made Crystal wonder if maybe it might be a tad too outlandish.

While his three girls were out on their shopping trip, Jean-Claude busied himself preparing tea. About three-quarters of an hour later, a slight man sporting a black bowler and umbrella arrived. From his dress and manners he was so obviously English, which is what made him such an excellent and discrete envoy for the Vatican, when the Vatican did not want to announce its involvement to the world.

"Charles," Jean-Claude greeted, although Charles was not his real name. They all seemed to call themselves either Charles of Vincenzo.

"Jean-Claude, my good man," his guest replied.

"Come in, come in," Jean-Claude urged, "I have put on tea, no?"

"My good man, if you are not sure if you have or not," Charles teased, "how can I help you? But in case you do have a drop of tea prepared, I take mine with lemon."

It was an old joke between them, and perhaps not that funny, as such things often were. Jean-Claude brought the tea service into the living room, where the two men settled in.

"Is this site secure?"

"It is swept twice weekly, Charles," Jean-Claude replied. "It is also a place of the Wiccan."

And thus warded against the supernatural.

"The Vatican has received your request and is curious as to why you think such a drastic step is necessary." Charles ventured, stirring his tea to maintain his English equanimity.

"The vampyre in New York number three times that of those in Transylvania during the Long Night of the Vampyre," Jean-Claude began, letting that sink in.

"That bad, old chap?"

"With modern transportation more could be moved here, no?" Jean-Claude shrugged. "Control here would give them the strongest position globally. We have suspected for some time they would make their move here in North America for a number of reasons, chief amongst them the dwindling strength of the Church here."

"Blood and vinegar, old chap!" Charles whistled. "I don't think my superiors realize it has gotten that bad."

"It gets worse," Jean-Claude warned, holding up his hand. "I have just confirmed that twenty-four years ago the eleventh Succubus was destroyed. All of the Incubus are gone according to our best intelligence. This girl is the last of her kind."

"You realize what you are saying, Jean-Claude?"

"If we fail here," Jean-Claude replied in a dead voice, "the Prophesies of Hsatan will override Revelations."

"I had not thought to see this day in my lifetime, old chap. The order to mobilize the Choir will go out immediately upon my return," Charles nodded, and then shook himself.

"Then may God grant you a safe and swift journey, mon ami."

They were at the Mall for a couple of hours before Crystal noticed the absence of the Goths. Certainly she saw youths dressed in similar black leathers and silks, but one look at their costumes and she could see they were pale imitations of the uniforms of the real Goths. And some were what Gwen referred to as Emos, whatever they were? Crystal wondered about the sudden absence of the gangs that seemed like her shadows since she had left the hospital, but not enough to let it spoil the fun she was having shopping with Gwen.

At last they had everything on April's list, including socks, and were making their way back home. Only because of the many bags and parcels they had with them, April relented and let them take a cab back home rather than the bus and subway. Crystal was as relieved as Gwen, both of whom were tired after a late night of talking and giggling, and a day long adrenaline rush that was the excitement of shopping. All they wanted now was something to eat, and to drop in front of the television until sleep and boredom finally overcame them.

Jean-Claude had a simple meal of soup, sour dough bread and cheese and sliced fruit waiting for them when they got home. The moment they saw him their hunger and exhaustion were forgotten. In a rush of excitement they disappeared into Crystal's room, and the fashion show began. Seated on a kitchen chair facing the living room, he watched as the treasures painstakingly recovered from the wilds of the mall were put on display. Tops, and skirts and jeans – all matched and paired up in a dozen marvellous outfits – ooohed and ahhed over until the owner of each was gratified and ready to replace it with another.

And, of course, this led to a council of war over tomorrow's wardrobe, upon which the fate of the rest of Crystal's life now depended. Various combinations must be tried, each tested on the proving grounds of a full length mirror, opinions sought and weighed and then rejected as too uncool. With some cajoling from April, they were convinced to sit at the table long enough at least to give the meal Jean-Claude had prepared a sniff and a nibble. All the while, they discussed combinations of colours and fabrics, make-up and the ever vital accessories, tongues wagging a mile a minute in their excitement. And finally the adults could stand no more.

They sent them off to Crystal's room with a plate of bread, cheese and fruit in hopes that at some point hunger would overcome the siren grips of fashion.

"And at last it is over for another year, no?" Jean-Claude sighed, reaching for the butter for his bread.

"You love it," April smirked, "you know it. I'm the one who has to give up my day off to drag them to the mall."

"And you hate this time with the girls, no?" Jean-Claude replied, a knowing look in his eyes.

"She's growing up too fast," April admitted. "Soon she will not need me at all."

"Never, April," he reassured her. "A girl will always need her mother, no?"

"No!" April teased, but knew he was right.

Later that night, when the girls were bathed and tucked in together downstairs in Gwen's room, Jean-Claude put on his trench coat and left the apartment. He left his car behind, choosing to walk. His destination was not far from where they lived, and the night air, although crisp, was exhilarating. A harvest moon hung almost full and gibbous in the October sky, peaking out between the silhouettes of the skyscrapers that dotted the distant skyline of New York.

It was in quiet times like this that he loved his adopted city the most. You knew she was there, alive and vibrant, her citizens asleep or tucked safely away in their homes. Or at least most of them. Always there was those too who prowled the night. Those without homes, and those who made their living in the shadows of the city – and, of course, those who preyed on the dregs of society, both human and inhuman. It was this latter group that had brought Jean-Claude here from his home in Montreal, and what now drove him out into the night.

The building he sought was old, and no longer inhabited. Even the homeless seldom ventured its rotting structure. It was perfect for tonight's business, and a place the two often used when their mutual responsibilities brought them together. Opening its warped, front door, Jean-Claude began the long climb up to its roof. Inside, the halls smelled of mildew, dust, and years of urine and puke that could never be washed away. Up above this grime and decay he rose, until he moved out of the miasma of human neglect and back into the crisp air of the freshly rain-washed city night.

"I see you have come unarmed, old friend," Vlad called from the deepest shadows.

Unperturbed, Jean-Claude moved to the edge of the roof. "If we cannot trust each other in this, there is no hope for our two people."

"There never has been, Jean-Claude," Vlad chided gently.

"And yet now is not the time for open warfare between us," the monk replied easily. "Your son and his flight have been seen on the surface. He is disturbing the Goths."

"As it always has been."

"He was spotted in a crowded shopping mall," Jean-Claude warned. "An incident between our young there would not be easily covered up. The panic it would cause...."

"What will happen will happen, sooner or later."

"We cannot let you have the girl, Vlad," Jean-Claude urged. "The Church will commit all its resources to protecting her. Please, reconsider your actions..."

"There is no such thing as the Prophesies of Hsatan," Vlad snapped. "Revelations are the ravings of a lunatic."

"And most scientists will tell you vampyres don't exist," Jean-Claude prodded.

"I cannot base the decisions for my people on the ramblings of two old men who sat around all day inhaling the vapours venting from the earth," Vlad snapped, moving away. "The war in Heaven was aeons ago. What is happening today is what always happens when the victor fails to utterly destroy his enemy. The vanquished is rising once again."

"I will speak to my son," his voice drifted out of the darkness.

And he stepped off the roof.

Chapter 12

School day mornings, Crystal was to learn, were an orchestrated chaos played out in quick time. April called from the diner at 6 am, and again at 7 am because she knew the girls had not gotten up the first time. From that moment it was a rush to the showers, and to put on their make-up and do their hair. Fortunately, their outfits had been chosen and laid out the night before. Somewhere in the mad dash to get ready and make it out the door before 8:30, they had to get their own breakfast. Jean-Claude, that silly old man, often worked until late in the night, and seldom made an appearance before nine in the morning. So he was no help.

Dressed, but not yet ready to face her first day at school, Crystal followed Gwen out the door to a glass rattling bang. As the climax to the crescendo that was their morning, it had a satisfactory clash. And the added bonus of rousing Jean-Claude from his sleep.

The Academy of the Apocrypha was only a few short blocks from their brownstone. Close, and difficult to find, to say the least. Located on a dead-end lane whose entrance was almost totally blocked off by the buildings on either side, whose construction had reached deep into the road allowance, Academy Lane had long since fallen off all city maps. In fact, most people passed by it daily without knowing it was there. And if she were not tagging behind on Gwen's heals, rushing towards school to avoid being late, she would have passed right by the narrow walk way without noticing it.

The school sat brooding in the shadows of its neighbours, dark and mysterious, daunting any an all who approached its doors. Built in the Romanesque style of brick and stone, its graceful arches, capitals and drum columns, finished with delicate friezes were as intricate as those of any building she had ever seen. . It taunted Crystal, as if it were saying to her that it would not let just anyone cross its threshold – not just a building, a challenge, a test she was not ready to face. The first sight of it stopped Crystal dead in her tracks, and Gwen stumbled several steps ahead before she noticed the weight on her arm was missing.

"Come on Crystal!" She urged. "We're going to be late. Yoda hates when your late!"

"Yoda," Crystal complained. "Wasn't he that little green guy from the movie we watched on Saturday night. I thought you said he wasn't real."

Gwen giggled and grabbed her arm, running towards the doors. "Yoda is the toad that runs this place. He's the principal!"

"A toad am I Miss Moonshadow!" A voice boomed out from the shadows created by the arch and columns at the door.

"Uhm, Mr. Rontgen!" Gwen squeaked. "This is Crystal Raven. She is starting school here today."

"And off to a good start hitching her wagon to a reprobate like you," he teased. "Three minutes to first bell, ladies. And no running in my halls!"

"Yes sir!" The girls chorused, walking quickly until his back was turned, then speeding up to a jog.

Her first class, and home room, was with Ms Bells, a tall, sparse woman with a hatchet nose and a severe and permanent scowl. She taught metaphysics, a subject far too weighty for first thing in the morning – especially a Monday morning, when the students were still recovering from the weekend jags. Because the room was already full, Crystal could not sit with Gwen. She found herself at the back of the room, seated in a corner surrounded by Drake and his fellow Goths, and felt immediately uncomfortable.

She studied him, curious. Like touching the scab of a

serious wound, she wanted to pick at it but was afraid to touch it. He was pretty, in that boyish way, with full, kissable lips, sinful eyes that promised everything and gave nothing, and shoulders meant to be leaned on. Today he wore a black, silk shirt over a white tee shirt, black jeans that hugged his form, tight over his butt and thighs. One day he would grow into a very tasty man.

Despite his slack attitude, seated with his chair tilted back and his feet resting on his desk, he was a surprisingly attentive student.

"St. Augustine," he replied to a question from the harpy at the front of the room.

Ms Bells the Banshee was a screamer. Her tirades punctuated the silence of the school periodically through the day. It was as predictable as the geyser Old Faithful, alerting the world to another of her classes giving into the impulse of hormones or teenage boredom.

Surviving her first class unscathed was a minor miracle. And her next three classes, Math, esoteric science, and Greek, made her morning an unrelenting nightmare. When she was finally able to join Gwen and the girls in the cafeteria for lunch, she was about as miserable as she had ever been in her whole life. If this was her future, she would rather go back to the hospital. Maybe even back into the coma.

In the line at the food counter the two girls ordered all the food April would not let them eat. French fries with gravy and cheese, called poutine, and a greasy burger that Gwen knew for sure her mother served at her diner, and would never let her order. And no salad. And a slice of pie for dessert. With their tray loaded down with fats and carbohydrates, and nothing with any real food value – only the stuff that tasted good – they moved to a table where Bobby-Lynn and Amy were already waiting. They settled in near the wall, where they could talk in private, see but not necessarily be seen.

Finally seated before her food, the initial edge of her

hunger sated, Crystal had a moment to look around at her fellow students for the first time. They were an eclectic collection. There were, as always, the ever present Goths. One wore goggles and a studded leather mask, another wore a purple top-hat, each finger tipped with an elongated metal ring shaped like claws. And with the girls with their black hair and tattoos, wearing more clothes here than they did outside of school. And the collection of other girls of all ages, Wiccans, with their hair streaked different colours, and crystals visible somewhere on their person, but otherwise dressed fairly normal. And the boys, Augustinians, as normally dressed as their Wiccan counterparts, but wearing wooden crosses around their necks.

And then there was her, sitting in the centre of the cafeteria like a queen holding court, surrounded by a flock of boys, shimmering in her beauty.

"Whose that?" Crystal asked.

"Oh her," Amy replied, dismissively. "That's Kristen, the sylph."

"Like a nymph?" Crystal asked, puzzled.

"She might as well be that too," Bobby-Lynn replied bitterly, "the way she hogs all the good looking boys."

"Her pretties," Amy replied in an unflattering imitation of the girl in question.

"I guess they are pretty," Crystal sighed, "for boys."

"I forgot," Bobby-Lynn giggled, "you only like men."

"Just one particular silly little man," Gwen teased, and quickly changed the subject. "Although she is sitting next to Drake in Home Room."

"Woot! Do tell girlfriend," Bobby-Lynn urged. "I'd love to jump that boy's bones and ride him until I break his hips."

"Bobby-Lynn!" Gwen scolded, "you're worse than Kristen!"

"Never mind her mouth," Amy headed off the impending argument, giving both girls a hard look. "Tell us, girl!"

"What's to tell?" Crystal asked. "I don't think he said a

single word to me the whole class."

"That's right," Amy broke in, "you have the Banshee for Home Room, don't you?"

"Oh, you poor girl," Bobby-Lynn sympathized.

"Hey! What about me?" Gwen complained. "I have her too!"

"But you don't have Drake sitting beside you," Bobby-Lynn pointed out. "There's nothing more torturous than sitting beside someone that salty and not being able to talk to him."

"Look Peterson, the guy is not planning to sell the girl to white slavers," Jablonski complained. "Not after dropping sixty large to put her into a private school."

Peterson could not let it go. She was the one that got away. Even though the courts had ruled, and he had no official standing in the case any more, he had been keeping an eye on the two. That weaselly little man was hiding something. He felt it in his gut.

"About this school," Peterson shot back. "Have either of you ever seen it? I've lived in New York all my life, and I can't find it. I can't even find Academy Lane on any map."

"It is registered with the state," Kraus ventured into the fray, "both as a corporate entity and with the State Education Board. It graduates over fifty students a year."

"How about that gang-banger who showed up at his place at two in the morning?"

"Look," Jablonski sighed, exasperated. "We know he works with troubled kids. Besides, there is another teenage girl in the household. Chasing away unwanted male visitors at inappropriate times comes with the territory. Believe me, I know. I have three daughters of my own."

"And the English guy?"

"It's not illegal to have visitors, even from another country. Look Peterson, do yourself a favour. Don't come back here unless you have something real on this guy. You hear?"

"I hear."

Returning to class after lunch was difficult, especially after eating such a heavy meal. Crystal felt sleepy, and her hip ached from sitting too long. Even with the lighter class load in the afternoon, she was beginning to think that 3:45 would never come. And her second class that afternoon was gym. Despite the note from her doctor, and her suspicions that her hip could not take it, she did not want to wimp out on her first day, when the initial impressions of teachers and students would set the tone for the rest of her year.

In their gym uniforms, white tee shirts, black shorts and running shoes – the school's colours – everyone looked relatively normal. The one concession to fashion, the different coloured laces some of the girls wore in either shoe, was the only hint of individuality here. Crystal's were cherry red and a powder blue, a pattern copied by Bobby-Lynn. This upset Gwen and Amy, but it did not bother Crystal. She knew that this was just how the other girl coped with her insecurities, and struggling with her own long list of personal demons, Crystal was not about to criticize someone who had found a way to neutralize them.

Right now Crystal's most immediate foible was volleyball. She had never played. Worse, she could not remember every having heard anything about the game until that very moment. And that was her main problem. There were just so many things she knew nothing about.

"Who here does not remember how to bump from last year?" Miss Sweider asked.

Miss Sweider was an overly healthy, blonde nature goddess who had the adolescent boys tripping over their feet trying to impress her. Despite this she was loved by her female students. She was fun to be with, was a good listener, and took pains to treat everyone equally. She even dressed to down play her more striking physical attributes, wearing little make-up and loose clothing to minimize competing with the young girls in her classes, who were at an awkward stage of their social development and often struggling with issues with their self-image.

Crystal tentatively raised her hand, "Uh, me."

"You're new to this class," and Miss Sweider gave her a warm welcoming smile. "Crystal, isn't it?"

"Yes."

"Have you played volleyball before?" She asked, standing before the girl with her hands on her hips. Perhaps she did not realize how intimidating she looked.

"N-no."

"Have you played any team sport before?"

"Uhm," Crystal ventured, spitting out the first game that came to mind. "May Pole?"

Miss Sweider quelled the student's laughter with a look, a mere lifting of an eyebrow, but the damage had been done. Crimson with embarrassment, Crystal hung her head and studied her shoes, wishing she could melt into the cracks of the hardwood floor.

"Morgana," Miss Sweider chose, apparently at random. But there was guile behind her thinking, and an intuitive understanding of teenage social dynamics. "I want you to take Crystal aside and show her the fundamentals – volley, bump and serve."

"Yes Miss Sweider," Morgana responded a little too quickly.

"And Morgana," the teacher added, "don't disappoint me."

"No Ma'am."

Whatever nasty turn Morgana had been planning, it had been nipped in the bud. Miss Sweider could spot a potential rivalry, and she did not let personalities interfere with her team. She could even guess the source of Morgana's rancour: Drake.

"You volley with your fingers, like this," Morgana sped the ball towards Crystal's head.

Her hand-eye coordination was superb, but that was to be expected. She sent a perfect volley back and earned Morgana's grudging respect. That did not mean she liked her, even when she proved to have a blistering, accurate serve. Given time she would make an excellent addition to the school team.

Half way through class Miss Sweider called the two girls back to rejoin the main group for a scrimmage. Divided into two teams of ten and eleven, rotating a new player in after each volley, everyone had a turn to play. Crystal was winning points with her excellent serve, especially with Drake, who was looking over at her and smiling too much to suit Morgana. And she was really starting to enjoy herself, her earlier faux pas forgotten in the thrill and laughter of the increasingly competitive game.

Just when she was beginning to think school was not such a bad thing after all, a low spike came spinning into her section of the court. As Crystal moved to intercept it with a bump, Morgana stepped into her with a crushing hip check. She crashed into the hardwood floor, landing on her injured hip with a sickening thud.

Enraged with pain, Crystal looked up with a hungry glow in her eyes. A low throated growl escaped her lips, backing the other students away. Only Morgana stood her ground.

"Drake is not for you," she grated. "Feed on someone else!"

"Morgana," Miss Sweider voice whiplashed with an order. "Leave. Now!"

Gwen rushed to help her friend up. "Don't you know she just got out of the hospital? You bitch!"

After class, as she was limping to English, Drake caught up with her.

"Crystal, wait!"

"Haven't you caused me enough problems?" She hadn't meant to say that. She was still angry and feeling a little sorry for herself. Now he would hate her too, and she really wasn't sure if that even mattered to her.

"I just wanted to apologize for Morgana."

"Shouldn't she be doing that?" Crystal snapped, realizing

she was taking her anger out on him, but unable to help herself.

"She really isn't that bad of a person." Drake tried to explain. "She's just afraid because of who you are? I'm sorry, I really shouldn't have said anything. It's not my place. Forget I said that."

But how could she? She asked his back as he walked away. It was all she could think about through her last two classes. Why would anyone be afraid of her? What was she that people would act so mean? Crystal was so upset and distracted that Gwen and her were half way down the school laneway before she realized she had forgotten to go back to her locker to retrieve her books from her morning classes.

"Oh shit," she complained. "I forgot all my books in my locker!"

"Don't worry," Gwen laughed, "just go back and get them. I'll wait here. Promise."

"You better, girlfriend," Crystal teased as she turned to run back into the school.

Empty and silent, the deserted halls of the school reminded her of a mausoleum. A trill chased itself up her spine as a distant locker slamming broke the stillness, and she jumped at the sound of echoing footsteps. She wished she had asked Gwen to come with her, not sure if she even remembered the way back to her locker after that mad dash to Home Room earlier that morning. And now there was no-one around to ask for directions.

God was this place big. She thought to herself as she took yet another wrong turn. And why had they built it like a Cretan Labyrinth? Maybe she should have brought some bread crumbs. They had certainly left enough all over the kitchen table that morning when they grabbed some toast for breakfast.

Turning a corner, she came face to face with a lone boy. Small, and dressed much like a Goth, he reminded her of the figure from her visions in the hospital. He both attracted and frightened her in the same breath, and in her confusion, she let out a startled squeak.

"You're not here to consume me?" He asked tentatively. "Because you can't. It's forbidden at the school."

"Uhmm," she stammered, wondering why everyone she met was so damn weird. "No thank you, I've already ate today."

Dressed in a long, flowing leather jacket, with a ruffled white shirt that enhanced the pale pallor of his complexion, he reminded her a little of Drake and his brother Razor. But there the comparison ended. His lips were a pallid blue, almost purple black, and his cuspid teeth ended in slight points that pressed against them. His eyebrows were high and arching, hidden, as was much of his face, by his long, flowing black hair. Despite his short height, not much taller than Crystal herself, everything about him and his costume suggested grace and flowing motion.

"Uhm," Crystal hedged. "Can you help me find my locker?"

His eyes grew wider, and in the next moment he turned and fled down the hall, leaving the flabbergasted girl standing staring after him with a startled look on her face.

Chapter 13

Far below the subways of New York City ran a tunnel lined with ancient bricks. If one followed its length, and one was fortunate enough to avoid falling prey to the blood suckers who haunted its confines, it would lead to a large vaulted chamber. It's brick lined walls stretched for stories up into the darkness, lined with dozens of other tunnels leading out into the marches of the mortal lands. It was lit with torches and oil lamps, an affectation – vampyres could see perfectly in the dark – the dim pools of light surrounded by deepening shadows that hid more than it illuminated.

From the centre of its floor a ramp rose up into the darkness, ending in a pool of light at the foot of a massive gate. Black with age, its bronze reinforced ironwood was polished to a gleaming ebony, reflecting ghosts of the torches and lamps off its surface. Beyond its locked leaves lay the antechamber of the High Council's palace. Inside a second set of doors Vlad Romanov sat in a meeting with the leaders of the eleven other Vampyre kingdoms, and at the moment matters were not going well.

Seated around a long oak table with him were the men and women who either were or represented the most ancient and powerful vampyres in the world. Inlaid in its surface were the emblems of the twelve Vampyre Nations. The representatives from each sat before their nation's symbol, grouped in their regional blocks.

To Vlad's immediate right sat the man he had replaced as head of this council just over a decade ago. Yoshio Kagawa was as inscrutable as the other two representatives from the Asian nations, and twice as dangerous. That he had not sought his rest immediately after his thousand year vigil was worrisome at the least, perhaps deadly for Vlad's plans. Leadership of the council passed to each regional group every thousand years, and much of what Vlad had set in motion over the last seven hundred years depended on his seizing control of this council. And on this man being in the hibernation sleep known as the crepusculum immortalis for the first two or three hundred years of his reign.

Along with the Chinese princess, so beautiful and small that she seemed a fragile doll, and a swarthy man from the jungles of India, Yoshio headed the Asian block. As a political entity on the council they were as apt to vote against each other as in favour. But when they voted as a block their unanimity was unassailable.

To Vlad's left sat an Egyptian, perhaps the most ancient vampyre in the room. For some unfathomable reason he had allowed himself to age an unseemly amount. Along with a man and a women as black as night, they voted for the African nations, and always in a block. He was the man who would replace Vlad as council chair in a thousand years, and the power Vlad's plans represented – should they succeed– was too great a temptation to ignore.

After the Asians on the right side of the table were the representatives from the Western nations. Other than that blonde bitch from the Roman Aristocracy, Vlad had little to worry about from this quarter. Nor did he expect much opposition from the Caribbean nations, led by a Carib woman and her two Polynesian hand maids. Their habit of animating the dead made them almost not polite company, and their reliance on casting bones before voting was tedious. But Vlad was not fooled. He knew the Voodoo Queen decided where their votes fell.

The council was at an impasse.

"The girl has fed," Vlad reiterated. "Killing her the traditional way will only mean she will be reborn. She is now the only one of her kind left - no other Incubus or Succubus has survived our pogrom."

"I say kill her anyway and buy us time," Sangri, the swarthy night hunter from India suggested.

"She could return in as little as twelve years," Vlad explained. In this he was the undisputed expert thanks to the tome that sat before him. One of three surviving copies of the Greater Key of Solomon, it had given him the knowledge to find each succubus and incubus at the moment they took corporeal form, and how to kill them. "And this time we may not discover where until it's too late."

"Why were we not told this?" Yoshio demanded.

"Because the failure of your ninja was an unforeseen circumstance," Vlad replied, reminding everyone just who it was who had failed to kill the girl when she was the weakest.

"And what is to be done about it?" Isabella, the Italian Ice Queen said in that tone of voice that made him want to slap her. If this succeeded, he would make her the chamber maid to the lowliest Nosferatu.

Swallowing his bile, Vlad forced himself to remain calm. "There is a way. But it will be dangerous. It will require liberating an item from the vaults of the Vatican."

Yoshio held only disdain for the Western Church. Back home his people contended with Shinto monks, whose knowledge was far more ancient, and who possessed more sacred items capable of killing them. But even he would not continence open warfare with the church, and said as much.

"With your help it would not come to that," Vlad baited. "It would give your ninja clans a chance to redeem their honour.

Ember was fourteen. Tonight she had been accepted into one of the Goth bands. Razor had just told her tonight and this weekend she would begin her training as a lure. She was so anxious to tell her best girls that she decided not to wait for the others, but to head home on her own. After all, it was only six blocks to her house. And now that she was a member of one of the Goth bands, or almost a member, she felt so empowered that nothing in the night scared her any more.

That should have been her first warning.

Her Doc Martins echoed loudly on the surrounding buildings. Dark shadows grew from the pool of light cast by the lone street lamp, casting lurid parodies of herself in a broken circle around her. Lost in her thoughts, she ignored these, as she ignored everything else in her surroundings. A cardinal mistake.

Delph reached out of the shadows and pulled her hair back, exposing her pale neck. "What do we have here now?" He brought his lips up to her face, and she could smell his fetid breath. "A baby Goth."

"Oh look," Nephafari sneered, "our little Goth baby has fainted. Shall we drain her anyway?"

"No," he instructed as the rest of his flight swarmed around their victim, poking and prodding in anticipation of the meal she would soon make. "Let's take her back to the tunnels and have some fun with her first."

There was a look in his eyes that made Nephafari and several others of his flight shiver. While the young of their kind often played with their food, there was something cruel and heartless in that look that made them wonder if they really wanted to be a part of this. It was one thing to let your victim escape to be chased down several times before bleeding him out, but he meant to make the girl suffer to pay back the Goths who had brought him into the bad graces of his father.

On the trip down into the dark netherworld below New York City, Ember woke from time to time. When she did, she managed to scream, a voiceless squeak or whimper that only made her captors laugh. They dragged her by her hair when she could walk, or took turns carrying her over a shoulder in her more frequent periods of unconsciousness. Had she been fully trained, she would have tried to keep her wits about her and memorize the path they carried her along. As long as there was life, there was always the chance that you could escape, and once free your only chance of survival was to know exactly where you were running to – because you were only going to get that one chance. For Ember, there would be no escape.

What they were doing could earn them a Council censure, if they were caught. Poaching a victim from the heart of Goth territory, especially a baby Goth, could lead to open warfare between the two peoples, and that might bring about the discovery of their existence by the general populace. That in turn would draw to them much greater penalties than a mere sanction.

To avoid detection many of the younger flights had staked out lairs in the little used outer tunnels of Upyr, and it was to one of these that Delph and his companions carried their victim. In a chamber of crumbling yellow bricks, its vaulted ceiling lost in the darkness, they had carried furniture stolen from antique shops throughout the Bronx. Stealing what they needed from the mortals appealed to their sense of adventure, and made the place all the more theirs, cut off from the ancients and their restrictions. Here they came to drink ancient blood stored in bottles much like mortals stored their wine, or to drain the odd live victim, like the girl they dragged here now.

Once safely inside their lair, Delph tied his victim to a straight back chair. Sitting on his heels before her, he waited for her to regain consciousness. Groggy with fear, Ember came to unaware of her surroundings or circumstances. Before she could sort out her confused thoughts, Delph struck. He bit her on the neck, but did not drink. Just enough to inject her with the poison vampyres produced to subdue their victim. It had one side effect. It coursed through the victims veins like liquid fire, burning a path through the body so painful that eventually the girl would beg for death.

 The smell of blood excited his flight. Their cries and jeers, interspersed with the first of her screams, echoed in the upper reaches of the chamber, sweet music to Delph's ears. Soon all the Goths would die like this....

Vlad was in the habit of walking the outer borders of his kingdom, the lonely byways seldom visited by others from the city, not even the lower castes. Today's council session had been especially stressful. His position was precarious, but not untenable. A High Lord had never been impeached, and Vlad was not anxious to see if it could be done. Instead he desired more than anything else to complete the work his father had begun so many centuries ago, a plot to propel the third youngest nation of vampyres above the ancients who had exercised too much power over his people for far too long.

Lost in his thoughts, he wandered along the dusty corridors, letting the silence lead his thoughts where it will. Raucous laughter and the screams of a girl drifted to him from the distance. `Some of the young one's having sport,' he thought, turning his feet towards the sound, his son and the trouble his young flights were causing never far from his mind. This far out from the heart of the city, those behind the sounds were probably up to something they did not want the elders to find out about. And that could only spell trouble for Vlad, who could not afford to be embarrassed while the representatives from the other nations were still his guests.

The screams of the girl led him to a passageway so old its bricks were crumbling from the walls. He frowned. Such tunnels could be dangerous. No-one should be using them, which meant he was in the oldest section of Upyr, abandoned nearly two centuries ago due to structural instability. His frown deepened, and he quickened his step.

Rounding a corner, Vlad swept into a chamber that was no longer abandoned. He took the tableau unfolding before him in quick glances, noting the young human girl, her ripped clothes and the heady fragrance of her blood.

"You caught yourself a Goth, have you, my son," Vlad said quietly, moving nearer for a closer look. "Where did you catch it?"

"In the upper tunnels," Delph lied, although everyone there knew it was almost impossible to lie to an ancient while looking directly in his eyes.

"You did not find this one in the tunnels," Vlad replied mildly. His hand struck his son's face, its motion so quick it was invisible. "She is much too young to have been let off the surface. Look! Where are her tribal tattoos? Do you know how you have compromised me? Do you realize that now I must make concessions to our enemy? Go to your chambers now! All of you! I will deal with you when I get back."

His son and his flight fled the chamber. There were twelve of them, their bloodlust up, but even they had no chance against an ancient one. Especially one as angry as Vlad was at that moment. If any of the others learn of what he needed to do now everything he had worked for would be undone. The loss of face would be complete.

Horrible in his anger, his visage as he bent to free the girl from the chair nearly stopped her heart in terror. Fortunately, she lost consciousness. Wrapping her near naked body in his own cape, he picked her up in his arms as gently as he would his own child. The speed at which one of his kind could move, especially one as ancient and as powerful as himself, would have shocked any mortal. That these little Goth children could think they were a threat to one of the Sanguinarians was too pathetic to be viewed as anything but a joke. Still, to the young ones and the lesser castes they were a danger, and these did look to the elders for protection. And so for their sake he must take the threat of the Goth seriously.

For his son to have gone against his strictures was unforgiveable. Preventing open warfare between the Goths and the juvenile flights was something he must accomplish to maintain the secret of their existence hidden. The young fool! Did he not realize that the mortals existed on the surface in the billions? And with those kind of numbers one could accomplish almost anything. No vampyre nation would be safe if they came out of myth and folk lore to become mainstream reality. It would be the end of everything.

On the surface Vlad moved like a shadowy blur. Speed and darkness helped keep the vampyre unseen while hunting, and when just travelling they could cover distances so rapidly that scholars throughout history had claimed they could fly. He doubted his haste would make any difference. The girl had already slipped into a vampiric coma, and it would take a miracle for the mortals to prevent what would happen next. She would either make the change or die. If she were not found, however, the search for her would not only bring the Goth into the tunnels, but the Brotherhood as well. And once there, the chances they would discover his plans were just too great. His fool of a son had left him no alternative, no matter what his true feelings in the matter.

He growled at the thought of his son's disobedience. Delph was not only headstrong and wilful, he was fatally stupid – incapable of forming rational thought. It was Vlad's own fault for marrying below his station. But the alliance with his wife's clan had been too important in those early days, those dark times when so many of the Sanguinarians had died in the bloody battles in Transylvania and Wallachia. His kind had barely maintained its mastery over the lesser castes, and although the sacrifice to obtain the Greater Key of Solomon was paying dividends, for decades it had seemed in vain.

He looked down at the girl as he reached his destination. The memory of the loss of face this represented and the heady fragrance of her blood tempted him to rend her to shreds. The ability to control his passions, however, was the major difference between him and his son. Turning a victim, and then bleeding her was considered a mortal sin under the Vampyre Code of Law – a form of cannibalism. If anyone from the council found out what his son had done Vlad would have no choice but to demand his head. Although it ate at his insides like a cancer, hiding his son's crime amongst the mortals was Vlad's only choice.

At Jean-Claude's he ignored the buzzer and simply pounded on the door. Lights came on in the first and second story windows, and he heard a door open and close. His sensitive ears picked up a voice that could only be Jean-

Claude's muttering something about waking up the dead. `Not yet my old friend,' Vlad whispered, `not just yet.'

Jean-Claude was definitely not aging well. With his thinning hair sticking up in a wild hedge, his myopic stare, and the laugh lines seaming his face he looked decades older than the man waiting for him.

"Jean-Claude," Vlad announced. Now wasn't the time to stand on pleasantries. "We have troubles."

"What has happened here?" The monk demanded.

"One of the young flights has disobeyed the council," Vlad explained simply. "I am restricting all flights below the third level from your subways. I will place the Praetorian Guard to watch every exit to enforce my edict."

"I knew this was coming," Jean-Claude swore, but there was no recrimination in his voice. He had his own problems dealing with the young Goths. He gently took up the burden of the comatose girl.

"I did take action on your warnings," Vlad apologized, civilized to the end. "Unfortunately, I misjudged the extent of my son's rebellion. If the girl dies, I will personally deliver you his head."

"Let's hope that is not necessary, my friend," the gentle man replied. "There's been enough bloodshed between us already, no?"

Downstairs, April was waiting at the door. As Jean-Claude carried the stricken girl inside, Gwen stepped out of her room.

"What happened?"

"One of the Goths has been hurt," her mother replied.

"Oh my God!" Gwen gasped. "That's Ember!"

"Go upstairs! Go, be with Crystal," Jean-Claude snapped. "And say nothing."

She had never seen Jean-Claude like that. He had not even called her a `silly little girl`. He was enraged. Meekly, Gwen ran upstairs to comfort Crystal, knowing the girl downstairs would probably lose her fight. The implications of that left her more frightened for not knowing everything than it might otherwise have, her imagination providing its own gruesome answers reality could never match.

Upstairs, Gwen found Crystal sitting alone in the living room, shivering. She moved directly to her side and wrapped her arms around her for mutual comfort.

"What happened?" Crystal whispered.

"One of the Goths has been hurt," Gwen explained. "They bring them to my mom because she is a homeopathic healer, and because they don't want the police to know."

"Was it Drake?"

"No," Gwen smiled at her friend, "it was a girl."

Downstairs, April was on the telephone rounding up her coven between setting up to assist the girl. With Jean-Claude's help, who was making his own series of calls to round up the leaders of the Goth bands, she had rolled up the rug to reveal the Seal of the seventy-two spirits of Goetia from the Grimorium Verum. Wiccan's used it solely as a meditation tool to help focus one's concentration, and not as a seal for an alchemy ceremony. It helped the Wiccan tap into the energy of their crystals. Vampyre venom was designed to not only incapacitate the victim, but to cause severe pain – resulting in a heightened sense of terror and an increased heart rate. Garlic, both as a poultice and taken internally, helped counter some of its effects; not because it was an apotropaic capable of warding off demons, but because it contained properties that helped boost the immune system. And, as always, she brought out her wooden box containing a wide variety of crystals she used in all her Wiccan healing.

"I don't like the looks of this bite, Jean-Claude," April commented. "I've never seen anything like it. It's as if it were purposely inflicted to maximize the amount of pain. It is just fortunate the poor dear is in a coma."

"Thank God for minor blessings," Jean-Claude replied, "but the coma is a dark thing. The venom will either kill her, or change her into one of them."

"We will need Crystal and the raven," April suggested. "It

is the only focal point strong enough to focus three complete covens."

Jean-Claude stood silent for a long moment, staring down at the girl as she lay on a low table built for healing. They had always hoped to let Crystal's memory come back to her naturally

"Only if you can do it without revealing her true identity, no?" Jean-Claude relented. "I must go prevent the Goths from doing anything crazy. There has been enough stupidity for one night."

Chapter 14

"I feel like my life is that Chinese curse: may you live in interesting times," Crystal complained to Mama Flo in her weekly session. "There are so many strange things going on around me, and so much I don't understand."

"Oh honey," Mama Flo sympathized. "Vampyres are just a subculture of Goths. Like Skaters, and Punks and Emos. There no less human than you or I, just some of my babies who like to play dress up. Sometimes two rival groups will fight. Gang fights are a very serious problem, and really something you want to try to avoid. And that strange boy in school, unfortunately he was probably on drugs. Probably thought he was a Twinkie, or something."

"Drugs?" Crystal asked, puzzled.

"Some of my more confused babies will take certain chemicals to alter their mental state," Mama Flo explained. "They call it getting high. It's another problem common at high schools, even private ones. Definitely something you want to avoid, sweetheart."

Crystal gave a tentative smile. Everything seemed so much more reasonable when she talked to Mama Flo. The young girl remembered something about opium dens from somewhere in her past life, and the strange behaviour of the people who frequented them. And both April and Jean-Claude worked with troubled kids.

"How about Jean-Claude's suggestion that you join a team sport to help you make friends?" Mama Flo urged. "Is there a sport you like?"

"I like volleyball, I think." Crystal replied. "At least I did the one time I played it."

After her physiotherapy and counselling sessions, Crystal

was able to return to school in time to meet Gwen and their girlfriends for lunch. Gwen had picked up her homework from the morning classes, and was explaining it to her when the other two girls joined them. Everyone was talking about what happened to Ember in subdued whispers, and it was the first thing out of Bobby-Lynn's mouth.

"Hurt Balls!" She shivered as she sat down, "imagine being snatched by vampyres! Right off the street!"

"Vampyres are just a street gang, right?" Crystal asked, not sure just how she should feel if she had been snatched from the streets by anyone or anything.

"Uhm," Bobby-Lynn hedged as she caught Gwen's angry look. The thing with the vampyres was suppose to be a secret. "Yes. They often fight with our Goths."

"April said she had a drug overdoes," Crystal explained, "but they had caught it in time and that she would be okay now."

She remembered the long hours staring into her raven surrounded by Gwen and a roomful of strange women and girls with their own crystals. April worked over the girl, who woke periodically to scream and scream into the night, curling into a foetal position as the pain of her drug withdrawal became too much to bear. Seeing how much Ember had suffered, Crystal vowed never to try drugs. Even now, pale and wane, the girl lay in bed, too exhausted from her ordeal to even raise her head. Nothing she had encountered in her young life was worth that kind of suffering. Nothing.

"Would you want to try out for the volleyball team with me, Gwen?" Crystal asked out of the blue, long since blocking out their further speculation about Ember.

"Uhm, random or what?" Gwen teased. "I guess. It might be fun. But do you think we're good enough."

"Come on Gwen," Bobby-Lynn complained. "The way you can spike a ball, I'm sure Miss Sweider would love to have you try out."

"And besides," Amy teased, "you get to go on road trips

with the boys teams."

"Woot," Bobby-Lynn hooted, and all four girls giggled.

They had an opportunity to put their plan into motion that day in gym class. The two girls cornered Miss Sweider with their question at the beginning of class.

"Why it just so happens we have a couple of open spots on the team," Miss Sweider enthused. "I was just about to announce try-outs. They will be today after school. Poor Ember. I'm actually glad to see there is some interest. We've been short handed all season, and I was afraid we would have to fold the team this year."

"Oh, I'm sure lots of other girls will try out," Gwen assured her in an effort to cheer her up.

"In this school?" Miss Sweider teased. "Let's just say our sport teams are not a top priority around here."

Gwen called April at the diner immediately after gym class to ask if it would be okay if they stayed after school for the try-outs. And of course, like any mother, she said it was a wonderful idea. Although they would need to come straight home right after to help with Ember, who would be staying with them for a couple of weeks until she was fully recovered. Over the years Gwen had given up her room on several occasions to one of her mother's patients, though it was much nicer to be able to share a room with Crystal than to have to camp out on the pull-out couch in Jean-Claude's living room. And sharing the pain – so to speak – helped ease the resentment she sometimes felt when asked to make these sacrifices.

When Gwen gave Crystal her mother's message her face clouded over for a moment, and then brightened in a happy smile. Something about the story with Ember just did not sit well with Crystal. Why hadn't they brought her to the hospital? Surely Doctor Gilmore and Mama Flo would take care of her, even if she were hurt during a gang fight. And just what would the police do if they found out? She knew gang activity was illegal, but surely they would help someone who was injured without arresting them. Wouldn't they? Gwen said that there were a lot of other people, like illegal immigrants, who used clinics and healers like her mother to avoid entering the system. She just couldn't help notice how people stopped talking about Ember whenever she came around, and it made her wonder about just what was true and what was a lie.

Jean-Claude's leave-of-absence had ended that morning, returning to his half-day teaching job and a class room full of excited kindergarten students. He would be back by two o'clock to relieve Mrs. Koinensberg – the oddest Wiccan that Crystal had ever met, the epitome of every Jewish Grandmother rolled up in one, with just a pinch of pagan mysticism to make her interesting – who was watching over Ember so that April could open up her diner. By four: thirty, when the girls finally got home, it would be a toss up as to which one of the two would need rescuing most, Ember or Jean-Claude. As sweet as the man was, he just didn't understand teenage girls; and admit it Crystal, she told herself, he could be boring at times.

Ember and volleyball was all she could think about all through her last two classes, no matter how hard she tried to concentrate on her course material. No matter how hard she tried to distract herself, the odd behaviour of her classmates kept intruding on her thoughts. Drake and his Goth friends were edgy and carried the threat of violence with them like soldiers on the eve of battle. When she walked the halls, or turned her head in class, she caught others staring at her or whispering behind their hands. Something was going on here and she wasn't sure she liked it, or why it had anything to do with her.

After school she was back in the changing room with Gwen and the other girls from the volleyball team. Bobby-Lynn and Amy had even stayed after school, and were now waiting in the gym to offer them moral support. Catching sight of Morgana and two of her Goth friends entering the locker room was the only damper on her growing excitement.

Morgana looked over and spotted Crystal. Still half wearing the black dress she was changing from, she slipped her tee shirt over her bra and walked up to where Crystal was concentrating too hard on tying up a shoe.

"I hear you helped Ember," Morgana said conversationally.

"April asked Gwen and me to help," Crystal replied shyly.

"I wanted to thank you," Morgana replied in a clip voice. "She's my little cousin."

"You should talk to her about the gangs and the drugs," Crystal offered, struggling to find something to say to the girl she knew did not like her.

Anger momentarily lit Morgana's eyes, until she remembered that Jean-Claude did not want anyone to tell Crystal what was really going on around here. Crystal had to remember on her own, and until she did, they were to treat her like any other civilian.

Morgana smiled and held out her fist, "sorry I was so harsh the first day. Good luck in try-outs. You're actually pretty good."

Miss Sweider watched the two former rivals bump fists and nodded in satisfaction. "Come on girls! Less socializing and more action ladies. Let's exercise something other than our tongues."

For a school whose student body was obsessed with quasi-military training and physical fitness, the competition on the volleyball team was intense. Besides Morgana, there was the sylph, Kristen, a set of six-foot Nordic twins, and a dark-haired, broody girl who Crystal thought must be from the rival gang, the vampyre Goths. Those four were definitely first string, and had been playing together for years. Finding two other players with the right chemistry had been a real challenge over the last year. The two alternate players they already had were good, but not quite the fit Miss Sweider was looking for to build that championship calibre team.

Two of the new girls looked promising. Gwen, despite

her lack of height, was a powerful jumper at the net, and had a wicked spike. And Crystal had a serve a coach could only dream about. They were both raw, though, and did not have the experience of the older girls. The other three who had turned out had equally good qualities, and at least one of them had more experience. It was going to be a hard decision, and she would have to carry at least three of them for the next couple of games before she made her final decision.

For Crystal the practice had not gone so well. While her serves were excellent, she had flubbed several volleys, and took a ball off her face when she misjudged a bump. Despite her moments of clumsiness, she had had a lot of fun. The girls laughed and giggled at each other, shrieked their excitement after good plays, and pushed and shoved and teased. Mama Flo was right. She was making friends and feeling better about herself, and for an hour or so she forgot about all her problems and just had fun.

When they got home from school Ember was awake, and Jean-Claude and April carried her upstairs so she could visit with the girls. Leaving them sitting quietly in the living room watching a video, the adults had retreated downstairs to talk over a coffee. Supper was a catch-your-own affair of frozen entrées and noodle packages, and a cold plate of vegetables April had put together for her and Jean-Claude. It looked like a perfect evening when for once they could forget about the problems of raising girls with special talents.

And then there was a knock on the door. April rose, holding a hand out to forestall Jean-Claude as she made her way to see who it was. Detectives Kraus and Jablonski were waiting outside on the front stoop.

"We're looking for Jean-Claude?" Detective Kraus asked, apologetically.

"What is this about?" April asked.

"We've had a report of an injured girl?"

"Oh," April cut in. "That was here, and not a Jean-

Claude's. I'm a holistic healer and work with some kids who are recovering from drug addiction. One of my clients came in last night in pretty rough shape."

"Can we see the girl?" Jablonski asked.

"Sure," April agreed. "She's upstairs watching a movie with our daughters."

At that moment the girls were playing volleyball in Jean-Claude's living room, and not sitting quietly watching a movie. At that exact moment the ball took a crazy hop off of the television set. A glass knickknack shattered with a resounding crash.

All four adults raced upstairs. Determine to uncover whatever mayhem was taking place upstairs, they burst in to find three girls giggling and trying to reattach the male genitalia to a shattered statue of David.

"Oh you silly little girls," Jean-Claude teased. "I've had that out on loan from the Louvre. Thousands of years it has survived earthquakes and wars, and you three break it in one evening."

"Oh, come away from there girls," April scolded. "And for God sakes Crystal, put that down. You look silly."

If Jean-Claude was not going to take it seriously, at least she was. The girls were old enough to know better than to rough house in someone else's home – although, April supposed technically it was Crystal's home too.

"Ember," April instructed, "you go sit in a chair in the kitchen. You shouldn't be jumping around so soon after last night. Crystal, go get the dustpan. And Gwen, fetch a broom."

While the other two girls cleaned up the mess, the two officers went over to talk to Ember. It looked like they were sent over on another wild goose chase by Peterson. The girl was pale and wane, just like any recovering heroin addict they had ever seen, and she was obviously getting good care here.

"Don't worry Ember," Crystal called over. "That's just Detectives Kraus and Jablonski. They're pretty tight."

Finding nothing that needed their attention, the two detectives apologized and made their way towards the door. At the door, Crystal stopped them with a question.

"Do you think the people who attacked Ember were the same ones who attacked me? I mean the street gang?"

"We don't know young lady," Kraus answered gently. "But we haven't stopped looking. I promise you."

Satisfied, she nodded and turned back to her two girls. She suspected they were in for a lecture as soon as the officers left, and she was only postponing the inevitable. And she was sure they needed to apologize to Jean-Claude for playing volleyball in his living room, no matter how fun it had been at the time. Sometimes being a teenager meant doing things without thinking.

Against April's better judgement, she allowed Ember to sleep upstairs on the pull-out couch with the other girls. Now, showered and changed into their pyjamas, they flounced into Jean-Claude's room, where he sat on his bed reading, surrounded by a sea of paper with strange diagrams drawn on them.

"You've come for a story, mes enfants. No?" He asked, looking up from his studies.

"No!" The girls chorused and giggled.

"Come, into bed with you," he replied, setting aside his book and rising. "And I will tell you the story of the first Goth, in honour of our guest, no?"

"It all began in France in the 15th century," he began as he herded them down the hall and out into the living room. "In a very dangerous and confusing time."

"It was the time of the Great Witch hunts. There is, of course, no such thing as witches –"

"I too so exist," Gwen interrupted.

"You are a Wiccan, silly little girl," and he reached out and grabbed her nose between his thumb and forefinger, pretending to steal it as he had when she was very young. "This was a sad time when thousands of innocent men and women were blamed for all the ills in the world, and either imprisoned or burned to death at the stake."

"There were those in power who believed that a conspiracy of Satan worshipers existed, when in truth it all was the work of one man – or demon I should say. He called himself Pierre de Lancre – but we know him best by the name Shax, the great deceiver."

"Now de Lancre was an ambitious man with a peculiar antipathy for the Basque. And in his position he uncovered a man who was believed to be a wizard – one of those who communicated with demons to learn the secrets of the world.

"He was put to the question and was broken. But seeing a chance to exact his revenge on his tormentors, he convinced de Lancre to let him demonstrate his arts. The wizard called forth Shax, one of the seventy-two spirits of Goetic, but intentionally did not set the seals.

Now the Great Deceiver is one to seize any opportunity to cause mischief. And seeing he was summoned without the restraints of the Seal, he spun a fantastic tale of a Grand Conspiracy of Satan worshipers – wizards and witches who plotted to overthrow the Church and the rightful rulers of the land...."

Her name was Rachael, Crystal began to remember, no longer listening to his voice. She was from a small village in the Bordeaux region of France, and until the witch hunters came and took her closest friend and confident, had never been further away from home then the nearest village. Now Wynne was gone, dragged away in the night in a gaoler's wagon by coarse, dirty men carrying swords and torches. And she was miles away from her home, propelled by anger and desperation to follow them.

And she was hopelessly lost.

The boy was lazing under a tree, idly tapping on his boot with the tip of a rusty sword. It was chipped, and blunt, and obviously stolen from the scrap heap of some smithy. Illegal for any but a nobleman or his retainers to carry, and obviously the boy was not either. But his clothes, while rough and homespun, were well maintained. So

Rachael was almost sure he wasn't a cut throat or brigand. Besides, what choice did she have?

"What are you?" He asked suddenly.

"I am a woman!" Rachael snapped, beginning to question his sanity.

"No, you are a girl," he replied pertly. "But of what type, is what I want to know. You see, I have the `second sight' and you are not like other girls."

"Shit! He can't help me after all," Rachael muttered to herself. "He is but a poor witless fool. Telling a complete stranger he has the `second sight' in days like these."

"In need of help are you?" He sprang suddenly to his feet, startling her. "Let it not be said that Bayard de la Blonde failed to offer assistance to a woman in need!"

He was dark complexioned, with the black hair and deep brown eyes that marked his Basque ancestry. That he chose the name de la Blonde- a claim of nobility- deepened Rachael's suspicion of his mental state.

"I thought you said I was a girl?"

"Same difference. You are seeking the witch hunters who passed through here last night," he announced, a mischievous twinkle in his eyes. "Come. My aunt can help."

At least she now knew she was on the right track, and she was tired and hungry. Maybe she could beg some food from his people, and ask directions. Everyone in this region could not be as slack witted as the boy.

"Once de Lancre got a taste of the wealth and power that the Witch trials brought to him," Jean-Claude's voice broke in, 'he was addicted. And to protect his position, the temptation to summon the demon became stronger and stronger. And without the Seal to protect you, summoning a demon carries the risk that you will become its slave."

"My nephew tells me you are following the witch hunters?" The dark woman sat in the shadows at the corner of the cottage, her face veiled to further obscure her identity. "If the one you seek has been taken by the witch hunters, you are best to forget her."

"She is one of the others, Tauntie," Bayard broke in, "she could do it."

"Are you sure, my nephew?"

"She is like the ones they don't find," he assured his aunt. "If we help she could do it."

"Very well," the strange woman replied. "If you swear to help us free my brother, we will help you free your friend."

"I swear on my life," Rachael replied.

"Take this and her to your uncle. The man you want to find is Pierre de Lancre. The judge from Bordeaux."

"But I will never make it all that way in time!" Rachael complained.

"He is not in Bordeaux, but in the village of St. Emilion." The Basque woman explained. "It is your only chance. You must take this medallion and press it to de Lancre's heart. Say: ` I revoke you Shax' three times."

"Of course," Jean-Claude's voice cut through her recollections again, "such a method, even with the medallion of a saint, will only send a demon back. To destroy one you would need a holy item, and only certain holy items will hurt certain demons."

In the woods not far from the cottage a disparate group of men were gathered about a fire, sharpening a collection of antique weapons and farm implements. All of them were dark and swarthy like Baynard, all of Basque descent. A tall unshaven man with broad shoulders and a striking resemblance to the boy stood at the centre of this group, sharpening a scythe as he spoke to the men around him in a foreign language. His brother, Alphonso, owned a piece of land the judge wanted, and when he refused to sell, had been taken away to the witch trials. Now, they were gathered here in a desperate attempt to free him.

"Tauntie says she can help," Baynard explained, "but we need to help her free her friend."

"A girl?"

"She can take care of de Lancre and the demon."

They left two hours before dark, heading west towards the small village of St. Emilion. To free their friends they would need to take on the armed guards of the witch trial, and break into the jail where the prisoners were being held. But always before Pierre de Lancre seemed to know when they were coming. If Tauntie said that the girl would hide their presence, then tonight maybe they would have a chance.

They hid in a barn to wait for darkness, and Armand sent two men ahead to scout out the village. So far the large group of twenty men had not attracted any undue attention, having made their way along back lanes and across open country, away from the main roads and heavy traffic.

Rachael was a Daughter of Lilith, cursed to consume the one she loved like some black widow. It was why she avoided any dalliances with members of the opposite sex, That was why her only friend was Wynne. She was helping her try to break the cycle, to end the curse and the heartache by not consuming the soul of the one she loved. That was why her presence hid them. One demon could not see the other one. It was why it was so easy for her to slip into the chambers of Pierre de Lancre, and to seduce him once she was there.

He never saw what was coming. Shax screamed as the medallion struck de Lancre's heart. His body floated above the bed, spinning wildly. Nothing would dislodge the medallion as it burned an image of itself into the man's chest.

"Daughter of Lilith," he cried, alerting the guards outside his door. "I know your true name. One day you will pay for interfering with my plans!"

Outside the door, Baynard was waiting with his trusty sword. That mad, chaotic dash to freedom with Wynne and the other prisoners was the beginning of a whirlwind romance between the two of them. A romance that ended in his death not too many years later, and her return to the planes of hel, the long years of a purgatory, the memory of which never survived her rebirth. And no matter how she avoided the memories, no matter how hard she fought against it, the heartache returned to her again, as fresh as it had been on the day of his death.

"Jean-Claude?" Gwen asked sleepily. "How do you always do that?"

"Do what, mon enfant?" He asked, pausing in the doorway.

"That story, it was from one of our past lives." Gwen continued.

"It was merely a story told to me by my grand meme, nothing more," Jean-Claude smiled in the darkness. "Now go to sleep, silly little girl. This silly old man has to work in the morning."

Chapter 15

Reality and fantasy had collided with such force that it was difficult to distinguish the pieces of one from the other. What was dream and what was real? Her struggles to unravel this puzzle left Crystal feeling confused and exhausted. Gwen had assured her that she had fallen asleep almost as soon as Jean-Claude began his story – although it hadn't felt like a dream at the time. Mama Flo said the people in her dreams were people she was remembering from her life before the assault. Her father, or maybe a boyfriend. The problem was the only memories she had were of Gwen and April and Jean-Claude. She had even started to make up memories to please Mama Flo and Doctor Gilmore, only nothing was really coming back to her.

Who was she before she was Crystal Raven and where had that girl gone?

She slumped her way through class that day, wishing she was anyone but herself. The only time she could forget about her problems was out on the volleyball court. In the first game she scored three points off the serve, and in the tie breaker set up Gwen for the game winning spike. Our Lady of Grace was a competitive squad, and the win over them sent the girls to the changing room in high spirits.

"Hey Gwen, Crystal!" Morgana called from amidst a group of Goth girls. "It's my b-day this weekend. I'm having a party at my house – just the girls. Can you come?"

Crystal forced a smile. She felt even worse than she had this morning. When was her birthday? How old was she even? Old enough to love and be loved by Jean-Claude? It was Morgana's birthday, and the Sylph's birthday two days before that. Crystal thought it was rude that they called Kristen 'The Sylph' just because the boys thought she was pretty, and made a point never to do it. She knew she did it now only because she was feeling so miserable and jealous, but she just did not care.

April and Jean-Claude had come out to watch their game, and the girls met them now to go out for a celebratory dinner. Jean-Claude even pretended he was disappointed that they had chosen volleyball over basketball. It annoyed Crystal. His treating her like a child only reminded her of her frustrations in the romance department, her doubts about her failing memory, and her lack of self-knowledge. Just when would she be old enough for him to treat her like a woman? And when was her bloody birthday anyway? She wished she could remember that at least.

If Jean-Claude was anything, he was at least receptive to her moods. As soon as the waiter had taken their order, he turned to her.

"Why all the backward smiles, mon petite? Are we not happy to have won our games, no?"

"No," Crystal replied with a sigh, her heart just not into teasing him.

"So?"

"It's Morgana's birthday next weekend," she huffed.

"And then Kristen's and the Nordic twins," Gwen supplied, knowing what was making her friend unhappy.

"When is my birthday?" Crystal complained. "Do I have to be this age forever?" However old I am, she tagged on in her thoughts.

"We shall have a family meeting about this, no?" Jean-Claude decided. He was big on family meetings. Neither girl saw the point of them, when the adults still made all the decisions.

"I think that's a good idea," April offered, rubbing Crystal's arm in sympathy. "If you can't remember, I see no idea why you can't choose one."

"She could have her birthday on the same day as me," Gwen offered.

"I don't think it's a good idea for you to share your birthday, dear," April suggested. "It's best if you both have separate days to yourselves, although it was very kind of you to offer."

"Hmmm," Gwen frowned, lost in thought. "You're probably right. But it would have been fun. And a party would be a good way to help Crystal make friends."

"So the sooner the better, no?" Jean-Claude suggested.

"How about the weekend after next?" April suggested.

"But mom!" Gwen complained. "That's Halloween!"

"Perfect!" April said. "Since the school dance is on the Friday, we can have a party on Saturday. Everyone will want to go to a party any way."

"Awesome! What do you say girlfriend? Are you as stoked as I am?" Gwen enthused, nearly bouncing off her chair.

"Uhm," Crystal replied, taken aback by the speed in which things were moving, "I'm completely stoked."

Talk through dinner revolved around plans for the party. Plans that quickly turned into a proposed sleep-over with eight to ten adolescent girls, and had Jean-Claude order a second glass of wine. Being Halloween, the girls would come dressed like monsters, of course, and Jean-Claude ordered another glass of wine. They would watch horror movies, and he agreed to rent a big screen television set, and eat pop corn and drink punch in his living room and be too many girls for him to handle. And then, when the party ended, eight or ten little monsters would be camping out in his apartment, and they would have to move all his furniture to make room for all their sleeping bags. Nothing but noise and dust and giggles. He wondered if he would have any hair left when this weekend was over.

When Jean-Claude got up to pay the cheque, April asked, "so Crystal, what do you want for your birthday?"

"Just once I would like Jean-Claude to kiss me like a woman," she complained.

"Me too girl, me too," April teased and laughed.

"Mom!" Gwen complained. "Gross!"

Even in the age of heightened security no-one noticed the influx of strange men and women landing at New York's two airports. Nor did the influx of diplomatic pouches from Vatican city appear on anyone's radar, not with the UN in session, and so many crises on the world stage. Slowly over the course of two weeks the mobilization of the Choir was reaching completion, and these men and women began to appear on the streets around the Academy and the brownstone.

At first Crystal did not notice these strangers. And then she saw groups of the Goths from her school, four or five at a time, following one of these hard looking men or women through the neighbourhood. Several times she came home early from school, or woke up late at night to find one of these strangers visiting with Jean-Claude. She knew he did a lot of research, and that from time to time professors and scholars from around the world came to visit him. But these men and women did not look like scholars. If anything, they reminded her of soldiers. And in some cases nothing more than killers who would be better off behind bars.

At first Crystal suspected Jean-Claude was involved with the gangs, like some sort of Mafia don. He did have more money than a part-time kindergarten teacher could make. Then again, he spent every night reading from ancient manuscripts, when he wasn't volunteering at the youth centre, went to church every Sunday, and was involved in dozens of committees both from the church and school. Between that, and taking care of her and Gwen, when did he have time to run a large criminal enterprise?

And then she became too busy getting ready for the parties to think about it anymore. First, there was Morgana's party on Friday. Gwen and Crystal were stressing about what kind of outfits to wear to a Goth party, ignoring April's advice to just be themselves. In the end they wound up with something that made them look more like Emos. That's what you got when you were working with wardrobes that included so little black, and a mother who just did not understand the need for new clothes.

Walking with Gwen to Morgana's, Crystal saw one of those odd men twice. Looking around as they strolled through the neighbourhood, she noticed a lot of these same people hanging about with the Goths. By the end of the third block, she was sure that they were following them. And it was beginning to freak her out. After what had already happened to her and Ember, she couldn't help but be a bit frightened. Gwen put her hand in hers, and together they increased their pace, hoping to get to the party before it got too dark.

Inside, they walked up to Morgana's apartment and pounded on the door. As soon as they were inside, Crystal gasped. "Oh my God! I think those strange men are following us!"

"Whatever," Morgana fluffed it off. "They're from that group, Guardian Angels. They're here because of what happened to Ember and you. Jean-Claude got a hold of them through one of his contacts down at the centre. He's got them working with us Goths, 'cause he says we're too gang like and need to get our act together. Like we're the ones who need to get it together!"

"Adults, lame or what?" one of the Nordic twins cut in. And all the girls laughed, breaking the tension.

It was a good night. Talking to boys on MSN, imitating the girls from the rock videos, and recording each other on the webcam dancing and singing. And then they paid for the fun when they returned home. April had them spend the whole weekend preparing for their own party, with only time off for homework. What party required a spring cleaning of two apartments, especially when no-one would even see the bottom apartment? And Crystal backed up Gwen when she swore that no-one would be poking into their closets, not when they had so many more important things to do, like talk about boys.

Halloween night. After a day trying to avoid three stressed out women, Jean-Claude found himself answering the door to a flight of hormone overdosing vampyres. They arrived just after dusk, as one would expect from a polite vampyre, overly made-up in white heat and black lipstick, with realistic plastic fangs purchased at the corner joke shop, and dresses that for all their material did not cover enough flesh for his comfort. Taking one look at this gruesome crew, Jean-Claude grabbed a bottle of wine and disappeared downstairs to what he hoped would be a quiet evening with April. His apartment, he was afraid, would be a write off by the end of the evening. Ce la vie.

Gwen and Crystal met their guests with growing excitement. Fifteen girls were invited, nine from the volleyball team, and six of their closest friends. Eight would be sleeping over. Having successfully talked Jean-Claude and April out of bobbing for apples – how uncool – the girls would be spending the night watching horror movies, talking and rating the boys and men in their lives, and holding a séance once the elders downstairs retired for the night. Gwen and two of the Wiccan girls were going to do a few past lives regressions, which April had approved as long as they avoid doing one for Crystal. Jean-Claude was adamant about allowing her to recover her memory naturally.

The first movie they watched featured a horrifying woman who oozed from the walls and the plumbing to drink the souls of her victims. With long, flowing hair and gown, she seemed more liquid than solid, and there was no way to stop her. When she discovered she could melt into the electricity, and crept out into the internet, the unwitting protagonists released her into the world. Laughing, the girls dared each other to turn on their laptops and become the next victims of this vampiric creature amidst giggles and squeals.

It was a deliciously creepy movie, and almost kept them from their next activity. Almost. The lure of talking to their boys on the internet far outweighed any superstitious mumbo jumbo from Hollywood. They put them all into one giant chat room, and spent the next ninety minutes teasing each other and the boys. When one of the girls was talking to her special guy, one of the other girls would type in something suggestive. Everyone would laugh at her outraged reaction or embarrassment, and laugh all the harder if the wrong boy answered back. It was all too much fun to give up, and they would have continued all night if most of the hottest boys did not have to go out on patrol, leaving the girls bored and listless.

After a second movie some of their guests started drifting home. For those not being picked up by their parents, Jean-Claude ran them home – the perfect harrowing experience for Halloween. It was well after midnight when he returned home and sought his bed. He was sleeping downstairs in Gwen's room to allow the girls the entire apartment to have `their space', and to escape the ten hormonal monsters who had invaded his home. Ten teenagers! Mon Dieu, it was enough to drive a man to drink!

Finally alone, the ten girls – Crystal and Gwen and their eight guests – broke out the contraband Ouija board. To get everyone in the mood, Gwen, Amy and Bobby-Lynn did a few past life progressions. In an impish mood, Gwen threw in a few extra lives while reading Morgana. Cleopatra, Mati Hari, Ralph the carwash guy... Laughing, Morgana shoved her over and pretended to do Gwen's reading. When she got to Charles, the nose-picking dweeb from grade nine, they collapsed on the rug in a tickle war.

It was time for the séance. The girls arranged black candles in a star formation, and after lighting them they turned out the lights. Six girls sat in a circle holding hands, while Crystal, Gwen, Morgana and Kristen sat in the centre grouped around the Ouija board. Fingertips lightly on the planchette, they sat hunched over ready to begin.

"What shall we ask first?" Kristen questioned.

"I know," Gwen replied with a mischievous grin on her face. "Has Morgana done the deed?"

The planchette drifted slowly but surely to the `No'. Amidst her companions' hoots and laughter, Morgana sputtered. "Oh, the board lies! I have too."

"Virgin!" Gwen shot back.

"Look who's talking," Morgana laughed. "Never been kissed!"

"Why give away the milk," Kristen replied prudishly, "until they have bought the cow?"

"That's what comes from living with a nun too long," Morgana shot back.

And the girls laughed all the harder. If there was anyone in the group they were positive had gone all the way, it was Kristen and all her boy toys.

"My turn now," Morgana proclaimed. "Who will be Crystal's first kiss?"

"Oh," Crystal complained, frowning, "that's no good. I already kissed Jean-Claude."

Morgana couldn't help but feel a sense of relief. Crystal had imprinted another. Despite a stab of guilt for not being more concerned for Jean-Claude, at least her Drake was safe, the whole reason she had suggested the Ouija board in the first place.

"That doesn't count," Gwen spoke up. "He never kissed you back!"

"Who will be Crystal's first kiss?"

The candles blew out, plunging the room in darkness. It suddenly grew chilly. Too cold for the short night shirts most of them were wearing. The four girls fell back from the board, where an even blacker darkness was oozing forth. Silhouetted by the faint light emanating from the window, it rose to fill the room.

Black hair flowing into a blue-black complexion of decay, a

nightmarish woman rose above the cowering girls. From a mouth lined with sharp teeth a haunting wail poured forth.

"Crystal Raven!" She hissed and wailed. "Did you think you could hide from me forever, Daughter of Lilith!"

Ten terrified teenagers screaming down a flight of stairs to storm your apartment in the middle of the night was a heart attack in the making. One pair of arms for those same frightened girls, April learned as they clung to her, was an impossibility.

"What happened?" She asked calmly.

"We had a séance," Gwen babbled.

"And something tried to eat us!" Bobby-Lynn finished through chattering teeth.

"Holding a séance with two supernatural beings and three Wiccan girls!" April whispered in a low voice that Crystal still caught. "I thought you at least, Morgana, had more sense than that!"

"Sorry," the girl muttered contritely. "I didn't think..."

"You're right, you didn't think," April hissed back. "We'll talk about this more later."

"So I must now chase a poltergeist from my home," Jean-Claude complained as he stumbled out of Gwen's room, his hair sticking up like two horns. "I wonder if it is not a better house guest than a horde of teenagers, no?"

"No," Crystal tried a brave sally that came out like a whimper.

Jean-Claude frowned at her. "Where is the crucifix I gave you?"

"In my room," Crystal replied in a small voice. "Hanging on my bed. I was home and...."

"No troubles, no?" And he gave her a smile.

Crystal felt a wave of pride rise in her breast as Jean-Claude made his way out the door without hesitating. Jean-Claude was unflappable. Not even ghosts scared him as he made his way up the darken stairwell as if he were on an errand to swat a spider. At the head of the stairs he paused before his open door. He stepped across the threshold, and the door slammed at his back as he knew it would. Ducking a thrown vase, he dodged towards the hallway. Completing a perfect forward flip over a second thrown missile that would have shocked those who knew him, he somersaulted into Crystal's room ahead of the closing door.

Reaching the crucifix, he turned and held it up toward the darkness seeping into the room beneath the door. The metal bordering the cross began to glow. Holding it before him like a shield, he advanced and the darkness retreated. The door opened, and he was advancing against the retreating black cloud.

"By the power of Christ I revoke you!"

He took another step forward, the glow from the crucifix growing brighter.

"By the power of Christ I revoke you!"

He stepped into the living room past the couch, the Ouija board visible in the growing emanation from his cross. A commanding male voice, incongruous with the apparition hovering before him, rose to fill the room.

"Jean-Claude Philipe Beaucour. I will be your undoing!"

"But, not tonight, Shax. By the power of Christ I revoke you."

He threw the crucifix. A blinding light filled the room as its tip struck the Ouija board, carrying all away with it.

"Not tonight."

Chapter 16

`You silly little girls and your silly imaginations,' Jean-Claude had complained, `nearly burning down my apartment.' Crystal still did not believe it was only their imagination. Yes, they had eaten more sugar than a human body could absorb. Yes, they were all exhausted and sleepy. And yes, the apparition had looked suspiciously like the woman from the first movie they had watched. But all ten of them had seen it. And who had broken the vase and the statue of Venus – the match to the doomed statue of David that fell prey to their volleyball obsession. Even in the dark, during their panicked flight from the apartment, she was sure no-one had come near them. Or almost sure.

And then there was the conversation she had overheard between April and Morgana.

"I needed to know," Morgana confessed.

"Needed to know what, girl?" April had asked patiently. Now that the panic of the moment was over, her anger and fear were gone.

"If Drake was safe from her."

"Oh sweetheart," April soothed. "She does not even realize what she is. And her heart is seeking closer to home."

Morgana knew that now, and April could tell by her guilty start. "You must trust Jean-Claude. The Church would never have sent him if he were not the right man for the job. And have faith in Crystal for who she is, not what she is."

What was she? She was always overhearing people whispering about her like this, but she remembered nothing of her past. It was so frustrating.

On Tuesday evening April had a meeting of her coven, an old biddies' knitting circle Gwen swore was slightly worse than death, and Jean-Claude was volunteering at the youth centre. The girls did not want to stay home so soon after the haunting, not alone, and decided to tag along with Jean-Claude. Reminded again of the supernatural warning, it was all Crystal could think about on the drive over. Even Jean-Claude's latest short-cut, through a scrap yard of all the other cars he drove over the past year, or so Gwen claimed, failed to jar it from her thoughts. `Daughter of Lilith', the voice had moaned. Was her mother's name Lilith?

Crystal was no longer sure what or who to believe. She would see and hear one thing, and then people she trusted would say it was the exact opposite of what she thought. The only thing she was sure of was that Jean-Claude was on her side. He wanted for her to live as normal a life as possible, no matter how abnormal his own life seemed. And when her doubts overshadowed her sense of self only he could find her again. He was the last thing in her life that still made sense.

At the centre about forty boys ranging in age from ten to sixteen dribbled basketballs, shooting hoops or running lazy lay-ups. Most of them were black or Hispanic, with one or two white boys to add colour to the ethnic blend. Not sure of herself, Crystal stuck close to Jean-Claude, shadowing him as Gwen, a social butterfly self, connecting with every cute boy. The boys began to show off, running furious drills and attempting board shattering jump shots. They got air on both ends, both beneath their feet, and with the ball as it missed back board and net completely. And while Gwen noticed, and smiled and flirted like a normal teenager, Crystal hid in his shadow.

At first he thought it was because these new kids were black and darker skinned Hispanics, where the kids in their neighbourhood were mostly white, lighter skinned Hispanics and Asian. She also ignored the white boys, and did not even seem to notice the young college volunteer who Gwen was absolutely swooning over. If he looked over his shoulders, there was Crystal waiting for a moment of his attention –

ready with a ball or the water bottle, and holding onto his clipboard like a swimmer to a life preserver in hurricane swells. He began to suspect they had an even bigger problem. Either she had imprinted him, and could not break the compulsion to feed on his soul, or she was a girl obsessed. And if the latter, she needed to let go of her infatuation or she would never develop a normal relationship and find real happiness.

"Hey Crystal! Watch this!" Juan cried as he approached the basket for a lay up.

"Watch me!" Another boy called as he dribbled through three or four of his team mates.

Neither boy earned more than a cursory glance as she turned immediately back to Jean-Claude. He realized they needed to talk. And as bad as he was with these kinds of delicate emotional issues, he knew he could not pass it on to April. It had to be him.

In the meantime, to get her involved with kids her own age, he organized a scrimmage game with the two girls on either team. He still had the magic, still knew there was nothing like a little friendly competition to loosen up that one reluctant nut on the tire. And with Gwen to egg her on, fouling her outrageously in the opening moments of the game, Crystal was soon laughing and screaming with the other kids as they chased the ball up and down the court. Changing the rules to suit the moment and their whims, the girls had the boys eating from their hands, and seemed to be the only ones winning despite being on opposite sides.

Too soon it was time to return to the brownstone and face a different set of demons. For the two girls, there was homework to struggle with, and for Jean-Claude a brief tete-de-tete with April, and a long talk with Crystal. Reluctantly, he followed the girls out to the car, and for once took the long way home. He even applied the brakes once or twice, and the girls were surprised to learn that they worked. And they said as much, a dozen times or so before he parked the car in the small garage attached to the back of the brownstone.

At home, while Jean-Claude disappeared downstairs to share a coffee with April. Alone, the girls set up their homework on the kitchen table upstairs. Gwen was full of the boys, even remembering many of their names. Crystal hardly cared. They were just boys, nothing to write home about. Jean-Claude, however, had made an amazing trick shot from centre court, bouncing the ball off one wall, off the floor, and nothing but net. She was repeating herself, and Gwen cut her off to recount the half-twist jump shot that Bobby Washington had almost made. Almost didn't quite impress Crystal, although he did have pretty eyes.

When the last binomial was factored, Gwen packed up and made her way downstairs to prepare for bed. She waited until Jean-Claude walked in the door, and made him stand there and watch until she was safely inside her apartment. One never knew what one would meet coming and going from Jean-Claude's house. Now that he was home, Crystal packed up her homework and made her way into the bathroom to get ready for bed. Jean-Claude kept himself busy in the kitchen, making up two cups of cocoa and steeling himself for the talk he hoped to have with Crystal.

"Ma petite," Jean-Claude called as she came out of the bathroom. "Come sit. We need to talk, no?"

"About what?" Crystal asked suspiciously, wrapping a towel around her wet hair as she made her way into the kitchen. "Yum, cocoa. With little marshmallows and everything."

She suspected this was not going to be something she would like.

"About boys, no?"

"What about them?"

This definitely wasn't going well. He wished he could let April do this, it all came easier to her. Plus, she at least had once been a teenage girl. Jean-Claude had barely ever been a teenage boy.

"Well, you should be noticing them more, no?" Jean-Claude tried another tact.

"I do," she shrugged expansively.

"You need to be more friendly, show you are interested in them, no?" He tried again, and fell short.

"Why, when I already know who I love?" Crystal asked frankly.

"Think of it as practice, like homework," he explained. "It helps you learn about yourself and what you want in an adult relationship, no?"

"Can I go now?"

"Promise me you will try."

Chapter 17

Jean-Claude's words echoed in her mind throughout the night and into the next day at school. Was that his version of one of those `I only want to be friends' speeches that everyone hated to hear? He didn't actually say that. What he said was he wanted her to practice having relationships, like with volleyball, until she was an adult. The problem was she only had feelings that way for him, no matter how crazy it was. Who said love had to be rational?

The time she spent on the volleyball court was the only respite from her emotional tumult. The action, the competition, and the intense concentration needed to follow the ball during a volley drove all other thoughts from her mind. If only she could live her life out on the volleyball court. Everything seemed so much simpler here. The rules were clear cut, with fault lines and sidelines clearly defined, and everyone's role all ready worked out for them. Everything was black and white. No greys. And she felt in control, especially when it was her turn to serve, and she could decide just where the ball would enter play. Where the whole world waited on her.

She was getting better, even at the volleys. Today she had a real good practice. She only wiped out once, twisting her ankle a little, and doing a skid on the hardwood floor that stripped the skin off her knee. She made three real awesome plays, though, setting up two spikes with perfect bumps, and slamming a third ball hard just inside the sidelines. And if her team won a few more games, Miss Sweider said they would get an invite to an Invitational Tournament down in Boston Massachusetts. A three day road trip on a bus, staying in a hotel, and possibly two days of games. And Jean-Claude had already agreed to pay for her and Gwen to go.

After practice Crystal realized she had forgotten her Greek text book in her locker. Gwen, forever organized, had all the books she needed in her backpack, so Crystal told her to go ahead and walk home with Amy and Bobby-Lynn. Retracing her steps to her locker she spotted that weird kid who thought she was going to eat him. His name was probably Wendell, or something, Crystal guessed. He did not look like any of the druggies she saw on the streets when Jean-Claude took her to the centre, far dweebier, like the president of the Chess club. And following him as he crept along the hallway wasn't exactly breaking her promise to Mama Flo to stay away from him.

There was just something suspicious about the way he crept down the hall, keeping to the shadows. Something mysterious that just drew Crystal after him. He went through a door on the main floor that Crystal had never seen before. Counting to ten, she made her way to the door and followed him. What was he doing in the school after hours? Besides a few after school sports teams and clubs, everyone had left more than an hour ago, and even these few were already making their way home. And she was pretty sure neither of them should be here, in what looked like the basement. She did not even know why she was even following him. It was not like she knew him, or even was his friend.

Not quite feeling right about spying on him, she kept to the deeper shadows and let him get further ahead of her. When he turned a corner, suddenly, she lost sight of him altogether. She hesitated. Almost she turned back. Something drew her further, and a few more yards down the creepy hallway, she saw a narrow side tunnel with a light at the end of it. She paused again. Continuing forward, more confident now, she came to the end of the hall.

She was standing on the threshold of a small room that had been furnished with Salvation Army cast-offs to form a cosy home. A converted utility closet filled with a cot, a dresser for his clothes, and a desk that doubled as a table, where the strange boy now sat.

"Hello?"

He turned, startled.

"What are you doing here?" He stammered. "You know you cannot feed on me here. It's sacred ground."

"Why would I want to feed on you?" Crystal laughed.

"Because I'm a vampyre."

"Shouldn't it be the other way around then?" Crystal teased. "In the movies the vampyres always feast on the innocent girls."

"But your not a girl," he stammered. "I mean, you're not just a girl. Oh never mind."

"Shite! Everyone always says that to me," Crystal complained. "I'm really beginning to hate it. I'm Crystal, by the way."

"If you're not here to feed on me," he asked, still keeping his distance. "What are you doing here?"

"I saw you creeping along the halls," Crystal explained, "and- well, it just seemed a little odd, is all."

The two stood staring at each other awkwardly. As the silence stretched out, Crystal began to feel uncomfortable.

"Is there really such things as vampyres?" Crystal asked shyly. "I mean like in the movies and everything."

"Yes. There's a whole nation living in the sub-tunnels beneath the city," he replied. "Thousands of us, really."

"Do you drink blood?"

"Yes. That's how I survive."

"Will you drink my blood?" Crystal asked, not really frightened despite the delicious chill running up her spine. "And turn me into a vampyre?"

"No," he laughed. "I couldn't turn you even if you weren't what you are. I'm a lower caste vampyre. That's why I live here. I am in exile from my people, and the Church protects me."

"The Church protects vampyres?" Crystal laughed. It was a game, childish, and in a moment of self-reflection she realized that she was only going along with it because of her desperate need to believe in something.

"My kind at least. I am not one of the Sanguinarians, I don't eat human blood." He explained. "And there are others, like Kristen, the sylph. A few lesser demons of one sort or other – although not all at this Academy."

They fell quiet, looking at each other warily, not sure if they trusted or even believed the other.

"My name is Brendan."

"Cool. Brendan. I like your name." Crystal fell silent, playing with her hair, pulling the bangs over her face to partially hide her eyes. "Will you take me down to the vampyre city?"

"No!" He almost shouted, half rising to his feet. "Sorry. It's not just because of what you are, Crystal. It's because it would be very, very dangerous. They want you dead. Dead, dead, and not just cast out."

"People keep saying, 'what you are', like it is something horrible and terrifying," Crystal was near tears with her frustration. "What am I Brendan?"

Jean-Claude had made the Goths swear not to tell her. He wasn't really a Goth, and had never made any promise. Probably an oversight, given that their two peoples were mortal enemies, and he had done his best to avoid her. Okay, it bent the spirit of Jean-Claude's wishes, still he could not deny her any more than any other of his kind could resist the allure of a Succubus. The pheromones she emitted were as irresistible as the sweetest nectar to a bee.

"Before any of my kind existed," Brendan explained, "the Children of Lilith ruled the night. They are more perfect hunters, harvesters of the soul and not just the blood. You are the last of her daughters, Crystal. You are a Succubus."

"Like some, sick ancient vampyre or something!"

"It's more complicated than that Crystal," Brendan

explained, wishing he had not said anything. But he knew all to well what it felt like to feel like an outsider. "Incubus and Succubus are more tragic figures than villains, while most vampyres are what you would consider evil. Your immortality was thrust upon you, like a curse, ours is something most of us chose. It's more painful and bitter than our own."

"If we're like cousins, or something," Crystal asked, "why do vampyres hate us so much?"

"Incubus and succubus emit pheromones that are irresistible to us, like that insect we learned about in science class that mimics the glow of the lightning bug to attract its prey. I guess you could say vampyres are a less painful meal for your kind."

"I like you Brendan," Crystal announced, "I wouldn't ever eat you."

"I like you too Crystal," he smiled. "You're pretty cool for a Succubus."

Oh damn!" Crystal looked up at the clock on his wall. "Look at the time! I am in so much shit! See you tomorrow."

It wasn't that bad. It wasn't dark yet, the street lights weren't even on. She was only a few minutes late for supper, even if, technically, she had been due back immediately after practice. And those creepy guys and their Goth ducklings were following her, or waiting on a corner they knew she had to pass by on her way home. It was only a game. There was no such thing a vampyres or demons, but if one of those creeps came too close she would eat him, if she could figure out how to do that. On second thought, she decided as she gave one of the ugly men a hard look, I'd rather eat chocolate.

She shivered at the thought. She did not know what to think about anything, and still something about what Brendan said sounded right. It fit everything that was happening to her. It was only a silly, childish game.

She sighed. She liked Brendan even if he was weird.

Six: fifteen. She wasn't too late. Crystal ran up the stairs and flung open the door, faking it. "I'm home!"

April and Jean-Claude were in the kitchen preparing supper and Gwen was setting the table. They stared at her grim-faced as Crystal threw down her pack and moved to help set the table.

"You're late," April said.

"I know. I'm so sorry," Crystal apologized, unable to stop talking. "I met someone at school, and we started talking, and I lost track of time…."

"Someone?"

"A boy. Brendan." Crystal replied.

April and Jean-Claude exchanged looks, not knowing whether to be happy that she was interested in a boy her own age, or concerned that it was this particular boy.

"You need to watch the time," April sighed, "even when you meet a boy. We didn't know where you were, and we were worried."

"I'm sorry. I will next time," Crystal promised. "Can I invite him over to supper on Friday? Only he's a vampyre…"

"What does one serve a vampyre, one would wonder, no?" Jean-Claude teased.

"The family cat," Gwen answered, winking at Crystal.

"Not funny!" Crystal complained.

"I can make up some blood pudding," April offered. "I'm sure he will be fine with that."

And she gave her daughter that look.

"And can he stay overnight?" Crystal asked hopefully. He really shouldn't be out of the school after dark, or the other vampyres might get him. She just couldn't bring herself to say anything to the others. It was just a game, and she was beginning to feel foolish.

"No boy sleepovers," April pronounced.

"Not until you are at least thirty, maybe forty," Jean-Claude continued teasing.

"How about me?" Gwen asked, teasing him back. "Can I have a boy over night?"

"Not until you are fifty," her mother answered for Jean-Claude.

"But can I have Stephen over for supper too?" Gwen asked, suddenly excited. "Then if would be like a double date. And we can watch movies."

"Brendan might not be comfortable," her mother continued.

"Oh mom," Gwen rolled her eyes. "Everyone knows about Brendan."

"I guess it would be okay," April relented. "If it's all right with Crystal."

"Oh yes, that would be sweet." Crystal started, then her face fell. "But how will he get home?"

"Do not worry, ma petite," Jean-Claude assured her. "We will see that he gets back and forth safely, no?"

The next morning Crystal met Brendan at the front doors of the school, and he walked Gwen and her to their homeroom. Between classes he was there again, and she worked up the courage to ask him over for supper. At first Brendan hesitated, his eating habits were a little disturbing to mortals, but by lunch time he could no longer stand the disappointed look in Crystal's eyes. And the smile she gave him when he said yes was worth any kind of distress.

They sat together at lunch with Gwen and Stephen, and several other couples. Friends, and companionship, and acceptance were new and strange, and he was not sure how he should react. Brendan did not smile much because barring your teeth in the vampyre world was a sign of challenge, and frowned upon by his overlords. Still, he managed to smile a few times for Crystal's sake. And once, after she teased him relentlessly, he even laughed. It had been a long time since anything amused him, or made him feel as happy as he found himself every time he heard Crystal's soft chuckle. How long? Decades ago, when he was still human, before the vampyres had turned him into a blood addicted slave to serve their whims. Long before the years of solitude, that endless stretch labouring in the darkness, carrying off the remains of their victims to the deeper underground, where the eaters of the dead lived.

Crystal and Brendan came to believe that they could only be with each other as long as there was no physical contact between them. They went to such lengths to avoid touching that their friends noticed and teased them about it, but only a little. Even they were aware of the dangers, maybe more so than Crystal, who still believe it was a fantasy – the vampyre prince and the last of the Succubus. While there was a romance in the scenario that was appealing, common sense, not to mention the reality maintenance mechanisms of the entire world she lived in said something else.

Crystal just figured he was shy. It was fun, even if it was make believe. This origin myth he spun about himself lent Brendan a tragic darkness that drew Crystal to him. They already shared so much in common, not having parents – although Jean-Claude and April were wonderful, and she could not wish for anyone else. Neither remembered anything of their pasts, and it created a bond that gave them both a sense of belonging. If he needed to flesh out their forgotten histories who was she to complain?

After school Crystal said goodbye shyly, and raced off to catch up with Gwen. He was Crystal's first boyfriend, and tonight was her first date. Both girls were excited. Stephen had said yes too. They chatted away animatedly, spinning dreams and exchanging ideas for their night together, dissecting every word and action of either boy, and teasing each other. They were so busy laughing and shoving each other, building a world so far removed from their current surroundings that they did not even notice when Peterson started to follow them. Just as they passed by Drake and his band assembling for their nightly patrols, Peterson moved up to intercept them.

"Crystal Raven?" He called out. "May I speak with you?"

"I don't think I have to talk to you," Crystal hedged,

backing away. "The judge said I was free to live with Jean-Claude and April. Why won't you leave us alone?"

"I just want to talk to you," Peterson explained.

"You're just trying to ruin everything!" Crystal snapped, turning away from him.

He reached out to grab her shoulder, and spun her about.

"Crystal," Drake asked, stepping out of the shadows with several other Goths. "Are you okay?"

"No," Crystal replied, "this man won't leave us alone."

"Is that true mister?" Drake asked, menacingly.

Peterson noticed he was outnumbered. He licked his lips, nervously. "I just wanted to talk to her for a moment. I'm from Children's Aide."

Even the badge did not intimidate these punks. They closed in, screening Crystal from him.

"Crystal is none of your concern," Drake replied. "You've also been giving Jean-Claude a hard time, and we don't like that. Maybe we need to teach you a lesson."

The hooded man from the `Guardian Angel's' stepped out of the alley, and if Peterson thought the man would intercede, he was disappointed. Turning a face lined with scars towards the two girls, he pointed towards their home without saying a word. Gwen grabbed Crystal's arm and propelled her along the sidewalk. She could tell her friend was angry, but whatever happened now was none of their business, and the further away when it happened, the better they would be. As soon as they were around the corner, she grabbed Crystal's hand in hers.

"Race you home!" Gwen yelled, and Crystal had no choice but to run with her or have her arm yanked off.

Friday morning Peterson arrived at work sporting a black eye and cuts and contusions on his face. One look at him, and his boss called him into his office.

"Are you all right Peterson?"

"Just a little misunderstanding with Crystal Raven's

boyfriend, Carl," Peterson sighed and sank into a chair. "It comes with the territory."

"Not this territory, Peterson," Carl snapped.

Carl was balding and slightly overweight from years of working behind a desk. Despite being a political appointee, he had spent his earlier years paying his dues as a field agent for CSA. He knew the signs of burn out when he saw it, and the man who sat before him, still wearing the clothes he had slept in last night, four days growth of beard barely hiding the bruises, and bags under his eye competing with the purple of the black eye, was past that point.

"What is going on with you lately, Peterson?" He asked, but he really did not need an answer.

"Just the usual investigations." Peterson replied.

"That's just it, Peterson. Your regular cases are slipping. You are obsessing over this Jean-Claude guy, and there's just nothing to find here. The guy is exactly as advertised, a monk."

"I know the guys dirty." Peterson interjected, pounding on his gut. "I feel it right here. He's hiding something."

"Florence Washington has reported that Crystal is settling nicely in school, with good grades – highest in her class in Greek and Latin." Carl returned, exasperated. "And by your own admission, she has a boyfriend. Her age I assume?" At Peterson's nod he continued. "I have three complaints here, including one by two officers – Kraus and Jablanski. You're on administrative suspension for one month, and if I hear you've been within a mile of these people in that time, don't bother coming back."

"But –."

"Don't but me," Carl snapped. "You're lucky I talked them out of filing a formal complaint, otherwise we would be having this meeting with one of the city's attorneys. We can't go around harassing innocent people on a gut feeling. And, if I need remind you, the girl is not in our system."

Autumn evenings grew dark early. Luckily, they only had to hold dinner until seven, when their last guest could leave the school building. As a vampyre, Brendan's skin could not take direct sunlight due to a severe reaction to a combination of vitamin D and ultra violet rays. While not lethal, direct sunlight could cause a form of light sensitive epilepsy in a high percentage of the vampyre population, the source of the myth that sunlight destroyed his kind. A smaller percentage, including Brendan, went into analectic shock, and so he had to wait until dusk to venture outside and make his way to the dinner party.

Outside the school, Drake and his band were waiting to escort him to Jean-Claude's. Stepping out of the door, he moved into the group and held out his hand to Drake.

"I wanted to thank you for what you did for Crystal yesterday," Brendan offered. "That guy has been causing problems for her family for some time."

Drake looked at the extended hand for a moment, hesitating. Goths and Vampyre's really didn't mix. He took it. "Anything for Jean-Claude. And I like Crystal. Nervous?"

"Yeah," Brendan looked out up at the surrounding buildings and swallowed. "I haven't been out of the school since Jean-Claude brought me here five years ago."

"Don't worry," Drake slapped him on the back, "we'll get you there safely, and no one messes with Jean-Claude. Besides, since Delph's little stink, we haven't seen a vampyre in almost two weeks."

Brendan was jumpy during the short walk between the school and the brownstone. It was strange to be out in the open, not surrounded by walls, with nothing but stars above his head. He had seen Drake and his band training, and the difference between the skills they displayed and the speed and power of a mature vampyre left him less than sanguine about his chances of surviving. As the irony of the thought struck Brendan, he smiled at a pun that was forming in his mind.

"Looking forward to spending time with Crystal?" Drake asked as he noticed the smile on the other boy's face.

"Yeah," Brendan replied, hesitating as his mind changed gears. "Strangely enough."

"Careful," Drake warned. "Not just for her sake, eh buddy."

"You said it," Brendan sighed. "This is kind of stupid, isn't it?"

"Girls are always dangerous," and Drake leaned over and gave Morgana a smack on the cheek, earning an elbow. "See what I mean?"

They left Brendan standing on the steps of the brownstone. For a long moment he hesitated, both knowing he was at risk standing here, and too nervous to knock. He had been taken as a teenager, and had never gone home to meet a girl's parents before. Would they like him? And why would they? He was a vampyre, and not even one of the sexy kind, like in all those Hollywood movies everyone was watching. No, he preyed on animals, spent his life as little more than a serf, and now lived in exile in a world no bigger than a high school.

Jean-Claude came down to answer his ring, opening the door with a warm, welcoming smile.

"Brendan," he greeted. "It is so good to see you again. You are looking good, no?"

"Thank you sir," Brendan returned nervously.

They went upstairs, where Crystal was waiting nervously at the door, and Gwen and Stephen were hovering in the background. Brendan felt better once he saw Crystal, and he moved to greet her. They stopped about a foot apart, smiling shyly at each other, leaning forward while leaving their feet firmly planted on the floor.

"Shall we eat?" April called from the kitchen, where she had been keeping their dinner warm.

Everyone moved into the dining room, taking seats around the table and waiting for that one moment that would dispel the awkwardness. April moved to join them, carrying out the last of the dishes.

"We weren't sure what you would like, Brendan," April said as she began to serve their guests, "so I made you a blood pudding."

"That sounds nice," he returned, wondering what exactly that was, and figuring it had to be an improvement over his normal diet of rats. Other than the goat the Church brought him once a month, they had been his only source of food for the past five years.

While she had followed the recipe, it was uncooked. She had merely warmed it up to body temperature, and then served it to him much like she would a soup. So he would not feel uncomfortable, she had made a cream of carrot soup and served it with little Enchiladas stuffed with rice and chicken. Brendan even agreed to try one, although April was afraid it wouldn't agree with his digestion. Out of politeness, she knew, he said it was delicious, but she could tell that the cooked meat didn't appeal to him.

"Thank you for the compliment, Brendan," she smiled. "I'm glad you are enjoying it, but please only eat what you like."

"She is as beautiful as her cooking is delicious, no?" Jean-Claude asked. And the two girls groaned and made a face, and there was that moment.

Laughing at Jean-Claude, the four kids opened up and started to talk about school and the upcoming volleyball game. The rascally monk winked at April, and helped himself to a third Enchilada.

After dinner the two adults made excuses to slip off downstairs and have a coffee. With a warning about a mother's innate ability to know when her daughter is being kissed, and a lie about the last four boys he had to bury down in the basement, Jean-Claude let two embarrassed and groaning girls shepherd him out the door. And once alone, Gwen and Crystal led their guests into the living room and popped a movie into the DVD. As Gwen switched off the lights, April called up from below.

"Put those lights back on!"

"Oh mom!" Gwen complained, "it's only to see the movie better."

And she rolled her eyes as she switched on the lights.

"Now I'm beginning to believe there are four boys buried in the basement," Brendan teased.

"Yes," Stephen joined in. "It seems to me that there are a few Goths missing. And what about that little Augustine kid from Grade nine?"

Gwen hit him. "That was you dweeb."

The movie was a bit of a dud. The four teenagers were too busy teasing each other and laughing to pay much attention to it anyway. They fell into talking about their class mates, and who was dating who, and as always lately, talk turned to what happened to Ember.

"You mean Delph bit her and just left her?" Brendan asked suddenly intensely. "I thought she was found on the surface."

"I thought she did drugs?" Crystal asked, confused.

"Yes," Gwen replied, giving Brendan a significant look, "he injected her with the drugs that made her sick. That man brought her back from the druggie hang out in the subway."

"That's not right," Brendan muttered to himself, recognizing Gwen's desperate signal, and still unable to hide his shock. "They don't bring them down there unless they plan to drain them. Does Jean-Claude know?"

"Does Jean-Claude know what, mes enfants?" He asked as he came upstairs to let the boys know it was time to go home.

"About Ember," Brendan answered lamely.

"Yes, mon couer," Jean-Claude replied quietly. "I know what you know. Come, tonight is not the time for such dark subjects, no? Time we get you home."

"Can I walk home with him?" Crystal pleaded. "I'll be with Drake and the scar-faced man from the Guardian Angels. And I have both the crystal and the crucifix."

"Perhaps you should let her, Jean-Claude," April suggested

as she came up behind him. "It should be safe enough."

"Oh, can I please?" Crystal urged.

"Okay," Jean-Claude relented. "Straight there and straight back, no?"

Crystal ran to get a jacket while Gwen went down to say good night to Stephen. His father was waiting in the car outside, and he honked the horn as the two danced around the issue of a kiss. Leaning in to give her a quick peck on the cheek, Gwen turned her head and met his lips with her own. Crystal, who had witnessed the kiss from the top of the stairs, felt a moment pang of jealousy. She wished she could say good night the same way to Brendan, or to any boy – and whether it was only because he was strange, or because what he said about her was true, she knew their date would not end the same way.

She and Brendan met Gwen coming up on the stairs, and Crystal reached out to give her friend a squeeze on the arm, signalling they would talk when she got home. Excited to be out alone, even if it was with an escort of Goths and one adult, she let Brendan hold the door open and stepped out into the crisp evening air. Everything felt fresh and clean after an early evening rain, and Crystal whirled around like a little girl, and then collapsed into a giggling heap with Morgana. Leaping to their feet, the two girls raced ahead, daring the boys to catch up with them.

They had pulled about half a block ahead of the others when they struck. Three shadowy blurs that leapt down from a roof top. Members of the Japanese assassins, on contract to Upyr to hunt down lone vampyres living outside the council's dominion, these three had been waiting five years for a chance at this target. Dressed in black like the Ninjas whose legend they inspired, they materialized out of the night like a mist.

They were fast, Crystal faster. Her eyes red with some inner rage, her answering hiss drowned out their own challenges. Fangs barred the first leapt at Brendan, and was intercepted by Crystal. As they made contact, she began to feed. Memory might be fragile, but instinct was everything.

Her world spun and changed. She was talking to a young blonde woman in a pink cabaret in downtown Tokyo. Later, in the alley outside the yakuza where they met, her teeth sinking into the soft, white flesh of her neck.... She was younger, running with a flight of her mates, raiding an orphanage in the Japanese countryside.... As Crystal drained his life force, more and more of his memories flooded into her mind. And then he was violently pulled from her grasp.

Drake reached out to help her up.

"Don't touch her! She's in a feeding frenzy!" Brendan cried, but his warning came too late.

She was kissing Morgana just hours earlier, playfully biting at her lip, hand sliding up the side of her shirt.... The memory was torn away from her as this one too was pulled away from her. Brendan faced her, holding his hands out to Crystal. Keeping his distance, he repeated her name over and over.

"It's okay Crystal," Brendan crooned. "It's Brendan and Drake. It's us, Crystal. Everything is okay now. Morgana, come take Crystal. Drake is okay, and she can't hurt you."

Morgana hesitated, unwilling to leave Drake.

"Morgana, she saved all our lives!" Brendan shouted. "She didn't hurt Drake on purpose. If anything it was my fault. So please, take her home now!"

Chapter 18

Home. Unaware and half blinded by tears, Crystal grabbed Gwen and Morgana by the arm and dragged them into her room. Slamming and locking the door, she threw herself onto her bed, buried her head in her pillow, and let herself cry. At first Gwen waited, gently stroking her back as she cried her heart out. Morgana, the oldest of the three, held her hand. And for a long time it seemed she would never stop weeping.

"What happened, Crystal?" Gwen asked soothingly.

Between her head being stuffed in her pillow, and her crying jag, Gwen thought Crystal had said something like `purple marshmallow paperweights.'

"It's okay now Crystal, you're home now sweetie!"

Crystal raised her head, tears streaming down her face, and complained through hiccups, "some creatures attacked Brendan. And I touched one of them, and I saw what he had done. Terrible sick things!"

"Japanese Assassin Vampyres," Morgana muttered.

Gwen turned white and began to shake. "Was anyone hurt?"

"I hurt Drake!" Crystal screamed.

"Drake's okay Crystal," Morgana soothed. "You saved all our lives. It was just instinct. He should have known better than to touch you then, with all his training."

"I'll go get my mom and Jean-Claude." Gwen offered.

Crystal wouldn't let her go, not at first. As much as Crystal wanted her right now, Gwen needed her mother.

Finally she let her go. Gwen ran downstairs like a whirlwind, doors slamming and walls shaking in her wake. She burst in on April and Jean-Claude, who were sitting quietly enjoying a coffee.

"Mom! Jean-Claude. It's Crystal!"

"Boy trouble, no?" That had been his guess when she had first stormed into the house and into her room.

"No!" Gwen breathed. "Japanese Assassin Vampyres attacked them and tried to kill Brendan!"

"Mon Dieu!"

His private cell rang just as he reached his feet. Answering it, Jean-Claude's features grew graver. "Hello? Yes. And everyone is alright? Okay. I will report this to the brotherhood. I need to go now. There is a crisis at home."

He followed the girls back upstairs, arriving moments after they did. "That was Razor on the phone. Drake is fine, Morgana."

"But I hurt him Jean-Claude!" Crystal screamed. "Why did you lie to me! Why didn't you tell me!"

Jean-Claude moved to the bed and sank down beside her. Although Crystal shrank from his touch, he took her hand anyway. "There has never been a situation like this, a little girl who has lost her memory…"

"They were not gang bangers! And I am not a little girl!" Crystal raged.

"Yes, Crystal," Jean-Claude soothed, "you are a little girl as much as Gwen and Morgana. And you are something more too."

"Am I a monster like that thing out there?" Crystal demanded. "Will I slaughter children like he did? Kill my friends, my family?"

She could feel Jean-Claude's concern for her through their physical contact, and although she felt inconsolable, his presence helped ease her pain.

"Demons," Jean-Claude explained slowly, "are also angels. They too are God's creatures. Like all of us, some are evil, some indifferent, and some are good. For centuries now there have been those Daughters of Lilith who have been friends of the Church – just like you, Crystal"

"I don't believe you are evil," Jean Claude continued with as much conviction as his voice could hold, "any more than I believe April or Gwen because they hold to the tenants of the Wiccan faith."

"What does it mean Jean-Claude," Crystal pleaded, "what am I? Brendan says I am cursed."

"There are two legends about the origin of the Daughters of Lilith," Jean-Claude began. "The first says that you are the daughters of Adam's first wife. The second says you are the daughter of an angel who followed one of the minions of Hsatan into hell for love. Both say you are cursed to consume the -."

"Jean-Claude," April interjected. "I think it is best if we do a past life regression. Better she see for herself."

"Yes," Jean-Claude replied. "I will walk Morgana home. We will probably stop in to see Drake on the way, no?"

"No," Morgana said through a smile. And she rose to walk with him out the room, leaving Gwen and her mother alone with Crystal.

Outside Drake's apartment building Jean-Claude stopped to talk to the scar-faced man, letting Morgana run up alone to see her boy.

"The girl is as strong as they say," the stranger said. "I watched one of those Jap monstrosities go from a teenager to a man in his late fifties before my eyes. And I ain't never seen anything faster than a vampyre."

"How is the boy?" Jean-Claude asked.

"Fine. Thanks to your pet, Brendan," the other replied. "She didn't even touch him, even in the midst of a feeding frenzy."

"I know your faction doesn't agree with our project, Gabriel," Jean-Claude replied.

"The Church shouldn't be meddling with these creatures," he replied. Gabriel was originally from Texas, but had lost his accent somewhere over the years. He had left at seventeen to join the marines during the Vietnam War. He still wore the

Special Forces tattoo on his right forearm, but after some of the things he had seen over the years with the Brotherhood, he no longer thought they were such hot shit. "After what I saw tonight?"

"We're going to have to call in the Specialists," Jean-Claude warned.

"This once I agree," Gabriel nodded and spat. "If the shit hits the fan here, I don't think the fighting can be contained to New York. Nothing we got here gonna stop that shit."

"Let us hope that Crystal-." Jean-Claude began.

"I know. I know. She's our nuclear deterrent." Gabriel complained. "But I don't have to like it. Send for your specialists."

"All God's creatures deserve a chance at redemption, Gabriel." Jean-Claude replied quietly. "Even us old warriors."

Back at the apartment, April and Gwen were setting up their crystals to take Crystal through a past life regression.

"Gwen is stronger at this than me," April was explaining, "but I have more experience. So we are going to channel together. I will lead and she will lend me some of her strength."

"Okay," Crystal said meekly.

"You may not like some of the things you see. I have no control over what you will remember, Crystal, so you have to be brave. We will go back as far as we can to help you recover as many of your memories from your past lives as possible, but I can't guarantee how far just two of us can take you."

"Anything would be better than the blank I'm living with now," Crystal replied. She was staring at a point on the ceiling, lost in a fog of her misery. "I feel so lost not knowing who or what I am."

"You have already seen one of our rituals," April continued, trying to prepare the girl as best she could. No-one in her coven had ever attempted this on an immortal, and it was difficult to hide the fear she felt for her daughter and herself. "So you know a little of what to expect. Are you ready?"

"As ready as I'll ever be," Crystal replied, following Gwen's instructions to lie down and relax.

Taking up position on both side of her, April and Gwen each held onto a focus crystal and one of Crystal's hands. They reached across until their crystals touched, completing the circle. As April's voice gently lulled her towards sleep, Crystal allowed herself to drift into a hypnotic trance.

She slipped into her past. Over a span of hours Crystal relived many of her past lives, all with a common theme. She fell in love, and slowly but inevitably consumed the soul of her beloved. Every one hundred and forty-four years she was reborn to replay the same scenario, sometimes dying old, bitter and lonely, sometimes cut down in a quick violent death. Only twice had she died before the man she loved, and of her host of lovers the one that haunted her still was her pope.

Her name was Meridiana. She lived in Rome with her lover, Gerbert d'Aurillac, a Catholic priest. Newly ordained, he had powerful friends in the Church, including his abbot – a man who would earn him the patronage of Borrell II of Barcelona – and Gerbert would not remain a priest forever. His potential to go far in the Church and one day become a powerful man was important to Meridiana's plans, for she had uncovered a dark secret and would have need of such allies in the future. Gerbert was also her confessor and knew what she was, and so she was careful not to feed on him. She had learned such restraint over the centuries, and there were others here she could feed on with impunity. For it was an age of chaos and change, a period when lesser demons and vampyres roamed the length and breadth of Europe.

They lay in bed, lounging over a half-eaten breakfast. Gerbert played with the locks of her hair that she had let out of its elegant coif and she leaned her head against his bare chest.

"Gerbert my love," she asked in a voice that came deep from her throat, "will you read something for me without getting angry?"

"Anything for you, my sweet," Gerbert replied, bending to kiss the nape of her neck.

She brought out a parchment that lay concealed beneath the blankets and presented it to him. The scroll was of ancient papyrus held together with a black ribbon and entitled: Prophesies of Hsatan.

"Where did you get this?" Gerbert demanded.

"I stole it when I was out feeding," she confessed. "Do you forgive me?"

"This once," he smiled down at her as she stretched seductively. "I must, since I have given my word."

He unrolled the scroll and began reading. "This is the exact reverse of Revelations. It is blasphemous!"

It spoke of a thousand years of war followed by a second of peace, the enslavement and slaughter of man kind, and renewal of the war in Heaven.

"But it is more, is it not?" Meridiana asked pointedly. "Is it not a blue print to subvert God's own plans? And as such, shouldn't the Church take pains to stop its author."

"I am but a simple priest," Gerbert replied gently. "To affect church policy at such a fundamental level I would need to be pope."

"Then you shall be, my love."

And they did just that, making him Pope Sylvester the second. They seduced, bribed and blackmailed their way through the Church hierarchy, eliminating all those who stood in his way. Such was the norm of European society of that time. It had taken years – happy, tense, exciting years. Some of the most content and satisfying days of her long life.'

Her death was brutal and bloody. The inquisitors who took her were in actuality four demons, beings more powerful than Meridiana, and they tortured her for months. Broken, her beauty torn away, Meridiana lay strapped to a stone table in the basement beneath a befouled church. The chamber they worked in was a wooden cage suspended in a larger chamber, a place between heaven and hell, and hidden from the scrying of the Wiccans. In the flickering torchlight a defrocked priest held a dagger with a sinuous blade, standing like a deformed parody of his own shadow. He chanted a Latin mass backwards, the blade held high above his head as he leered down at his prostrate victim.

Shax's voice cut through the chanting, "little cousin. Did you think you could betray us with impunity?"

"I am not your cousin," Meridiana coughed past the blood pooling in her throat. "And nothing you do will prevent what has already been set in motion."

"A pity you will no longer be around to save your little pet," he taunted. "See that blade in the mortal's hand? Do you not recognize it? It is Abraham's knife, the same blade he used in his failed sacrifice of his son."

One of a handful of items that could destroy her, ending all future incarnations.

Pope Sylvester and the members of his fledgling brotherhood found her. Led by a wild, red-haired, green-eyed Wiccan who studied under the Druids of Ireland, they burst into the concealed chambers, weapons drawn. With his crook staff, the emblem of his office, Sylvester struck down the first of the four possessed inquisitionist, the Irish Wiccan took the second. In a short time the other three men in the room were subdued or slain, but it would be years before the brotherhood learned how to slay a demon rather than just exorcize him from this mortal coil.

Sylvester was at her side, helping to free her from her bonds. One look at her and he knew that his Meridiana did not have long to live. One of his retinue handed him the dagger.

"Careful my love," Meridiana coughed. "That is one of the few things in the world that can end my existence."

"Then I shall place it in the vaults beneath the Vatican and see that it never sees the light of day." Pope Sylvester promised.

In another hundred and forty-four years she would be reborn. Her love would be dead by then, but at least she had seen her Gerbert one last time. There would be another to replace him in her heart, such was a nature of the curse that was her existence, and yet he would remain her soul mate forever. One day, because of him, she would be free to live out a normal life, to find true love without sacrifice. For now she could live for her revenge against the four demons who had taken her away from him.

She found Agares playing bandit lord on the steppes of China.

Her name was Jiao. Together with a band of shoaling monks, led by her current lover, Tai-Shan, they had been tracking these marauding cut-throats for weeks now. Tai-Shan carried the sacred staff of Varian, the deity who taught the Shaolin their famous staff methods. His nineteen followers were armed with bamboo staffs whose centre had been filled with iron. (An ancient temple secret he had shared with Jiao, it allowed the staff to turn the blade of a sword.) Tai-shan told Jiao that he brought nineteen others because twenty-one was a lucky number, and it was certainly their lucky day.

"They are not far ahead now," he looked up and smiled at her, pointing to the tracks.

"Soon my love," Jiao promised, "and the villagers will be safe again. We will bring those who killed your mother and sister to justice."

His eyes glowed with an inner light of a zealot. Since that day two years ago, when he returned to find the village of his birth burnt to the ground by bandits, and an injured Jiao the only survivor, it had been his mission to end this monster. He fought hard against his desire for revenge, struggled to make sure his motivations were noble and honourable, as a true Shaolin monk should. And when he floundered, Jiao was there to help him work through his confusion. A porcelain doll with those strange blue eyes, and the heart and perception of an ancient soul, she had become his constant companion and one true confident.

By dusk they had found the bandit's lair. Creeping through the brush and rocks, they surrounded the camp, taking out the guards with swift blows to the neck. The cry of a laughing thrush disturbed the night's silence. Breaking from cover, the twenty-one warriors raced from the hillside, meeting the rousing bandits with their staffs. Flailing bamboo and swift kicks cleared a path for Jiao and Tai-shan to the tent at the centre of the camp. With a roundhouse kick, Jiao knocked a bandit from their path. A low sweep of Tai-shan's staff took the feet from beneath two more.

Finally, they stood before the tent unopposed. Tai-shan faced the demon Agares with the staff of Vajrapani, a mortal carrying a sacred item to send him to his death. Tonight, he would learn that two could play that game, and that love was a far greater motivator than fear. Her lover fought with the supernatural strength and speed of his deity, countering all of the demon's sword strokes with his flashing staff.

"I will kill you little mortal," Agares taunted, "just as I killed your family."

"Don't let him taunt you, my warrior," Jiao called. She ducked a sword and struck its wielder in the throat. "The demon knows he cannot beat you if you keep you discipline."

And the anger drained from his mind. And the demon met his death....

One-hundred and forty-four years later she found Caim in a ruined temple on mount Arafat. Her name was Cassandra, and she was here with her lover, the Italian Explorer Vincenzo and his four Sherpa guides. They were here searching for the fabled Noah's Arc, said to be hidden somewhere in these mountains, when a sudden blizzard drove them into a cave for shelter. Studying their surroundings as the guides struggled to light a fire, Vincenzo determined that it was not natural, but a man-made tunnel. The explorer in him wanted to follow it to its end, and Cassandra encouraged his ambition, despite the storm, despite the mountain. Only because she loved and admired his spirit of adventure.

First, they needed a hot meal to help warm themselves up. If he was alone, Vincenzo might have set out immediately, but he needed to look out for his lovely Cassandra. He could see she was cold. So he let her draw him down beside her and placed an arm around her shoulder. The meal was a simple stew made from salted goat and dried vegetables. The snow melted quickly in the fire, even at this altitude, and they were soon packing up their gear, making torches from the wood they had lugged up the mountain so they could follow the tunnel.

The Sherpa did not like it. There was something not right about a tunnel carved so high up in the mountain. Although they had climbed this mountain many times, they had never heard tell of such a place. Vincenzo laughed off their concern. He was carrying his good luck charm, a strangely shaped crucifix made from the walnut tree under which Saint Anthony of Padua had died. Ever since the day his sister, a nun in the Benedictine order, had given him this *simple gift it had brought him good luck. As long as he had it and his Cassandra, Vincenzo did not fear anything. What could happen to a man surrounded by such love?*

The tunnel was rough hewn for three quarters of its length, and then was lined with sandstone brick that must have been hauled up the side of the mountain. It represented years of hard labour. The workmanship looked Middle Eastern, and was misplaced in this time and this region. It was the find of a lifetime. And when it ended in a set of brass doors adorned with pictograms in bas relief of some unknown origin, he knew he had found his Tombs of the King.

"This, my love," he said, turning towards Cassandra "is a significant find. It will make a name for me!'

"It is beautiful." She breathed.

Inside, waiting for them, was a temple of jade and marble to rival any in the world. And one strange old man with glowing eyes, who ripped the head off of the nearest guide.

"He's a demon!" Cassandra cried, for she knew such things. She could smell the sulphur on him, the stench from the pits of hell that was unmistakable to another of his kind. "Use the rosary."

The demon looked old and frail, and moved with lightning speed. He climbed the walls and disappeared up into the darkness of the ceiling. Quickly forming a circle around Cassandra, the four remaining men raised the pointed shafts of their ice picks up into the darkness. In his one hand Vincenzo held the rosary with its dagger-shaped crucifix, in the other the last remaining torch. Eyes scanning the inky black above their heads, they waited for the next assault.

The demon fell on one of the Sherpas. That was his last mistake. Even its supernatural quickness could not avoid three descending ice axes and the crucifix. Dodging the three obvious weapons, he placed himself in the path of Vincenzo's strike. His sudden cry of pain echoed in the darkness. Caim had learned the same lesson as Agares, and he too sacrificed his existence as his reward.

They never made it off the mountain. With the death of the demon the temple began to collapse. One of the two remaining Sherpas was crushed beneath a falling boulder, Vincenzo's arm was shattered, and the last of their guides took off in a panicked flight that led him over a hidden ice chasm. Although she was not to know of it until years later, he had fallen to his death. Cassandra was unable to carry her lover any further than the entrance of the tunnel, where they collapsed in an exhausted huddle. Unwilling to leave the man she loved, the two lovers froze to death on the mountain top, wrapped in each other's arms.

Caim was in the temple looking for something. Crystal needed to remember that when this was over....

Her name was Amelie. She lived in Paris France with her lover, Gabriel. He was a musketeer, a member of the Maison du Roi, and led a small company of ten men. They found Berith in a basement of a Paris tenement. Along with a dozen rough men and women, part of a salon dedicated to the occult, he was brewing a plague that would have killed millions. Tonight they were preparing to sacrifice a young, black-haired girl who was tied to a wooden table that had been dragooned into service as an altar. At the moment Gabriel and his men broke through the door, Berith, acting as high priest, was just about to plunge a wicked dagger into her breast.

Gabriel was carrying Durandal, the sword of Childe Roland. In an age where few outside the service of a lord or the king carried arms, all the men here drew swords to meet the intruders. Swords against drawn pistols were a long shot. Three of the cultists fell in the first volley, and then it was down to just the swords. Gabriel's blade caught Berith's dagger as it descended, and he was forced to turn and deal with the intruder. As her lover drew the demon away from his victim, Amelie moved to free the girl. In the years that followed, the two would become best friends, the closest companions through a life that would bring Amelie great heartache.

Tonight her heart was victorious. Outnumbered after the initial moments, the cultists fell back, their numbers reduced further. Once they pushed their way through the door and into the basement proper, the musketeers were able to fight five abreast, cutting the demon off from his supporters. Without Berith the cultists were no match for trained and disciplined troops, and soon were dropping like lemmings off a cliff. Alone, facing the determined mortal with a sword he now suspected was not a normal weapon, Berith began to look behind him for an escape. More and more blades faced him, and although he did not fear the mortals in themselves, the very bulk of *their numbers in the tight quarters blocked his way.*

He fought with desperation, wounding some of the men before him, and always Gabriel and Durandal were there to push him back. Steel on steel, ringing loudly in the close space. Back and back and back. Grim faced, Gabriel pressed, and as the demon made his move towards the two women to use as a shield, Gabriel ran him through.

Only Shax, the Great Deceiver, had managed to escape her vengeance. Crystal now knew he was here, in this time with her, and she was standing over a source of power that could make her stronger than a legion of hell....

Chapter 19

They called him the Wandering Jew. Some claimed he was cursed to walk the earth, wandering until the Second Coming. Hard, blue-eyes, seamed face framed by long grey locks, and a mouth that never smiled. He arrived in New York in the early evening, a strange haunted man wearing a long cloak over black leathers, and white linen shirt like some Mexican gunslinger from the West of the 1800's. Airport security and customs saw all kinds come through this airport, and although they gave him a hard look, they passed him through without more than the usual hassle he encountered in modern airports. And his paperwork was impeccable, issued by the Vatican, a diplomatic passport even Homeland Security could not question.

She was a Sylph with a special ability to make anyone believe what she said. Anastasia served as the Specialists press relations officer, ensuring their secrets never reached the attention of the public or the press. Tall and willowy, with long golden hair and stunning grey eyes, she dressed in the latest fashions from Paris or Milan – always conservative, always with a suggestion of sex. She was the second to arrive, again on a Vatican passport with diplomatic privileges. Anastasia flew into New York's second airport, arriving on a domestic flight, as others would reach the city by bus or by train after flying into the United States through other airports in multiple cities.

He was a guardian angel who had failed to protect his ward. Known to the mortals simply as Angel, he was one of the first exiles to hide within the church. Black hair and black eyes, with the face of a warrior who had seen too many battles, he arrived in the city wearing a three-piece business suit on a commuter train from Jersey City. Angel spoke to no-one, moving through the crowd with the step of a man who knew his destination. It had been over a hundred years since he had been here last. No-one from then would be alive from that time to recognize him, as no-one in this time would remember his passing.

He was a Stregoni Benefici, a vampyre who only drank the blood given to him voluntarily. Although a member of the Sanguinarians, he never drank blood directly from a victim, never injected a mortal with his venom. Alvaro de San Carlos was one of several vampyres who had sought sanctuary within the Church, an urbane gentleman who wore Italian cut suits in colours that suited his swarthy features. Black hair and brown eyes, he could blend in with the population of any Spanish nation, appearing no more than the playboy he was.

She was Djinn. Cantara was unlike the others who sought sanctuary in the Church. She cared nothing for salvation. She cared only for her vengeance on the vampyres, who once held her captive for eight hundred years, and her lover, the man they called the Wandering Jew. Dark, brown hair and eyes, dark Arabic features, she was short and slim, and utterly feminine. Cantara was also cold, and rapacious and heartless as a desert night. Blood was her religion, violence her creed. Mortals meant little to her, civilian or otherwise, and if not for her lover and rescuer, even the Brotherhood could not control her thirst for killing.

These five and twenty others of their kind made up the Specialists. All supernatural creatures, they found homes within the vast church infrastructure, where they were hidden and protected. Called together only in the direst of circumstances, they seldom crossed paths with one and other. Almost three hundred years had passed since last they had come together, some incident in Japan, where they had been sent to retrieve a sacred item.

Gabriel was waiting with April and Jean-Claude when these five reached the brown stone. He was a hard man, these creatures harder. There was no humanity to leach away as his had. None of them were human. Alien and difficult to read, he did not like working with them.

Alvaro came out from Crystal's room, where he had gone to check in on the girl. For two days now she had lain in a coma, absorbing the memories of scores of past lives, assimilating the knowledge and experiences into one coherent whole.

"She has fed on one of my kind," Alvaro pronounced, "and recently."

He had some medical experience, and still Gabriel did not trust him. Even if the girl was one of them. "She took out one of Yoshio Kagawa's Ninja like he was a rag doll. Aged him five, six decades. Might even have killed him."

"We need to watch she does not drain too many," Alvaro warned. "It would be like a nuclear pile going critical – or, more appropriately, like a five year old who ate a ten pound bag of sugar. She would be a danger to any living creature near her."

"That is bad, mon ami," Jean-Claude assured him. "It is our job to see none of Vlad's people reach her, no?"

A knock sounded at the door. Yet no-one had rang the buzzer below, and everyone was accounted for in the apartment at the moment. Who? With a questioning look, Jean-Claude moved to answer it.

He found himself facing Peterson.

"May I help you?" He asked, rather annoyed.

"What have you done with the girl?" Peterson snapped, barging his way into the apartment. "I demand you let me see her now!"

"You do not want to see the girl now," Anastasia interjected.

"I do not want to see the girl," Peterson replied, as if it were his intention all along.

"You have only come to check on her before you go away," the Sylph continued.

"I am leaving the city," Peterson explained, "and just wanted to check in on her before I go."

"Now that you have some time off," she continued to lead him, "you have decided to finally take that trip to Hawaii. You have been saving for it for two years, and plan to be gone for at least a month."

"I'm heading to Hawaii," Peterson continued as if she had not spoken. "Works been a little stressful, and I plan to chill on the beach for a month."

"Thank you," Jean-Claude replied. "Unfortunately, Crystal is feeling a little under the weather, and is sleeping now. I'm sure she would have wanted to say good bye."

"Sorry for bothering you," Peterson moved to the door. "Have a good night."

The room fell silent after he left.

"Someone better arrange to put enough money into his account for a month in Hawaii," the Wandering Jew commented dryly.

"It can be done," Jean-Claude replied, distracted.

"You should have let me deal with him," Cantara commented. "Less expensive and more permanent."

"The Vatican frowns on civilian casualties, my love," the Wandering Jew replied. "And even such as he would have someone who misses him. Questions would be asked we would not want to answer."

"There is a place for you and your people down in the basement," Jean-Claude explained. "We will discuss our plans more fully tomorrow, no?"

Crystal lay in a coma for three days. Worried, they watched and waited for her to recover, needing her more than ever as tensions continued to mount. Waking up on Tuesday morning, however, she refused to get out of bed or to leave her room. Severely depressed and despondent, Crystal was convinced that there was no escaping the long existence of heartache and killing that waited for her. And worse, she had already begun to feed on Jean-Claude and Drake, and now knew she would eventually destroy one or both of them. It was her nature. Aeons of existence had taught her that she could not control the compulsion to fall in love, to feed, and leave nothing behind but a soulless husk.

How many men had she killed? Already most of what she had seen during the past life regression was fading from her memory. While it may still be there, somewhere in the recesses of her mind, she could recall less and less with each passing hour. All that remained was the bitter taste of heartache, lingering like a cancer waiting to eat at her insides. Crystal struggled to find the energy to get dressed, and once dressed, found she was not interested in doing anything except sit in a chair and stare out her window.

After school Gwen went into her room to try and cheer up her friend. She had never seen Crystal like this, dark and morose. Gwen was out of her depth, unable to comprehend let alone understand how much Crystal must hate herself right now. She tried to imagine kissing Stephen so passionately that she sucked his soul from his body, and failed. What kind of friend could not relate to the others problems? She felt useless.

"Maybe it would help if you talked about it, Crystal," Gwen suggested, taking a seat on the arm of the chair and putting a comforting arm around her friend's shoulder.

"I'm a real evil person, Gwen," Crystal replied quietly, a single tear rolling down her cheek. "I kill everyone I love."

"Maybe we should not have done the past life regression," Gwen said slowly, "maybe it would have been better if you did not know."

"No!" Crystal replied sharply, and then paused. "Maybe for me, Gwen. But now I know that I have to avoid falling in love... Only, I've fed on Jean-Claude and Drake. It means eventually I will destroy one of them...."

"If you don't want to," Gwen suggested, "you don't have to. I mean, forewarned is defended, or something like that."

"Something like that," Crystal smiled through her tears.

"We've had this conversation before, you know. Several times, and always it ended up with me still falling in love, still killing someone...."

"Maybe if we were celibate like Jean-Claude," Gwen ventured, "become, like some kind of nuns who live on top of a mountain away from boys."

"I suspect we tried that before," Crystal answered wryly. "Besides, you have to be Catholic to become a nun."

"Well," Gwen defended her idea without a lot of conviction, "I could become the first Wiccan nun. Or we could become like dike lesbians, and put on a real hate for men."

"You like boys too much," Crystal sighed, frustrated. "I do too."

"Hey!" Gwen brightened. "If you lived all those past lives, that means you've done it before!"

"You have too," Crystal pointed out. "To both of those, Miss `Doesn't-He-Have –Cute- Buns'. And I bet you don't remember any better than I do."

"It doesn't help much, does it?" Gwen admitted. "What's the point of having lived before if you don't get to remember any of the good stuff?"

April suggested Jean-Claude let Crystal take the week to work things out for herself. Sometimes teenagers were better at dealing with angst and depression than adults. First the girls, Gwen, Morgan and little Ember came over to sit with her. There was nothing like having someone around who worshipped the very ground you walked on for to feed your self esteem. Jean-Claude experienced that feeling often with the little ones from his kindergarten class, who gave their hearts completely. And for Ember, who believed Crystal had saved her life, she was the world's coolest person.

Seeing the various lives she had touched without harm helped Crystal, at least a little, except everyone of them was female, and she was a Succubus not an Incubus. Surely there was other good she had done in her past lives. And, as

Morgana pointed out, she was as much a victim of the curse as were the men whose souls she had consumed. It was natural to fall in love, and maybe not just for humans. And she did not harm these men intentionally, but in fact the opposite.

Still Crystal was not ready to leave her room and face the world. She struggled not only with an overwhelming sense of guilt, but heartache, bitterness, and an equal part self-pity. It did not seem fair – and don't tell her that wasn't the word for what she was feeling. Why did her life have to be this way?

Just when April and Jean-Claude felt that they needed call in professional help – there were members of the church who specialized in such matters – Crystal received a surprise visitor. Drake came on Friday night to see how she was making out. He brought her a bouquet of blue roses from him, and a letter from Brendan. He would have come himself, Drake explained, but the Brotherhood did not think it was safe at the moment.

Drake and Crystal sat in her room talking.

"I'm sorry I hurt you Drake," Crystal said, a catch in her voice. "It was the last thing I ever wanted to do."

"I know Boo," Drake smiled at her, and she thought he had a beautiful smile. "It really was my fault. I'm the one with all the training and you didn't even know you could do that."

"But –."

"Come on Crystal," Drake chided. "You did not even remember anything about our world. I've been able to see demons since I was a toddler. Some of those monsters under my bed were real. I should have known better than to touch you while you were feeding. Or without asking permission."

"If it wasn't for–." Crystal began shyly.

"You being a demon," Drake teased. "Don't sweat it, girl. You still got it going on."

"That's just the influence of the pheromones," Crystal replied wryly.

"You got me under your spell, is that what you mean?" Drake laughed. "Girl, I grew up with a Sylph in my class since grade school. No irresistible scent gonna turn my head."

"I bet you say that to all the girls," Crystal laughed.

"Well," Drake admitted with a mischievous grin. "Just two."

The two teens talked well into the night, and were later joined by Gwen and Morgana. Jean-Claude ordered pizza, and he delivered it to her room with a warning to Drake not to be kissing any of his girls. He retreated in the wake of a groan from the teenagers, and several thrown serviettes. But he heard laughter coming from Crystal's room for the first time in a week, and knew he had accomplished his mission.

Once she was alone with Gwen, Crystal nervously picked up Brendan's letter.

"Are you going to read it," Gwen urged, dying of curiosity.

"I don't know," Crystal hesitated. "I'm so nervous. What if it's like one of those `Dear John' letters, or something. I mean, after what I did...."

"Well," Gwen teased, "wasn't that what we've been talking about all week? No boys?"

Crystal gave here a playful shove, careful not to crinkle Brendan's letter. Finally, even she couldn't stand the wait any longer.

> *My Dearest Crystal,*
>
> *It crushed me to see you so hurt. Of all the beings I have met, your heart is the truest. How proud I am to have had the privilege to get to know you.*
>
> *If I knew saving my life would cause you such pain I would gladly have gone to my death. And yet, saving me, one of your natural enemies, only goes to prove that we can rise above our natures.*
>
> *Jean-Claude was right when he said we all deserve a chance at redemption.*
>
> *And no-one I've met, human or otherwise, deserves to find salvation more than you. And I am not just saying that because you have the most beautiful eyes in creation.*

I believe in you Crystal.

Our free choice was stripped from us by the curses that inflict us, but it wasn't taken from us completely. We are still free to choose who we become and how we conduct our lives. Follow your heart Crystal. It's one of the purest and beautiful hearts I've come across in my life.

It's the heart I choose,

Brendan

By the time she finished the letter there were tears streaming down Crystal's cheeks.

"What's wrong?" Gwen asked, concerned.

"It's so beautiful," Crystal replied, smiling through her tears. "Here read it."

Another page fell out as she handed it to Gwen.

"It's a poem," Gwen said, handing it back. "Read it, Crystal."

Chapter 20

The time was now. No more hesitation. Time to strike a blow against the Western Church. Word had come from Vlad's people that the four supernatural creatures that guarded the vaults beneath the Vatican had left Rome. Drawing these four to New York almost made up for the dishonour of his clan for failing such a simple assignment, Yoshio Kagawa thought, but not quite. His grandson was now physically older than he was, and that was too public a reminder of his disgrace to allow him to live.

"The boy still lives?"

"Yes, Sama Kagawa!"

"And why did you allow this thing to happen?" Yoshio continued his interrogation.

"I failed to anticipate the presence of the succubus when we made the attempt," his grandson bowed, touching his grey hair to the floor.

"This stain on the clan's honour must be removed," Yoshio pronounced.

"Hai!"

His grandson bowed his head one last time. The sword flashed, one swift powerful stroke. And the head rolled to Yoshio's feet.

"Send in the Hand," he ordered.

Five Vampyres dressed in black tenugui, worn over ring mail or lamellar, they looked much like the ninja from a Hollywood movie. When they infiltrated Rome, they would look much like any business traveller flying between Japan and Europe. Even their passports would be the best the Yakuza could provide – failure in this matter carried a price even these mortals feared to pay. Canadian passports were often preferred, although in this case they probably had them printed by the Japanese government, bribing or threatening some bureaucrat into providing them.

"It is time," Yoshio pronounced.

"We will not fail you," the middle of the five vampyres replied.

"There have been too many failures lately," Yoshio answered. "One more will be intolerable. The honour of your clan rides with you."

The five bowed and turned, leaving as they had come. The Hand was composed of the most skilled spies and assassins in the clan, five men and women who were masters of every weapon, and possessed the mystical powers of their ancestors. Matters forgotten and dismissed in this age of science, they could meld with the shadows, run up walls, and become a mist that could slip through the smallest crack. From these vampyres came the legends surrounding the mortal ninja, and exploiting their talents had earned the clans of the Iga and Koga regions a reputation that would outlive the clans themselves. Yet call these vampyres ninja and you will earn a fate worse than death.

The leader of the Hand was an ancient vampyre known only as Shadow. Some claimed he was older than Yoshio, that he was in fact a true demon who had taken a mortal form and was then turned into a vampyre. He killed with a ruthlessness never matched on earth or in hell. The lacquered mask he wore was never removed, and travelled in a fashion even the members of his own Hand knew nothing about. Always he was there to meet them, dressed in the traditional tenugui, unseen by those about them as was the air they breathed. Shadow cared for nothing and no-one, yet still kept the other four members of the Hand with him – an extra blade was occasionally useful. None had dared fail him in years, and those who had in the past died screaming.

The youngest member of the Hand was but a girl. Some said Aiko was Shadow's daughter because they both shared the same cold dispassion, and the same love of blood and pain. It fell to her to escort the mortal Yakuza to Rome. A short, slight man with two fingers missing from his left hand, he was covered with tattoos that advertised his profession. Almost she killed the worm at first sight. And if his death would not mean the failure of her mission and the dishonour of her clan, nothing would have saved his life. Nothing blemished her creamy white skin, and she looked young enough to pass for a school girl. She could become anything and anyone with few alterations of her appearance, and only one of her kind would recognize her for what she was.

Yi was a small time thief, and sometimes safe cracker. He had lost his two fingers when too much sake and a pretty girl had loosened his tongue enough to brag about his most daring exploits in a night club. Now he let his tattoos do his bragging. They covered his entire torso, images and Japanese symbols that chronicled his criminal exploits. Dressed as a tourist in a loose fitting shirt that covered much of his ink, his school girl daughter in tow, he was about to board an airplane for the first time. He had never been out of Japan, never even thought of travelling beyond the familiar confines of the underworld where he lived.

If the Japanese customs officials recognized him for what he was, they chose not to complicate their lives with the business of the Yakuza. It would not remain the same elsewhere. The farther they moved from Japan, the source of the Yakuza reputation, the less the fear of reprisals would motivate airport officials. Aiko was in high dungeon. While she could not kill this man, yet, the one who supplied this fool would die the moment she returned to Japan. And his dying would take days.

On the plane, waiting for take-off, Yi could not take his eyes off of the beautiful creature beside him. He knew she was a demon. And still, her features were so perfect his heart ached when he looked at her.

"What should I call you?" He ventured.

"My name is of no concern to you," she replied in a voice that did not disguise her disdain.

"If you are to play my daughter," he pressed, "surely someone will ask me your name."

"Daughter will suffice."

The thought of taking a mortal for a lover was so insulting as to almost make it laughable. She could break him with a whisper. Aiko had not even bothered to take a lover in three hundred years – matters became messy when it was time to kill and free herself of their presence when they bored her. She saw how this repulsive slug looked at her, and she toyed with the idea of ripping out his eyes. Surely he did not need his eyes to complete the mission. After all, they would do all the real work of stealing the item. But Shadow would not be pleased, and even as oblivious as most mortals were, someone would surely notice a man walking around with two bleeding eye sockets. Still, the thought kept her amused through the first leg of their long flight.

Their connection was in Amsterdam's Schiphol airport. During the twelve hour flight between Tokyo and Amsterdam Aiko had taken some time to meditate. The light trance would feign sleep, as was expected from a teenage mortal girl, and would allow her to channel some of her growing anger. She awoke to find Yi's head on her shoulder, his right hand cupping her breast. Instinctively, she snapped his wrist.

"If you cry out mortal," she hissed, "I will cut out your tongue!"

Yi nodded through his pain. Hopefully he would not need more than one hand to carry the object. This was only the beginning of their problems, however. In Amsterdam, one of the customs officials at the boarding gate for their connecting flight questioned Yi's passport. Even real, their passports could cause problems as the names on them were fictitious. Unfortunately, his had the same name as the man who had just passed through the gate ahead of him, and the stupid mortal panicked. Aiko had no choice but to kill the custom's agent. Even burdened with the weight of the mortal, she knew she would be too fast for any of the security agents to catch her. And with the night deepening outside the airport, there were plenty of shadows where she could disappear.

It would be far easier for her to just kill the mortal and disappear. That unfortunately was not an option she was at liberty to take. And on the unfamiliar territory of the airport, she was at a disadvantage. Even with all her speed, she did not know where the exits were, and they did. Radioing ahead, these were locked down and blocked before she could reach any of them. So she made her own exit, jumping out a second story window in a spray of shattered glass. The cloth of her skirt billowed out like a parachute, helping to break her fall as she landed on the balls of her feet, bending her knees to absorb the shock.

Running across the runways towards the distant city, she dodged beneath the body of a plane as it skidded to a landing. No-one was chasing them yet, but that would not last long. These mortals were everywhere in their cars and their carts, and the radio allowed them to move assets ahead of her to cut off her escape. Once over the fence, and into the outskirts of the city beyond, even the radio would not matter any more. And they dare not follow her here, onto the busy runways, where planes were constantly landing and taking off.

Brianna was a seventeen year old high school drop-out who recently took up hooking to support herself. With long, honey-blonde hair, blue eyes, and a well proportioned chest, attracting clients was not too difficult. She took up residence in a small flat above a café in the red light district. She had forgotten to turn out the lamp with the red bulb at the window, although at four am there was little chance of receiving a customer, and she decided to leave it. A knock sounded at her door, startling her from her doze. She was really too tired to service another client, and had just decided to say as much as she rolled out of bed to answer the insistent knock.

A Japanese tourist and his daughter stood facing her. Japanese tourists were good tippers, but Brianna was not into that kinky stuff, and said as much.

The girl moved towards Brianna, their eyes locked, and she found she could not break the stare. There was no resistance as Aiko took her hand and led her towards the bed. Yi closed the door and locked it. At first he was turned on. The smaller Japanese girl was on top of the European girl, who was wearing only bra and panties, both moving in suggestive rhythms. He mistook her withering for the throes of passion, and was soon disillusioned. Her back arched in unspeakable pain as the venom from her slayer burned through her veins, paralysing Brianna's throat muscles, and trapping the scream. Aiko turned towards Yi, the blood of her victim dripping from her fangs and chin, her eyes lit like two red suns. He backed away, until the wall stopped his retreat. Unable to tear his eyes off the grizzly tableau unfolding before him., he was witnessing a foreshadowing of his own death, and was unable to find the courage to run from it.

Killing the girl helped relieve some of Aiko's growing rage. Sending that foolish mortal out to dispose of her body was perhaps a mistake. She had no fear that he would run, there was no place for him to go, trapped in Amsterdam as he was without her contacts to its underworld. Yet the feeble-minded mortal would probably go no further than the dumpster in the back alley to dispose of the remains of her meal. No matter. They would only be here in the flat they had acquired until tomorrow night. It was time to call Shadow and inform him of the delay.

Her throw-away cell had one number programmed in it. It was picked up after three rings.

"The package is delayed. It will arrive tomorrow evening by train."

Aiko listened before speaking again. "The package is severely defective. We will need to speak to the supplier when we return home." After a short pause, she continued, "I was hoping to do that myself."

His blunder at the airport had cost her some of her favourite disguises. Fortunately, her equipment had been shipped in a different fashion, sent to a post office box as collectibles. Another from the Hand would be picking them up even as the thought crossed her mind. The bedding had blood stains on it. Aiko frowned, removing the sheet with the worse of these, and wrapping herself in a blanket as she waited for Yi to return. She always felt cold after she fed, a chill that settled in bone deep and would not leave her for days. She did not let it bother her. Such was the price she paid for the strength a feeding brought her.

Yi returned. He was too frightened to do anything else. He had dumped the body into one of the city's canals, weighed down with cobblestones he had pried up from a sidewalk. It would be weeks before it was found, if ever. The demon was asleep on the bed, her back to him, and he was unsure whether he should disturb her with such a trivial report. Instead he moved to the corner furthest from her, sinking down to the floor to wait out the long day that followed.

The train station the next day went more smoothly. Aiko looked older, disguised as Yi's wife, and she had used her skills with make-up to age him. Getting new passports was not difficult. Two Canadian passports for a couple from Vancouver had cost her ten thousand Euros. It was ten thousand more reasons to slay the man who brought this disaster into her life, a useless tool that the yakuza most likely thought of as expendable. Looking at him now as he sat staring out the window of the train, all but drooling, the ache to kill him returned.

Shadow would not be pleased. With neither of them. The click, click of the train wheels against the track became the heart beat of her anxiety as it carried her closer to a meeting with her master. Her worry etched itself onto her face. Her gaze kept returning to the source of her troubles, her thoughts turning darker and more violent with each passing mile.

Two of her fellow Hand were waiting for them at the Rome train station, and she knew Shadow's displeasure was worse than she had anticipated. They had a car waiting for them outside the station doors, and since they had no luggage, they went directly to the vehicle. After the delays of the past day things were now moving too fast for Aiko's liking. She was not afraid, not really, but the loss of honour before Shadow was an embarrassment she did not want to face. Especially, when his censor would come in such a public fashion.

At the villa outside Rome, where Shadow had set up headquarters, he sent for Aiko first. Not daring to keep him waiting, she moved into the library he was now using as his office, and came to a stop just within his reach. Shadow's eyes drifted over her as she stood at attention before him, studying her from foot to crown.

"You kept me waiting, daughter," he grated.

"Hai!"

His hand struck her, knocking Aiko off her feet and into the wall.

"Send in the mortal."

Two of her fellow Hand bowed, and backed out the door. They returned moments later, the human stumbling between them. Shadow frowned. He had seen healthier specimens in the palliative care ward in a hospital.

"Perhaps my censure was a little premature, daughter."

It was not an apology, and did not sooth her dislocated jaw. Too sore to speak, Aiko nodded.

"Go and rest mortal," Shadow ordered. "We will enter the Vatican tonight. Fail me and I will make you beg for death."

Turning to Aiko, he continued. "The one who sent him is yours. Make his death historic."

She nodded again, bowing by touching her forehead against the marble floor. The cool of the stone eased the ache in her cheek – a little. Aiko fought her tears as she made her way out of the room and up the stairs to the bedroom that had been set aside for her.

On the bed she hugged a pillow to her chest. Thinking she was alone, she let her tears escape, cascading down her cheeks like twin waterfalls.

"Are you okay, my lady," Yi asked tentatively.

Seeing the mortal, she wiped the tears from her face, ignoring the pain. Of course they put the mortal in her chambers.

"Humble apologies," he bowed, "if any of this is my fault."

"Of course it is your fault," she snapped.

"Again I apologize," Yi replied. "I am but a simple man and have never flown before. I am a very good thief. I will not fail you in this."

"The next time will be the last thing you do," she replied dismissively.

The wait through the daylight hours was long and tedious. The human slept, and he snored. Aiko once had a lover who snored like that. She slit his throat on the third night, and left his blood to pool on the floor. While most of her kind was fastidious about draining another vampyre, Aiko ate whatever she killed. Almost always. This one she just wanted to kill, although she supposed waking him would put an end to the racket he was making. Only then she would have to endure his hang-dog expression and constant tongue wagging.

When darkness fell Aiko said a small prayer of thanks to her ancestors. It was the first time she had prayed in her life, and she was not sure how one went about it. Threatening to hunt them down in the afterlife and destroy them was probably not quite right. At least the snoring had stopped, and the mortal was too frightened of the Hand to speak in their presence. A small mercy that soon wore thin. For this mission they had acquired a small Italian van, and it was overcrowded with the six of them inside. The smell of the mortal was intolerable. Like rotten fish and urine.

They parked at the end of Viale Vatican, beneath some trees across the road from the corner of the Vatican wall. Climbing a wall for a vampyre was child's play, and Aiko could have done it in her sleep. Even carrying the human on her back, the smell of his putrid breath hot in her ear, it took no real effort. Speed was important at this phase of their infiltration, and as quickly as these vampyres moved they easily avoided detection. Even on the security monitor they would appear as nothing more than a brief blur. In moments they were hugging the wall of St. Peter's Basilica, hidden in a blind spot between two of the security cameras.

Without the human their entrance into the Vatican would have been through one of the air vents, disembodied mist flowing down into the vaults below. With the human they would need to access a door, and move down into the archives from there. They needed to access the Tower of the Winds, where a wire elevator led down to the reading room of Leo XIII. The elevator was the key. Gaining entrance into the Tower of Winds was the problem. Hidden in the court yard of the papal residence was a set of brass doors carved with scenes celebrating Egyptian papyrus, medieval manuscripts and monks' scrolls. It was the only way visitors were allowed to enter, but there was a way in through the Hall of Lagorio.

At the door one of the Hand dematerialized. As a mist he slipped under the seal between the door and the sill. Yi had barely deactivated the alarm when the door opened.

"Do not move, idiot!" Yi hissed, forgetting himself.

For a moment it looked as the rematerialized vampyre would strike the mortal, and then Shadow spoke from the darkness. "Do as the mortal says."

From his bag of tricks Yi removed a garden variety bee smoker. He lit it, quickly filling the hallway with smoke, where the red beams of alarm sensors became visible.

"Step carefully over the beam," Yi instructed. "Careful. Do not break it or you will set off the alarm."

When the vampyre was outside the door, Yi turned back to the hallway, saying, "follow me and do exactly as I do."

As he began to crawl beneath the first beam, the five vampyres dematerialized, drifting as a mist through the field of beams. On the far side they rematerialized, turning to watch the human. Aiko had to admit it was amusing watching him crawl under, over and contort himself around the beams. For a mortal he was surprisingly agile, bending backwards almost double to stand on his hands, then slipping beneath a second with his legs remaining perfectly perpendicular to the floor. He was muttering about vampyres the whole way, unaware that their acute hearing was picking up every word. But the human was not totally to blame – almost no vampyres outside their clan could take the form of mist or smoke.

She bent to help him up. Aiko still had to kill him – he had seen her cry, and caused her dishonour amongst her Hand – perhaps now his death would be quick and clean. They let the human lead the way into the Tower of Wind, disabling the alarm on the door and unlocking it. Here, one of the Hand took the lead, disappearing into the darkness to disable the cameras. As instructed by their pet mortal, he carefully clipped pictures of the empty room taken at the angle of the camera, his motions so swift the human eye could not follow them. At his silent signal, a gesture only the vampyre with their night vision could see, the other five joined him.

Yi worked to disable the sensor on the door of the elevator. This one was more complicated than the ones on the other door. In his youth he had worked in the factory that made the chip that was its main component, and with two alligator clips attached to either end of a wire he bypassed this chip. Yi took a deep, calming breath and struggled to open the elevator doors. One of the Hand stepped up and pulled them open as easily as turning the page in a book. Above them, the elevator car was locked in position for the night. Taking one look to ensure it was there, the vampyre stepped out into the elevator shaft and disappeared into the darkness below.

Before Yi could recover from his shock, another Vampyre picked him up and dropped him into the shaft. The sound of his startled yelp drifted up to the four standing at the top of the shaft, and they chuckled to themselves. Below, the first vampyre caught Yi before he hit the concrete floor of the shaft. One by one the other four jumped down to join them, led by Aiko, Shadow bringing up the rear.

In the darkness directly above their heads was a door. One floor above it was the bottom floor of the archives. Here was the entrance into a truly secret chamber within the Vatican, the vault of the Brotherhood. Here they stored manuscripts, scrolls and artefacts considered dangerous to humanity. This was their target, and reaching it was a simple climb up near the nearly smooth sides of the elevator shaft – easy for a vampyre assassin, who had honed their natural climbing abilities from the time they could walk into a skill that made vertical walls no more difficult than a small hillock.

Once again Aiko was forced to carry the obnoxious mortal on her back. The climb was a simple one, and was over in less than a minute. Setting him down, Aiko looked around at the chambers beyond with a sense of awe. The damage they could do to the Brotherhood here, if they had the time. And if so many of the artefacts hidden in niches around the room were not so dangerous to her kind. Even the item they were sent to retrieve could only be handled by a mortal, which explained Yi's presence amongst them. Aiko took one last regretful look around, and joined her brothers in a search for a statue of Saint Dismas, the guardian saint of thieves and murders.

Aiko found it in the furthest room of the vault, calling to her brothers and the mortal to join her. The item lay under the base of the statue. Finding the trick to moving it was the job of the mortal, and the five vampyres stood back in the shadows, away from the light he was using to inspect the statue. They did not want to ruin their night vision, and there was always the possibility the hiding place of this particular artefact was booby trapped. A bit of a lead might just save their lives.

Yi ignored his supernatural companions and concentrated

on the statue. This is why the Yakuza had chosen to send him, one of the lowest members of their society. He had a knack for finding hidden compartments that bordered on the magical, and the trigger on this one was hidden with more craftiness than any other he had encountered. The statue was of marble inlaid with precious woods and gems. The designs created depicted scenes from the saint's life, most notably his death on the hill of Calvary beside the Christians prophet Jesus. Yi knew little of Christian mythology, but the amount of space allotted to this one scene led him to suspect the trigger was hidden somewhere within this collage. Focusing, he studied the pattern of wood and gems inlaid into the marble to create this scene, ruling out the gemstones as too obvious. There, the one piece of black wood that formed the cross he had died on.

With a click the base of the statue moved. It was too heavy for his slight form, so Shadow signalled Aiko to go and help. Reluctantly, she joined the human. Together they pushed the statue away from its pedestal, revealing a small chamber. No fireball rose to incinerate them, no stakes or other instrument of death sprang from the floor or walls. Yi reached in and retrieved a box of gopher wood about two feet long and ten inches wide. He held it up to show his companions.

"Very good," Shadow pronounced. "Push the statue back in place and let's make are way out of here."

The climb back up the elevator shaft with the mortal riding on her back seemed endless to Aiko. She did not like to have the box and its contents so close to her. Even through the wood she could feel its malignant influence. Death lay only inches away. Her death. Something she had managed to avoid for almost four hundred years, and she was looking forward to her five hundredth birthday. Although death was a common thing in her profession, she had never imagined it would happen to her until this moment. It sent a chill down her spine. A chill she could not shake.

Their exit from the Vatican was a reverse of their entrance.

At the elevator Yi removed the wire from the sensor, one of the Hand moved around the chamber removing the pictures, and rejoined them in the Hall of Lagorio. All trace of their presence was removed, and still someone from the Brotherhood would notice their theft in the morning. How? It did not matter, by that time it was already too late.

At the villa, Shadow called Aiko into his study.

"There will be no repeats of yesterday's disaster." It was not a question, but a command.

"No Sama," Aiko replied. "I have hired a private jet that will fly us directly to New York."

"Very well, daughter," Shadow nodded. "Two of your brothers will drive you to the airport. Return to me in Japan when your mission is complete."

"Hai."

Aiko collected the mortal and led him out to the car. Again they were disguised as a Japanese couple, matching the passport and visa they had used to gain entrance into the country. With their Canadian passports and passage on a private airplane, they had little difficulty with the Italian customs. Employees from the private airline took their luggage, purchased and assembled in Rome by two members of the Hand just for this purpose. Yi carried the box and its priceless artefact on board as part of his carry-on luggage.

Paperwork claiming it was part of the Japanese Royal collection on loan to a New York museum had been provided by the best forgers in Europe. The work was flawless. On the plane they disposed of their current passports, tucking them under the cushions of their seats, and collecting a new set that were hidden in the same place. Aiko removed some of the grey from Yi's hair, carefully adding a small beard on the cleft of his chin. She could do nothing about his multiple tattoos except hide it under a long-sleeved button down shirt and suit coat. In the washroom she changed her appearance, transforming herself into a young Japanese business assistant – a girl starting her first job and on her first trip away from home.

Satisfied that she had achieved the right balance between efficiency and vulnerability, she returned to the cabin. She chose a seat near the back of the plane, signalling to her companion that she did not want his company. Soon after take-off the fool was asleep again and snoring. Aiko doubted she could stand nine hours of that disgusting noise, not while trapped in the small cabin, and not without doing violence to its author. She looked on it as penance for her loss of honour during the trip in from Japan, a test of her discipline and endurance that would redeem her, if not in anyone else's eyes, at least in her own.

American customs was more difficult than she had anticipated. At the initial queue the discovery of the artefact, a dagger, caused a small disturbance. They were flagged by the customs officer for further search, and led off to a small room. In keeping with her disguise, Aiko pretended not to speak English – and in truth her grasp of the language was not as strong as the Yakuza's. He took the lead, his mannerism so fidgety and nervous she wanted to slap him. It was no wonder he had roused the American's suspicions.

"Mr. Yakamoto," a tall, broad-shouldered man entered the room and greeted them. Unlike the others they had seen so far, he wore a three-piece suit without any sign of a name tag. "I apologize for the inconvenience."

"No apology is necessary," Yi replied, playing up his role too much for Aiko's liking. "It is merely your job."

"And this is?" The customs official indicated Aiko.

"My daughter, Mai-ling." Yi replied.

"The box you were carrying?" the customer official questioned. He still had not introduced himself, and merely nodded to the uniformed officer who brought in the artefact.

"It is from the Emperor's personal collection." Yi explained. "A rare blade said to have been used by one of Japan's most notorious ninjas. It has never before been displayed outside our country."

Aiko gave him a hard look. Every time he opened his mouth he gave her one more reason to kill him. She hated the word ninja, as did all the members of her clan, and the slur was so intense she found herself struggling to contain her anger.

"You seem nervous, Mister Yakamoto?" The customs agent suggested.

"Hai," Yi replied. "It is a very big responsibility. Transporting an item worth many millions of yen. I am much afraid it will be stolen."

"And why no security?" He pressed the Japanese gentleman.

"We are travelling, how do you say, incognito," Yi replied. "We are attempting to avoid drawing attention to ourselves and the `Death Blade'. A diversionary transport was attempted with a copy of the blade, and it was stolen at the Tokyo airport despite all the security. Much honour was lost that day."

"I see," the customer agent frowned. It sounded plausible. Such methods were often used when transporting such high risk items. "And what museum are you bringing it to?"

"I believe you call it the Goodenburg?" Yi tried.

"Gutenberg," the other corrected

"Ah, much apologies," Yi bowed. "I meant no disrespect."

"Well," the agent continued after a long pause while he studied their papers. "Your documents seem to be in order. I wish you good luck. My cousin has a security firm here in the city, should you decide to hire any."

"Hai," Yi replied, bowing as he accepted the card.

Outside the airport doors, Aiko hailed a cab. They did not have far to go, only as far as the nearest subway entrance. Apparently, she thought, Yi could be a good liar when he was properly motivated. It made his slip up at the Amsterdam airport seem all the more deliberate. Their time together was drawing to a close, and she vowed to keep his betrayal in mind when it came time to bid him farewell.

They had already dumped the luggage at the airport. Aiko doubted anything in it would either fit, or be miss. A man's idea of a woman's shape and size was always too big in the breast and too tight in the waist, and revealed more than it covered. Unencumbered by anything except the box and its precious cargo, Aiko paid off the cabbie and led the way down into the subway. She ignored the man's offer to take them all the way to their destination. He did not want to take that fare, Aiko thought darkly, but if he did not stop his yipping she vowed to drag him along anyway. A gift to her hosts. Two such pigs were more than she could bear. He had spent the entire trip from the airport using his mirror to look down her blouse, the smell of his unwashed body polluting the air in the cab.

The men of her era were different, taking what they wanted. So were the women, for that matter. She had never been that meek, killing her first lover at sixteen. Of course, blood was nothing new to her. A vampyre born, she took it in with her mother's milk, and made her own first kill at the precocious age of six.

From the subway, making their way into the under tunnels that led to Upyr was easy. The way was marked for those who knew what to look for – a door scribed with graffiti written in Latin, or the skull of a rat wedged into a certain collection of pipes. Without light the mortal stumbled and bumbled about like a drunk on a three day run, but he had displeased Aiko, and it soothed her ruffled feelings to let him suffer. Only the box and its contents had to arrive at Upyr safely, and so far the fool had been fortunate enough not to drop it.

Three levels down they ran into the first of Vlad's patrols. Their leader assigned three of his men to escort their visitors down to the city – now that they were so close, he did not want a chance encounter with a band of Goths or the Eaters of the Dead to ruin everything. Aiko was glad to have some company, though she spoke little, her jaw still aching from

Shadow's blow. The Praetorian Guard included some of the best specimens from Vlad's people, male and female vampyres in their prime, strong and lithe in their leather and chain mail armour. At another time and place Aiko might have considered a momentary dalliance with one or all of her three escorts. The sooner they were finished here, the sooner she could rid herself of this odious mortal – and killing one of Vlad's people would surely cause an incident Sama Kagawa would frown upon. Some peccadilloes were just too personal to share.

Vlad was waiting for them in his personal office, a smaller room that led off the council chambers. In one corner an empty pedestal waited for the item they were delivering.

When his guests arrived, he dismissed the guard. They knew enough to return to their patrol without having to be ordered – the members of his personal guard were chosen for their intelligence as much as their fighting skill. Turning his attention to the two remaining, he studied the girl for a long moment – the Lotus Blossom, the only female member of the Hand, Kagawa's elite group of assassins. Her reputation for killing her lovers buried any romantic thought that might have crossed Vlad's mind, and brought him back to the task at hand.

The human was a reprobate, a cast-off from his own society. Vlad doubted he would survive the night, and briefly considered whether the assassin would bleed him when she killed him. He couldn't afford that kind of body to turn up on the surface, not after the agreement he had made with Jean-Claude. One last glance at the girl and he could see she had recently fed. This one would merely be slain.

"Please open the box," Vlad instructed the human.

Yi bowed, and with his head still lowered, lifted the lid of the box. Inside, lying on a pillow of black silk, the Akedah knife, a dull blade about eight inches long of forged steel. Abraham's knife. Vlad nodded and the human closed the box.

"Place it there on that pedestal." Vlad instructed. As the Yi turned back, Vlad handed him a bag of gold coins. "Go with her. She will take you back to the surface. Please send Kagawa my regards."

"Hai." Aiko bowed and turned, drawing the mortal in her wake.

He still wore the robe from his time with the Brotherhood, this strange deluded man who lived picking things out of dumpsters and garbage cans. He spoke to no-one. Accepted no charity. When he remembered, his name was Clive, and if his disposition was not enough to drive people away, the smell of garbage and back alleys that followed him like a miasma did the job. Clive was in his time the most experienced agent in the Papal intelligence department, assigned to collecting data on the movement of demons around the world as others kept track of human governments and other organizations. Until he lost his wits while interrogating one of the demons he had captured.

That was his talent. No-one knew how he managed it. Clive just had a knack for ensnaring some of the more elusive and dangerous minions of hell. He no longer had the money and resources of the Vatican to rely on – now he had to find what he needed in the dumpsters and garbage littered alleys of New York to build his devices.

As he watched the diminutive Japanese girl snap the man's neck, Clive knew her for what she was. Moving from his mountain of garbage that was his current home, he attracted her attention. She whirled and walked right into his net.

What? Aiko thought. This foolish mortal thought he could hold her with a collection of twine and crystals! Angry, Aiko struggled against the netting and found she could not free herself. Why could she not rend this collection of garbage to shreds? Fear teased the edges of her thoughts.

Since coming to New York, Gabriel had brought his patrol of Goths by to check on Clive at least twice a night. They arrived to find Clive sitting on top of his garbage heap, mumbling and cackling at a girl he had trapped with one of his toys. One look and he knew she was much more than a girl...

"Clive," he called gently. "Clive you can not keep her here."

"Mine!" Clive snapped.

"Come Clive," Gabriel urged gently. "Let's bring her to show to Jean-Claude. You know how much Jean-Claude would like to meet your guest."

"Jean-Claude?" Clive asked, a moment of sanity shining in his eyes. "Yes. Show my pretty to Jean-Claude."

Aiko found herself surrounded by enemies. Not normal mortals, skilled hunters from the Brotherhood. And one from their Special squad, a vampyre like her. Still no real challenge was she free, and yet the old man took up the netting and led her out of the alley like a pet dog.

Chapter 21

Banned. The girls were not allowed down in the basement of the brownstone. It was no-man's-land, and those who had come to live there were forbidden fruit, and all the more sweet a temptation. Lately, they had developed an attachment to Alvaro de San Carlos. He was suave, and he spoke with an accent, and told wonderful tales of his travels. He even treated them as young ladies, and not little girls, occasionally flirting with them in an innocent way, reciting Italian poetry until they blushed.

That was how they discovered the room with the girl in it. And that was why Morgana was now down in the basement with them, teaching Gwen and Crystal how to pick a lock. It was not as sophisticated as Morgana had first suspected. The lock was there to keep people out, and not keep the girl in. Other, more supernatural means were keeping the vampyre from escaping. Embedded into each wall was a piece of the true cross, and the chains that held her were forged from two links of Saint Peter's chains. Even as she noticed the two humans and the Succubus she knew there was no escape.

The two humans, a Goth and a Wiccan were nothing to Aiko, even in her weekend state. Her jaw was now swollen and a fever ravished her body. Even healthy she would have found the Succubus a difficult obstacle, although it was weak itself, hardly having fed. Aiko raged against the injustice. The humiliation of being fed to her people's enemy to strengthen it.

"Crystal," Morgana warned, "she's a vampyre."

"I know." Aiko watched the creature come up to her, and still she was too weak even to find her feet. It reached down and brushed a lock of her hair from her face. Didn't it know it was impolite to play with your food? "She's hurt. She has a fever and her face is all swollen. Heal her, Gwen."

"Wiccan medicine is not like magic, Crystal," Gwen complained, laughing. "I can't just heal her like some elf from a movie or a video game. All I can do is ease the pain so she can sleep and her body can heal itself."

"What are you young ladies doing here?" A voice asked behind them.

Startled, the three girls whirled and were relieved to see Alvaro standing in the door way.

"Don't you know it's dangerous to be here?" He asked again.

"Yes," Crystal sighed. "But she's hurt, real bad, Alvaro. I don't think she could hurt any of us, even if she tried."

"Perhaps I can be of some help," Alvaro relented.

He moved towards Aiko and she shrank back. There was something about the man that frightened her, a little. He brought his hands up to Aiko's face and gently probed her swollen cheek.

"Her jaw is dislocated," Alvaro pronounced, and seeing Crystal's cold gaze continued. "It's an old wound, something that happened several days before she came to be our guest. The fever is from a slight infection. Antibiotics ought to clear it up, but I am going to have to reset the jaw, and that's going to hurt."

"Oh, I can help with that," Gwen replied eagerly, and touched Aiko's forehead with her crystal. "Oh, she has been a busy girl, hasn't she?"

That was Gwen, always putting the best spin on anything she saw. Shaking his head, bemused, Alvaro reset the girl's jaw. It clicked back into place with a loud snap that made the others in the room wince, and thanks to Gwen, Aiko felt almost nothing.

"Come, Aiko," Alvaro chided, "that is hardly a charitable thought, given what these three have done for you."

Aiko's eyes widened. How did he know her name? And how did he know she was thinking of bleeding all three of these Gaijin? He was a mind reader.

"Oh come now, Aiko," Alvaro scolded. "That is hardly how one thanks one's benefactors, now is it?"

"Stay out of my thoughts," Aiko grated.

Alvaro taunted the woman with a smile, and turned, saying, "I will come by with some antibiotics soon. Come now, this really isn't a place for young ladies."

Crystal shrugged and led the girls out of the cell. They had plans to go dress shopping anyway, the Harvest dance now only a few days away, and not one of them with a decent dress. Jean-Claude had given Crystal and Gwen a credit card, and they planned to share his largess with their friend. Nothing compared with a trip to the mall when you had money. Imitating Wilma and Betty from the Flintstones, the girls ran up the stairs yelling `Charge-it!' just loud enough to carry to April and Jean-Claude where they sat in the living room over a coffee.

"Keep it to a dull roar," April called back. "Don't spend more than the national budget of a small country. A very small country."

"We won't!" Gwen called back. "Just dresses, shoes and a few accessories."

Anastasia and Cantara had volunteered to shadow the girls during their shopping trip, and immediately discovered their charges planned to ditch their plans to go to the mall. Instead they hopped on the subway and headed for a store in Long Island known as Magic Moments. As soon as they sat down, Crystal got up and walked over to the two women. Even if she had not seen them around the brown stone, she would have recognized them for what they were – perhaps not as a sylph and a djinn, just demon spawn like herself.

"We want to go to a store in Long Island," Crystal explained. "Can you take us? April won't let us go out of the Bronx unless an adult takes us."

"You don't really want to go to Long Island," Anastasia tried.

"Yes we do. The stores there have the best dresses for proms, and Magic Moments is amazing!" Crystal replied, and the two women shared a bemused smile. "We saw it online."

"Okay, just this once," Anastasia relented.

As Crystal returned to her seat to share the news with her friends, Cantara turned to her companion. "You should have just killed her."

"I think that runs counter to our goal of protecting her," Anastasia teased. "You should spend some time with our little guest, you two seem to share the same philosophy – kill everything and sort it out later."

"It keeps everything simple," Cantara shrugged. "Have you ever taken teenage girls dress shopping? You'll be begging for death before this day ends."

"Come on," Anastasia teased, "it will be fun."

"That doesn't work on me either."

The trip to Long Island was an adventure in itself. Long Island, of course, translated to Jefferson Port Station, and involved a brief ride on the LIRR. Arriving at the famous dress shop was like reaching their personal chapel perilous, and finding the perfect prom dress was the goal of their quests. Two thousand square feet of dreams. Keeping track of three excited girls in a crowd of others, and all this for merely a sweetheart dance, took protection to all new frontiers. Lost in a world of fashion that made them feel like princesses, the girls tried very hard not to go overboard. Morgana found a platinum beaded dress, strapless with front slits and a skirt with a train; Gwen chose a blue dress with a sequined bodice with a ruched knot style waist band, a low open back with a train.

And Crystal outshone them all. With her black hair the crimson satin of the dress stood out like she was standing beneath a spot light. The full length, shimmering dress with a beaded straps on a high neckline, a cut-out bust, a low back accented with beadings, and a slit so high that it would be a toss up who objected to it more – Jean-Claude or April. She looked like sex incarnate, and Anastasia wanted to say something, then seeing her happy smile found she did not have the heart to puncture her dream. Let April or Jean-Claude try it, if they had the spine. There had been few enough happy moments in her life lately, and less in her future.

Arriving home later than expected, the three girls found Jean-Claude and April waiting for them with some Chinese take-out. Putting the meal on the table, the two adults moved into the living room and waited as the girls changed into their dresses to show their treasures. Walking the living room like runway models, the three girls looked so grown up at that moment that it brought a tear to Jean-Claude's eye. April's eye had another look altogether. Her girls looked like they were ready to go night clubbing, and not to a high school dance. She did not know how in good conscience she could let them out of their rooms in those dresses, let alone out of the house.

"Mes jeune filles," Jean-Claude breathed, "you look so very beautiful. You did very well indeed."

"Jean-Claude," April sighed. "Those dresses are way to much for a high school dance. Sequence, open backs, slit skirts."

"Non," Jean-Claude shook his head. "Our babies are growing up, no? It is time for them to break a few hearts. And what can happen with so many eyes on them, eh?"

"Okay," April relented. "This once, but next time I go dress shopping with you."

"Thank you mom!" Gwen beamed happily. "I feel like a rainbow in this dress."

"Oh God, you're lame," Morgana teased. "I feel like the Goth Queen, and I will deign to allow you two to be my hand maidens."

The three girls retreated toward Crystal's room, giggling and laughing. Crystal had forgotten how difficult it was to walk in high heels, falling into first one and then the other of her two girls.

Jean-Claude looked at April and said, "and they are still girls at heart, no? We will let them play dress up and practice."

"No Jean-Claude," April teased.

Later, with the adults downstairs having a coffee, and her two friends watching a movie as they did their homework, Crystal grabbed a bag from her room and snuck down to the basement. The lock on the door to the cell was not as easy to pick as Morgana had made it seem. Somehow she managed to open it, and was at a lost to say how she had done it. Slipping inside, she stood just inside the door waiting for her eyes to adjust to the darkness.

"You again," Aiko grated.

"I thought you might like some fresh clothes," Crystal explained. "Your blouse is ripped. I brought you a blanket too, in case you get cold."

"I am a vampyre," Aiko replied. "I don't feel the cold."

Then why are you shaking, Crystal wanted to retort, but she had not come here to argue. She handed the other girl the bag. Aiko looked at her suspiciously, and reached out to pull out a beautiful kimono. Sky blue silk hand painted with a gold dragon, cherry trees and a bridge, it must have cost a fortune. Aiko let the succubus help her change, a little difficult with the chains around her wrists and ankles. Her enemy was so close she could smell her breath, could reach out and rip out her throat, and was still too weak to take advantage of the opportunity.

Crystal saw the calculating look in her eyes, and smiled. "You would never hurt me. I am still faster and stronger than you, little cousin."

Crystal put her ruined clothes into the bag and wrapped the blanket around Aiko's shoulders. Aiko was too ashamed to look up, not for thinking about killing her enemy, but because she was too weak to do it.

Turning, Crystal almost ran straight into Alvaro. "You do

have a tough time staying away from here, eh?"

"Her clothes were torn and she was cold," Crystal explained.

"And she smells delicious," he teased, "and you were thinking of a midnight snack, eh?"

"Get real, Alvaro," Crystal complained, "I don't go around eating every vampyre I meet any more than you eat every pretty virgin who crosses your path."

"Just those who have a problem obeying rules," he continued to tease.

"I am safe with her, honest," Crystal replied. "I can't explain it, Alvaro. I just have a feeling that our fates are linked somehow. I won't harm her, and she cannot harm me."

"As much as it is a good thing to trust one's instincts, Crystal," he replied, leading her to the foot of the stairs, "it is always wise to remember who she is. She is not just a vampyre - she is an assassin who lives to kill."

"Then you take care of her for me, Alvaro," Crystal replied.

"I will."

Friday night of the dance Drake and Stephen came to meet the girls at the brownstone and escort them to the school. Because her own date could not come to pick her up, Drake had volunteered Stephen and his services. Besides, he teased Crystal and Morgana, walking into the dance with a girl on either arm would only enhance his reputation. The girls were not over dressed after all. Everyone at the school had gone all out for this dance, even if it was not their prom. This was a school whose student body knew they were on the eve of a war, despite the adults' effort to keep it from them, and they knew that some of their older classmates could be called up to the Choirs to replace those lost in battle. Tonight was a celebration of their last days of innocence.

Brendan was waiting for her at the door to the gym. He had rented a black suit from somewhere, and although Crystal was not sure how, since it was the twin to the one worn by Drake, she could make a pretty good guess. She gave Drake's arm a squeeze to say thank you and walked over to talk to Brendan. He was still unsure about physical contact between them, but thanks to Alvaro and Aiko Crystal now knew she could touch a vampyre without feeding. She did have self-control, and continued to believe that right up until she came close enough to smell his sweet breath. Maybe Brendan was right after all.

Many of the dances did not involve touching, as this first song from some hard driven Goth band.

"Would you care to dance?" Brendan asked.

"Uhm," Crystal hesitated, and then laughed as Gwen pushed her towards the dance floor. "I don't think I know how, but I'll fake it."

The night was perfect. Crystal did not think it could get any better. She had danced with Brendan and with Drake and Stephen, and even a couple of times with just the two girls. When the band played slow songs, a staple for a sweetheart dance, Crystal and Brendan would meet at the punch bowl to talk. The evening went on in this fashion until the band announced it was taking a break between sets.

"I'll be right back," Brendan said.

As he walked away, Crystal suddenly noticed she was all alone. All her other friends had disappeared, leaving her standing there by herself. It did not matter. She couldn't be happier.

A light flicked on at the stage. A single spot light that lit Brendan as he sat on a wooden stage, a guitar on his lap and a microphone in a stand by his face. Crystal was mystified. She did no know he played guitar, and he had told her nothing about playing during the dance.

"I'd like to play you a little something I wrote," he began quietly. "This one's for you, Crystal."

He plucked the strings of a G chord, fingering a soft rhythm that dropped down to a D minor. When Brendan sang his voice was clear and mellow, a soft and sweet sound that filled the gym.

Close your eyes and dream with me of a world of simpler times,
We laugh, we cried, we skinned our knees, had adventures in the park
Close your eyes and dream tonight of a world that passed us by
We had carnivals and butterflies to chase away the dark
Stay with me, don't drift away, don't lose yourself again
We'll find gentle hearts and gilded dreams, and laughter in the rain.

For the chorus, all her friends moved on stage – Gwen and Stephen, Drake and Morgana, even Amy and Bobby-Lynn and their dates. A tear trickled down Crystal's cheek. She had never been more touched in all her life.
Heart to heart, we'll sing to you
Now brush away those tears.
Heart to heart, we'll pray for you
And chase away your fears.

And then just Brendan singing alone, his voice rising:
Heart to heart I'll be yours girl
And rock your little world
Heart to heart I'll be yours girl
And rock your little world.

He was just beginning the second verse when Delph and six members of his flight crashed the dance. A shocked gasp migrated through the crowd. This was sacred ground. If they would come here, then no place was safe – and worse, the treaty was broken.

Delph and his companions pushed their way through the crowds, working their way towards the middle of the gym. No-one had weapons here. No-one could stop him, he could do what he pleased. Kristen and her dates – well muscled, athletic boys who looked to be the entire football team, if the Academy had a football team – moved to block their path. The vampyres stepped up their pace, as only their kind could, brushing past the sylph and her retinue as if they were paper dolls.

Crystal was angry. Brendan's song had been so beautiful. It seemed that every time something sweet and gentle happened in her life, something dark and brutal destroyed it. She was pissed beyond reason. She moved to intercept Delph and his thugs, a thunderhead of violence riding before her. She knocked them back a step.

"You do not belong here," Crystal's voice was ice and steel.

"Who's going to stop us?" Delph taunted, a trace of false bravado in his voice. Down in Upyr it was said she had destroyed three of Kagawa's assassins.

"We are!" Drake grated.

The sylph and her crew, Drake and his band, Gwen and a dozen Wiccan girls, and Brendan moved up behind Crystal to form a solid wall. Delph wasn't worried about any of the others, they were merely pawns on a chess board. He had never expected to see the succubus at the dance, not with his people actively planning to destroy her. He figured the church would have her hidden away somewhere. Her presence skewed the whole dynamic of this show down.

"We have come to have some fun, and we are not leaving until we have had a dance," Delph drawled.

"You can dance with me," Crystal replied, suggestively, both of them knowing he would not survive that dance.

Bruno was a throw-back amongst his people. Broad-shouldered, heavily muscled like a linebacker, and still as quick and light on his feet as a dancer. Because of his size he feared nothing, and because his father was Second Chair on the council, and Vlad's most important ally he did not worry about the consequences of his `little accidents'. He was the one who had snapped the neck of the Praetorian Guard who watched the tunnel they had used to reach the surface – after all, what could his family do against Bruno's own larger and more influential clan. Unfortunately, for all his strength and swiftness, none of it carried over to his mental capacities.

Crystal intercepted him as he made his move towards Gwen and the girls standing behind her. Where moments ago sweet music filled the rafters of the gym, his cry reverberated through the school. Like the distress call of a stricken crow, the sound was so hopeless and wrenching it was hard for anyone there to hear. Gwen reached Crystal as Delph and another of his flight pulled their stricken friend to safety. He was badly aged and nearly crippled, half his former size, with snow white hair and rheumy eyes that stared at the world in terror. Horrified, Delph and his flight fled the confrontation.

Crystal was cold and shaking. In shock, she kept repeating, "I'm okay. I'm okay."

The dance was over, ruined for the evening. The girls swarmed around Crystal, Gwen taking Drake's jacket to wrap around her friend's shoulders. Brendan had gone off to call Jean-Claude to take the girls home, while Drake, Razor and the other Goth leaders led their bands off to their lockers to change and arm. Whatever plans they had for the evening were changed. The Academy was now on full mobilization, and already a hastily armed band of Goths guarded the doors to the gym. Only a miracle would keep this incident from turning into a full scale war, and at that moment the young demon hunters were too angry to care.

"It's okay Crystal," Gwen soothed.

"Really, Gwen," Crystal replied. "I'm fine. I'm just really, really angry."

"Pissed," Kristen returned, shocking her friends. "It's okay to say what we are all feeling. Just this once."

And the girls laughed, releasing some of their stress and fear.

Soon the school was swarming with members of the Choir, Goth patrols, and most of the Specialists. When Gwen and Crystal arrived home, the leaders of the Brotherhood were meeting in the living room with Jean-Claude and April. With the Specialists either out on patrol, or upstairs in the meeting, the basement was deserted. Crystal seized the opportunity to sneak down and visit Aiko, drawn to her for some inexplicable reason that had nothing to do with her instinctual need to feed. Despite her promise to Alvaro, despite her revulsion for the girl and what she was, Crystal found a sense of peace and belonging when she was with the vampyre.

"You have fed on one of my kind," Aiko greeted her, still slightly afraid of this girl, and yet feeling lonely. "And recently."

"A little," Crystal admitted, muttering.

"How do you feed 'a little'?" Aiko's tone of voice was snotty, but she was truly curious.

"He's still alive, is all," Crystal replied, shrugging.

"The other one you aged is dead," Aiko lashed out, trying to hurt the girl to overcome her fear.

Crystal sank down to the floor, hugging her legs and resting her chin on her knees. "Did I kill him?"

"No," Aiko admitted.

Looking at Aiko was like looking in a mirror at her exact opposite. The anger was there in both women, only the source was different. And the way they dealt with it.

Crystal handed her a bottle of blood she had borrowed from Alvaro's private stash. Aiko felt like a lamb being fattened for the slaughter, and still she took the blood. She would need her strength if she had any hope to escape this place.

"It's AB," Crystal explained, "if that makes any difference to the taste."

"Blood is blood," Aiko replied, shrugging her indifference.

"Alvaro says you killed every lover you had," Crystal began. "Brendan, the boy who took me to the dance, he's a vampyre like you. I am afraid I will kill him."

"If you love him," Aiko answered, "why would you let anyone else have him?"

"You're messed, Aiko."

"And you are not?"

Crystal paused at the door, turning back to look at the girl within. "You're probably right."

Chapter 22

The score was twenty to eighteen in the tie breaker. The winner of this game won a place in the Salem Invitational Volleyball tournament in Massachusetts. Crystal had the serve. The pressure was intense, sweat dripping off her forehead into her eyes, which she wiped away with an equally sweaty arm. She could feel the hopes of the other girls resting on her shoulders, could see the tension of the opposing team as she studied the far side of the court.

Thump! It was a booming serve, barely clearing the net in a line drive to the far court. It landed in the inside right corner, a girl in the green and red uniform of Saint Xavier's diving, the ball just out of reach. Twenty-one.

They had won! They were going to Salem! For a whole second the gym fell quiet, the girls pausing in exhaustion. And then Morgana's scream rent the silence. Fists clenched, her face uplifted, she fell to her knees. Released from their paralysis the other girls began adding excited screams of their own, rushing onto the court to hug Crystal and Morgana. They were going to Salem! They were going to Salem! The first team from the Academy to play in an invitational tournament in over twenty years. It was unbelievable. The two Nordic twins dumped the Gatorade over Miss Sweider's head, drenching her moments before all the girls buried her in an excited hug.

In the stands Jean-Claude was frowning. Although he was excited for the girls than he could express, the logistics of a tournament in another city were a nightmare. He could not deny them this triumph after they had worked so hard, and he had promised. Gabriel and the others were not going to like it. Not everyone agreed with his strategy to let her live as normal a human life as she could, given that she was not human. And still he saw her as the little girl she was when she first came into his life, one with so much potential if she were only given the chance. Even now Crystal snuck down into the cellar to show their guest small kindnesses, this to a girl who lived for her death, and who would slaughter everyone she held dear.

And with that thought Jean-Claude knew his answer would be yes. He would have to contact the Salem sect, a faction of the Brotherhood that believed that all demons and supernatural beings needed to be destroyed. With them involved there would be killing, and the war he fought so hard to prevent for so long would be one step closer. Jean-Claude felt like the British Prime Minister Neville just after he learned that Hitler had betrayed him. Was there never any other way? If there was it rested with this girl, on her living out a life without killing, and somewhere in the process finding her redemption. And so he could see no other choice but to activate the Salem sect, to allow them to guard Crystal and the girls while they participated in the tournament.

Crystal ran up and jumped into his arms, wrapping her legs and arms around him. "Did you see it, Jean-Claude? Did you see it?"

"It was a perfect serve, ma petite. Had it been a buzzer beating three-pointer," he teased, "now that would have been a thing of beauty."

She jumped down, pushing him away. She called back as she ran off to change. "Oh, Jean-Claude! You and your basketball. Nobody likes it, it's too boring!"

"Are you alright?" April asked, smiling.

"She is learning to control herself, no?" And she had not tried to feed. He felt her prod at the bond between them like a scab on a wound, and no more.

"If you say so," April replied sarcastically. "I doubt either one of us will survive our two sixteen year old daughters."

"We will go with them to Salem, no?" Jean-Claude

changed the subject. "It will be fun, and they will need parents to volunteer."

"Jean-Claude -."

"Oh, pooh," he responded, "the diner will survive one weekend without you. Gabriel can look after things on this end."

"Getting them away from here might be a good thing on many levels," April relented. "It might allow them time to be just girls, and maybe let things cool off back here a little."

"Bon."

The girls poured out of the change room and into the gym. Jean-Claude had invited the whole team out to dinner to celebrate, and had chosen a more upscale restaurant. Miss Sweider came out of the change room in her street clothes, the first time most of them had seen her without her customary shorts and tee-shirt. In a white blouse, and a black skirt that showed off her legs to advantage, she looked like a goddess – more sylph than Kristen. The male students in the gym were not the only ones with breast envy, and even Jean-Claude seemed to forget himself for a moment, lost and confused as he tried to place the super model who had suddenly stepped off the runway and into the gym.

"Miss Sweider," April supplied with a tolerant smile.

"Has she done something with her hair?" Jean-Claude asked, innocently.

"I would imagine," April replied, still smiling. "Amongst other things."

"Well, shall we get this horde off to the restaurant?" Jean-Claude suggested.

"I think that might be best," April agreed, "before some of the boys have and apoplectic fit."

"How many are going in our car?"

"No-one have volunteered so far," April teased.

At the restaurant the waitresses had pushed together several tables to accommodate all twelve of them, the nine girls on the team, their coach, and Jean-Claude and April.

They were a noisy group, perhaps a little too loud for the setting, and they got a few nasty looks from the other patrons. Pumped by their victory, and excited about the upcoming trip to Salem, the girls just brushed it off. They grew louder with every passing moment. Jean-Claude ordered a bottle of champagne, and allowed each girl a small amount to make a toast to the team and its victory. Throwing alcohol into this volatile mix was probably not the smartest move, but Jean-Claude was a regular customer, and he tipped well.

"Attention girls," Miss Sweider rang a fork on her glass. "I have some good news. Since the athletic budget is hardly used, the school has agreed to pay half our way to the tournament. Each girl will only have to pay one hundred and fifty dollars."

"And I will pay the balance," Jean-Claude announced, sitting back with a smile on his face as he collected hugs from all the girls. "A small price to pay for the attention of so many lovely ladies, no?"

"No!" The girls roared back, and started laughing.

The Brotherhood supplied a small twelve-seat bus and driver, the engine and body modified for speed and protection. Excited about what was for most of the girls their first trip out of New York, the team and its three adult escorts boarded the bus at six in the morning. Exhausted, but too keyed up to sleep, Crystal leaned her head against Gwen's shoulder, staring out the window at the gathering light. Jean-Claude and the bus driver, a burly man who moved as if he wore armour beneath his uniform, loaded their luggage into the cargo space at the side of the bus. For a moment they stood at the door of the vehicle, talking in urgent whispers. Finally Jean-Claude nodded and boarded the bus.

"Ah mes enfants," he rubbed his hands together, "off we go onto the wild black tarmac, off to find adventure, mystery, and maybe a little romance, no?"

"No!" The girls groaned.

It really was too early in the morning for Jean-Claude's

lame humour, and their laughter was a little forced. At least they had laughed, and some of their stress and worry had fled with it. This promised to be such a wonderful trip, and if they were going to be away from home for the first time for three days, at least they had three adults they knew and trusted going with them. And despite their answer to Jean-Claude's sally, boys were exactly what were on most of their minds. Perhaps not at that exact moment, just every other second during the long hours of planning, packing and choosing outfits over the last few days.

The bus started up with a roar and rolled into New York traffic. The trip would take between three and four hours, with an estimated time of arrival around ten am, giving them plenty of time to check in to their hotel and do a little sight seeing before their first game started at two that afternoon. Four hours in a bus did not seem so long, and they had all brought fully loaded IPods, crosswords, novels and card games. Right at that moment, however, most were too tired to do more than lean back in their seats and let the sound of the tires on the tarmac lull them to sleep. Despite their coach's instructions to get a good night sleep, there had been very little of that as they spent much of the night on MSN, chatting excitedly.

Following the mortals, even while they were travelling in daylight, was childishly simple. In a blacked out van with a mortal driver, a five man team of vampyres followed several cars back. As long as they kept the bus in sight, and could keep track of what exits their quarry took, the vampyre surveillance team did not have to get any closer. And a vampyre could see for a long distance.

Druegar had his own set of orders, orders he took directly from Lord Jaeger of the Sanguinarian clan of Bluidthane. Lord Jaeger was disturbed by what had happened to his son at the hands of this girl, and no longer agreed with High Lord Vlad's plans to wait for the eclipse of the moon. For the good of all vampyres, the girl had to die. He carried with him an ancient blade thought capable of killing the succubus, and forged sealed orders in Vlad's handwriting ordering her death. He watched the bus through the tinted windshield, studying his prey from five miles away as it disappeared and reappeared on the hills and vales.

On the bus, Crystal felt an itch in the centre of her back. She squirmed, trying to scratch it, and a chill suddenly ran up and down her spine. Turning, she looked back out the rear windows, watching the cars and trucks stretched out for miles behind her. Just nerves, she decided. For Crystal, this too was her first trip out of New York City, at least in this lifetime. Unlike the other girls, the only parents she knew were travelling with her, and Gwen and her would be sharing a room with Morgana and Kristen in Salem. Nothing really for her to worry about, so she wondered what was making her feel so edgy.

Afraid her fidgeting would wake Gwen, she got up carefully from her seat. She and walked up to the front of the bus to where Jean-Claude and April sat. She flopped down on the seat next to him and cuddled up beside him, her head resting on his chest.

"What is wrong, ma enfant?" He asked, rubbing her back.

"A little nervous, I guess." Crystal said through a yawn.

"A little sleepy too, no?" Jean-Claude teased.

"I was too excited to sleep," Crystal admitted. "Thank you for letting me have this, Jean-Claude."

"Ah, ma petite," he chided, "you earned this, no? You kept your room clean, you did your homework and dishes without complaining, and you have a wicked serve, no?"

"No," Crystal teased, "but I'll clean my room up as soon as we get back. And I'll hardly complain about it."

"That would be a miracle," April interjected, reaching over to brush the bangs out of Crystal's eyes so she could check her temperature. "And maybe it's time for a hair cut to, no?"

"April," Crystal complained, "not you too!"

By the third hour all the girls were up and chatting away

like magpies. Jean-Claude rolled his eyes and got no sympathy from April, who he had dragged along on this trip. If he wanted to read he would have to wait until he got into his hotel room that night. Until then, the nine over-exhausted and wound up girls were all his responsibility. April was only here for the scenery. And maybe to help with a twisted ankle, bumped knee, or bruised heart.

By the fourth hour everyone was anxious to get off the bus. A collective groan went up as the bus pulled up beside a small church in the middle of nowhere.

"Mes petites," Jean-Claude raised his hands to silence them. "Please remain on the bus. I will be no more than ten minutes."

A long low boo followed him out of the van. Shaking his head in frustration, he walked up to the church and inside. Jean-Claude would never understand girls, and if he could not understand them as girls, how was he expected to understand them as women? Surely they could not be that bored, not with all the electronic gizmos and whirly gigs they had dragged onto the bus. Between that and their make-up, there was enough in there to build themselves their own boy.

Brother Fallon, the Master at Arms for the Salem Brotherhood, had aged like the bark of an ironwood tree. His skin was brown and leathery, his muscles long and sinewy from years of hard work and training. He was a man with no give, stubborn as a mule, and as unforgiving as a blizzard on the prairies. His faction had no use for demons and their kits, and if Fallon had his way, he and his men would be putting paid to the two on the bus. At the moment Jean-Claude and his ilk set the policy for the Brotherhood, but their time would not last, and when more saw the light, Fallon would lead them onto the true path – ridding the world of all things evil.

"Brother Fallon," Jean-Claude greeted.

Fallon grunted a reply that may have been a greeting, or a slur.

"Your people are in place at the hotel, no?" Jean-Claude

continued, ignoring the other man's petulance.

"We know our duty," Fallon spat back.

"There is a van with perhaps five vampyres following us," Jean-Claude explained. "Our satellite surveillance team spotted them on its last pass over. They are about five, maybe six miles behind us."

"Do not worry, Jean-Claude," Fallon replied harshly. "They will not even see the girl. My men are ready."

"Try to avoid any killing," Jean-Claude requested, but he knew it was useless. The man would listen to no-one's counsel but his own.

Watching from the window of the bus as it pulled out, Crystal studied the people moving about the church. They were large, burly men and women who moved, like those in New York, with the gait of a warrior. They did not fit the contemplative life they pretended, and Crystal knew they must be more of these 'guardian angels' Jean-Claude had protecting her and the other students at her school.

At the hotel the girls charged into the lobby, leaving Jean-Claude and the driver to sort out their luggage while April and Miss Sweider helped them check into their rooms. The moment they crossed the threshold, the four girls were on the phone to their boys back home, Kristen booting up her laptop to add to the blog she used to keep in touch with the small entourage that called her their girl. Crystal smiled as she found a text message waiting for her from Brendan. He must have got a heads up from Drake, who had been texting Morgana constantly for the last two hours of the bus ride. She quickly dialled his number, dropping onto one of the two beds as she waited for her turn in the bathroom.

"Hey Brendan," Crystal said shyly, twirling a lock of her hair with one of her finger. "What's up?"
Brendan told her a lie that did not match the tension and fear she remembered from only four hours ago.

"Don't play me Brendan," Crystal complained. "How is it really?"

Crystal was relieved to hear that no other vampyres had been seen since the dance. Brendan was now working in the communications centre, and all the Goth patrols were carrying two-way radios so they could expand the radius of their patrols. The vampyres could enter the city from any of the subway entrances, and the fact was, there just wasn't enough of them between the Goths and the Choir to cover the entire city. Right now they were more concerned about the immediate area around the Academy and the brown stone. Gabriel was expecting some kind of move to free Aiko, although so far nothing had materialized.

"Oh, don't let that happen!" Crystal exclaimed, and then covered. "Jean-Claude would be upset."

She listened for a moment, frowning. "Of course I know she is not my friend. I could never be friends with a stone cold killer like her. It's just...."

After checking in, the girls gathered for a little sight-seeing and shopping. The adults decided to get a coffee at a nearby café, giving the girls a little room to breathe. Crystal knew it was a pretence. They were not really on their own. Everywhere they went a small knot of men and women followed, spread out like secret service agents to cover every angle of approach. There, at the corner, leaning up against the wall pretending to read a newspaper; there, midway down the block, the woman who seemed to be window shopping. Crystal was getting good picking them out of a crowd.

Even if they did meet any interesting boys, Crystal knew none of them would get a chance to sneak off alone to do any of that heavy kissing they were bragging about. The only thing they were likely to suck face with was an all day sucker. Crystal really didn't care either way. Jean-Claude was the only one she would ever seriously consider kissing that passionately, and April and Miss Sweider had him held under lock and key. And besides, the museum and display about the witch trials were kind of interesting.

They were due back at the hotel at one, and they were only

slightly late. Jean-Claude said that was like being slightly dead, dead was still dead and late was late. There was no slightly about it. He sent them up to their rooms with a comical scowl that probably didn't even intimidate his kindergarten class either.

In a rush of forgotten knee pads and missing jerseys, the team tumbled into the van. Miss Sweider, who had been to one or two of these events when she was their age, had a few extras of each for just such an emergency. They were `slightly late' arriving at the arena where the tournament was being held, and rushed to find their dressing rooms and change before their first game. Two strange women were waiting there, pretending to be volunteers from the tournament there to assist them. Crystal doubted anyone was fooled between their leather bands at wrists and neck, and the suspicious clank and clang when they moved that could only come from light weight chain mail.

Crystal put it out of her mind and got ready for her game. It was just a part of the weirdness that had infiltrated all aspects of her life, and it was beginning to fade into the background as it had long ago for the other girls.

They drew the top seeded team in the tournament for their first game. Jean-Claude suggested they go man-on-man until they got a lead, and then switch to a zone defence. A typical basketball reference that was growing a little old, but the laughter loosened them up. Miss Sweider, smiling a little too much at Jean-Claude for Crystal's liking, gave a pep talk and discussed strategy for the game. The girls were now ready to focus on her words and not on the Amazons who made up the other team.

By the time they won back the serve the New York girls were already down seven to nothing. And then Crystal delivered a blistering overhand serve that was untouchable. And the Academy girls began to rally, showing those girls from Boston why they had been invited to this tournament. Her second serve was returned, the volley blocked at the net by Jade, one of the two Nordic twins on their team. What followed was a six point run, capped off by a spike by Gwen set up by a perfect bump by Morgana. They lost that first game twenty-two to twenty, and then stormed back to take the next two games, winning the last one twenty-one to four.

Having taken their first set two games to one, they were guaranteed to play in the round robin on Saturday. Jean-Claude suggested they all go out to celebrate, effectively putting the kibosh on their plans to sneak out to a night club. Crystal gave him a hard look. Jean-Claude had a way of being totally sneaky, and pulling it off with such an innocent air that you were left wondering if he really knew what was happening. He was a dangerous enemy, Crystal thought, much too crafty for either Gwen or her future romances. She wondered if any of the other girls saw through his charade, and knowing them as well as she did now, they probably did.

He chose to bring them to Cap't Waterfront, a restaurant with a view of an old sailing ship bedecked in lights. They found seats out on the patio, and the twelve of them sat at three tables pushed together, still the boisterous sports team even in the dresses they had brought down for their aborted evening of clubbing. As lady-like as they looked, they were still fifteen, sixteen and seventeen year old girls who had just kicked butt on the volleyball court, thank-you-very-much. And even if the adults in their lives were being wet blankets, they intended to celebrate. And celebrate they did, waving to every cute boy they saw, flirting with the waiter, and generally cutting up. Tonight, at least, they were the queens of the universe, and for once the world was marching to their drum.

Even with a ridiculous curfew, Saturday morning seemed to come way too early, ambushing the girls amidst pleasant dreams of boys and rock concerts. The scramble out to the van was less chaotic this time, all the equipment and the girls managing to make it inside in some semblance of order. Showered, breakfast eaten, dressed, and still applying make-up in the van – in case some Chippendale dancers gyrated through the gym, Jean-Claude teased – the young warriors prepared for a day of battle.

At the arena hundreds of girls and their parents milled about, getting changed for the games that were due to start in less than an hour, or just waiting around, mourning the dearth of eligible boys and expending their nervousness in boisterous chatting. Amongst them, like weeds amongst a field of roses, the strange men and women from the Salem sect kept vigil. Their presence was beginning to raise a few eyebrows, although the rumours currently being nosed about suggested the Academy was some ultra religious school for children destined to be nuns and priests. The number of chaperons was a bit excessive, but these days, who could blame them?

Before the game Jean-Claude met with Michael, the brother in charge of on site security. So far there was no sign of the vampyres. They were out there, somewhere, waiting out the daylight hours in some shadowy corner of Salem or the surrounding countryside. If they did make a move it would be sometime after dark, at or near the hotel. The brotherhood would be ready.

The Academy's first game was at ten, two hours after they arrived. Watching some of their competition killed a little of that time, although that got old rather fast, and the rest of the scenery was rather lame. Cell phones and IPods came out then, and the girls gave their thumbs a vigorous work out to prepare for the game. Brendan sent a text message wishing Crystal and the other girls good luck, and tagged it with a personal message that made her blush. That would never happen, even if she wanted to. Not as long as she was what she was, and he was what he was.

The afternoon progressed. The girls took their first set of the day in two straight games, and split the second, winning two out of three games. It was enough to advance them into the Sunday's match as the fifth place team, and they were scheduled to meet the fourth place team in the one set elimination round. Only two more wins separated them from the championship game. This time Jean-Claude could not induce the girls to spend another night celebrating with the adults, and they insisted on hitting the town alone. April interceded with Jean-Claude on their behalf, and convinced him to let them go out to a local café only a few blocks from the hotel.

"Bon, mes enfants," Jean-Claude decided, "you may eat out at this fine eatery on your own. I shall return to the hotel with your coach and April, where we will no doubt starve to death, no?"

"No!" The girls chorused happily.

"No later than ten," April warned. "Miss Sweider and I will be conducting bed checks at ten-oh-five, and if anyone is missing, we will be heading straight home."

"Oh mom!" Gwen complained, giggling with her friends.

"And if you are missing, young lady," Jean-Claude teased, "it's straight to the convent for all of you, no?"

Gwen just rolled her eyes and shared a look with Crystal. Jean-Claude could be such an ass sometimes.

The café was a little Italian place with outdoor tables that offered the best boy watching opportunities. What the boys back home didn't know, couldn't hurt them. Besides, Morgana offered up, what happened in Salem, stayed in Salem. Laughing and teasing Morgana by threatening to tell Drake what she had said, the girls spilled out of the hotel and onto the street. Free, or as free as they could be with an invisible escort, they strolled happily down the street towards their destination of choice. The night couldn't be any more perfect, warm with gentle zephyrs stirring the skirts of their dresses, and a canopy of stars overhead. The odd dream strolling by to be picked over and divvied up, and nobody but their best girls for company.

At the café Kristen tried to order a glass of wine – she didn't see why she shouldn't indulge, being nearly twelve hundred years old – but the waitress didn't buy it. Still laughing and teasing, they all pretended that their sodas where alcoholic drinks with suggestive names. The Fuzzy Navel, the Slow Screw Against the Wall, the Screaming Orgasm. Morgana seemed to know them all, which led to another round of teasing, with her as the target. Playing it up, she pretended to be a regular patron at all the hot New York night clubs, many known only by name.

Ten o'clock was really a lame curfew. It came far too soon, and before they knew it they were dividing up the cheque and looking for change to leave for a tip. If they did not hurry, they would be late again. Running in high heels was a skill not all the girls had mastered, and they were soon strung out for almost a block in their mad dash to reach the hotel in time. Crystal, the newest to this fashion torture, was near the back, running with Gwen, finding herself walking on her ankles more often than the thin heel of her shoe. Frustrated, she paused to remove the shoes.

This was the moment Druegar was waiting for. The girl was alone and vulnerable. His forged orders had been distributed, one of his team waited a mile away with their van, ready to make a fast break, and the other three were here. He nodded to his flight and leapt out of hiding.

She came from nowhere. A woman in chain mail with a strange weapon shaped like a crucifix, two more men leaping out of the shadows to help her. All over the street these mortals, armed and ready, poured out of buildings and alleyways. Crystal, seeing the fight, picked up Gwen and ran for all she was worth in her bare stockings.

"Run!" She screamed as she caught up with the other girls.

Druegar and his flight were caught up in a pitched battle, and could only hiss his frustration as he watched his quarry disappear. Already one of his men was down and another was badly wounded. It was a perfectly executed ambush, with the girl used as bait.

"Retreat!" He called, climbing up the side of a building to escape the five who had trapped him near the mouth of an alley. He never looked back. The others would have to fend for themselves.

Jean-Claude was fuming when Michael came to make his report. The girls were safe, tucked into their rooms and watched over by April and Miss Sweider. The death of one of the vampyres was a disaster. There was little hope of avoiding an open war in New York. It might be what Fallon wanted, but the man was a fool. He knew or cared little for the fall out such a war would cause. His recklessness may just trigger the End Times, and coming this early, it could only strengthen the probability of the Hsatan prophesies overriding Revelations. Even if the vampyres were following their own agenda, there was nothing preventing others from hijacking that agenda for their own ends.

Sacre bleu! Fallon should learn to pay more attention to what was written in the ancient texts and less to his own rhetoric.

Despite the evening's disturbance, Jean-Claude decided to let the girls continue on with their tournament. Any real danger had left with the vampyres after their failed assassination attempt, and Anastasia had worked through the night convincing the witnesses that they had seen nothing more than a drunken brawl between a group of tourists and some local toughs.

At breakfast the next morning Jean-Claude spoke quietly to the girls.

"Last night there was an incident with some vampyres," he began quietly. "While they may have been here for one of you, we have no real way of knowing what they were after."

"Does this mean we have to go home?" Morgana asked, the disappointment heavy in her voice.

"No, ma enfant," Jean-Claude replied gently. "I do not believe any of us are in any further danger. So why spoil your fun, no?"

For once the girls were in total agreement. And while they remained a little uneasy, having lived with the threat of vampyres all their lives, they found a way to put it out of their minds. After all, there had been vampyre attacks in the past, and there would be vampyre attacks in the future, but they may never have another opportunity to win a championship. And they trusted Jean-Claude completely. Even if he could be a complete dweeb sometimes, and his jokes were about as funny as a nightmare during a blackout.

Their opponents had the first serve in the opening game. This made the girls a little nervous, their defence having been a little weak over the course of the last two days. And the first rally only served to illustrate this. At the net they were strong, led by Morgana and the two Nordic twins, and no-one on the courts were as fast as Crystal and Kristen with their supernatural reflexes. They were down eighteen to three when Crystal got the serve, beginning a run that led to the tournament's most exciting come back.

It set the tone for the next two games. After winning the next game and taking the set, they played off the third for positioning. In case of a tie, their three wins would determine who played in the championship game, and who received the all important first serve. Theirs was the only upset in the first four games, leaving them the lowest seeded team for the final two games. It was a handicap, but coming into the tournament, they were actually higher seeded than the second placed team, who were playing the tournament of their lives.

Two sets left. Gwen scored the opening point, returning a serve with a squib of a bump that managed to fall between two girls on the opposite team. Kristen took the first serve, and she had no compulsion against using her natural strength and reflexes when competing. Her first blistering serve left a scorch mark across the wooden floor. On impact the ball exploded. The game halted as tournament officials gathered to rule on the point, having never encountered something like this before. It might have been a defective ball, or a sliver on the floor and a very powerful serve. Coach Sweider knew what had really happened, and she took Crystal and Kristen aside for a private discussion while the officials deliberated.

"While it really isn't cheating," Miss Sweider explained patiently, "if you two make too many serves like that, it's going to be a little hard to explain. Remember, our overriding concern is to keep the civilians from discovering our existence, and especially yours."

"Sorry Miss Sweider," Kristen responded with a fierce grin. "Sometimes I just don't know my own strength."

"Just ease up a little," her coach responded. "But not too much. We want to win this bloody thing."

The girls returned to the court grinning. The officials had decided that the point would be replayed with a new ball. Kristen's next serve was almost as fast, bouncing off the defenders arm just above her hands and straight up into the air, where it hit the ceiling. Their rivals luck had panned out. Kristen ran her serve for a six point lead, and Hillmount public school only managed to gain two back during their serve. Then Crystal took the serve. The Academy added twelve points with the ball in her hands, and after conceding a point, Morgana came in to finish the game. The second game was closer, ending twenty-one to sixteen, and the Academy was in the finals.

Their opponents for the championship game, Coral Gables Senior High School from Miami, were the second seeded team in the United States. They had smoked their rivals in every game leading up to this one, having not dropped a single game in the run up to the championship. Besides the tans, they did not look any different from the girls who stood on the other side of the court, although their confidence was translating into a kind of arrogance. Yet they had earned it. Many of the girls had been on the team for three or four years, attended training camps in the summer, and had ambitions to make the US Olympic team. It was enough to make you feel sick, Crystal thought.

The Academy dropped their first game in convincing fashion. At least they were convinced they could never beat these girls. Vampyres were less difficult to deal with. With them you only had to worry about losing your immortal soul, and not looking like a bunch of losers in front of all these people.

"I think we can beat them," Crystal suggested between games.

"Were you here for the last game?" Morgan asked, incredulously.

"Well, if Jade and her sister drop back to the middle, and we move Gwen and Nancy to the net," Crystal explained. "And let me serve first. You'll see."

Crystal had the most accurate serve of any girl at the tournament. She bounced her first two just inside the baseline at either corner, giving the Academy its first two point lead. The next two points were hard fought, and split between either team. These two points set the tone for the entire game, a gruelling marathon that the Academy won twenty-two to twenty, setting up the tie breaker.

Game point. Twenty to nineteen. Crystal held the serve. She felt a terrible sense of déjà vu. This was exactly the same situation that had won them the invitation to the tournament, but no-one could be that lucky. She studied the girls on the far side of the court. The girl in the middle, a senior and one of Coral Gables best players, was favouring her left ankle. Her coach should have pulled her out and sent in a substitute. Crystal had her target. She took a deep calming breath and wiped the sweat from her brow. It all came down to a guess, whether the opposing coached had guessed wrong keeping in her best player, the best defensive player of the tournament, or if Crystal had guessed right, suspecting the injury was worse than the girl had told her coach.

The ball left Crystal's hand. Fast and true, it made a beeline toward left of centre court. The twisted ankle failed to take her weight as the girl shifted left. The ball bounced once, and spun over the head of the two girls moving up to support her. The Academy had won the tournament.

Chapter 23

"We are the champions! We are the champions! We are the champions, of the world!" The girls half-shouted, half-sang like a clowder of drunken alley cats, filling the hall of the hotel with their caterwauling.

Jean-Claude and April escaped to his room, where three mysterious people were waiting to meet with him. Father Abraham was a hundred and twenty years old, and looked twice that age. He was so stooped and arthritic it was amazing he could move at all, let alone travel half-way around the world to meet here tonight. The other two women were in their eighties, and looked like school girls next to him. Leaders in the local Wiccan community, and representatives of the National Convocation, they came to consult with Jean-Claude on the eve of what looked like open warfare. While it had fallen out of fashion to believe in evil and monsters that go bump in the night, these women knew differently.

"I don't see what they were after," Jean-Claude was saying. "Surely they understand that they cannot kill her outright, no?"

"Perhaps they only want her out of the way temporarily," Father Abraham suggested.

Just then the object of their conversation burst into the room. Finding strangers there with Jean-Claude, Crystal stopped in confusion.

"Oh," she stumbled, "I just came to ask if we could order room service. I didn't know you had guests."

"By all means, ma petite," Jean-Claude put aside his worried scowl and smiled for her. "Charge it to my room. Have a big victory celebration, no?"

"No!" Crystal cried excitedly, turning and running from

the room.

As Jean-Claude crossed the room to close the door, Sister Harmony spoke up.

"There is a girl who has recently met her soul mate."

"Mon Dieu!" Jean-Claude swore. "Do I not have enough worries on my mind? Can you tell me who it is?"

"Not without seeing them together, Jean-Claude," Sister Harmony gave a tolerant smile. "The crystals have their limits."

"As problematic as that is, Jean-Claude," Father Abraham chided gently, "perhaps we best get back to the matter at hand."

"Yes," Jean-Claude replied, turning back to his guests.

"We know the vampyres mean to make a move against her," April summed up their discussion to date. "Is there any way they could do her any permanent harm?"

"No," Jean-Claude said, and then stopped himself. "Maybe one way. But it would require an object that is hidden away and guarded by the church. Besides, they could not even touch this object."

"They could kidnap her," Sister Willette, the second Wiccan suggested. "There are certain herbs they could use to keep her in a stupor and helpless. There would be little risk that such a concoction would kill her, and it would take a long time for her body to build up immunity, so they could keep the dosage low."

"She is the key, no?" Jean-Claude interjected. "Without her we cannot prevent the war, and if there is a war can the End Times be far behind?"

"What do you suggest, Jean-Claude?" Father Abraham urged.

"We must protect her at all costs," Jean-Claude returned, "but we dare not move her from New York. She is our only deterrent to Vlad and his wild ambitions, no? We must change our rules of engagement. We must no longer be concerned with just driving any threat away, it must be eliminated."

"You sound like Brother Fallon," Father Abraham teased.

"Yes, and his actions helped drive us to this, no?" Jean-Claude replied bleakly.

In the room Crystal shared with three other girls, the players' high spirits were dwindling with the last of their supper. They would be heading back to New York soon, victors with their spoils. And although Crystal was anxious to see Drake and Brendan again, she was ambivalent about returning home. She wondered why Drake was the first one to come to her mind, the first person she thought to miss if she did not return to New York, but it was a momentary distraction. Larger, more weightier matters occupied her thoughts.

"I almost don't want to go home," Crystal voiced her doubts.

"Why?" Morgana teased. "You and Brendan fighting already?"

Crystal felt a momentary pang of guilt. "He's not my boyfriend, and no. I do want to see him more than ever. It's just all this vampyre stuff, and all the talk of war. It's kind of -."

"Frightening?" Morgana replied when Crystal found herself at a loss for words. "My Mom says they almost had a war back in the fifties. And they actually fought a pitched battle back in the seventies during the black out. She says they always manage to back down before things ever get to that point."

"It's kind of weird," Gwen offered. "Everyone talks about 9/11 and the war on terror. If they only knew what we knew."

A shiver ran up her spine, like a premonition of disaster. Gwen sunk back into Crystal's arms as the room grew sombre.

"What if one of you got hurt because of me?" Crystal asked. "I don't think I could live with myself if that happened."

"We'll just have to keep a sharper eye out for those Vampyres," Morgana soothed, showing more confidence than she felt. "We'll form a pact to look out for one and another, and protect each other no matter what. After all, we are the Ghosts, and no one messes with the Ghost Sisterhood."

"Isn't that too much like the Sisterhood of the Travelling Pants," Kristen complained. "I think I'll just let all my boys walk me home for now on."

Kristen ducked a shower of pillows that suddenly flew her way, and stuck out her tongue when they all missed.

"Let's make it official," Jade suggested when the laughter died down.

"What do you mean?" Morgana demanded. Like all Goths, she was still suspicious of anything Wiccan. She was still recovering from what happened at the séance. "Make what official?"

"The Oath." Jade replied.

"How?" She had spoken a little too offhandedly, and now all of Morgana's alarm bells were ringing.

"Well," Jade elaborated, "there are three Wiccans here, and we all have our crystals."

"A blood oath!" Gwen objected. "Jade, that's very dangerous!"

And suddenly the idea appealed to Morgana, to that small voice that was always getting her in trouble, and that somehow always seemed to overrule her common sense.

"More dangerous than a flight of vampyres?" Jade countered.

Gwen thought about it for a long moment. Admittedly, even she would feel better knowing that the eight people she trusted most in the world, her girls, were watching her back. On the other hand, a blood oath could create compulsions. If one of them were to get into a really dangerous situation the others could find themselves forced to follow. In the end, the frightened looks on the other girls' faces made the decision for her.

"Okay." Gwen relented. "Only if I lead the ceremony."

The others nodded their agreement. Her talent was by far the strongest, and with all that extra training, Gwen was naturally the logical choice.

"We'll need a knife and a crystal to accept out oath," Gwen explained.

"Use mine," Crystal offered.

"And I have a knife," Morgana supplied, responding to the startled looks from the other girls. "What? I am a Goth, you know."

"That will make you the oath keeper, Crystal," Gwen explained, giving her one last chance to back out.

"I am the oldest. I think it should be me."

Chapter 24

Within minutes of the surveillance team's return home word of the failed assassination attempt reached Vlad. Almost immediately he called for Hrathgar, his agent on the team and its nominal leader. As he waited for the vampyre to report, Vlad sat perfectly still, struggling to contain the rage that was overcoming his reason. Why were so many ignoring his orders? Was it simple over-enthusiasm, a too keen desire to please, or was there something deeper and darker behind it?

Hrathgar looked unruffled when he arrived in the High Lord's study, unlike the other three who returned with him, two of them wounded.

"My Lord!"

"Report," Vlad demanded with barely contained anger.

"We proceeded to follow the girl as per your initial orders," Hrathgar began.

"My initial orders!" Vlad exploded.

Hrathgar blinked. Why had the use of the word `initial' set his lord off? "Upon arriving in Salem, their destination, Druegar produced a second set of orders. They were contained in a black envelope sealed with your personal signet."

A black envelope always carried a death warrant. Ordinary, such an order required the full backing of the council, and the council had not met prior to his sending out of this mission. This was a double-edged sword, a trap meant to cut him two ways – if successful, it would destroy his overall plans, and if it failed, blame could be laid at his feet.

"Tell me more about these orders," and seeing the danger, Vlad calmed down as his cold, analytic mind began to study all the angles.

"One wonders why My Lord did not trust me with such orders." Hrathgar ventured.

"Because I never issued those orders," Vlad replied flatly, all the while wondering who did, and calculating who had the most to gain by it.

Hrathgar nodded. He understood the implications and Vlad could see it in his eyes.

"The orders appeared to be in your hand writing," he continued his report, "ordering an attempt on the girl using the Deadalus blade. Thinking I had fallen out of favour, I arranged to take the lesser role, guarding the mortal and the van."

"I see," Vlad chose to see the act for what it was, and not read anything lesser into it. As his agent, Hrathgar probably wouldn't have survived the assault – coming to a tragic accident that would prevent his report. "Very honourable. I appreciate the show of loyalty, especially in light of this news. Go, take a squad and arrest Druegar and the others, and then have my Tipstaff assemble the full council.

It was a dangerous gambit, one that could explode in his own face, but Vlad thought he saw a way to turn this to his advantage.

"And Hrathgar," he called after the retreating vampyre, "bring me a copy of this order."

"I have it here, My Lord," Hrathgar turned and bowed, producing the black envelope.

"Excellent."

In fact perfect, Vlad thought as he watched the vampyre retreat to do his bidding. A full council meeting was rare, bringing together all one hundred and forty-four household heads. In spirit they represented all castes of vampyre society, in truth they were the seventy two men and women who represented the top six castes. Prejudice played as large a part here as it did in the mortal world, and with deeper roots. After all, one could barely tolerate the eaters of animals, let alone the loathsome eaters of the dead. The bottom six castes were only animals – one only had to look at those who metamorphosed into their prey at each full moon to see proof of this.

A full council meeting meant he would see his lady wife for the first time since he had censured his son. As lovely as she was, the simple-minded bat did not grasp the complexities of council politics. She refused to see how Delph's continued disobedience threatened all of them. She was blinded by, of all things, emotions. They would talk before this council meeting, and if she failed to understand that her unwavering support was what was needed, he would simply have her tongue removed.

Vlad regretted having married the women, political expedience aside. He had not uttered her name, even in private, for over three decades. He had weightier issues on his mind, and could not dwell on his loveless marriage. Not at the moment.

Bells tolled throughout the caverns of Upyr. Traditionally they would continue to peel until the last of the councillors arrived and the Tipstaff locked the doors of the Council Chambers. All members of the guard, both Praetorian and Household, moved to the outer passages to guard against outside influence, and to prevent them from applying their own influence on the deliberation. Most tasks, except those considered essential to the running of the city, came to a halt, and the citizens of the city gathered in or near the central square. Historically, they were there to await the council decision, but over the years it had been an excuse for a celebration.

Arriving last to the council chamber had long ago become a power play, one that Vlad normally won due to his position as High Lord. Today was no exception. He waited in the wings, in a small auxiliary office he used only for these occasions, until his aide came to let him know the Tipstaff had locked the doors. Vlad kept them waiting another ten minutes, sitting at his desk with his fingers steepled against his brow, collecting his thoughts. Before him lay three orders, two in the black envelope of the council, one in the blood red that signified his office of High Lord of the Twelve Vampyre Nations.

It was time. Vlad entered the council chambers in full regalia, the crimson-lined black cape trailing behind him, the small sceptre of office held in his right hand. He stood before the council for a long moment, studying the faces of those assembled before him for minute telltale signs. He knew every nuance of every member here. Vlad had been playing council politics for over four hundred years, and his skill here had led to his rise of power.

Vlad took his seat, gavelling the session to order with the base of his sceptre.

"These are orders calling for the death of an enemy of state using the Deadalus blade," Vlad said calmly. "These orders were never issued by this chamber."

"This outrage must be investigated to the fullest!" Lord Gruefang, a corpulent vampyre beginning to show his age shouted in a near apoplectic rage.

"That is why this council has been summoned, my Lord Gruefang," Vlad replied calmly, drawing a chuckle from the chamber. "If you would be so kind as to let us proceed."

Vlad drew up a second black envelope. "This is the order this chamber issued at my request for the death of this same individual using the Hallaf of Abraham."

Vlad paused, studying his audience again.

"The council will call as its first witness, Hrathgar de Boulainvilliers, the vampyre entrusted with the initial orders for this surveillance team." Vlad held up the third envelope as the Sergeant-At-Arms tolled out Hrathgar's name.

Hrathgar wore his full Praetorian Guard uniform. He would not dare appear before council in anything less. He stood straight, with the bearing of a soldier, his eyes front and glued to a spot on the wall above Vlad's head.

"Hrathgar de Boulainvilliers," Vlad began. There was no point asking for his oath to tell the truth, everyone knew the penalty for lying to council. "How many times have you taken a death warrant from me?"

"Seventy-two, My Lord."

"And," Vlad continued in a casual, conversational fashion, "where were every one of these orders delivered?"

"My Lord?" Hrathgar questioned, puzzled. Everyone in the room knew the answer. "Here, My Lord, in these chambers, before the entire council."

"And what orders did you receive before your last mission?" Vlad pressed, leaning forward.

"My orders were to follow the girl and determine if the Church was hiding her outside the city," Hrathgar continued with more confidence.

"And what orders were carried out?" Vlad concluded.

"At first those you gave me in the Crimson envelope," Hrathgar explained. "The orders I just explained to this council. And then Druegar Fruggar-Polignac produced a second set of orders in a Black envelope."

"Very well," Vlad replied. "I thank you for your report at this moment. Before I offer this witness to the floor for questionings, I would like to make a statement of my own."

Although many would like to have objected, no-one knew enough of what was going on to stick out their necks. Vlad was too wily a political opponent to bring any of this up if it led back to his door step. Much safer to wait and see where this all led.

"This order," Vlad held up the order he knew to be a forgery, "calls for the death of Crystal Raven using the Deadalus blade. I had nothing to do with this order, but I would like to make a confession to this council."

Vlad's pronouncement caused a stir amongst the gallery. This was a case of high treason, a case that carried death to any and all involved. What could the High Lord be thinking?

"The Deadalus blade is a fake." Vlad continued when the

chambers fell quiet. "It is my family's most embarrassing secret, and one we have kept for generations. Only I and I alone could know it would do no harm to this individual."

Lord Jaeger blinked. Such a small gesture, but it was enough. Vlad had known him, both as a brother-in-law and a political crony for centuries, knew every nuance and habit of his like he knew his own

"Some of you perhaps doubt my word?" Vlad asked with no animosity in his voice. "So I will demonstrate. Hrathgar, please fetch the Deadalus blade for me, and let any of the council members who choose to handle it."

The Deadalus blade was brought in from an antechamber. Many of the councillors took it up, studying it minutely, searching for some trick that they knew must be there. Vlad was too crafty a political animal for there not to be one. They could find nothing, although that did not prevent some from taking a closer look, holding up proceedings for nearly twenty minutes.

"Do any of you feel any ill effects?" Vlad asked pleasantly, and the lord currently holding it all but threw it to the ground. "I assure you there is no poison on it. There is nothing in fact that could harm even a child."

"Another demonstration if I might ask this august body to indulge me?" Vlad suggested, nodding towards the Sergeant-at-arms.

A second door opened. Four Nosferatu stumbled into the chambers bearing the pedestal that held the box taken from the Vatican. Even contact with the pedestal caused their skin to wither and bubble, staggering them with unbearable agony although the whole could weigh no more than forty pounds. A gasp of horror chased itself about the room, and many fell back as their gruesome burden neared them. Setting it down at the centre of the council chambers, the four porters fell to the floor, crawling away from the source of their torment and leaving trails of blood behind.

"No vampyre could withstand the touch of a true

apotropaic," Vlad pronounced. "If the Deadalus blade were a true weapon, all those who touched it would look like those poor wretches. Sergeant-at-Arms, remove these creatures from our presence please."

"This council calls Druegar Fruggar-Polignac before it," Vlad announced.

Druegar knew he was in trouble from the first moment he was summoned to council. The failure of his mission guaranteed the loss of his benefactor's support, as it should be. He was still a good soldier, and knew how to play his part for the benefit and glory of his clan and house. And Druegar still had one more card to play in this game.

"Druegar Fruggar-Polignac," Vlad demanded, "who gave you these orders?"

"You did, My Lord." A simple statement. Druegar had no way of knowing what had happened before he entered the chamber, and thought nothing of the reaction his words caused.

"I," Vlad laughed, asking the council. "Knowing what you now know of the Deadalus blade, does anyone here think I am that simple-minded? I, scion of a family who has worked and bled for generations to raise our people to their true birthright! Does anyone here believe that I would throw everything away and order the death of our enemy with a blade that I, and I alone knew could not harm a sparrow?"

Outraged screams and yells were his reply. Most of these in the negative.

"Druegar Fruggar-Polignac," Vlad threatened, "we will have the truth from you! Send in the Inquisitionists."

Four vampyres born with the ability to read the truth and cause pain with their minds, they were the most feared members of Upyr society. Dressed in black robes with cowls that hid their features, they entered the chambers chanting in a procession. They came to a halt in the centre of the chambers, their leader bowing before Vlad. Their robes were so shapeless none knew if they were males or females, and they spoke in an ancient dialect long since forgotten, and then only in whispers.

"Proceed." Vlad ordered.

The leader of the four Inquisitionists bowed once again and turned to the other three. They took up a stance at the four cardinal points surrounding Druegar, their leader scribing a circle in chalk on the floor. Bowing on last time, he closed his eyes and led his companions in the opening ritual.

Druegar smiled. This was his last card. He was a void, one of a few very rare individuals whose mind was shielded even from the strongest mentalists. They would learn nothing of value from him. It was Druegar's last gift to his clan, and the true reason he was chosen for this mission.

"We can tell you nothing, My Lord," the leader of the inquisition replied, "save that he is lying."

"Very well," Vlad returned, hiding his disappointment. "You may go."

Leaving as they came, the four cowled vampyres turned and marched in procession out of the chambers. When they were gone Vlad turned back to the council.

"I ask this council for a warrant of death for the traitor, Druegar Fruggar-Polignac."

"Consider it given, My Lord," Lord Jaeger was the first on his feet, sacrificing this pawn in an effort to hide his own complicity.

"Kill the traitor!"

"Death to the miscreant!"

The council chambers erupted in a bedlam. The cries for his death grew louder, and Druegar knew that this too was coming. The price of failure could be no less. Vlad let it go on for another few minutes before calling a vote. It was unanimous. For one so low to attempt to usurp the power of the council could demand no less a penalty.

"Throw him to the Eaters of the Dead," Vlad commanded.

The Sergeant-at-Arms drew his sword to take Druegar's head, and Vlad's harsh command halted him.

"I did not say kill him!"

The council grew deathly still. A small circle of stone met the radiating rays of alternating stone at the foot of Vlad's dais. Four members of the chamber guard moved to take up position around its perimeter, each taking up one of the four handles carved in its surface. The gaping maw of a pit was revealed. Many stories below, three of the most ancient Eaters of the Dead waited, winged, misshapen creatures that long ago had lost all semblance of humanity. Sharp teeth and claws, sightless eyes and sickly white skin of cave dwellers, they moved towards the opening, where a fresh breeze brought them scent of new prey. Into this pit the guards threw a struggling Druegar.

Vlad stood, speaking over the screams rising from the pit. "My friends and countrymen, I thank you for your cooperation in this matter. And for your patience as our collective dream draws towards completion. One more ingredient is lacking before we are ready to move, and soon I will issue orders to bring that ingredient here. By the dark of the moon, our victory will be complete."

The council meeting ended, and, having sent a strong message to his enemies, Vlad could now deal with his son. Despite the embarrassment he had caused him, Vlad believed he had found a way to turn his son's disobedience to his advantage. And although he knew this would most likely kill the boy, sometimes such sacrifices were necessary. As long as Jean-Claude continued to believe Delph and his flight of hooligans were responsible, Vlad saw a way to weaken his enemies. By stretching out the Church's resources, causing them to guard more and more targets, the way to the girl would be open to him.

As he waited for his son, Vlad remembered those cold dark days after the Troubles. The only ships they could hire were shallow draft cogs sailed by the scourge and reprobates of the Northern Sea, and Greenland was the furthest they could sail in those days. These cut throats did not realize what they had brought on board. When the first Captain had tried to cross him, Vlad fed him to his people and turned the crew, making them the first Loogaroo and Nosferatu. Two of the seventeen ships had failed to make port, and four of those that did were missing most of their crew. Vlad had no choice but to order the deaths of all the survivors, and have the ships scuttled a mile off shore.

Greenland had been a harsh, barren land with few inhabitants. Vlad and his people were forced to make raids on the people in the land to the north to feed his people, and there were few enough of those. He sat here wondering if his own war with the Church would end any better than his father's had. Patience was the watch word, and for creatures who are so long lived, his people seemed to be in short supply of it lately.

As New Amsterdam grew, and eventually became New York, he was able to move more and more of his people to North America. When the first sewer system was put in place, Vlad and his people built their first settlement there, and the rebuilding of their nation had begun in truth. The losses during those long years of wandering the wilderness had been catastrophic, and soon Vlad was one of the oldest and most powerful vampyres in his nation. It helped him rise to power so quickly, but even then his position was precarious.

His weak position led to his marriage to his wife, the eldest daughter of a Civatateo lord with the largest clan. It was a decision he had learned to regret over the years, especially after the old lord's death. He had known his place and did not forget the old ways. The same could not always be said for his son, and today's fiasco was the culmination of his over reaching ambition.

Delph knocked on the door and entered.

"You wish to see me, father."

"Yes, my son." Vlad cleared the haunting visions from his mind and focused on the here and now. "Your actions of the past few months have nearly ruined the work of generations of your family. You and your flight have become a liability to our people. You have brought shame to our family and our clan. And so, I am assigning you and your flight to patrol the nether tunnels and keep the Eaters of Dead in check. And while you are down there, you will see to it that Lord Jaeger's son has a fatal accident."

"But-."

"No buts!" Vlad roared. "It's time you grew up and learned that disobedience to your lord has consequences. Penalties must be paid! His life is your forfeit."

Lessons could be taught to more than one pupil at a time.

Chapter 25

The bus ride back from Massachusetts was long and uneventful. Most of the girls were sleeping, exhausted from the stress of the tournament, the excitement of bringing home the school's first trophy in twenty years, and the eight hours of travel. Unable to sleep, Crystal sat up watching the stars through the window as the bus sped down the highway. One man and two boys tumbled through her mind as she let her thoughts wander. Things had been so much simpler when she was younger. Was that only two months ago? She teased herself.

It was no wonder she could not remember a childhood, she had never had one. Not really. Even after untold thousands of years, she had always reincarnated as a sixteen year old girl, a woman by the standards of most of the societies she had lived in, but not this one. This is the closest she had ever come, and it was thanks to a man she wanted to see her as a woman more than anything else in the world.

And then there was Brendan. Theirs was a friendship that could never blossom into a romance, not unless they planned to be celibate, and they both had hormones screaming against it. He came the closest to understanding what she felt since she had discovered her true nature, and as much as he tried, he could never truly understand her heartache. Brendan was just too young. He had never had his heart broken. Had never fallen in love, having been taken by the vampyres young and the lived in a world where love could not blossom.

Drake. She refused to even think about him. That one brief moment they had shared, that moment when she was feeding on his soul, and could feel his love and desire for Morgana.

She remembered that feeling oh too many times. Crystal longed to feel it again, and feared it. As long as she was who and what she was, she could not afford to follow her heart. And yet she was so lonely. So very lonely.

It was after midnight when they arrived home, and the girls had school in the morning. Crystal had already missed too many days. April sent them both upstairs to get ready for bed, letting them off with their unfinished math homework just this once time. She and Jean-Claude retired to her apartment for a coffee and a little alone time, escaping from girls and responsibilities for one hour. Their two sweethearts were old enough by now to get themselves showered and into bed, and if any real emergency happened, they were only just downstairs.

As tired as she was, Crystal still couldn't sleep. Within minutes Gwen was sound asleep, and she was feeling lonely. Jean-Claude was still downstairs when she looked into his room. Crystal slipped on a pair of jeans and tucked her nightgown inside, sneaking out the door and down into the basement, where she knew she would find people who could understand something of her angst. Everyone there was a supernatural being, had lived centuries at least, and most of them lived much of their lives alone – sometimes by choice, like with Aiko.

In the rooms that had been converted into a living quarters for the twenty-five members of the specialists, an arrangement that included a concept called hot swapping of beds that had the two girls giggling for twenty minutes, Crystal found Alvaro, Cantara, and the Wandering Jew. Cantara was sitting in her lover's arms, leaning against his chest as she sharpened a knife with a whet stone.

"What are you doing here, little angel?" Alvaro asked, "Shouldn't you be in bed?"

"I couldn't sleep," Crystal admitted, tucking her feet up under her as she sat on one of the beds facing Cantara. She watched fascinated as the djinn swept the knife back and forth over the stone.

"Something bothering you, little cousin?" Cantara asked, using the diminutive she had adopted to tease Crystal. Both knew the girl was probably thousands of years older than the woman, and it struck Cantara's warped sense of humour.

"Just my life, the vampyres, the world we live in," Crystal replied with a weak smile.

"Is that all?" Alvaro replied with a full toothed smile. "The answer to all those questions is lemonade."

"Thanks," Crystal gave him a fake smile, "that was a real big help. How do you do it? I mean, falling in love with a mortal, or even an immortal, knowing that one day they will die and you will be alone."

"When my Isabella died," Alvaro replied with a sad, broken smile, "I spent a year wandering drunk and naked through the streets of Rome."

"No way," Cantara laughed. "Did he really do that?"

"I don't know." The Wandering Jew replied. "I don't think he liked me back then."

"Yes," Alvaro replied tartly, "I thought he was a douche."

"Me," Cantara replied, "I'm sitting on the fence,"

"Hey!" The Wandering Jew exclaimed, digging his fingers into her side, "I represent that remark."

"You guys are just a font of wisdom," Crystal complained. "I think I'll go talk to Aiko. At least I know when she asks me to kindly drop dead, it's from the heart."

"Only your heart can answer those questions for you, little cousin," Cantara soothed. "And now, off to bed. You have school in the morning."

"I wonder how many times I've completed high school in my life time," Crystal complained.

"Probably not as many times as you think," Alvaro pointed out. "Women were not educated in most societies."

"We don't have to tell Jean-Claude that when I try to convince him to let me give it up," Crystal suggested.

Cantara's laughter followed her back upstairs.

Morning came way too early for Crystal. Her eyes refused to open, even when Gwen bounced on the bed beside her, and April called for the third time. In desperation, Gwen finally dumped a pail of water on her. With a startled squeak, Crystal leapt from her covers, and chased the other girl through the apartment, threatening bodily harm. Laughing, she made her way into the bathroom for a quick shower, and then threw on some clothes while shoving a piece of toast down her throat. Without make-up, and feeling like a bag lady, she grabbed her back pack and raced out the door to catch up with Gwen.

"Wait up girl!" Crystal complained.

"If you would have got up the first fifty times we asked," Gwen yelled back over her shoulder, "we wouldn't be late."

"The least you could do after nearly drowning me," Crystal shot back, laughing, "is slow down a bit."

Brendan was waiting for them, even though it meant that he too would be late for class. And being late, the three of them automatically received a detention after school, no exceptions for athletic stars. Groaning and grumbling through their morning classes, they got no sympathy from their fellow Ghosts when they all met for lunch. They were all tired and a little grumpy, and it was kind of nice to know someone else was having a worse day then they were. Crystal thought their attitude stank, especially when she was the one who was having that bad day that made everyone else's seem so much sweeter.

After lunch, in gym class, Miss Sweider actually gave the girls a bit of a break. She set them to cleaning and organizing their gear from the tournament, and storing it all neatly in the equipment locker. Crystal was working in the store room with Morgana, untangling and folding up one of the two nets for the volleyball court.

"I don't know what to do about Drake," Morgana was complaining. "He hardly ever calls, and when we are together, all we seem to do is fight. I just can't seem to get him to notice me. It's always vampyre this, vampyre that."

"He loves you Morgana, very much," Crystal replied.

"How could you know?" Morgana harrumphed.

"When I -." Crystal began, and found herself at a loss for words. She really didn't want to tell Morgana what she had seen and felt when she had touched Drake's soul. It was too personal, and a little embarrassing.

"When you feed," Morgana helped. She was really curious to know what Crystal had seen when she touched Drake, and afraid to hear the answer.

"That vampyre who attacked Brendan," Crystal began again, feeling she was on safer ground here. "When I touched him, I saw every victim he had ever murdered, felt everything he had during his life."

"And with Drake?" Morgana asked, turning her back in case she did not like the answer.

"Maybe I shouldn't say anything," Crystal hedged. "Maybe he should be the one to tell you. But I wish someone felt about me that way."

A single tear rolled down Morgana's cheek as she turned and gave Crystal a quick hug. "Thank you."

And so the afternoon dragged on with Crystal feeling tired and awkward and unloved. She and Brendan had not had time to talk since she got back from the tournament, and now they had an hour to sit through detention, trying to reconnect under the watchful gaze of Mrs. Henderson. Crystal lugged a full backpack of books down the hall with Gwen and Brendan, not looking forward to the two days of homework she had to catch up on. She would get some of it done in detention, but probably not much with the distraction Brendan would offer.

Brendan slid a note to her as soon as the two sat down. It simply said, missed you. Smiling, Crystal passed it on to Gwen, who was sitting on the opposite side of her. Mrs. Henderson cleared her throat menacingly, and Crystal looked back at her homework guiltily. A few minutes later Gwen passed the note back to Crystal with a comment of her own.

Reading it quickly, she scribbled an invitation for Brendan to come to dinner, if he could clear it with the security detail assigned to him, and Crystal could clear it with Jean-Claude and April. After what happened last time permission on either front was an iffy thing.

Worried about the calls each had to make as soon as they were freed from this slow torture, and anxious to spend some real time with Brendan, Crystal found she could not concentrate on her math homework. It seemed as if her new lifetime was nothing but homework and school projects that she somehow had no time to complete. When did she get to the good stuff? Like kissing the man she loved. Or just hanging with the girls at the mall, or at a movie, or – should all the stars line up – at a night club. Of course, that would require Jean-Claude to be struck blind, and April to suffer a sudden bout of senility.

Permission to have Brendan over for supper, especially after both girls were in detention, took half a dozen calls back and forth. Too exhausted to fight on they agreed he could come if one of the Goth bands were free to escort him, and at least one of the Specialists were with them. Crystal immediately called Cantara, and begged her to come and walk them home, then called both Drake and Morgana, and arranged for his band to swing by the school at roughly the same time. With all the calling and the detention, it was nearly five-thirty and growing dark before they left the school. Perfect timing, Crystal thought, given Brendan's aversion to the sun.

Gwen and Crystal conceived this brilliant plan to invite Alvaro and Aiko to eat with them so Brendan would not feel uncomfortable. And being as earth shattering as it was, they could not understand why it was greeted with blank stares by the two adults waiting at home for them. April even went as far as to feel their foreheads, checking to see if they were developing a fever. Brendan laughed, and assured both girls he would be fine. And Alvaro, hearing of their proposed invitation, asked how either could think he could dine with anyone else when two such beauties would be their to monopolize his attention.

Crystal and Gwen frowned. Obviously everyone else in their lives had lost their marbles. It was a perfectly reasonable invitation, and the only polite thing to do. Here were two people perfect for each other, both vampyres –albeit the one did have the slightly bad habit of killing all her lovers. And Alvaro was so charming and handsome you would be totally out of your mind to dump him. Jean-Claude pointed out that Aiko was a prisoner-of-war who would like nothing better than an opportunity to kill the other six members of the proposed dinner party, and that three of those would make a better meal than the casserole April had prepared.

The battle lost, the two girls settled down to dinner with only Brendan and the adults for company. April had managed to get a quart of cow's blood from a local butcher, a man who was accustomed to such strange requests, and she had warmed it up in a kind of consommé served at room temperature. With the increase of non-human dinner guests over the last few weeks, the four residents of the brownstone had grown use to the strange diets of their guests. Crystal and Gwen really did not have to worry about Brendan feeling uncomfortable, dinner past with pleasant conversation and companionable laughter that led to all five into the living room to watch a movie together.

Crystal and Brendan snuck off to her room while April made some popcorn. Knowing they could not touch each other, neither adult raised an eyebrow. This once they would bend the 'no boys in your room' rule.

"How have you been?" Crystal asked shyly, sinking onto her bed as Brendan crossed the room to lean against the desk.

"Other than missing you," Brendan replied, "pretty good."

"I missed you too," Crystal teased, "when I wasn't chasing all those hot Salem boys."

"Was that during or after the games?" Brendan asked

playfully.

"Well," Crystal laughed, "you know. After the first hour I had a harem bigger than Kristen's. That's why the two of us had to throw down."

"Oh, so that's what happened to you," Brendan replied, ducking the pillow she threw at him.

"I'll have you know these are muscles of steel," Crystal bragged, flexing her biceps.

"Steel just gets shoddier and shoddier," Brendan clucked his tongue and laughed.

"Watch it!" Crystal threatened, still flexing, "or you'll be the first vampyre who actually can fly."

Their laughter died out, and for a long moment the two stood staring at each other across the room.

"What's wrong, Crystal?"

"I don't know, Brendan," Crystal replied quietly. "It's just what am I going to do? Our lives are so constrained by what we are that we really don't have the freedom to discover who we are. And just by living I am dragging everyone I know towards a war that seems so impossible, and so much bigger than all of us."

"None of that is really any of your fault, Crystal," Brendan replied earnestly. "You know the vampyres have been planning this war for more than seven hundred years, and you are really only a pawn on their chess board. The House of Romanov have this crazy dream that the vampyres can control the surface world. The Church and the vampyres have been dancing around this issue long before you came along."

"But -."

"Crystal," Brendan interjected, "I know you have lived many lives before this, but this has been building probably before the time of Christ. And this is not the only group of demons the Church has to contending with. This is more of a three way war, like Mr. Shepherd was explaining to us in Metaphysics class. As much as the vampyres and demons fight against us, they fight amongst themselves, and each side plays the others against themselves."

"As to your bigger question, Crystal," Brendan smiled weakly, "I haven't figured that out myself. We are both pretty young in this lifetime, and maybe we just need to give it some time."

Crystal and Brendan rejoined the others in the living room, where they watched a comedy. Crystal wedged herself in between Jean-Claude and Brendan, leaning up against Jean-Claude's shoulder and trailing a hand out towards her friend, her fingers almost brushing his thigh. The movie was a light-hearted comedy of errors that kept two high school sweethearts apart, so reminiscent of her own relationship with Brendan that Crystal could not help but shed a happy tear when the plot brought the lovers back together again. It lightened Crystal's dark mood, and by the end she was holding Jean-Claude's hand and smiling at Brendan.

Alvaro knocked at the door at ten pm to come and collect Brendan. After the movie the three students had moved into the kitchen, where they had done more chatting than homework, and now begged for more time to complete their assignments. Jean-Claude was not biting. Jean-Claude was not biting. Pouts and hang-dog expressions aside, they wanted to have Brendan back at the school by midnight, the dark of the night, when the vampyres were strongest. And April reminded the two girls that they needed to be in bed early, having been late for school that morning. A promise was a promise, and how would they be able to believe them in the future if they broke their word at the first opportunity?

It was logic Crystal and Gwen were not prepared to counter. At this age, they were learning, it was best to pick their battles. If ever they had children of their own, the two girls swore, they would at least let them finish their homework. But that kind of emotional blackmail was not going to win them any points here. Not against April.

Crystal walked Brendan down to the street door, where they had a few moments alone to say good night. After what had happened the last time there was no way Jean-Claude would allow Crystal to walk Brendan home, no matter what kind of pheromone storm she unleashed on him. Even God would have difficulty arranging her parole tonight. And with the kind of day Crystal was having, He was probably grounded for the next two weeks as well.

Sometimes Crystal regretted that Jean-Claude and April were so determined to raise her the same way they raised Gwen, and not like some demigod who would eat their souls if they did not pander to her every whim. Especially at times like this. But she respected and loved the two of them to ever behave like a spoiled princess. Even when they forced her to take Math.

Razor, Drake's little brother, came with his band. Alvaro, Cantara and the Wandering Jew came up from downstairs to escort them. They would then continue the patrol until three in the morning, when Dragrar and his band would relieve them. It was a perfect night, dark and cloudy with pockets of deep shadows littering the landscape. A perfect night for the hunter, and vampyres were nothing if not night stalkers.

"I don't like this, Alvaro," Cantara whispered as they began the walk to the school. "The vampyres have been too quiet lately."

"I agree with you," Alvaro replied. "It has been two weeks, they must be getting hungry. You two drop back to cover our six, I will take point. Razor, keep your people tight."

They were two blocks from the school and reaching that point where over-confidence warred with embarrassment to undermine their vigilance. Two parties of vampyres struck. Five in the rear, chased off by Cantara and the Wandering Jew, a second between Alvaro and the lead elements of the Goths. Both groups broke off after a couple of minutes, with the three specialists in pursuit.

The second attack came as the Goths were rushing Brendan towards the school, their column stretched out and vulnerable. Without the specialists, they were easy pickings.

A hard, sharp fight began. The thirteen Goths and Brendan outnumbered their five attackers three to one, and were still hard pressed to hold them off. Two of the vampyres reached Brendan, hammering at his ribs and head. His knee was broken, his elbow shattered. It was only minutes before the Goths fought their way back to his side, but the damage was done.

Razor sent Ember running back to the brownstone to fetch Jean-Claude and the others. Panicked, she ran back as fast as her legs could carry her, looking neither left or right, terrified that at any moment another group of vampyres would jump out of the darkness. She was crying by the time she reached the door to the brownstone, her mascara running down her cheeks and creating a racoon mask. Jean-Claude and Crystal came down to the door. Ember fell into his arms, sobbing.

"Calm down, ma petite," Jean-Claude soothed. "Take a breath, one deep breath, no?"

"Brendan's been hurt," Ember sobbed.

Crystal was already half way down the street by the time Ember and Jean-Claude thought to chase after her. Her eyes red as two pools of blood, her mind screaming with so much rage she could not form a rational thought, Crystal ran with only her desire to reach Brendan keeping her feet moving in the right direction. She ran faster than a mortal could keep up, arriving in two minutes. Jade and her sister intercepted her, holding her away from Brendan.

"He's okay, Crystal," Jade soothed. "He's still alive. And the vampyres are gone. Everyone is safe now."

Crystal was irrational and stronger than the two of them. Fortunately, Cantara and Jean-Claude arrived at the same moment. He moved in front of her, and raised a hand to catch up her chin. "Go wake up April! Go home now, Brendan needs her healing."

Snarling, she turned and ran back down the street, her nostrils flaring, catching the scent of her enemy. Almost she ignored Jean-Claude's orders, and only the knowledge that

Brendan needed help kept her from following her instinctual need to hunt. Soon. Very soon she would find those who had done this, and when she did she would not stop herself from killing them. Slow, and painfully, the way a vampyre kills its prey.

At the brownstone April shook her head in dismay, muttering to herself. She gave Crystal a quick hug, and then turned to the matter at hand. "Gwen, since you are up, you can help me ease his pain until the others come. Call Mrs. Langdon, not the younger one, but her older sister who is the registered nurse. She can set any broken bones."

After Brendan and his healers arrived, Crystal stormed about the apartment like an enraged kitten that had gotten its tail stepped on. Jean-Claude caught her up by both shoulders and looked directly into her eyes, still red and baleful.

"You cannot kill a vampyre that way, no?" Jean-Claude soothed. "Brendan is only hurt, ma petite. Remember, there is only three ways to kill a vampyre. Now go downstairs and be with the others until you calm down. April needs to concentrate if she is going to ease his pain, no?"

"There are four ways to kill a vampyre, Jean-Claude," Crystal called back as she stomped out of the apartment, slamming the door behind her. "Four ways to kill a vampyre if you are a succubus!"

In the basement Crystal ignored the others there and headed straight for Aiko's cell. Banging the door open, she looked across at the vampyre girl.

"You will take me to Vlad now!" She demanded in a petulant voice.

"I am sorry to hear that your boyfriend has been injured," Aiko replied calmly.

"Brendan is not my boyfriend!" Crystal release just a little of the anger she was holding like a ball of molten lava in her heart.

"I see," Aiko nodded. "Not even you could defeat two hundred thousand of my kind. Revenge is a dish best served cold. Very, very cold."

The numbers staggered Crystal. "I only want Vlad and that whelp of his. I will tear out their eyes and rip off their ears, then beat the both of them to death with their own intestines!"

"Our guest is right," Cantara said from the doorway.

"I am not your guest," Aiko returned, a chill in her voice as she held up the chains she wore.

"Of course you are," Cantara retorted. "We just don't want you to leave before you've overstayed your welcome. Besides, eating vampyres is bad for you little cousin. They're nothing but carbs, and will go straight to your hips."

"Not funny, Cantara," Crystal snorted.

"And yet she laughs?" Aiko commented, raising an eyebrow.

"I definitely heard a laugh too," Cantara agreed.

Crystal's eyes were beginning to fade, the blue of her irises showing at the edges. "Well, then Aiko can kill them for me. She's an assassin."

"She cannot even escape from here," Cantara pointed out. "Not even with her mist trick."

The Djinn was right. Even the one time the girl had forgotten to replace her chains, she could not cross the barrier created by the pieces of the True Cross. Embedded in the walls and doors, they effectively narrowed her world down to a four by twelve space that left her barely enough space for her exercises. But Cantara was wrong. It was not that Aiko could not reach Vlad, more so that she doubted that she was powerful enough on her own to kill such an ancient vampyre. And she very much wished to kill the one whose plans had led her to this place.

Chapter 26

It was a long night at the brownstone. They did not get the girls off to bed until well after midnight, and Jean-Claude still had work to do over the fall-out from the attack. In the debrief Razor and all three of the specialists took the blame for having fallen prey to the well co-ordinated three prong attack. While younger vampyres still felt the need to hunt their prey, Jean-Claude wasn't convinced it had been their work. The planning was far too sophisticated, and the damage had been rather superficial. Something else was going on here, and he just could not see it.

Nearing three o'clock in the morning Jean-Claude met with the three Goth leaders, Gabriel from the Choir, and Alvaro from the specialists.

"Gabriel," Jean-Claude decided. "I want you to start drawing up plans to pull back your people. I want a tighter ring around the brownstone and the academy. It feels like someone is trying to stretch our resources, and right now the Vatican cannot afford to send us any more of its Choirs."

"We will have to abandon the outer boroughs," Gabriel warned, "and that will give them staging areas on the surface should the real fighting start."

"And as long as we can keep Crystal safe," Jean-Claude countered, "we can prevent the outbreak of war. You know what is going on in the Middle East right now. There are just too few resources the Vatican can pull away from there if we fail."

"Okay," Gabriel nodded, "my people will be repositioned by the end of the week."

"Alvaro," Jean-Claude continued, acknowledging Gabriel

with a nod. "I want the specialists to concentrate on establishing control of the roof tops and alleyways. I want you to make it as dangerous for them to operate in our immediate area as possible."

Drake, Razor, Leatherface," Jean-Claude turned to the three young cadets. "I'm establishing a curfew for all students of the academy."

The three boys could not hide their dismay. No more Friday night dates at the movies, necking in the balcony or in the parking lot behind the mall.

"I am activating the three reserve bands," Jean-Claude replied, smiling at their reaction. "Drake, I need three names of those most qualified to lead them."

"Wild Willy, Doppelganger, and Black Rose," Drake replied without a second thought.

"What are you thinking, bro? Black Rose is a girl," Razor objected before Jean-Claude could say anything.

"She can kick your butt three ways to Sunday, little brother," Drake teased.

"Yeah, that's the problem. She's right spun," Razor complained. "She's as likely to trash all of us as any of the vampyres."

Black Rose was a very angry young girl. At seventeen she had been suspended from the Academy three times, all for unsanctioned violence. The last time involved their hand-to-hand combat instructor, who she had hospitalized with a broken pelvis and dislocated shoulder. If the Academy went in for such things, she would have multiple black belts in several disciplines. No-one knew why she was so angry, or anything else about her, because she seldom spoke, and then only in vulgar Latin.

"If we have to put up with Vlad's problem child, perhaps it is time he has to deal with one of mine," Jean-Claude concluded, accepting Drake's recommendations.

"Sometimes, Jean-Claude," Drake grinned at the diminutive French Man, "you're pretty devious for an old guy."

"You're not too shabby yourself," Jean-Claude teased, "for a young guy. I want two active patrols for each watch with overlapping patterns. No further out than the border of Zone B."

The Academy was a sea of very unhappy faces over the next week. By lunch all the students had heard of the attack on Brendan, and the morning announcements reminded students daily of the new curfew. Jean-Claude's name was taken in vain a thousand times of day, but their anger was feigned, barely hiding the growing fear that had gripped the student body. The attack on Brendan only confirmed what they all suspected since the dance- they were targets in these growing troubles with the vampyres. And the efforts being made to protect them were proving less than effective, leaving them feeling abandoned and distrustful.

Precisely as Kristen had promised the girls of the Ghost Sisterhood, she began to insist that all her boys walk her home each night. She lived not far from Gwen and Crystal, in a red stone five-story apartment building with a retired nun. Now in her late eighties, Sister Mary-Beth was frail and of failing health. She depended on several medications, including an inhaler that injected steroids into her system to help with her breathing. Once home, much of Kristen's evenings were taken up with caring for the elderly lady, preparing and helping to feed Mary-Beth her supper, cleaning up the apartment, and keeping the sweet old lady company until she dozed off in her chair.

In the evenings her only contact with the outside world was through chat rooms and her Facebook and My Space web pages. When Sister Mary Beth's breathing became laboured, and her inhaler was empty, Kristen panicked. She was on her cell phone immediately, first to the local pharmacy to arrange another prescription, and then to Morgana to ask her to have one of the Goth bands come by to escort her to the store. Unable to wait until they arrived, Kristen started out and hoped she would meet them before she had gone too far.

Black Rose was slim, with a boyish figure. She had a single tear tattooed beneath her right eye, and a second of a black rose that started beneath her chin and went down all the way to her iliac crest. Even in the coldest weather she wore clothing that revealed a large portion of her ink. When she got Morgana's call she scowled. She did not like the Sylph, could barely tolerate Morgana, and thought the other members of her band were a total waste of skin. If she didn't have to issue orders, she would never have spoken to any of them. She never even bothered to learn their names. Gutless Wonder seemed to work so well for almost everyone, so why bother cluttering her mind with meaningless dribble.

The night was cold and rainy. The cloud cover made it seem much darker in the ground between the pools of street light. Kristen was frightened. Her defences were not primarily physical ones, she could release a cloud of pheromones that would cause anyone caught in it to lust after her. She could also convince anyone to believe whatever she wanted them to, but even that was not very effective against a flight of hungry vampyres. Up ahead she saw a band of shadows moving towards her and at first was frighten half to death until she realized they were moving too slowly to be anything other than her friends.

And just when she was feeling comfortable the vampyres struck. Kristen used everything she could remember from her self-defence classes. She screamed to startle her attackers, she kicked, and blocked their attempts to grab her, managing to throw one into two of his companions. It was enough to give Black Rose and her friends time to catch up. Black Rose showed no mercy. She never did. She and two other Goths took up a defensive posture, staging a fighting retreat to give the others time to drag Kristen to safety. When they were far enough away that she knew the specialists and the Choir would reach them first, Black Rose sent the other two away.

Alone against five vampyres, some injured, Black Rose

fought with a tenacity born of pure hatred. As fast as the vampyres were, as strong as they were, she knew how to use their speed and strength against them. In the end, even her skill was no match. Her ribs were cracked, her knee was shattered, both arms were broken in several places, and both lungs were collapsed. She died on that cold wet sidewalk that night, but she took three of her killers with her. No one student in any of the thirteen academies had ever amassed five kills before graduating to the Choirs, and few in the Choirs outside times of crisis and war had managed such a feat. Hers was a talent the Church would surely miss in the days to come.

Two members of the specialists escorted Kristen to the drug store and back home while their companions stayed behind with the survivors of Black Rose's band to guard her body. Nothing had to be done to clean up the bodies of her killers since soon after death a vampyre begins to crumble into dust, the older the vampyre the quicker the decomposition begins. These three disappeared much too quickly to have been under two centuries old, and that information would not be long in reaching Jean-Claude.

The girl's body was another story. It was taken to the neighbourhood church, where a sympathetic mortician would prepare the body and provide a coffin in a room in the church's basement. If one wanted to hide a body whose death could not be easily explained, where better than a graveyard? Death, while tragic, was too commonplace to rouse suspicion, especially when wrapped in the usual packaging. Her blood would be washed off the sidewalk and all trace of the fight swept from the scene. No-one outside the community would ever know that Black Rose had lived, or how heroically she had died defending one of her school mates. And that's the way it needed to stay.

Black Rose had been an orphan and a loner for so long there was no one even to notify. No one to really mourn her passing except Jean-Claude. She was one of the few children he could not reach, and she spent most of her short life alone and unhappy. The only thing she had going for her was the Academy, and even there she made no effort to fit in. She was uncompromising in her hatred of the world and all humanity, and yet in the end she had done the right thing, the noble thing.

She lay in state at Saint Dismas Church for three days. The first morning after her death the entire student body of the Academy cut class and swarmed the church to mourn the death of one of their own. Father Murphy understood their hurt and their confusion, and asked if they would like him to lead them in prayers. With nothing more than their faith to fall back on, they gratefully accepted. When prayers were complete, he asked if any of the students wanted to come up and share a memory from Black Rose's life.

When no one came forward, Kristen rose and walked to the front of the church. She went up to the pulpit to the left of the altar and fought with the microphone. Two of her boys raced to assist her, the one who arrived late turning back disappointed, hanging his head as he made his way to his pew.

"I didn't know Black Rose very well," Kristen began, tentatively. "I guess none of us really did. Margaret was a very private person."

At the mention of her real name a confused murmur worked its way through the assembled students.

"You see," Kristen smiled, a tear beginning to well in her eye. "Most of us did not know her real name. She was a very difficult person to get to know, and I am afraid we never really made much of an effort until it was too late. There is a very important lesson there I think."

"We take each other for granted sometimes. We make snap judgements about each other and don't really know what someone is truly capable of, sometimes until it's too late. For me, Black Rose will forever be the girl who saved my life, the girl who might have been my friend had I taken the time to really get to know her."

Despite the tradition of male pall bearers, the Ghost Sisterhood insisted on carrying Black Rose's coffin. With Kristen reinforcing their desire, not one of the boys at school voice an objection. This, of course, meant new dresses for Crystal and Gwen, who, unlike their Goth friends owned almost nothing black. This time April brought them out shopping, escorted by Anastasia and Cantara as security. The dresses were pretty, and demur, and very reasonably priced. And as pretty as the two girls looked as they dressed the morning of the funeral, they felt no joy in wearing them.

A limousine came by the brownstone to pick them up and drive them to the church, even though it was only a few blocks away. The full Choir was in attendance, providing security for the event. As pall bearers, Gwen and Crystal sat in the front pew with the other seven members of their volleyball team. Directly behind them, Jean-Claude and April, and most of the twenty-five specialists sat. Beyond the adults, in the pews of a church that seldom saw more than forty parishioners, the entire community surrounding the Academy and the Brotherhood filled every seat and spilled out into the street. The crowd inevitably attracted reporters, who were met by Anastasia and a story about a popular girl from the local high school who lost a three year battle to cancer.

Father Murphy was joined by Bishop O'Malley to celebrate the Requiem Mass. Had any of the reporters been allowed to enter the church, his presence might have caused a sensation. As it was, they celebrated a beautiful ceremony for the daughter of the church that had fallen in a war that would forever be unknown. A choir made up of students from the Academy sang Amazing Grace to open the ceremony. Three time state champions, their voices rose to fill the small church like a host of angels. The tears started somewhere in the opening two lines and would continue throughout the mass.

At one point Jean-Claude was called up to deliver the Eulogy. Crystal and Gwen had never seen him look so crushed.

"Few of you here would know Margaret's story," Jean-Claude spoke in a quiet voice that had all of his listeners leaning forward in their seats. "Margaret was an orphan found in the wilderness sixteen years ago...."

The killings had started with sheep. When the first child had disappeared with only the bloody blankets in his cradle remaining, the local priest had written a letter asking for a priest who specialized in exorcism. As a matter of course, the letter and his suspicions about his fellow priest were forwarded to the Brotherhood.

Jean-Claude was studying documents in the Vatican Archives when he was asked by the Commander-General of the Brotherhood if he would take the lead in the investigation. Along with Gabriel and Cantara, he took the first flight out of Rome to the United States. Their destination was a rural and wild area of Wyoming. The Snowy Range, as much of Wyoming, was a wild majestic place of independent people and long, lonely stretches of open country.

Arriving in the small church in a small town of four or five buildings, they found the local priest butchered, his body tied to the crucifix over the altar, his entrails wrapped around his neck. On the befouled altar, an infant girl lay naked and tied to a strange device. It seemed obvious that they had arrived just in time to interrupt some perverse ceremony. Of Father Xavier there was no sign. Nor was there another living soul in the town. Only blood, and blood. The walls and floors of the other four buildings painted red with the blood of humans and animals and no sign of any bodies. In fact, they found no-one for miles around.

They stayed in the town for three weeks, following the scent of possible demon activity. Taking turns caring for the infant, they investigated the village and surrounding areas, searching everywhere. And then, with Cantara bird-dogging the scent for them, they followed the trail up into the Snowy Mountains to a small, lonely cabin. Here they found their first bodies, and evidence of something dark and terrible. Someone had been using the Grimorium Verum to summon demons and feed them human sacrifices. And the only living person missing, as far as an extensive search of local church records could uncover, was Father Xavier.

They also found evidence of a baby recently born to the cabin's household. Her name was Margaret.

"We brought her here to the Academy, where she lived her entire life. The Academy was her home, its student were her only family. Those of us who taught her over the years have grown to love her as a daughter. As we watched her grow, an angry, sullen child with more skill and potential than we had ever seen, we feared we would never reach that tortured soul inside."

"In dying, she taught us a lesson. In sacrificing her life for that of someone she had more reason to hate than any of us, she brought honour to this Academy, to the entire Brotherhood. She showed us despite our differences we are all God's children, and there is hope that someday we can live together in peace."

The church was utterly silent as Jean-Claude walked away from the podium. So few knew anything about the tragic beginnings of a life that had come to such an abrupt end. Many felt ashamed of what they had thought about the girl while she was alive even before Jean-Claude had shared her story with them, and now felt truly guilty. Even Crystal had never given the girl a second thought when they were in school together. She was a weird, silent girl who was slightly scary.

"We will now be making our way to the grave side, for any of you who would like to join us," Father Murphy broke the heavy silence. "For any of those not joining us at the Holy Cross Cemetery, the Brotherhood invites you to join them at the gym of the Academy for a reception."

The funeral director came up to Crystal and the girls, instructing them to come up to the front where the casket waited. Six of them would lift it onto a wheeled gurney, and then all nine would escort it out to the hearse. The girls would then travel to the cemetery in a limousine that would follow close behind. In front of the hearse, and immediately behind the limousine. In front of the hearse, and immediately behind the limousine, two heavily armoured van loaded with musclebound monks escorted the body to the funeral. Behind followed a procession of eclectic of vehicles, including Jean-Claude's battered and rusty Forenza. The odd procession attracted some attention between the church and the graveyard, but for most of the New Yorkers who saw it, the funeral was just another bloody delay in the endless traffic tie-ups the plagued the city.

Gwen and Kristen stood at either end of the casket, Morgan and the other girls at its side, and Crystal led the procession. April was right to insist on flats. Crying, walking and carrying a casket were hard enough without having to contend with the heels the girls had wanted to buy. Crystal eyed the open grave. It seemed so far away, even though it was only twenty or thirty feet from the roadway where the hearse had come to rest. Black Rose had always been a small girl for someone capable of so much violence, and her remains were not very heavy. The coffin was another matter altogether, but with one of the two Nordic twins on either side it was not the problem many thought they would experience.

Father Murphy had baptized Margaret, so it seemed only fitting that he gave the graveside prayers. `Ashes to ashes, dust to dust.' The words echoed through Crystal's mind. How many times, in how many languages had she heard those words over the years. It never got easier to say good bye to friends, and was even harder to say good bye to someone you only got to know after they had died. `You'll bloom again, black rose,' she thought as the casket was lowered, and one by one the mourners came to toss a handful of dirt on the casket. `Somewhere.'

Chapter 27

The reception broke up just before five pm, as it was starting to get dark. Until darkness fell was beginning to become a watchword amongst the households of the Brotherhood community. Jean-Claude saw his girls safely home, and waited until April got them organized with their homework before slipping out. He was immensely proud of his two youngest. Crystal and Gwen had done a good job as pallbearers, and later had acted as hosts at the reception. All the girls from the volleyball team had done well, but it was a task none of them should have had to shoulder, and Jean-Claude's rage was simmering.

It was hard enough to bury a child, and this poor lamb had suffered so much in life. Vlad was worse than a fool. His over-reaching ambitions were bringing their two people to the edge of a bloodbath that could only become genocide. There were billions of humans on earth, and while the majority of their weapons could not kill, they could hurt enough to allow more primitive means to finish the job. And there were even greater dangers here, ones that could destroy everything. They two were not the only players in this war, and the others were bigger and more terrifying than both peoples combined.

Jean-Claude had sent the usual signal for a meeting. Over the years a series of methods had been developed to communicate, all of them ridiculous when the two could have used a cell phone or drop each other an email. But electronic communications were monitored, and could be far too easily intercepted. And with all that steel and concrete between them wireless was a major miracle. Both sides depended too much on secrecy, for differing reasons, to trust any non-secure form of communication. Far better to tag a subway train with apparent gang graffiti, or release a goat into the lower tunnel. Perhaps not as efficient, but too commonplace on the one hand, and too bizarre on the other to raise any real suspicion.

Vlad was waiting for him on the chosen rooftop.

"My condolences, old friend," Vlad greeted. "I assure you the council has no part in these attacks."

"Your son again?" Jean-Claude asked mildly, hiding both his incredulity and his anger. He no more believed Vlad that he believed Martians were controlling the White House.

"Yes," Vlad frowned, a look of distaste crossing his features. "He has – how do you human phrase it – run away from home. He has taken a small dissatisfied group with him. Even with my people there are those misguided individuals who are pushing for war."

"We all have our problem children," Jean-Claude concurred. "Fortunately ours grow out of it so much sooner. Do you require assistance searching the tunnels for him?"

"I do not believe he is still underground," Vlad replied, brushing off the offer. "If he were my patrols would have found some trace of them – unless they have gone into the underdark. If so, the Eaters of the Dead will take care of our little problem. In light of these attacks –. There are places on the surface where my kind can hide."

"I see," Jean-Claude nodded. `Did he think I am that much of a fool that I would waste resources searching every abandoned building in New York?' "I would send you the three bodies of those who Black Rose killed, but you know they do not survive. Perhaps one might have been your son?"

"Three?" Vlad hissed at the obvious dig.

Jean-Claude shrugged. "We each have our problem children. Black Rose was a very violent young girl with demons of her own, no?"

….violent young girl with demons of her own… The phrase echoed through Vlad's mind as he made his way back to Upyr. Jean-Claude had delivered his message, but what the devil did it mean? Was he telling him there were more specialists than Vlad was aware of, or that his own people had been compromised? It was rare, but not impossible. Even vampyres could be possessed by demons. Fortunately, Vlad had kept his true plans close to his vest. No-one knew the entire plan, and those who knew anything were only told enough to carry out their orders.

Shadow was waiting in his office when Vlad arrived. That was another way he was protecting his overall plans, by using outside contractors whenever he could. The Hand spoke with no-one. Outside of Shadow, none of the other four would know the object of their mission until the very last minute.

"How is your master these days?" Vlad asked, opening up a locked drawer on his desk to retrieve an envelope. It contained nothing more than a bank draft.

"He is anxious to see you succeed," Shadow bowed politely, "as we all are."

"Very soon, my friend," Vlad replied. "Very, very soon. There will be one more job for you and your Hand when this one is complete. It would be wise not to return to Japan too soon after this one."

"Very well, Sama Romanov."

Shadow left as quietly and unseen as he came. Drifting as a mist through the tunnels, passing by guard posts, sensed but not seen. As he returned to his family, his thoughts returned to his daughter. Aiko had not returned to him after their last mission. Having drunk her blood, as he had the blood of all his children, he was sure he would have sensed her death. Even now he could sense his four children who were waiting for him in a farmhouse at the edge of the city, still feeding on the family who had lived their. Of Aiko he felt nothing. She was either hiding from him or captured. If hiding, he would find and kill her. And if captured, he would kill her for having dishonoured the clan. Either way she was dead to him.

Ji, his new son that had replaced her, was bulkier and stronger than any of the others. While not as fast as Aiko, his strength would prove useful on this mission. It was the first time he had attempted to break into an American prison, let alone free a prisoner from death row. He imagined it would be a bloody night's work. He smiled at the thought. Shadow thought nothing of killing, not in the same way his children in the Hand relished it, but the challenge of each mission was electrifying. The more challenging, the greater the gift from the gods, the larger the adrenaline rush he would ride.

The living room of the farm house was a bloody mess. The desiccated bodies of their victims still lay where they fell, the dismembered pieces scattered like chaff across the floor. Shadow retired up to one of the rooms to meditate. Tomorrow night they would begin the first leg of their cross country trek, one that would carry them to the ranch of an arms dealer in Arizona. There they would meet up with the Mexicans, and arrange for some of the equipment and services they would require to free this man. The arms dealer and his business were legal, his clientele anything but. While there was always the off-chance that some law enforcement agency was watching, the ranch seemed the perfect place to set up their meeting. Out in the open, surrounded by outbuildings in the dark, there was little chance of their words being intercepted.

Father Xavier sat in a cell on death row of a Texas prison. He no longer referred to himself by his old name. He was tried and convicted of the ritual murder of twenty-seven children under the name of Jute Wilkins. The authorities had finally caught up with him on a small religious commune somewhere outside of Waco Texas. He had said nothing throughout his arrest, trail and conviction, merely sat smiling his knowing little smile. Even as each and every appeal failed, his smile never wavered. He knew that his overlords would deliver him from his enemies and reward him with their deaths for all his years of faithful service.

He admitted to himself some small moments of doubt with his execution only two weeks away. The defrocked priest renewed his faith with memories of the children's cries of pain as he cut out their entrails, offering up their small pain wracked bodies to his masters. How skilled he had become in these last years at prolonging his victims pain, at keeping them alive long enough for the great ones to feed long a deeply on their terror. He relived his disappointment at each death, when his sacrifices were delivered from his tender mercies, and the sense of power and sexual tension slipped away from him. Xavier would know moments of great depression as these memories returned to him, memories of his ultimate failure, betrayed by the frailty of the human physiology.

His lawyers claimed he was insane. But no. He was a true visionary, a man on the verge of creating a new world order. A man always betrayed by the weakness of his victims. That is why this new offer intrigued him so. To be offered a Succubus to play with. It could be nothing less than a sign from his masters. He drooled at the thought, becoming aroused as his mind created such delicious images of what he could do to her....

In two weeks they would find the house after a nosy neighbour alerted the authorities. The press would dub it the `Vampyre Murders'. Had the discovery occurred a week earlier it may have changed the outcome – such were the plans of men and demons. In the same van once used by another team of Vlad's operatives, Shadow and the Hand drove down the highway heading west. They would drive only at night, finding shelter along the way at various out of the way motels or farmhouses. Empty buildings were preferred, although the added bonus of a quick meal was never turned down, except when the Hand was trying to hide its trail.

Their first stop-over was at a small motel well off the main highway. Nestled in a grove of ancient trees, whose orange, yellow and red foliage was still thick enough to leave the building and parking lot deep in shadows, the motel looked dark and deserted. The day was exceptionally bright and sunny, even for this late in the fall, a day a vampyre absolutely hated. With the blinds closed, and the beds pushed away from the windows, the five members of the Hand sat around waiting out the sun. Ji and Dan-hu were playing a game of Chopsticks, tapping each other's hands at lightning speeds. Shadow was meditating, still aware of the others as they played games or cleaned their equipment.

His eyes flew open with the knock on the door. His sons quietly tucked their equipment under the beds, and sat up, ready for action. Signalling for them to stand down, Shadow moved to answer the door.

A state trooper stood in the threshold, his face shrouded by the brim of his hat and the sunglasses he wore. Shadow did not approve of anything that impaired the vision. Any advantage you gave your enemy was foolish.

"Officer," Shadow greeted in a soft, quiet voice. "How may we help you?"

"Charlie, who owns the place," the state trooper replied, "was a little concerned. We don't usually get strangers here, and five men booking one room made him a little suspicious. May I ask what you are doing in these parts?"

"Just passing through," Shadow explained. "My sons will be attending the University of Phoenix."

"Four sons in university," the officer whistled. "That must have put you back a pretty penny."

"Only two," Shadow replied. "The others are too young yet. Fortunately, your American Universities are much cheaper than those in Japan."

"May I ask why you just didn't fly directly to Phoenix?" He asked.

"Sightseeing." Shadow replied. "We were told the drive across your country is very scenic. Unfortunately we flew into New York quite late, and spent most of the night driving."

"Sorry to have disturbed you," the officer apologized. "I'll let you get back to your rest."

The remainder of the trip to the ranch in southern Arizona went without incident. Two of the remaining three days were spent in abandoned buildings, the last in a farm house well away from the highway, the old man who was it's lone occupant conveniently having a heart attack when they broke in. On the fourth night they arrived at the ranch. Home of one of the most eccentric mortals they had ever encountered, he met them on a Harley Davison that had two machine guns mounted on either of the front forks, and a flamethrower off of a backrest that rose nine feet into the air and ended in a dragonhead. It looked formidable, but was too unstable to ride.

The man was a clown who sold well-made weapons. The men they were meeting were anything but. Hard and pitiless, they feared death as little as his own Hand, and cared for their fellow mortals about as much as a mosquitoes. Not men Shadow would normally trust. Then again he trusted no-one. He merely killed those who failed him.

"Have your other guests arrived?" Shadow inquired.

"In the main house," the ancient biker cackled. "What do you think of my toy?"

"I think it will one day be the death of you," Shadow replied, leading the way into the house, the lunatic laughter of his host following him.

Jesus Morte was wanted in almost every Latin American country. A prominent scar about an inch thick ran from one side of his collar bone to the other, a small revolver was tattooed on his right cheek, a pair of tumbling dice on his left. The scar was how he got his name – Jesus is dead in Spanish, Dead Christ in English. Most men were afraid of him, but Shadow was not most men. The scores this mortal had killed could not match the numbers Shadow had accumulated in one of his centuries of life.

"Mi amigo," Jesus greeted in a show of bonhomie. "You have arrived at last."

"As we said we would." Shadow replied. He had no intention of becoming this man's friend, and wished only to get down to business.

"A drink?" Jesus offered, snapping his fingers at one of the women he and his people had brought with them. "Our host has an excellent bar."

"No." Shadow replied.

"I do not like to do business with a man who does not drink!" Jesus declared menacingly.

"Nevertheless," Shadow replied calmly. "You will do business with us."

Jesus laughed suddenly. Whether he recognized the threat behind Shadow's words, and saw something darker and more bloody than himself, or was truly drunk and bipolar, he let it go.

"Bueno! Let us talk business."

"Shall we take in the night air?" Shadow suggested. He trusted nothing. The mortals had too many means to overhear a conversation for them to talk within a building. Outside would be safer.

Four of Jesus' thugs followed them out into the darkness, hands on the guns they wore beneath their jackets. Shadow left his four sons behind. Five mortals represented no real threat, especially when none of them had Brotherhood training or weapons. Let the mortal think he was safe for the moment.

Outside, the two men stopped behind one of the larger outbuildings. Jesus waved to his men to halt just outside hearing range.

"What you want will cost ten million." Jesus opened up the discussion.

Shadow handed over an envelope with the bank draft.

"What is this shit?" Jesus demanded.

"It is a bank draft on a bank in the Cayman Islands as you requested," Shadow replied. "Half now, half when the job is completed."

"You do not trust me, jefe?" Jesus demanded.

"I trust no-one," Shadow replied, never losing his cool. This man was a fool, always loosing his temper. He wondered if Vlad had made the right choice, although he was not in the habit of questioning his superiors.

Jesus laughed loudly. "Bueno! Come, let's go toast our new business arrangement, eh, amigo."

Half a night and a day with this egotistical cockroach was almost enough to make Shadow rip out his throat. If this man crossed him he would need no motivation to kill him. Too many of his missions lately had relied on mortals, and the last one had cost him one of his favourite daughters. As soon as politeness would allow, Shadow retired to one of the rooms to meditate. He let his thoughts drift until he had centred himself, and then sought the link to Aiko. She was still a blank, a void that had dropped off the face of the earth – neither dead, nor living. The only people who could do that were the Brotherhood, and that left only one question: was she a voluntary guest or a prisoner.

Jesus and his crew were just kicking their drinking into high gear when Shadow and his Hand were preparing to leave.

"Hey Jefe!" Jesus called. "Where are you going, amigo? The party is just starting."

"It is time for us to leave," Shadow replied, still centred.

"What? At night?" Jesus asked, laughing. "Are you like vampyres or something?"

"Something like that," Shadow replied, showing his fangs as he turned from the mortal.

Back in the van, Shadow returned to his meditation. Ji was driving, and Dan-hu was riding shot gun, his two older sons working over their equipment. He had long since determined that Vlad was a fool, trusting the very ones he sought to destroy. Even the knowledge he used to move the Vampyre nations on this dangerous path had been collected by the humans. Mortals were food, a source of pranic energy that gave him strength, and a wise man did not play with his food. First, they were sent to fetch an item only a mortal could wield, and now a mortal to wield what could only be a weapon. Only sorrow could lie down this path.

It took two nights to drive from Arizona to Texas, two nights and a day for Shadow to meditate and find no answers. When they reached the cabin they had rented, he turned his mind to the mission at hand. Tomorrow night they would enter the prison. With their ability to dematerialize, to become a mist, entering was no problem – exiting with the mortal would all depend on timing. And depending on mortals was too dangerous. If the Mexican and his people failed to show up on schedule, their mission would fail. Shadow hated to have his honour rely on something so fragile as a mortal, and so unreliable as Jesus had seemed.

The night of the assault the five vampyres began to prepare early. Bowing before a shrine set up to their ancestors, they began dressing in the traditional garb of their clan. First the shinobi shozoku of a blackish grey colour to better blend into the shadows, the split-toed tabi boots, and the obi belt. They bowed and prayed before slipping on each set of clothing, armouring themselves with the honour of the clan against evil spirits that wished to bring them ill luck. And next their weapons, the throwing star, the katana, tanto daggers, and tekagi-shuko – a claw like weapon good for close quarters.

Prayers completed, the five slipped out into the night, heading for the prison on foot. As the night deepened, they crossed the wilderness, avoiding roads and settled areas where unwanted eyes might linger. If all went as planned, they would reach the prison just before midnight, when their powers were the strongest, and the guards just coming on shift were settled into their routine. But getting in to the death row facilities had never been the problem. Any ventilation shaft or unbarred window would offer them unseen access, coming out with a mortal who could not become incorporeal at will had always been the problem.

The prison, a four hundred and seventy acre facility surrounded by chain link fence and concrete towers, sat shrouded in pools of light and shadows. It sombre putty-grey concrete buildings stood out like cardboard silhouettes against the lighter black of the night sky. From their vantage point on a low rise not far from the imposing chain link and razor wire fence, the facility looked deserted. Not even the guards in the nearest tower were visible. Human interlopers would need to cut the wire of the fence, and would run the risk of discovery at each point between the hill and the fence, and again from the fence to the shadows of the buildings beyond. The visibility gave the prison a security many others might not enjoy.

A small pocket of mist drifted down out of the hills towards the fence. No one noticed that it moved in the opposite direction of the breeze that was blowing fitfully from the south. It was not something anyone was looking for, they were there to keep people in – or out when the protestors gathered to mark an execution. Unobserved and unnoticed, the mist continued its progress in towards the buildings. Its meanderings unerringly centred on a two-story building, where it seemed to hover, as if studying its approach. It crawled up the wall, disappearing into the darker shadows that clung to the roof. Here, a ventilation shaft seemed to vacuum it up, even though here too the flow of air was in the opposite direction.

Only one pool of mist remained on the roof, and soon that too disappeared into the shadows nestled about the ventilation shafts. Inside, on the second floor, where the most dangerous offenders were kept locked away in a special isolation ward, the pool of mist solidified into four ninjas.

"Holy shi-." The guard clutched his throat, his words drowned in a gurgle of blood as a throwing star found its mark.

A second fell, a dagger embedded in his eye. There would be no alarm for the moment, but that would change the once they opened the door to their targets cell. Everything from this point on depended on precision timing.

"Now my son," Shadow whispered towards the roof.

Above, the mist resolved itself into the fifth member of the Hand. He worked swiftly and silently, unravelling a string of C-4 putty already rolled out and ready to shape. He pressed this into a rough circle on the chip dust surface of the roof. Primer cord and detonator were quickly assembled, and word passed down to those waiting below.

Ji moved up to the cell bars. Other prisoners attempted to look out through the slots they were fed, but the solid doors offered little visibility. In a show of strength that would have given the designers of the cell a heart attack, the youngest member of the Hand ripped the door off its hinges. Alarm bells rang throughout the prison. No sooner had the claxon shattered the silence of the night, no sooner had the four vampyres ducked out of the hall and into Xavier's cell, then a loud explosion rent the air. Dust and debris filled the hallway, obscuring the sight of the guards responding to the alarm. Before the dust cleared, the four vampyres and their escapee were up through the hole rent into the ceiling, and were standing on the roof.

Spot lights lit the prison grounds and swept the rooftops. The six stood, looking up at the night sky, waiting. As the first shots rang out towards them they were still waiting, Shadow experiencing the first of many qualms. Where were that Mexican and his people?

The thump thump thump of a helicopters blades rose above the noise of the sirens and gunfire. Black as the night sky, it swept out of the hills and over the fence of the prison. It stopped, hovering above the six fugitives. As it circled, Shadow took Xavier up onto his back and leapt aboard. Two others of his Hand leapt aboard when the co-pilot complained.

"We are too heavy!" He screamed over the whine of the engine. "We can take no more!"

Shadow nodded, calling down to his two remaining sons.

"Meet us at the cabin. Go, with the wind."

In a blink of an eye they dematerialized, a strange mist that disappeared into the darkness. When the helicopter turned and raced over the night enshrouded hills, there was nothing left of the five invaders who had engineered the escape of the most dangerous prisoner at Allan B. Polunsky Unit. Scheduled for execution in a little over week, the A.P.B. was out over the wire seconds behind the disappearance of the helicopter. A call went out to the sheriff's department, and it had two of its own helicopters in the air within fifteen minutes of the break out, but the fugitives' aircraft had disappeared.

Those who escaped by foot were already at the cabin when the helicopter touched down. Shadow jumped out of the aircraft, Xavier riding on his back, and ducked beneath the whirling blades. The moment his feet touched the ground, he was off on the run across country, leading the four members of his Hand towards the distant state border. The initial search would be in the immediate vicinity of the prison, and within minutes road blocks would be set on every highway leading out of the area, with the strongest presence towards the Mexican border. Helicopters from other counties were already on the way, searching for the aircraft the fugitives had used in their daring escape, and monitoring traffic on the highways and back roads, where a lone vehicle would stick out this late at night.

Unfamiliar with the speeds at which vampyres could travel on foot, the drag net would fall short a good fifty miles. Just before dawn they crossed the border into Oklahoma, and took shelter in an abandoned barn. A new vehicle would be waiting for them in a small town about half a night's run from their current location. In another three days from then, they would be in New York City, their fugitive hidden deep within its tunnels, where no mortal law enforcement agent dared to go. What happened then to the creepy little man, with his knowing smile and bloodshot eyes, Shadow did not care. He had one more task to complete until he was again on a plane headed toward Japan, where the mortals behaved with some level of sophistication, and his ancestors were close at hand to protect him.

It was two in the morning. Everyone was sleeping in the Beaucour residence, both girls camped out in the living room amidst the refuse of their homework. The throw-away cell phone at his bedside screamed for attention. Switched up every week, Jean-Claude was usually guaranteed twelve uninterrupted hours after each new phone came into service. All that had changed after the death of Black Rose. Everything had become more immediate, more real, and his people were displaying a new efficiency that would have made him proud at any other time.

Groping sleepily for the cell phone and his glasses, Jean-Claude swore in French under his breath.

"Yes, no?" He answered groggily.

"Which is it?" Gabriel teased. "It can't be both."

"It is late, no?" Jean-Claude complained.

"Turn on CNN then call me back."

This meant turning on the light, of course, and immediate blindness. During the trip out to the living room, where his babies were sleeping, he barked his shins so many times he ran out of swear words. Sometimes God tested him in ways that would drive a lesser man insane. He had brought the brownstone thinking it was more room than a simple monk would ever need, and now he doubted the White House was large enough to contain all the children in his life.

Crystal woke as he turned on the television, immediately turning down the volume to decibels more suited to human ears. MTV would be the death of everyone over thirty in the near future, and the way his heart was slamming against his ribcage, his fiftieth heart attack was only moments away.

"Jean-Claude?" She asked through a yawn. "What is it?"

"Nothing to worry about, ma petite," he replied. "Just some news about a man I used to know, no?"

She plopped herself into his lap, blankets and all as he

changed the channel. She was getting too big for this. If she did not outgrow it soon, Jean-Claude would have to invest in a bigger lap.

"....again," the announcer from CNN continued in an excited voice, "we have confirmed reports of a daring prison break-out from the Allan B. Polunsky unit near Livingston Texas. As you may remember, John, this prison houses the state's death row inmates."

"Sorry to interrupt," the anchor broke in. "We have just received word that the escaped prisoner is Jute Wilkins, who was convicted of the ritual slaying of twenty-seven children in 2005. He was scheduled for execution next week."

"That's right, Pauly," John continued from the field. "Early reports indicate that an unknown number of assailants dressed as Ninjas broke into the prison. They then blew a hole in the roof -."

The camera panned to take in a view of building twelve, now crowned by ring of mobile lights and the stark shadows they created.

"All the suspects then escaped in a helicopter...."

"Who is it? Crystal demanded, resting her head against his chest.

"Just a real bad man Gabriel and I once knew," Jean-Claude replied, stroking her hair. "Come, let's get you settled back down. I need to call Gabriel, he will be upset."

"He was the man who killed Black Rose's parents, wasn't he?" Crystal asked, displaying that moment of intuition that always surprised parents when it came from their children.

"....authorities believe that one of the assailants may have been wounded, judging by the blood found on the scene...."

"Merd!" Jean-Claude breathed as he switched off the television, turning back to Crystal. "Yes. We will talk about it more, tomorrow. Right now I need to call Gabriel."

In his room, Jean-Claude picked up the cell phone, hitting one number to dial Gabriel.

"Did you catch the part about the blood?" Gabriel asked as

he answered the call.

"Send someone down to clean that up," Jean-Claude made a face, as if he had just eaten something very rotten. "We can't let them test that. And Gabriel, start making plans to strike Upyr. A, how do you call it, pre-emptive strike. I do not want that man reaching there."

Chapter 28

A long night with no sleep and still Jean-Claude had a classroom of little angels to care for the next morning. Unfortunately, someone had released the demon sugar amongst his flock of lambs. Some of them were vibrating so much that at first he feared they were possessed. A rousing game of Duck, Duck, Goose, one that involved more chasers than sitters, burned off much of their excess energy. It also robbed him of the last of his own. After the last of his charges was picked up and on his way home, hopefully for a long nap, Jean-Claude sat in his office over a well deserved coffee. He looked up at a knock on his door to find a small, Chinese man standing in the threshold.

"May I help you?" He asked.

"Our mutual friend in Rome asked that I stop by," the other man replied.

"How is my dear friend?" Jean-Claude asked, his expression neutral.

"Not well, I'm afraid," the Chinese gentleman replied. His English was well cultured. "He has misplaced an item that is of concern to both of you, and feared he might have left it here in New York."

"Please assure him that I will make an immediate search, no?" Jean-Claude replied, a chill running up his spine. "May I offer you some tea, or coffee?"

"I thank you for the offer," his guest replied. "Unfortunately, I have other messages to deliver, and an early flight to catch. I wish you luck, Jean-Claude."

When his guest had left, Jean-Claude picked up his cell phone and pressed a familiar number. "Gabriel, get a hold of Alvaro and Cantara. Pull the six cadet leaders from class. Meet me at my apartment. I will be there in twenty minutes."

Those he had summoned were still arriving when Jean-Claude's car screeched to a halt in front of the brownstone. What was going on here, and how did it all come unravelled so fast? He ran up the stairs, taking them two at a time despite his bad knees. The last of those summoned to this meeting were climbing the stairs just behind him, and the others were waiting in the living room, where April was serving coffee and cold drinks. He accepted the hug she greeted him with, and then turned, grim-faced to the assembled men and women.

"The Hallaf of Abraham was stolen from the Vatican," Jean-Claude began without preamble. "Our sources believe it is already here in New York."

"Christ!"

"Yes," Jean-Claude replied in a mild rebuke. "We can use all the prayers we can get right now."

A forced laugh rose, everyone recognizing it for the gallows humour it was.

"Gabriel, I want you to move all our people to block every entrance to Upyr," Jean-Claude ordered quietly. It would be him who started the war after all.

"We only know of eight entrances," Gabriel warned. "There is no guarantee that there are not more."

"Move five of the specialists to the school," Jean-Claude replied after a moments thought, "another five here at the brownstone. Take the rest down into the tunnels. Have them rove around looking for any sign of another entrance. We cannot allow Xavier to reach Upyr. I want him killed on sight."

The room fell silent. In all the years these people had known Jean-Claude, he had never issued a kill order. He was a pacifist. A man of peace.

"Are you sure, Jean-Claude?" Alvaro asked, making sure the man knew what was in his heart.

"No, Alvaro," Jean-Claude replied honestly. "How could we ever be sure about such a judgement, no? The man is either a tool of Vlad, and will kill the child. Or he will betray Vlad....."

Alvaro nodded, accepting Jean-Claude's judgement.

The Academy was beginning to look more like a military base preparing to deploy than a high school. The Goth bands ran around gathering equipment, moving out to their muster points, not as organized units, but more like a gaggle of teenagers heading to a hockey tournament, or a baseball game. All the Wiccan girls were busy helping their covens preparing for the expected casualties, charging crystals, organizing first aide kits, and cleaning off the evocation grids. At first Crystal helped Gwen and April, until her lack of understanding of what was happening began to make her feel useless. And then she escaped, as she had all too often over the past weeks, down into the basement to spend time with Aiko. Two fish out of water, exiles lost in a world neither felt like they belonged.

Vlad sat in his office, waiting word of his latest project when a guard burst in looking harried and travel worn. Vlad frowned. Had something gone wrong?

"My Lord!" The guard cried. "The mortals have blockaded the city. Large bands are at eight of the entrances!"

That left only three entrances clear, one of them Vlad's private escape tunnel. Of the two known to the general public, one was an emergency exit that came out on the Hudson River.

"Gather sixteen flights," Vlad ordered. "You are to fight them, but no deaths. It is important they believe they have us pinned in. Do you understand?"

"Yes, My Lord," the guard captain replied. "No deaths. Make the mortals believe they have us pinned in."

"Good, go now!"

Vlad sat back and watched the guard move off. Shadow and his people were still two days away from New York City. If his people could only keep the Brotherhood distracted until then, Shadow and his Hand could slip in through the last undiscovered tunnel. If only he could avoid any deaths, except for that of the girl. His plans were far more sophisticated than his father's had ever been, and had never really included a pitched battle with the Church. There was more than one way to conduct a war, and not all wars were won on the field of battle. The Vietnam War was a prime example of that, where the rebels had won the propaganda war back home in America, and taken the heart out of their enemy.

His victory would be even more subtle than even this. His enemies would not even know they were at war until it was over, and New York City would be the proving grounds for his new strategy.

Deep underground, the opening moves in what would become a two-day running battle were in progress. The vampyres' strategy was simple, break out at three points with two or three flights, and retreat back into the city. Periodically, they would probe the Brotherhood lines at different points, keeping them guessing, and unable to consolidate their own troops at any point.

Drake and his band were with Gabriel and two squads of the Vatican Choir, guarding the nearest entrance to the brownstone. He was thinking of Morgana, who leaned against his side, and Crystal, who waited in the apartment above their heads. He thought a lot about Black Rose, who might still be alive if he had not recommended her to Jean-Claude, and Brendan, who was alive because she had been where he had placed her. All his life he had been training for this moment, and now he wondered if all that training would mean anything. Who really knew how many entrances to that ant warren the vampyres called home really existed? Even now, as they waited here, they could be making a raid on the brownstone, and everything they had sacrificed and struggled for over the years would be for nothing.

'Pre-battle nerves,' Gabriel had called it. He suffered from the same doubts before each mission, he had confessed to Drake, even when the opponents were merely human back in his days with the Marines. The combat-hardened veteran who led one of the Vatican's elite Choirs stood leaning against the wall of the tunnel, an unlit, half-smoked cigarette dangling from his lips. Gabriel didn't look as if anything in or out of this world would phase him.

The first vampyre to emerge leapt out almost on top of them. Gabriel tripped him up with a bolo-type weapon, taking his feet from under him. Drake was in the forefront of those who moved up to assist Gabriel, armed with a shillelagh. Most of the opponents on both sides were using blunt implements, his fellow Goths using baseball bats. The whole engagement reminded him more of an old school rumble than a pitched battle. Drake jammed his nearest opponent in the ribs moments before some kind of club slammed into his shoulder.

Even though the Brotherhood outnumbered their opposition three-to-one, they were pushed back three levels before they could contain the break out. Morgana and Drake limped into the Brownstone, where Drake insisted on reporting to Jean-Claude before he would except any treatment for his shoulder.

"Okay Monsieur Drake," Jean-Claude greeted the cadet, "let us hear your report before April grounds the both of us, no?"

"The vampyres broke out in three locations," Drake replied, holding up his arm to illustrate his point. "We managed to contain them at all three locations. We took some injuries, but no deaths have been reported on either side."

The apartment looked more like a war room than a home. Alvaro and Crystal stood over one of the only maps of the tunnel system, moving coloured markers over its surface to plot the movement of both factions.

"I should be down there, doing something," Crystal complained.

"You are doing something," Alvaro winked at her. "You are keeping me from panicking. Besides, your presence would only make things worse. Your beauty is too tempting."

April and Gwen came up to collect Drake.

"Come along now, young man." April said firmly. "We'll put that arm of yours back in place. A little boneset will help with the pain, and some camomile tea will help you relax."

When they were gone, Jean-Claude turned to Alvaro. "Any word from Cantara and the specialists?"

"Nothing yet," Anastasia replied, straightening up. "They are deeper down than any of our other patrols."

If any other entrances existed they would begin deep in the tunnels, down in the area the vampyres referred to as the Underdark. There was no messing around with non-lethal weapons here. Cantara and every member of her fifteen man patrol carried swords, and the dagger-shaped rosaries of the Church issued apotropaics. This was the territory of the Eaters of the Dead, where even the other vampyres treaded lightly. More demon than human, they came in more shapes and sizes than even the Church lore masters could catalogue, and all of them deadly. They were not fussy about how their prey died, as long as the body rotted enough before they actually fed on them.

Cantara paused. She held out a hand to halt those following behind her, perhaps a useless gesture in the dark tunnel. A rustling sound came from up ahead. Maybe only a rat. Maybe a set of leathery wings. The kind that came attached to a brutal hulk with large teeth, white fishy skin, and claws eight inches long.

"Did you hear that?" She whispered.

"Hear it," the Wandering Jew complained. "I can smell it."

The faint smell of sulphur and rotten flesh drifted down the tunnel, propelled by a sweep of his wings in the stagnant air.

"How about I go high you go low?" The Wandering Jew suggested.

"Okay," Cantara countered, "I go high and you go low."

She ran forward, calling back as she caught the first sight of their opponent, "or maybe middle!"

The Vetal was a brute. His wingtips brushed the roof of the tunnel, and his shoulders were not much lower. He had no eyes, a flat nose that was mostly nostril, and a mouth full of jagged teeth that stuck out in every direction. It was a good thing three of her companions had followed behind, but in the close quarters the brute had the advantage. It screamed a challenge and charged.

Cantara met its charge with her sword, the curved blade of her Saif cutting a deep slash just above its rib cage. It bellowed a challenge. The Wandering Jew's dagger struck its left knee cap. It roared and charged again. Three shots from slings bounced off its head, and Cantara opened a slash across its abdomen and forearm. The bloody ghoul was not even slowing down. Three daggers left the Wandering Jew's hands, two of them finding marks on its muscular body. Using his hand as a stepping stool, Cantara leapt through the air, sword flashing. Her sharp blade sliced through its neck, black ichor spurting in a fountain that drenched the djinn as the two parts of its body fell on either side.

"Damn!" Cantara swore, wiping the black liquid from her eyes and hair, "I've been slimed!"

"It looks good on you," the Wandering Jew teased.

"In that case," Cantara threatened, teasingly, "come here and kiss me."

"Not on your life." He replied, offering her a rag he carried to clean his daggers.

"That brute was too ancient to just be wandering around these tunnels," Khalil commented. "He was guarding something."

The Almas was right. The Sanguinarians treated the Eaters of the Dead like pets, and often used them the same way humans used guard dogs.

"We must be close," Cantara ordered. "Keep your eyes sharp and your weapons sharper."

"My Lord Vlad!" Lord Jaeger burst into his office, near purple with rage. "The Guard has just reported that a band of the Church's specialists are nearing the Emergency exit. They are all here! It is time to strike, not cower behind our wives skirts!"

"My dear brother-in-law," Vlad replied calmly. "You have never been one to grasp subtleties."

Vlad paused, studying the other man. What little reason he may once have possessed seemed to have left him since his son's death. "Did you think that all of this was ever about waging a war against six billion mortals, a war we cannot win along traditional lines?"

"But -."

"Why, my dear Lord Jaeger, do you think we have invested so much of this nation's wealth into genetic and stem cell research?" Vlad teased. The man was really a odious fool, much like his sister. "Did you imagine our breeding program was designed to create some hulking brute of a super-soldier? Someone to fight our battles in the daylight?"

"Certainly we cannot control the surface world without that," Lord Jaeger replied in a pompous show of outrage.

"The Church's need to keep our existence a secret is there greatest weakness and our greatest strength," Vlad explained, ever so patiently. "No, my friend, this has always been about one death, and one death only. Once the last of their allies who can truly see us for what we are is dead, we are free to move as we please."

"If your New Breed are not soldiers," Lord Jaeger demanded, "what are they?"

"In two years there is a Mayoral campaign in New York City," Vlad explained. "Our candidate will have the charisma of our people, the wealth of a nation, and a platform of law and order the citizens will be crying for."

"All that money to take control of one, measly city!"

"Very well," Vlad conceded, or seemed to. "Since you are so insistent on seeing battle, you can lead the flights against the specialists when the time comes. You can even take my son and his rabble with you."

Shadow and his Hand had taken shelter in an old, abandoned school house. The search for the mortal had gone national, and all day police cars passing on the highway not far from where they were hiding were watched with a jaundice eye. The vampyres could escape only at night, and the human only with a vehicle or by hiding somewhere where the other mortals would not think to look. So far no one had stumbled upon the van they had hidden in the nearby woods, no one had stopped them along the highway, and there was always somewhere to hide out during the daylight hours.

By dawn they should be back in New York City, back underground where none of this would matter anymore. With his mission so close to completion, Shadow could not help worrying. Something was jangling his nerves, especially something about the odious mortal that they were travelling with. His soul was so rotten in his soul that a vampyre would not eat him, throwing him away like that grape that had shrivelled to a raisin and had spoiled the bunch. One more task, just the one, and he and his Hand could return home to Japan.

This Gaijin country was enough to knock anyone off centre. Shadow sat up in the rafters of the one-room schoolhouse, cross-legged, eyes closed as he meditated on all that he had seen. The first mission for Vlad had cost him his favourite daughter. What would the price be for completing this one? Already a full Choir armed with apotropaics were waiting for him in New York, and getting past them would rely on some scheme of Vlad's, a scheme he had no more faith in than he did in this mission. Thinking about the Church and Aiko led him to an unexpected revelation. He now thought he knew where his wayward daughter was. It would be nice to see her one last time before she died.

All through the night sporadic running battles continued unchecked. So far the only fatality had been a vampyre, who had fallen into the shaft of a giant sump pump and been decapitated. Jean-Claude remained in the brownstone, pacing the living room as he waited for word of Xavier's death. So far there had been no word. He knew they could not keep up the blockade much longer. Both sides were exhausted, tempers were frayed, and the probability of a true bloody battle increased with every passing hour. If they did not find the defrocked priest by dawn, Jean-Claude would be forced to draw his forces back three levels. They would need to concede defeat.

Jean-Claude paused to look down at Crystal as she slept on the couch. He knelt and tucked the blanket around her, smiling as she turned and stretched like a cat, her eyes remaining closed. It would all rest on keeping her safe. No matter how important to the Church and the safety of the world, he could not help but want to keep her safe for purely personal reasons. Jean-Claude had not realized that he had been missing something in his life all these years, not with April and Gwen already filling so much of that emptiness, and then she had arrived. For a demon, she was really quite an angel. And she could get into such innocent mischief even going to the mall to buy school supplies.

"At dawn," he called over to Alvaro, who was still monitoring the map, "have everyone retreat to the third level below the subway. Leave Cantara and her people where they are. I have a feeling that's where we will find them."

"We still could get lucky," Alvaro offered.

"In this case we might have to make our own luck," Jean-Claude sighed wearily. "When Gabriel reports back, I want you two to start planning an assault on Upyr should it become necessary. Our staging area will be the level just below the subway entrance down the street."

"Good choice, logistically speaking." Alvaro agreed.

As the wait continued throughout the night, reports coming in every twenty or thirty minutes, the two men counted down the hours of nothingness. It looked like their gamble was not going to pay any dividends. It was all coming to Cantara and her team. Even if they failed here, everything was not lost. It just increased the danger to Crystal. And by increasing their security precautions, they could counter any move Vlad was planning. After all, there were only so many days ceremonies of these kinds could be preformed....

Deep underground, Cantara and her team continued to press forward along the same passage. They paused at each cross tunnel, every crook in the tunnel as it snaked its way beneath the city. A few smaller ghoul-like vampyres had crossed their path, one scuttling off into the darkness before they could engage it. The second was brought down with a well placed sling stone before Cantara severed its head with her sword – a clean decapitation. Dead vampyres were not always as dead as you thought. It was always smarter to wait until the body crumbled into dust, when circumstances gave you the opportunity.

The vampyres struck where the tunnel dog-legged sharply to the left. It was a well executed ambush, but their victims were no mere mortals. Reflexes as quick, just as tough, and armed with specially designed apotropaics, only the Wandering Jew was wounded in the initial onslaught. Despite the three quick kills, the Brotherhood specialists were hard-pressed by the fifty-seven others coming up behind the fallen three. As Cantara fell back to help the Wandering Jew back down along the tunnel, Khalil and two others moved forward to cover their retreat.

It was hopeless. They were going no further along this tunnel, and it was beginning to look like they would not make it back to the surface. Cantara set down her lover, and turned to face a vampyre who had broken past the lead three. Swords and fangs drawn, he charged – a darker blur in the blackness of the tunnel. Cantara smiled, a cold, feral thing with the promise of death. She was killing vampyres when this one was still a cold glint in his father's eyes.

A whirlwind of steel and sparks, the two met. So fast and so deadly, even if the tunnel were not shrouded in darkness, no human eye could follow. Ducking below one of his sword, bent over almost backwards, Cantara caught his second sword arm on the point of her own. A vicious twist of her blade ripped the hand from his wrist. There were no niceties here. Bringing her feet up in a perfectly executed back flip, she kicked him in the chest. He was still falling backwards when she found her own feet. Leaping after his falling body, she swept his head from his shoulders. For Cantara, there was only one way to kill a vampyre.

"Go!" Khalil shouted.

Lord Jaeger moved forward. He still preferred the Great swords used in the Middle Ages, loved the way its weight shattered bones, its edge rent flesh. No one was stupid enough to use a firearm down beneath the city, where pockets of methane could ignite the air, sending fireballs racing in both directions along the narrow confines of the tunnels. Chain mail and raw steel was where it was at.

Khalil leapt forwards into the massed ranks of the vampyres, ignoring their drawn blades. Lord Jaeger's blade slid into his chest.

Twenty feet down the tunnel, where Cantara was struggling with the weight of her lover, a gale force wind came rushing back in the opposite direction. It was like all the air in the tunnel was racing to that one point where Khalil stood dying on the length of Lord Jaeger's sword. Excited molecules vibrated at a thousand times their normal rate. It was hard to kill a vampyre, but not even they could survive tons of falling concrete. The implosion that ripped through the tunnel at the moment of Khalil's death detonated in the midst of the vampyre ranks.

Cantara and the surviving specialists were in a race for their lives. Falling slabs of concrete and flying pieces of debris filled the closed confines of the tunnel, peppering them with small cuts and contusions. The only consolation was that nobody and nothing could follow them through the collapsing length of tunnel behind them. Choking on the smoke and dust, sweating from the stress and heat of the fire filling the tunnel, the surviving fourteen specialists stumbled up out of the tunnels, and made their way towards the brownstone and safety.

On the surface, the tremor was felt as far away as Jersey City. People reported dust and smoke rising from sewers, reports that were dismissed as the panicked imagination of a city that had survived the 9/11 terrorist attack. A small tremor, authorities would claim after the hard work of Anastasia, and for the majority of New York City and the world that was all it remained.

For those waiting in the brownstone it was a sombre occasion. When Cantara and her exhausted band staggered into the apartment, looking like refugees from a dozen natural disasters, and two dozen wars, April and her coven were busy caring for the wounded.

"The tunnel is a write-off," Cantara swore. "I don't know Jean-Claude. I've never seen nothing like Khalil's death."

"He was a nature spirit," Jean-Claude replied, "a child of the air, the only one I've ever met."

"We were so damn close," she swore, the closest he had ever seen any djinn to tears.

"It's not over yet, ma petite," he promised. "The mouse had not yet roared, no?"

It was almost dawn when Shadow and his Hand entered the tunnels. Three levels down the tremors struck. Their way down into Upyr was unimpeded. One more mission and he was on his way home to Japan, where maybe he would seek a long deserved rest. Just for a century or two.

Chapter 29

Most of the items placed on the Vatican's Anathema list were books and texts. Xavier was the only human on that list, in a special section never released to the public. His inclusion on the list amused him. He had long since stopped caring about what those weak sisters in Rome thought, and no words on a piece of parchment could either hurt him or stop his work. His masters had made that clear, and should he waver, the pain they sent him – pain that seared through his very soul itself – kept him on his path.

Vlad wanted him to perform a ritual at the lunar eclipse. The concept of the ritual amused him, and the thought of the pain he could afflict sent an undeniable shiver through his loins. Killing was easy. Inflicting enough pain to force her to surrender her soul voluntarily, that took true skill. And with a supernatural being that could take days. Xavier closed his eyes and relished the thought.

The ritual itself was complex. The preparations could take weeks, but Vlad was only giving him a few days. Xavier frowned. He hated working with amateurs. They were always in a hurry, always ready to interfere with his pleasures. And deadlines in this business caused mistakes, mistakes that could take more than just your life. Xavier was not ready to leave this life. His masters had promised him immortality, and all the victims he needed to continue his work, work he hoped one day would give him the power over life and death, and everything in between. Yes, what he could do with that power.

His latest victim was fifteen when she was taken by the vampyres to serve in their city. Her name had been Orchid in the life before she became a Loogaroo, a vampyre often referred to as a werewolf by the mortals. Luring her down into the room Xavier had taken over as his laboratory had been ridiculously easy. The lower castes were trained well to obey commands without question, and Vlad had made it clear to all his people that his orders were to be obeyed implicitly. And once she was in his lab, how reasonable it seemed to stand next to the steel slab at the centre of the room, just to help him test its length and restraints?

Locked in place by steel wrist and ankle bands, Orchid stood suspended against the steel table. As Xavier lowered the table to its horizontal position, he crooned.

"Do not worry, my pretty Orchid. This will not hurt for some time yet."

He smiled. Her eyes reflected the terror she knew enough to feel, and it pleased him more than he could say. Fear was such a strong motivator, and the promise of a release from that pain and the fear it caused made his subjects so much more tractable. His first supernatural victim. This could last forever, as long as he was careful to use a regular knife and was careful with how and when he used Abraham's Hallaf. Xavier would use the hallaf, or course, both to test it and for the undeniable pleasure of watching his victim withering in pain. Pain that scourged her very soul. Pain he could only dream of causing his mere mortal victims.

"You will help me prepare for the ritual, my pretty Orchid," Xavier commented conversationally. "And together we will learn so much. You want to help me learn what I need to know, don't you my love?"

Her frightened eyes followed him as he walked over to the wooden chest Shadow and his Hand had stolen from the Vatican. He opened its lid and stared down at its contents for a long time. Orchid watched, fighting the whimper that threatened to overwhelm her self-restraint. Making noise in the presence of one of the Sanguinarians could earn you a very painful chastising, one that could take months to recover from. And if you did not work, you did not eat – making your convalescence last all the longer.

First, her shirt and leather chest armour had to go. Clothing was so constricting when one was operating, Xavier mused, cutting both from his prostrate victim. He returned to the chest and took up Abraham's Hallaf, a raw iron blade of nine inches. Knowing what it could do was so essential to planning the ceremony. Pressing its blade against Orchid's exposed belly, he smiled a sickly sweet grin, watching fascinated as the skin beneath the blade bubbled and blistered. Her screams of agony felt like a lover's caress, exciting his quiescent libido.

"No!" Xavier chided himself. I must not lose focus, he thought, shaking his head as he lifted the blade from her skin. I must not allow her to die too soon. There was so much for him to learn to throw it all away like a teenager with his first lover. Turning, he fled the room, leaving his sobbing victim behind. His footsteps took him to the central chamber, to the foot of the great stairwell that led up into the council chambers. In his monks robe and sandals, he stood out from the well-dressed denizens of Upyr, and thus all knew to avoid the mortal in their midst.

About his waist, dangling from the rope cinch he wore as a belt, he carried a collection of leather pouches that contained dusts and sands composed of many things. The smallest contained bone dust ground from the bones of those murdered by loved ones, and from this pouch Xavier drew out a handful, and began sprinkling it on the flagstone floor. The first object he drew was a diamond, almost a parallelogram that encompassed the stone altar that would be the central stage for his ritual. He worked slowly, patiently, punishing himself for his impatience with his victim. He had waited too long, dreamed of this moment for decades to rush it with unbridled enthusiasm.

When the white outline of the diamond was completed, he reached into a second pouch, a pouch containing the dried blood of slain children. With infinitesimal patience, working with a mere pinch at a time, Xavier began to colour in the inside of the diamond. Blood red and glistening in the candle light as if it were freshly spilt, his work soothed his jangled nerves. Already he was envisioning the next gift he planned to bestow upon little Orchid. Such a pretty thing, such a small incision on either breast that would make such a vast improvement to her beauty. And the joyous music of her screams would be a heavenly choir to reward him for his labours on her behalf.

In his office above the main square of Upyr, Vlad sat reading over the reports from the two days of fighting with the Church. They were hurt, as he had intended. Humans took far longer to recover from their wounds than his own people, and took far more resources and manpower to care for. Only one more step remained before the last of his plans were in place, and the first steps of his real campaign – in more than once sense of the word- could begin. And the fighting had had one other small feature to make his victory all the sweeter, he had gotten rid of his annoying brother-in-law. Even his disappointment of a son was still missing after the tunnel collapsed, and if he was lucky, Delph too was buried beneath the tons of rubble.

Not everyone was happy about the battle losses. His wife was one of these, and she meant to voice her displeasure. She swept into his office, still looking like the sweet young woman he had married, but more bitter and soured by her long years of marriage to this man.

"Are you proud now that your little blunder has cost me the life of my son and my brother?" She demanded, hissing at her husband like a harpy.

"Our son has merely run off to sulk," Vlad returned dismissively. "And, as for our brother, if he had followed my orders all those who died would still be alive. What did he think would happen, killing one of the Church's specialists within these tunnels?"

"And you expect me to believe any of this?" His wife

demanded. "You were taught deception as you took in your mother's milk-blood!"

"I care little for what you believe, dear wife," Vlad waved a hand in the air. "I gave all our guards the same order. They were to wound and main, but not kill. A dead mortal is less distracting than a wounded one, and more than anything else I need our mortal enemies distracted."

"Everything for your cause, Vlad," his wife hissed, "and nothing for your family and people. As long as Vlad gains the power he seeks!"

She turned to leave, then whirled back. "Oh, and husband. One of my handmaidens is missing. I better not find you have stooped so low as to bed the lower castes, now!"

"I will look into it," Vlad sighed.

Xavier was back in the forecourt, giving both himself and a subject a rest. Her pain tolerance was remarkable, and forced him to plumb the depth of his skill and knowledge to bring her to the sobbing, orgasmic agony that they were both learning to love. He was working about ten feet out from the northern point of the diamond, working on a six-point star. Xavier paused in his work on the centre hexagon that formed the foundation of the star, reliving those precious moments he had spent with his victim. From yet another pouch he drew forth a pinch of iron blue, a soft sandy element he was using to paint the inside of the hexagon. The black outline had been formed with obsidian sand obtained from the doomed city of Pompeii, the iron blue from a mine where seventeen men had been crushed to death.

The defrocked priest loved the feel of the elements he used to form his evocation diagrams, so soft and sensual like the skin of his subjects. When he returned again to his research he would take her toes. It was a long, gruelling process that would take hours to complete. First he would rip the nail from each toe with a pair of pliers, letting his sweet Orchid experience each exquisite moment of pain. A shiver ran up his spine at the mere thought, and he revelled in it like a gourmand at a buffet of chocolate. And then, the flesh of each toe was expertly peeled away – a procedure that took a delicate touch if one wanted to prevent his subject from passing out. And finally, with loving care, each exposed bone was cut away.

It was such a precious gift he was contemplating bringing this sweet Orchid that he almost lost his focus on the task at hand. Xavier could not let that happen. Too much was at stake in the real ritual to allow his personal gratification to interfere. His masters would not like that. No, they would not like that at all.

The yellow of the star's six points was of finely ground sulphur, and the stench of rotten eggs soon filled the chamber. Such noxious smells never bothered the diminutive little priest. Xavier relished each and every moment of his work, never letting the smile slip from his face. He would duplicate this same pattern at each of the cardinal point, where important prayers and offerings would need to be made during the ritual. Small details, like a sliver of liver here, a gall bladder in the south, but extremely important to the overall goal. And equally important to his safety. One did not work with such powerful demons without paying a price, and it was the demons and not the sacred item who would rend the victim's soul to pieces.

His work was done for the moment. The symbols in each star he had so painstakingly drawn would require fresh blood, and it was time to return to his subject. In both arts Xavier was a perfectionist. He would not compromise on either the materials he used, or tools that went into their making.

After Khalil's death Crystal tried hard to avoid the specialists, but that was proving difficult now that they had become her personal protectors. They stood at the door outside her classroom, at least one of their numbers at the back of each class, and camped out in the living room each night after she retired to her room. She had not known Khalil, not like the others, and she could not help but feel that his death was her fault. And feeling responsible for his death, she could not avoid the almost crippling guilt that was giving her nightmares every night. While no-one would ever say anything, she was beginning to think everyone would be safer if she were dead.

Cantara stood outside her door, listening as the girl within woke up screaming again. Alvaro was right. She blamed herself for the deaths of Black Rose and Khalil. Guilt was a powerful emotion, and Cantara did not agree with Alvaro or Jean-Claude when they suggested she needed to work it out on her own. Guilt could lead someone as naïve as a sixteen-year-old girl to do something foolish, and that could lead to many more deaths.

Cantara opened the door and walked over to the bed. The Wandering Jew was so much better at this than her, and she wished he was here now. At least he was human, and understood something of human emotions. Djinn did not think along those lines. They were natural warriors. Uncompromising.

"Hey, girl," Cantara shook Crystal's shoulder. "Wake up."

"What? Oh, Cantara," Crystal grumped, sleepily. She sat up, not really needing a light to see anymore than her visitor did.

"You were screaming." Cantara supplied. "The mortal's need their rest."

"Sorry," Crystal pouted.

"You are not sleeping well?" Cantara tried again, on a different task. Her lover really was so much better at this than she was.

"I keep having this dream where this dark, shadowy figure is trying to hurt me," Crystal complained, "and everyone I know dies trying to save me. Sometimes I think it would be better not to have been born than to be the cause of your friends and loved-ones death."

"Khalil," Cantara explained, frowning at her choice of words. "He was like you, the last of his kind. He was obsessed with redeeming himself and his people. This obsession with redemption is foolish, and brings you to a bad end. It is no sin to be who and what you are."

"What if that is someone who kills everything she loves?" Crystal asked doubtfully.

"All creatures choose to fall in love, Crystal," Cantara frowned again. "Even djinn. If one day that love ends, or that person dies, to love or not love was their choice."

"And if your man died because of me?" Crystal pressed. "They're all dying because the vampyres want me dead."

Cantara laughed, bitterly. "This war started long before either of us was created. Crystal, with the vampyres, one objective is never the sum of their whole plan. They are crafty creatures. They want you dead only to make way for whatever their next objective is in a plan that has been in the works for centuries, if not longer. Nor are they the only others involved in this spat."

"So," Crystal replied, choosing to be difficult, "everyone is trying to keep me alive because the vampyres want me dead."

"For me," Cantara replied, winking, "that's more than enough reason. For Jean-Claude and April, I think they kind of like you. But they're mortals, and you know mortals don't have good judgement."

"Apparently not," Crystal laughed, "if one chose to be with you."

"For that, I'm going have to hand you over to the vampyres myself," Cantara teased. "Penalties must be paid. A djinn must maintain her dignity."

"Whatever," Crystal replied, pulling the covers over her head.

"And Crystal," Cantara paused at the door, "remember that surrendering yourself to the vampyres is not an option. With those bastards one objective is only the ends to a means. You would only be allowing them to do something that will be more deadly and damaging to the friends you care so much about."

"Yes Ma'am!"

Near midnight Vlad stepped out into the forecourt to check on the mortal and his progress. The human was busy crafting a large yellow circle with a coiled snake running through it. Vlad frowned. Did the mortal think he was a fool not to recognize the nearly completed Grimorium Verum? Vlad realized that such diagrams were used in many different rituals, but its main purpose was to summon one of seventy-two demons. And demons were no more friends of vampyres than they were of most mortals. All that was missing was a sacrifice, and that brought to mind his wife's missing handmaiden. She preferred young girls still in her teens, and so did the mortal down on the floor. Xavier had been on death row awaiting execution for the murder of twenty-seven human children.

Remaining out of sight, Vlad moved back into the council chambers and tracked down two or three of the Praetorian Guard. He brought them back with him to the forecourt, where they stood together in the shadows, watching the human as he worked on the latest addition to his diagrams. The yellow was again sulphur, the smell rising to overwhelm the vampyres over-developed senses. Xavier would be a while, there was still more than a third of the image to complete, but vampyres were a patient lot, and hours meant little in a lifetime that spanned centuries. And this time Vlad could not leave until he knew for sure.

Xavier was savouring his last session with Orchid. His thoughts were split between the meticulous task and memories of the girl's screams as he tried a technique he feared to use on a mortal. She had passed out about a dozen times, the agony of their experiments together exceeding even her pain threshold. They would be delving into more new territory when he continued their next session. None of his previous victims had ever survived this long, and if he could take a vampyre this far, how much further could he take a succubus?

At last his task was completed. Xavier could not deny himself anymore. It was time to explore further the depth he could take an immortal, and he feared that soon even she would voluntarily give up her life. Such a pity. They were learning so much together, expanding his necessary knowledge if one day he was truly to control the power of life and death. And one needed to know death, to truly understand it in all its guises, before one could know life.

Vlad followed the mortal into his laboratory. The girl was still alive, barely. He had eviscerated her, leaving her entrails hanging around her neck, her hands and feet were ruined, and every inch of her legs and body were covered in small cuts. Xavier had not touched her face. He had left that pretty and unsullied.

"What do you do here, mortal?" Vlad spat. "Do you really think I would let you summon a demon, here?"

"My lord," Xavier replied blithely. "I needed to test the efficacy of Abraham's hallaf, did I not?"

"Yes, I see that you have tested it, and much more," Vlad replied sarcastically.

"This is a delicate ritual. It would not do to accidentally kill her before the right moment. She must voluntarily surrender her soul precisely at the beginning of the lunar eclipse. Only then will she be truly dead." Xavier explained.

"You will use no more of my people for your perversions," Vlad ordered. "You are lucky I have not decide to turn you over to the girl. You could be her first taste of human blood. Centurion, take the girl away. Have my personal healer put her back together, and see that she feeds regularly."

'Yes, My Lord."

"And for now on this man does not move around unescorted."

Chapter 30

Shadow sat in a pool of darkness on a rooftop, staring down at the brownstone. From sunset to sunrise, his target remained behind its locked doors, guarded by no less than ten specialists. Every fifteen minutes a patrol of Goth, reinforced by Choir soldiers, made a circuit along the street. They checked every door, every window, every shadow in the alleys – weapons drawn and ready for action. Even the rooftop he was on would not be safe in another five minutes, for there were those who patrolled up here as well.

Shadow had faced another target with this kind of security once in the past. In a modern version of a Trojan horse, he had one of his Hand delivered inside the empty shell of a refrigerator – boxed and sealed. That would not work here for two reasons: one, the brownstone was accepting no deliveries; and two, that had been a suicide mission with an objective of killing the target. Here, he would need to get both his people and the target out of the brownstone alive. And a large scale assault was not an option.

In frustration, he turned and slipped off into the night. Somehow they would need to get the girl to come to them, and without most of her escort.

Three blocks from the brownstone he dropped down to the ground in front of a startled drunk. With a polite nod, he turned and walked off towards the nearest subway entrance. This late at night the tunnels were only populated by the homeless and the transit cops who chased them away. Making his way through a door marked `Authorized Personal Only' and down into the maintenance tunnels was an easy task. Night was truly an appropriate time for his kind, with so few people around to observe, and unfettered mobility. Even if he were not a vampyre, prone to anaphylaxis shock when exposed to sunlight, Shadow knew he would still live much of his life in the dark hours.

From the maintenance tunnels an unmarked door led into the sewers and utility tunnels, and from here into the warren of chambers created by the many high rise buildings. At one point his travels carried him along a stretch of railway tracks built to transport a crippled President Roosevelt into the city in secret. It was a testament of humanities vanity, and its weakness. A vampyre would never allow himself to live as a cripple, or to become a burden to society, but then, their lifestyle was far more unforgiving than that of the humans.

His thoughts turned to Aiko. She had been captured and had dishonoured the clan. There could be no forgiveness. Shadow was convinced now that she was in the brownstone, and although he could not sense her, the probability had become a certainty. He could show no weakness when he delivered the coup de grace. Already he knew when he would be able to enter the brownstone. For once Vlad's plans corresponded with his own.

Vlad was waiting in his office, still studying the Greater Key of Solomon, comparing it to sketches of the growing diagram in the central forecourt. Shadow glided into the room unseen. Still preoccupied with his thoughts, it was several minutes before he looked up.

"We have problems, Shadow," Vlad offered in way of greeting.

"Yes, My Lord."

"I was afraid we would encounter something like this once my son began to stick his fingers into our plans," Vlad sighed. "I've had a little project on the go in anticipation of just such a contingency."

Even in Upyr the computer was commonplace. Many used an intranet connection to stay in touch, and for the day-today administration of a city of two-hundred thousand. There were places in the upper tunnels, however, where Vlad's operatives could tap into the World Wide Web, hijacking a connection from one of the local cable companies. Here they had hacked into the social networks and chat rooms used by many of the students from the Academy – a task made easier since so many of them accessed the internet through the school gateway site, as so many grade and high school students did across North America.

Sometimes a security measure became a point of vulnerability. In a secret base on the upper levels hidden in a converted tool crib, three vampyres monitored the entire social network of the Academy student body. From their hacking and eavesdropping of cell phone calls, Vlad's operatives had learned about the blood oath taken by the nine girls, including the Succubus, Crystal Raven. They were even now synthesizing the voice track that would lure the girl out of the brownstone alone, splicing it together from intercepted cell phone calls. They even had some past dealings with the girl whose voice they had chosen.

"Have your people at this intersection," Vlad instructed. "Two nights from now. Precisely at eight pm. The girl will come to you."

"That is only hours before the conjunction of the planets and the lunar eclipse," Shadow noted.

"So we will only have one chance at this," Vlad replied equanimously. "Do not fail me."

"Hai."

Crystal snuck down to visit Brendan in April's apartment, where he had been convalescing in Gwen's room. It was an activity that she would have repeated more often, if Brendan had not been in a coma until yesterday, and one the adults would have been more concerned about if Brendan was still not afraid to touch her. Sometimes, she thought, you just couldn't have your cake and eat it too. The irony of the thought struck the warped bent her sense of humour had taken lately, and she entered Gwen's room with a mischievous smile on her face.

"What are you thinking about?" Brendan asked, a mischievous look of his own rising to match her own.

"Wouldn't you like to know?" Crystal taunted.

"That's why I asked," Brendan retorted.

"Ah," Crystal wagged a finger at him, "but what you don't know won't hurt me."

"Is that how it's going to be now?"

"Oh, always," Crystal smiled, showing her teeth as if she too had fangs.

"Oh," Brendan complained, "now you are picking on the invalid. Can you sink any lower, I ask you?"

Crystal leaned over until their lips were only an inch apart, his sweet breath her own, their eyes locked. "Would you care to find out?"

"Hmmm, hmmm," April cleared her throat from the doorway. Her arms crossed, she gave Crystal a disapproving looking.

"What?" Crystal rocked back, laughing. "It wasn't like I was going to kiss him or anything. Not much, anyway."

"No kissing my patients," April chastised. "That's my job."

"How come you get all the boys?" Crystal complained.

"Because I'm older," April teased as she turned to leave the room.

"I beg to differ," Crystal shot back.

"At least in this lifetime." April concluded. "And that's all that counts."

They were taking Brendan back to the school tonight. Three squads of the Choir via a less obvious path, counter-ambushes set along the entire route. Those in hiding would be armed with crossbows, the bolts made of gopher wood, glass tips filled with holy water from the Nativity Church in Bethlehem. Not always lethal, but very, very painful. The weaponry in evidence had become increasingly more lethal as the night of the lunar eclipse approached, and despite the wishes of the Vatican, Jean-Claude had issued orders of operation that included the use of lethal force. The time for games was over.

With communications only through couriers, and only then through word of mouth, it was difficult to convey to the Vatican officials just how drastic matters had become in New York. And with two other serious demon outbreaks elsewhere in the world, incidences that were given a higher priority than their own, preoccupying those who normally offer Jean-Claude council, he was the one who needed to make these decisions. Jean-Claude was a scholar, not a man of violence. He had been chosen for this mission because of his extensive knowledge of the subject, knowledge that was spotty at best.

April carried a cup of coffee into the living room, and handed it to him. Jean-Claude ran his fingers through his thinning hair, sighing with frustration and exhaustion.

"You caught the teenagers kissing, no?" Jean-Claude gave a tired smile. "How unreal something as mundane as that could seem against the backdrop of all this, eh?"

"Maybe it is the only thing that is real," April suggested, "or really matters."

"No matter how this ends," Jean-Claude replied, "this may ruin us all. If we can somehow keep the girls innocent, that may be the only victory we will see."

"Two more days and it will be over," April soothed. "At least for six months."

"And then it starts again, no?" Jean-Claude leaned forward. "We need to find a way to end this permanently. For Crystal's sake."

That night was one of the biggest test of their new security regime, and one of the few moments of true vulnerability.
With so much of their attention and resources focused on the neighbourhood surrounding the brownstone, and not at the apartment building itself, it was the perfect moment to make an assault. Gwen and Crystal were up in her room with Cantara, Alvaro and the Wandering Jew. Alvaro was keeping the two girls distracted while the djinn watched the window,

and her lover covered the door. Even if an attempt was made, the five of them could hold out long enough to allow others to come to their aid.

Jean-Claude and Gabriel were accompanying Brendan to the school. They went downstairs to help him out of the apartment, each taking an arm as they assisted him up the stairs. Outside, a group of hard-faced men and women dressed in the ochre robes of the Vatican's elite Choir waited in a loose formation to begin the escort. With the speed and strength of vampyres, a close formation was a death trap. It offered too many targets in a small space, while keeping spread out offered only one.

Delph had not perished beneath the falling rubble that had slain so many of his companions. He and the survivors had taken almost two days to dig themselves out, an eternity in that dark prison, feeling his sense of betrayal grow. He used the time to convince those survivors with him that Upyr was gone, destroyed by a small nuclear device carried there by agents of the Church. He was a member of the Sanguinarians, and they members of lesser castes, bred and raised to believe and obey every word their betters spoke. Centuries of conditioning demanded nothing less.

Once out, Delph recruited a band of Eaters of the Dead to swell his numbers – two hulking Vetals, four Kuang-shi, and almost a dozen of the small, gnome-like Kasha. They would be his storm troopers, his shock troops as he delivered his final vengeance on those who had taken his whole world from him. Of the original sixty Lord Jaeger had set out with, Delph still had twenty-eight, most of these Loogaroo and Nosferatu. Four Dearg-due and one Empusae made up his officer corps, and all had sworn allegiance to him as his father's successor. Vengeance was what he preached, and vengeance was all they lived for, believing as they did that their families and their homes had been destroyed by the one nightmare that plagued all vampyres.

On the surface his people settled into an abandoned

building close to the brownstone to wait for the darkness. Like acolytes in a death cult, they sat grim-faced and silent, waiting for the fate they knew would come for them with nightfall. To take as many of their enemy with them, to find an honourable death was all they had left.

As the first blush of darkness brushed the sky, Delph and his troops moved out to a rooftop closer to the brownstone. Their movement was marked by one of the specialists, a djinn who could become part of the shadows around him. Oblivious, Delph placed his men in position and went on alone to study the headquarters of his enemy, where he arrived in time to watch Jean-Claude and Brendan leave under escort. He knew where they were heading, but they left by a different route, a round-about way that would eventually bring them to the school from the opposite direction. From the rooftops Delph could move faster than they could, and knew exactly where to place his people.

Jean-Claude and Gabriel received word of the vampyres moving in on their column, and turned towards where the concentration of their own people was the strongest. They knew, without having word sent back, that their stalkers would follow.

Delph sent half his forces ahead, and signalled the other half to stay with him. At a crossroads created by two alleys, they dropped down off of the rooftops....

And right into a crossfire. From both sides bolts exploded into their ranks. From the rooftops they had just left, specialist and Choir members dropped into their midst. Angel landed onto of the largest Vetal. Unlike its wings, Angel's were real. He swept down, the sword that was as much apart of him as were his wings, burst through its body. A pulse of light flashed into the sky, sending shreds of its ghoulish skin and black ichor in every direction. A guardian angel, even a fallen one, was a sight to behold. In battle he glowed with a heavenly light, he was everywhere at once, and death followed with each swipe of his terrible sword.

Delph saw that he had led his people into an ambush. Seeing his moment, he leapt onto the rooftop just ahead of a flight of bolts, disappearing into the night....

Back at the brownstone word of the ambush reached the girls. Crystal was inconsolable, her eyes glowing red, her desperate efforts to race off to rescue taking the efforts of all four to contain.

"Mom!" Gwen's desperate wail reached April as she was climbing up to the second story apartment.

Racing into the room, April took in the problem with one glance. Grasping Crystal by the shoulders to force her to look into her eyes, she called.

"Crystal! Listen to me!" April called. "Jean-Claude and Brendan are safe. They are not involved in the fighting. Angel and Gabriel have the situation under control. They don't need you to make it any worse. Now Think!"

"She's right Crystal," Cantara interjected through clenched teeth. Christ, was an enraged Succubus strong. "This could be a diversionary attack to draw you away while everyone else is too far away to come to your aid."

"But Jean-Claude needs me!" She screamed. "Why won't you let me go to him?"

"Jean-Claude is fine," April soothed. "He graduated from the Academy a long time ago, and this is not his first run in with vampyres or demons. He knows what he is doing, so do the others."

"They walked right into our ambush, Crystal," Alvaro offered. "We had more than a hundred men waiting for them. There was no chance they would ever reach Jean-Claude or Brendan."

Brendan reached the school safely, and Jean-Claude returned back to the brownstone unscathed. It had been, in Gabriel's words, a turkey shoot, where thirty vampyres had been destroyed. Other eyes had been watching and learning. Security was heavy in a three block radius of the school and the brownstone, layered so that each position could support the other, and hidden from both the vampyres and the local authorities. Shadow took it all in. They would need to lure the girl outside of this perimeter, where they would have a chance of escaping with the girl before her guards could adjust.

Shadow returned to the bolthole he and his Hand had found in an old warehouse. No one used its upper floors anymore, condemned more than a decade ago, and the lower levels were barely used as the rest of it slowly followed suit. Once there he returned to his meditations. Despite his reputation with weapons, Shadow had always believed the Sheishinteki kyoyo – the spiritual refinement – was the most important part of a warrior's development. Although he was a vampyre, his first sensei had been a human many centuries ago. If he held himself still enough Shadow could still hear his voice, old and blind and frail, and still capable of fighting a warrior a fifth of his age. He was the first and only human Shadow had met that he had not killed.

`...knowledge is the key to victory...' the old man's voice echoed in his mind. `...and when complete knowledge is not possible...the perception of complete knowledge...' Just fragments of lessons from so long ago. Why were these words coming back to him now, at this time? Just hours before his last mission in this strange gaijin land? The mind could play such tricks on one in the moments before battle, could lead one's thoughts to a thousand irrelevant moments in your life. Never before had he thought about that old human in these pre-battle meditations.

Tonight he would talk with his daughter one last time before returning home to Japan. The outcome of the ritual meant nothing to him. He had never cared for politics. Instead, his thoughts turned to the first time he had met Aiko, an orphan in the sewers of Tokyo, wandering with a pack of lower caste Animal Eaters. Shadow could still remember the first time he had seen the dirty-faced three-year-old Sanguinarian, fighting with a pack of Nosferatu for the carcass of a rat. She was the best student he had ever trained, obedient and dedicated, and always respectful. He would be greatly saddened by her death, but for the honour of their clan, she would have to die.

Crystal had stayed late at school. Only by forty-five minutes, just long enough to visit Brendan and make sure he had settled into his basement apartment. Now, back at her own apartment, she was in her room with Gwen, getting ready to have a shower. As they talked, she removed the crystal raven and the apotropaic rosary Jean-Claude had given to her, setting both down on her dresser. With housecoat and towel, she made her way into the bathroom, and cranked the hot water all the way. She let the stress of the last few days wash down the drain, the steaming water loosening the knots in her muscles, and she felt herself relax in what had felt like the first time in weeks.

Her three evening body guards were downstairs in the basement when she re-entered her room. A towel wrapped around her hair, she had only began to dress when her cell phone rang.

"I'll get it!" Gwen offered.

The voice on the other end was Ember's. "Morgana's been hurt! They were escorting Jean-Claude to the church, and some vampyres attacked. Please come. Hurry!"

"Oh my God!" Gwen breathed. "Morgana's in trouble!"

Crystal threw on a pair of jeans and a sweater, stuffing her bare feet into a pair of sneakers as she raced out the door. It never occurred to either girl that had Jean-Claude really been attack a call would have gone out to either Gabriel or Angel, and would not have come from Ember. She was in Razor's band, who were currently guarding the school. All they knew was that one of the nine in the Ghost Sisterhood was in trouble, and they had to go help her.

"Wait up!" Gwen called, nearly half a block behind Crystal. Gwen hated when she did that red eye thing. Any other time Gwen would be the one in the front, and Crystal would be the one yelling for her to wait up. It just wasn't fair.

Realizing that the girls had left the house when she came up to check on them, Cantara caught up Crystal's cell phone and redialled the last call. Every cell phone the Brotherhood used automatically recorded each call, and hearing the panicked voice of Ember, she led the rest of the specialists out of the building to give chase.

Crystal was two blocks from Saint Dismas' church and beginning to wonder how much further it was to the scene of the attack. Gwen was still half a block or more behind her, too far to help, yet far enough away that she was not caught in the attack when it came.

Ji leapt to the sidewalk directly behind the girl. Shadow knew his great strength would prove vital to this mission, still holding the girl as she fed on him. He held on long enough for one of his brothers to inject the girl with anaesthesia, and continued to hold on until the powerful drug took effect. Only then, aged and withered, did he fall on his knees and then blow away in a cloud of dust. Shadow picked up the girl's prone form and leapt up to the rooftops, watching the human girl race away to raise the alarm. And looking that way he saw the ten specialists charging towards them. He turned to his remaining three sons, gesturing with his chin at the approaching enemy before he turned to flee towards the nearest entrance to the subway.

Cantara raced at the head of the specialist as they leapt across the rooftops towards the vampyres who had kidnapped Crystal. She met the first vampyre while she was still in the air, swords drawn, coming at each other from two different directions. These Vampyre ninjas were lightning quick, but djinn were children of the air. Her sword extended, she ducked both of his blades. Hers found its mark. Pulling up on her sword as she flipped up over his head, she tore his torso to the neck – not fatal, but painful and debilitating enough to take him out of the fight.

Alvaro took out the next vampyre, leaping on him and

tearing his throat out with his fangs. Totally unexpected. Even Cantara was shocked. Alvaro did have a sword, after all. A far more civilized method of slaying someone's enemy. These Spaniards were animals. Cantara would have to revisit her Christmas invitation list because she would just hate to see what he would do to a turkey. All her humour fled as they came up to the third and final vampyre, a much older and more experienced warrior. The older the vampyre, the stronger and faster he was. And this one was fast enough to keep all six of them occupied long enough for Shadow to disappear off the rooftops and out of sight.

Frustrated, Cantara turned to her opponent. With two swords, stronger and faster than she was, he had everything going for him but her incredible temper. And she was pissed. He attacked in a blur. She cut through his assault with her larger, heavier blade. He flipped over her head, she somersaulted away. Flipping backwards over his thrust to her spine, she brought her own sword forward, scoring a large scratch across his cheek.

They turned, facing each other again. Every time another tried to get past him, his blades were there to stop them. Cantara was tired of playing around. Whirling her blade one handed, twirling it around like a baton, faster and faster. A windmill of steel, she advanced on her opponent. Even djinn had their little tricks, and this was a little something from her homeland. Steel, served up with a little spice.

Wherever and whenever his blade met hers, she immediately changed the direction of her spinning. First one of his swords, then the other spun out of his hands. He backed away, blocking her blade with his steel wrist guards. Still grinning, she continued to advance, walking him right into the point of Alvaro's sword.

"So you do know what to do with that after all," Cantara grinned, slicing the vampyre's head off as he wriggled on the blade that impaled him. "I was beginning to wonder."

"Enough chatter woman," Alvaro teased. "The last one's

getting away with the princess."

"Just try not to get in my way," Cantara retorted.

Chapter 31

Shadow had entered the subway tunnels when he felt the death of his last son. He knew those that had killed him would be following close behind, but thought he had enough of a lead to escape them.

"Halt! Police!"

Shadow spun so fast the officer had not raised his gun all the way before the throwing stars took him in the eye and the throat. He turned, looking for an exit down into the lower tunnels before any more of these mortals threw up further road blocks. Bullets might only be painful, like a bee sting to him, but they were fatal to the girl he was carrying over his shoulder.

Shadow just managed to slip through a utility door when Cantara and her companions raced into the subway. Whatever speed advantage he might normally have over his pursuers was negated by the weight of his burden. A straight run to Upyr was iffy at best, a death race at worse. He would need to take a more devious route, and the first stretches of these were populated by mortals. A mere inconvenience, Shadow thought as he contemplated the final section, a stretch of tunnel populated by those even the Eaters of the Dead feared.

Even here in the underdark there were Urban Legends. This one existed in every one of the twelve Vampyre nations Shadow had ever visited. Legends were ticklish things. Even the wildest, most improbable started with some kernel of truth. A demon bitten by an ancient vampyre – a vampyre from the First Times, who had somehow survived in a Vampyric sleep for aeons. Never mind that no vampyre could sleep for more than three hundred years at a stretch, or that no demon had ever been affected by vampyre venom, this bite was said to have created a creature so twisted, so terrifying that he held the same place in his peoples legends as dragons and kraken did in mortal myths.

Shadow had other matters to contend with at the moment. Ahead of him a wall completely covered in graffiti marked the beginning of gang territory. Not two hundred feet further along the tunnel, dark shapes were leaning against the walls and stretched out on the floor, their raucous laughter drifting back to him and putting a frown on his face. He really did not have the time to play with these mortal pups right now, but given his current emotional state, he might just come back to teach them how to dance. Before he wanted them to the young boys noticed his approach. Leaving their mating games, they stood in a loose horseshoe, completely blocking the tunnel.

From a secret pocket in his shirt, Shadow withdrew three pyrotechnics. He threw two, filling the tunnel with a thick, cloying smoke. The third was something with a little more kick. A small explosive device that worked very much like a concussion grenade. By the time the smoke cleared, Shadow had slipped off into the darkness at the far side of the tunnel.

Cantara came pounding up the tunnel ahead of her companions. The street toughs were just pulling themselves to their feet, and felt a need to recapture their manhood when they caught sight of a hot woman alone in the tunnels.

"Chica," the largest of them grabbed his crotch. "Come over here and I will make a woman of you!"

He was obvious their pack leader judging by the hoots and catcalls his verbal sally had generated. Others were gesturing with pelvis and making vulgar references to her body, their crude suggestions more amusing than insulting. Any other time and she might have stayed to play with them.

"I'm sorry," Cantara threw out a hip and winked, "but I'm afraid all this is just too much for little boys like you."

The one they called Lobo drew his knife, leering. "But we

insist you stay and play, mi chica caliente."

If he thought he was impressing her with all that wrist wiggling and a butterfly knife, he was either younger than she thought, or just stupid. She drew her sword. Faster than the human eye could follow, she slapped his wrist with the flat of her blade, and then the side of his head for good measure. His posse moved up to back his play just as Cantara's companions came up behind her, dampening their ardour.

"I'm just a little busy now, boys. Maybe later I'll come back and rock your world," Cantara called out, winking at the retreating toughs with a smile that promised violence.

"You know Cantara, you might get more action if you tried to act more lady-like," Alvaro suggested as she raced on up the tunnel, calling after her. "Maybe lose the sword, and maybe a half dozen of those knives you carry."

She sent one of her knives whizzing back towards his head as her companions' laughter chased her up the tunnel.

Some distance ahead Shadow left the main tunnel. He climbed up to a second, smaller passageway, the rounded surface of a pipe making up the floor, its ceiling so low he had to run doubled over at the waist. Forced to carry the girl cradled in his arms, her weight upset his centre of gravity where balance was everything. The sedative would only keep her under for two hours, and already he had wasted an hour in these tunnels barely three levels below the surface. Shadow needed to find a way down to the deep tunnels, and his choices were being limited by his pursuers. Ahead, there was a steep drop. A drop that would kill any mortal but meant little to a vampyre. A drop that would take him even deeper than the territory of the Eaters of the Dead.

Cantara raced up the tunnel, passing the point where Shadow had left the main passage when Alvaro's voice called out.

"Djinn, wait!" Alvaro stopped listening for a long moment. "He went up there."

Cantara looked up at the narrow passage and swore.

"When we catch this slimy sewer rat I am going to mount his head in our living room!"

"His head won't survive his death," Alvaro grunted in reply, climbing just below her. "Vampyre. Death. Dust. Remember."

"Then I'll brick the bugger into the wall and use his face as a dart board," Cantara replied, smiling pleasantly down at Alvaro.

"And they say there is nothing sweeter than a woman scorned," Alvaro breathed, and his companions laughed again.

And they say humans have a dark sense of humour during times of stress, Cantara thought as she climbed into the narrow tunnel above. None of them had ever worked with these specialists. They made gallows humour look like a knock-knock joke. And a clean one at that. She stared ahead at the darkness. She hated cramped spaces. And not just because of the slime and the spiders, or even the millions of tons of rocks and concrete lying above her head. But because the cramped space reminded her so much of the lamps and bottles and other small spaces human stories always claimed could imprison her people. What kind of sick mind could envision something so insidious? It gave her the creeps.

She slipped and slid on the concave surface of the floor, wondering how the blackheart she chased managed to stay so far ahead of them. It was almost impossible to run bent over double at the waist, and the smaller pipes hanging down from the ceiling were a constant hazard to the unwary. Cantara had already smashed her head on them a half dozen times. Her growing migraine was not improving her mood.

Cantara came up to a sharp drop. Alvaro running up behind her almost knocked her over the lip of the abyss. As they teetered on the lip, unbalanced, he suddenly wrapped his arms around her waist and leapt.

"Yooou –son-oooooooooooooooof!" Cantara screamed as they fell.

The splash at the bottom was more of a plop as they landed in a pool of sludge as thick as porridge. A mixture of clay, water and oil, it stuck to their clothes and hair and skin, oozing down their bodies in waves. Turning as she gained her feet, Cantara punched her tormentor in the jaw. Smiling his charming, toothy grin, he rubbed his jaw and pulled her out of the way as their four companions landed in the sludge just were they had been standing – Angel gliding down on his wings. He landed knee deep in the sludge, and indulged in one of his rare smiles as he caught sight of his two companions encased in the noxious liquid.

"Don't you start!" Cantara snapped, wiping more of the goop out of her eyes and whipping it at the grinning guardian angel, "or I'll knock that halo off your head!"

"Angels don't wear halos," Angel teased. "It's so passé."

"You will when I'm through with you," Cantara grumbled. "I'll hit you so hard, you'll find yourself back before the Big Bang!"

"See," Alvaro chided, backing away from her as he studied their surroundings, "you act more lady like and men show more interest in you."

"Yeah," Cantara retorted, "introduce me to one, and I'll show you a lady. Until then, shut the fuck up."

His pursuers were making so much noise that Shadow knew they were less than a hundred yards behind him. And what lay ahead would give even him nightmares for the next decade. Slinging the girl up onto his shoulder, he tied her in place with some of his sashes and climbed into the rafters just out of the monstrosity's reach. Two pipes stretched out over the large chamber where it made its lair, ending about two-thirds of the way across. Shadow threw the last of his smoke bombs into its lair and waited. Sometimes it was better to let one problem solve another.

Down the passageway Cantara and her companions were just pulling themselves out of the molasses when the smell of the smoke reached them.

"This way!" And she was off like a hound on the trail of a fox.

Ahead, a larger darkness marked the entrance of a chamber. For each of them, the black was no different than daylight, the images taking on sharper edges as the lighting changed. Where humans would have missed the large head and open jaws of the creature waiting in the threshold before them, the six specialists saw it as plainly as anyone else would have seen a truck heading straight for them at noon.

"The Saints preserve us!" Angel cried. "What in heaven's name is that!"

"Damn!" Alvaro breathed, "I think that head is gonna be a little too big, even for your living room Cantara!"

"Yeah," she replied, backing away. "But that claw would make an excellent dining room table. Of course, I'd need to pick up twelve more place settings. And a few more chairs."

"Just a few," Angel chided, drawing his sword.

Overhead, Shadow waited for the six Brotherhood warriors to engage the creature, and then crept out along the pipe over their heads. He watched a djinn leap out from beneath one of its massive paws, clipping a claw with the massive curved sword she preferred. She was good, but he doubted even he could take out the massive demon/vampyre mutant that blocked its way. He only needed them to keep it occupied for ten minutes, just long enough for him to escape out the other end of the tunnel. And if Shadow did not keep moving, he would find himself trapped, facing its undivided attention.

Counting slowly to ten, Shadow dropped down silently behind the mutant. Still on his feet as he landed, the noise of the battle covering his fall, he sprinted off towards the far entrance to the tunnel. Halfway to safety, the girl roused enough to cry out. The beast began to turn.

Cantara saw the vampyre drop behind the creature. She watched, horrified, as Crystal's cry alerted the beast to their presence. It was like fighting a hill of sand, and she was no bigger than a flea. Desperately, she took a running start, leaping off Alvaro's back, catching him in the head with her trailing foot. Sword plunging, she landed on its neck. Or maybe its shoulder.

The creature roared, lifting is head towards the ceiling. As it spun to dislodge its tormentor, Cantara decided this was not such a good idea. She found herself dangling from her sword, two hands gripped on its hilt. `Don't worry girl,' she told herself, `you've been in worse situations than this.' She couldn't exactly remember when, not quite at this particular moment, but as pep talks go it really was one of her better ones. It just really didn't help as the creature began spinning her one her sword like strippers tassel!

Angel leapt to her defence, twin blades growing out of his hands. The bigger they are the harder they fell, just as long as this bitch doesn't fall on me, he prayed. Oh cripes, this is really going to hurt.

Alvaro leapt across the void, knocking Angel aside as the demon fell to the floor. Not even close to out for the count. With the day they were having, they just couldn't get that lucky. It roared to its feet, Cantara still clinging to the sword embedded in its back. One-handed she drew a knife from her chest armour, plunging it into the demon's neck again and again as it turned towards her companions. Another of the vampyres in her group leapt on its back beside her, plunging his two swords deep into the chorded muscles on its back.

"What is it going to take to kill this bugaboo?" Cantara screamed in frustration as she went flying into one of the walls. `God this is going to hurt!'

"We just need to find its soft spot!" Alvaro screamed back, stabbing it in its heel as it turned towards the djinn.

"Or hit it with something even bigger than it," Angel suggested as he spotted a large stalagmite hanging above its head. Sometimes the ability to fly was the bomb, no matter how many times his companions called him a fairy.

Cantara and Alvaro were in trouble. There was only so much space in the chamber it had made its lair to dodge its huge feet, and their companions sling stones and bolts were not even distracting it any more. It belched suddenly, filling the chamber with the smell of rotten eggs and old gym socks.

"Damn!" Cantara swore. "What the hell does this thing eat?"

"Us! I'm guessing!" Alvaro yelled back, diving beneath its claws and rolling head first into the wall.

Far above their heads Angel smashed against the base of the stalagmite with the largest sword he could project. Again and again with desperate strength. Yes, he wanted something hard, just not this impossible to cut through.

"Try to lure it into the centre!" Angel called down to those below.

"Any suggestions as to how?" Cantara retorted, hitting the mountain of flesh with two of her daggers to draw it away from Alvaro. She winced, hoping it wasn't male as the second of her daggers found its mark.

"Try asking it out in your most lady-like fashion," Angel shot back.

"Oh, you are so dead, fairy boy!" And she leapt out of its grasp, the tip of one of its claws scraping across the back of her armour.

And as it turned back to chase Cantara this enfant terrible moved beneath Angel and his missile. One last stroke of his sword and it detached from the ceiling. For a moment it seemed to hang suspended in mid air. And then it fell. Science tell us that objects fall at a steady rate of 9.81 meters per second, to those watching above and below it seemed to gain speed as it fell. The monstrosity looked up, sensing a threat. Too late. Like a spearhead it pierced his head, throwing ichor and guts, exploding in every direction like a geyser.

For the third time in too few days, Cantara found herself slimed.

"The vampyre is probably in Upyr now," Alvaro asked as he helped her to her feet. "Or he will be by the time we catch up to him. What do you want to do?"

"Let's follow him and stir up the shit a little," Cantara suggested.

"I don't think we were invited to the party," Angel suggested as he floated down to join them, his armour untouched by the slime storm he had created.

"Yeah," Cantara suggested, "but they've left their backdoor open, and you know how I hate to miss a party."

"Sneaky, sneaky," Angel replied.

Crystal felt like she was swimming through Jell-O. Her thoughts were sluggish snails that crept along, disjointed and unconnected. She must be back in the hospital. Why was she in the hospital and where were Jean-Claude and April? Someone forced a cup of bitter tasting liquid down her throat, and it hit her empty stomach like a ball of fire. Crystal didn't like the nurses here, they had terrible bedside manner. As she drifted toward unconsciousness, she felt herself being dragged along a hallway. Something wasn't right here, but she was too doped up to remember.

Chapter 32

Gwen was more terrified than she had ever been in her life. At any moment as she raced back home she expected a vampyre to jump out and stop her. She no longer knew if the exertion of the run or her fear was causing her heart to beat so erratically against her ribcage, and her breath to come out in ragged gasps. She was on the edge of hyperventilating. Tears and sweat dripped from her face, and Gwen only realized she was sobbing when the taste of mascara reached her mouth. Never cry with make-up on, she thought, but it failed to cheer her up.

She pounded onto her street, the slap of her running shoes on the pavement keeping time with her heart. Even if someone was chasing her like she feared she would never hear them over the thunder in her ears. Almost there. Past the bodega three doors down from the brownstone, its front window dark, security bars on and door locked. The apartment building two doors down dark and deserted. Why were all the lights out? It was only eight o'clock! Where did everyone disappear to when you were alone and afraid and fleeing from your own imagination?

She pounded up the stairs of home, running straight up to Jean-Claude's apartment. The door was still open, the way Crystal and her had left it when they had raced out, running to save Morgana.

"Jean-Claude!" She ran into the kitchen and living room, finding both empty. "Cantara! Alvaro!"

Sprinting down the hall, she checked its room, flicking on the light to confirm it was empty. She dashed across the hall and into Crystal's room. It was empty too. She paused long enough to collect the crystal raven and the cell phone from the dresser, then dashed back down the stairs. Where was everyone? Didn't they realize she was a young girl and she needed them? Of course, that only worked when she felt like an adult, and didn't want them around.

Down in her own apartment she raced through the rooms, calling out to her mom. No one was here either. Where should she go? What should she do? She was already auto-dialling her girls on the cell phone. Brendan was the first number programmed into the cell phone. It figured. It was Crystal's.

"Brendan! Brendan!" She screamed into the phone.

"Gwen?" Brendan's voice came over the phone. "Calm down. What's wrong?"

"They got Crystal! The vampyres got Crystal and I can't find anyone." Gwen yelled, pausing. "Stay there, I'm coming. Call everyone and have them meet us there."

Before leaving her apartment Gwen moved into her mother's room. Wiping her hands on her jeans, she approached the closet, the one she was never allowed to go into. Gwen felt like she did that time when she was five, and she had crept into her mother's room to peak at her Christmas presents before they were wrapped. On the top shelf, hidden way at the back was a teak wood box, the one she was never ever to touch outside of her mother's presence. Except in an absolute dire emergency, she tagged on in her head. And if there ever was a time that qualified, Gwen was pretty sure this was it. Flipping open its lid, she removed the metal rod and stuck it beneath her jacket before dashing out the door.

Scribbling a quick message, she grabbed up the cell phone. Gwen was on the phone to Morgana as she ran towards the school. It was the second number programmed into the phone. She was a little insulted that her own number did not make the top five on Crystal's phone, but she guessed it made sense. They did live together, and were hardly ever out of each others presence.

"Morgana! The vampyres got Crystal. Tell Gabriel, and

then you and Drake meet us at the school. We're going after her!"

At the church, Morgana ran up Gabriel and Drake. "They got Crystal. The vampyres have Crystal." Gabbing Drake's hand, she pulled him after her. "Come on, we need to get to the school!"

Gabriel watched the Goths run off, ignoring his calls to return. Shaking his head, he issued a few orders to his own men, and moved into the church to inform Jean-Claude. It was about to hit the fan, big time.

At the school, Gwen met with Brendan and Kristen in the gym. Already others were gathering, wearing their spelunking gear and weapons. Now that she had someone to share her fear with, Gwen was not as afraid as she had been. And given what they were about to do, she was no longer so terrified she would pee herself. She was either growing up or growing insane, and when she shared this with her friends the jury seemed to be split.

"Man," Drake breathed as the girls filled him in on their plans. "We'll be slaughtered."

"Not with this," Gwen said, removing the metal rod from her jacket.

"What is that?" Morgana asked, "some kind of fairy wand or something."

"Something like that," the Nordic twins replied in sync. "It's a kind of cathode we Wiccans use to charge are crystals."

"But it can be used as a weapon if you reverse the polarity," Jade finished alone. "Gwen, it's against the Three Fold Law."

"I don't think it applies to this situation," Gwen hedged. "I mean rescuing a friend from evil creatures and everything. Just wait until those vampyres get a load of this."

"Well then," Morgana suggested. "Let's go get our inner demons on!"

Laughing for about if long as it took them to reach the nearest subway entrance, the collection of twenty teenagers set out on a quest to rescue their friend. Drake was right, Gwen thought, this was crazy, but the compulsion set in place by the blood oath would not let the eight girls do anything less. And if the girls were going, Drake, Brendan and the ten other boys would not stay behind. And they did have an advantage. Well, two really. No one would expect anyone to be following so soon after the abduction, and Brendan knew exactly how to get into Upyr unobserved.

Every Nosferatu and teenage vampyre knew of ways in and out of the city, ways too old or too narrow to be considered useable by the adults. Without it the young vampyres could not outgrow their urge to hunt, and those who served the thriving metropolis as little more as slaves would not survive. The way that Brendan was taking his friends was a path only known to the sub castes of Upyr, a way so twisted and tortuous that even the most desperate of the teens in the city considered it unusable. It was dangerous in parts, so rubble choked in others that you could only crawl on your belly, and led almost right to the main square.

There were a few mortal road blocks to contend with first. A utility repair worker took it upon himself to try to flush these interlopers out of the dangerous under tunnels, chasing them for most of twenty minutes. Brendan led his friends along a long, arching path, turning often to try to shake their determined pursuer, but always leading back to their original path. Two turns from the original tunnel in which the young pit bull originally took up the chase, Brendan began to fear they would never shake him.

"Why don't I just go back and eat him," he asked, stopping to catch his breath.

"Ah," Kristen took a stab at it, "because you don't eat humans."

"Oh yeah," Brendan agreed, straightening up and leading his friends into a hidden side tunnel. "There's that."

This last trick worked, fortunately, because they had run out of room. When the utility worker sprinted by them at full tilt, the teenagers slipped out of hiding and quietly moved into a second tunnel just a little further down the main path. They were back on track, but only long enough to run into the same gang who had molested Cantara.

"Oh criminy!" Brendan swore.

"Criminy," Drake complained. "What kind of a curse word is that? We're in deep doo doo and all you can think to say is criminy. I need cooler friends."

"What's the problem boys?" Kristen smiled at them sweetly, "I'll take care of them."

Adjusting her shirt to show a little more cleavage – not that she had much to work with to begin with – Kristen sashayed out from her nineteen companions.

"Chica!" Lobos called, saying something in Spanish Kristen just didn't choose to translate.

"Hello boys," Kristen smiled sweetly, her eyes red, releasing pheromones into the air no male mortal could resist. If she did not get on with it, Gwen thought, watching from behind, she would have their own boys running off on some wild goose chase to please her. And my Stephan better not be one of them!

"I was wondering if you could help me." She shifted position, showing a little leg. Well, a little ankle, she was wearing jeans. "My friends and I are really, really thirsty. Could you just run up to the bodega and get us some drinks."

Lobo and his posse were falling all over themselves to be the first one to bring her a drink.

"And boys," she called after them. "Could one of you get me an ice cream?"

Morgana slugged her.

"What?" Kristen complained. "I have a sweet tooth."

Brendan chose a different route than the one Shadow had led Cantara and her companions down. It started at a grate in a utility closet, and impossibly narrow space that was dark, and stank and looked to be full of spiders. Gwen took one look at it and slugged Brendan.

"You did this on purpose!" She hissed. "You know I hate spiders!"

"Then you better let me go first, Brumhilda," he smiled, giving her hand a squeeze. "I promise I will sweep all the spider webs aside."

"Oh good," Gwen complained, "and then I won't know where those little critters are hiding, just waiting to suck my blood."

"Oh, come off it," Drake teased, rolling his eyes.

"I have really tasty blood you know," Gwen retorted, realizing she was babbling – a little bit. "Every spider in the world is conspiring to get a taste of this morsel."

"Well," Stephen teased, "if the spiders have already laid claim, then you won't have to worry about the vampyres."

"Not funny, Stephen," Gwen grumbled as she followed Brendan into the narrow vent. "Boys! I wonder why we even bother to date them!"

"Is she always like this?" Drake asked Morgana.

"Only when she's feeling brave," she replied smartly.

"And what does she do when she's scared," he muttered to himself.

"Oh, you won't like that," Jade teased, pushing him towards Morgana's retreating feet.

The vent really was not that bad, not compared to the crumbling ledge Brendan led them to next. If you could call something barely longer than your thumb a ledge. And Gwen really did not mind heights, and she had really good balance, having practiced on the balance beam for hours back when she wanted to be a world class gymnast. It was just that the pebble she had thrown over the edge still hadn't struck bottom, and she wasn't sure whether she should cross facing the fall or facing the wall. None of them were, except Brendan. And since he clung to the wall, where he could find handholds amongst the cracks and splits, it seemed like a good idea.

Right up until the point a crack and the brick under her

foot disintegrated at the same time. Someone screamed, and she was afraid it might have been her, but she was too busy balancing on one toe to worry about it at that point in time in her life. She really did have good balance. The problem now was that she really wasn't much of a climber. Her tomboy stage had not lasted long enough to include rock climbing, or even tree climbing. I mean, she debated with herself, there's only so much you can do in three weeks. And being a princess was way cooler.

"Gwen!" Brendan called softly. "What are you doing?"

"Well," Gwen said in a perfectly conversational voice, "I'm a little stuck right now, and am really not too sure what I should do. All I know is I really don't want to lose my balance right now, cause that pebble I dropped still hasn't hit bottom, and I don't know how much longer I can stay balanced on one toe like this. So, if you have any suggestions, I think now is a good time."

As scared as they all were, her companions couldn't help but laugh.

"Okay," Brendan smiled in the darkness, which she could not see because at that moment the light on her helmet was pointed pretty well straight down. "Slowly reach out your right hand until you feel the wall. Very easy now."

"I found it!" Gwen was really proud of herself at that moment, but it was probably not the best time to celebrate. Brendan's hand found her wrist before she fell.

"Well, not quite what I had in mind. Can you find the ledge again with your feet," and it really wasn't long before he felt her weight ease up on his arm.

When they had all reached the far end, Gwen sat down on a pile of rocks, ignoring the spider webs hanging inches from her head. "That was pretty exciting, but next time you take me on a date, Brendan, can we just go to the movies or something."

"Hey now! That's my job," Stephen complained.

"Girls!" Drake teased, "they're always complaining we

don't take them anywhere, and as soon as we do...."

Morgana slugged him in the shoulder. "Let's get going Romeo. We have work to do."

For the next quarter mile Brendan led them along an old bricked tunnel that might have been the remains of the sewer system. And for a while, they could hike along almost like normal humans. If normal people commonly took their evening stroll through a sewer populated with the odd Eater of the Dead about the size of an average rottweiler with an appetite for human flesh. A large party such as their own, however, had nothing to fear from the creatures, who ran off ahead of them, or scrabbled into crevices to hide. Somehow, none of them thought their encounters with the vampyres would be so easy once they reached the city proper.

They were counting heavily on the element of surprise. And the artillery Gwen carried with her. The cathode was the Wiccan version of the apotropaic the Goths used, and powered by the crystals of five Wiccan girls just coming into their powers, it carried quite a kick. Just how much of one, she did not know, having never used it like this before. But the plans she and Drake had mapped out called for her and the girls to create as big of a diversion as they could, while he and his Goths raced in to free Crystal. Once Crystal was free, the fear she would cause would create enough chaos for all twenty-one of them to slip away unnoticed. At least that was the plan.

Plan B was to create enough of a ruckus to delay the ceremony until Jean-Claude and the Choir made their rescue attempt. It was the plan Gwen liked the least, because there was a strong possibility some of them might get eaten – and she wasn't too fond of the idea.

The next stretch of tunnel was too unbelievable to imagine. It was not only a sewer, but a sewage pipe, and apparently vampyres produced sewage too. All the shampoo in the city would not wash that smell out of her hair before prom. And eeeew, Gwen thought as Stephen helped her up at the other end of the pipe, even her date would smell like that! If the vampyres did not see or hear them, they would certainly smell them from a mile away. And washing up in that green, scummy water that had pooled up at the opposite end definitely wasn't an improvement. The things a girl went through for her friends.

When this was over Crystal was going to owe her big time. She was thinking breakfast in bed for a month, and her chores for at least the next two years. Oh, she really shouldn't have thought about food quite at that moment.

"What's wrong Gwen?" Stephen asked. "You look a little green."

And there went her cookies. And pretty well everything she had eaten for the last three years. And she had company. Glad to see she wasn't the only one totally grossed out by the sewage pipe.

"Uhm," Drake suggested, stepping away from Morgana as she added to the mess, "maybe we should move away from here."

"And no more smelly pipes," Gwen complained. "Is a pathway strewn with rose petals too much to ask for?"

"It gets easier from here," Brendan replied, grinning. "I promise."

"You also promised me dinner and roses," Gwen teased, "and I don't see them either."

Well, it was easier than the sewage pipe. And if you were a mouse, and not a healthy human girl –kind of on the pretty side, if I say so myself – you might believe Brendan was keeping his promise. The only problem is, that unlike mice, girls had hips, and right now Gwen's seemed to be stuck between a rather large piece of rock and a stubborn slab of concrete. No matter which way she wriggled, there just did not seem any way to free herself. How embarrassing! Coming all this way to crash a party only to end up starving to death, trapped under a pile of rubble. She sucked in her gut, but her gut really wasn't the problem here. And if she was having this much problem, how were the Nordic twins going to get those enormous breasts all the girls were jealous of through here. Could someone tell me that!

And then someone gave her a push and she was free. It better have been one of the girls, Gwen thought as she wiggled and squirmed her way through the last stretch of this mouse hole. Because nobody touches my butt, except a select group of movie stars, and maybe one or two of the cuter rock stars. God, she was only a size three. Three!

"So what now?" Gwen asked, "A short swim through lava? Maybe wrestle through a few of the alligators people claim live down here?"

"No, we can pretty well walk from here," Brendan replied. "But we better keep a sharp eye out. It's not too far until we reach an area where sometimes Delph and his cronies like to hang out."

"Okay," Drake ordered. "Crossbows loaded. Crosses ready at hand. You and your girls better do whatever you do to make that thing work."

Gwen took a giant gulp of air and nodded. "Okay."

"Okay boys and girls," Brendan announced, "sneaky sneaky time."

The next section of tunnels was referred to as Old Town in Upyr. Parts of the city that were condemned and no longer inhabitant, that part of any community that became the haunt for its teenagers and juvenile delinquents. It was the first part of their journey into the underworld where the chance of discovery existed, and that knowledge slowed their steps. At any moment they could run across a flight of young vampyres, down in this deserted stretch of tunnels and chambers to escape the restrictions of their elders. Here there were footprints in the dust, there a room with slightly newer furnishings, and the refuse of past parties. At any moment the cry of discovery could greet them around every corner, and their mission would end.

And then that moment was now.

Face to face with a flight of three vampyres, both parties froze. Someone screamed, releasing everyone from the spell. Whoever it was, Gwen wished they would stop that. And then the vampyres turned to flee. The cathode that was the Wiccan Apotropaic whooshed. If they expected lightning bolts, or a twenty foot tongue of flames, their companions were disappointed. There was no visible sign it had been fired, but they certainly felt the concussion. The lead vampyre exploded in a shower of dust. The two following fell to the ground, giving Drake and the Goths time to catch up.

No-one was faster than Brendan. Years of abuse at the hands of vampyres much like these welled up into an infernal of rage. Leaping down the tunnel, all but flying through the air, he landed on a second vampyre. Although a Jaaracacas, stronger and faster than he was, because of his human birth, Brendan could wield one of the rosaries every Goth carried. This, and his anger, allowed him to overpower his opponent. He drove the crucifix into its back again and again and again. He was still stabbing at the body as it began to crumble into dust – but with vampyres, as their instructor was fond of saying, better safe than sorry.

Three bolts flashed through the air, catching the last vampyre in the back. Drake and Morgana moved up, apotropaics drawn. The vampyre stumbled over the disintegrating body of their first kill, slowing him, but not enough to allow the two to catch him. Frustrated, Morgana swore, throwing her crucifix – a definite no-no in vampyre hunting. Trailing its beads like the tail of a kite, it streaked through the air, catching the fleeing vampyre in the back of the leg. As he stumbled, hobbling off, Drake managed to catch up with him. One, swift blow to the back of his neck, and the vampyre fell to the ground, dead before he completed his face plant.

Retrieving the rosary from the body's leg, he straightened, turning to Morgana. "If you ever do that again, I'll kick your ass."

"See this," Morgana cocked a hip, drawing one of Drake's finger to her cheek. "This is the butt of an Irish girl, and this is the closest you are ever getting to heaven."

And she sauntered off down the tunnel, hips swaying as she led the way deeper into the city.

Chapter 33

The backdoor into Upyr proved to be exactly that. The end of the long climbing tunnel carried Cantara and her companions to the heart of the city, where they found most of its inhabitants moving towards the central square. At the end of the corridor a guard blocked their path. Angel moved up behind her, one blade slashing her throat, a second bursting through her chest, deflating her lungs and preventing her from crying out. Quietly, and efficiently he dragged the body back into the darkness of the tunnel, and lay her down. Fortunately, with vampyres one never had to worry about leaving bodies behind to be discovered. They had the consideration to disintegrate and disappear, leaving only a pool of dust that would blow away in the first draft.

"Jean-Claude and Gabriel will be using tunnel three and tunnel seven," Cantara whispered. "Let's go see what Vlad left to greet them."

She smiled and winked. Tip-toeing, she led the way out into the main corridor and off towards the nearest crossroads, where they disappeared around the corner. Alvaro, who had visited the city in the past, took the lead, patting her on the backside as he past and just avoiding the knife aimed at his crotch. The two smiled at each other. Creeping through the heart of Upyr was almost as delicious a chocolate, Cantara thought, and wished she could see Vlad's face when he discovered what they had been up to.

Shadowy figures hid in the darkness just off they main intersection leading to the main square. Any rescue attempt would have to come through here. It was a natural choke point leading to the council chambers, and the square where the vampyres planned to conduct the ritual and kill Crystal. Exactly where Cantara would have set such an ambush, but no-one was expecting an attack from the other direction. Her smile turned cold and feral.

Turning, she signalled to her companions. Angel and one other would slip across the corridor and come behind those waiting in the other arm of the T, Alvaro and the second vampyre would sweep past those directly ahead to take out the guards in the main corridor as soon as Cantara and the water nymph put paid to those directly ahead. It was a simple plan, one that could only go wrong in a dozen ways, but the kind Cantara loved best. She drew her sword. Nothing topped a plan that called for taking the heads of vampyres. It was clean, it was pure, and it was violent.

They gave Angel and his companion the count of sixty to get into position. If they couldn't do it in that time, Cantara thought, it was time for them to think about changing professions. Maybe a nice flower shop in Queens. Her sword took the first vampyre in the neck. Not a clean cut, but what could a girl do? He ducked. You just couldn't trust a man to do the right thing. At least he was out of the fight, for the moment, and with his head hanging by a thread of skin, he wasn't going to be raising the alarm any time soon. Nasty shaving cut that.

She met the sword of the next vampyre with her own blade, slipping a knife under his guard and up into his abdomen. Stepping back, she took his head with a quick stroke. Cantara was good at this, and frankly was a little disappointed to see that her companion had already put paid to the other two. She pouted as she moved back to finish off her first kill. Bloody spoil sports.

"Where to now, sweet princess?" Alvaro teased. "I swear the woman is glowing."

"We are heading down that way," Cantara retorted, "I think you might be safer heading in the opposite direction. I just have this awful premonition that one of your not so secret detractors means to do you harm."

"See," Alvaro appealed to his companions, "this is what I

have been talking about. When you act more lady-like you win the admiration of more men."

"I see only fools. Perhaps us ladies should seek more fitting dance partners down this way." And Cantara smiled ever so sweetly that Alvaro could not help the shiver that ran down his spine.

The further they drew away from the main square the more deserted the city became, and the easier it became for them to travel. It was like fair day in a small town. There were some who could not attend, the guards and the slaves who worked to keep the city running, and those who chose not to consort with their fellow vampyre. These were easy enough to avoid. At least for the moment. Cantara and her companions had a job to do, had very select targets to destroy to open a path for those who would follow. They were the Church's fifth column, a silent shadow stalking through enemy cities and demon lairs, causing havoc, and collecting intelligence. It was what they lived for, and the price of the sanctuary they received in return.

As they moved through the city they began to collect items and gear – oil from the lamps, lengths of rope, and a small handcart. Anything they thought might be turned into a weapon. The ambushes set ahead would be larger, with a greater chance of someone escaping to raise the alarm, and so they needed something to even the odds a little. And with all the noise going on in the central square – it sounded like New Year's Eve in Times Square – who would hear a little pyrotechnics. And Cantara and Alvaro had a little something they were cooking up she was sure the vampyres were going to love.

In the Middle Ages they called the weapon a springald box-ballista. And whether an urban legend or true weapon, the designers had not had explosives and metal pipes to send rebar stakes flying through the air. Nor were they ever designed to roll down into their enemy ranks after discharging its missile, a fiery chariot behind which Cantara and her companions would close on their enemy.

Angel went ahead to scout out the enemy position. Along the way he eliminated a few potential witnesses, returning them to the human form they had been born to, and then to the dust which we all must return. They were there, at a manifold, where eight tunnels led off from the chamber. It was a full flight, some hiding up in the rafters, waiting to leap down on the unwary. Perfect, Angel thought. There little surprise would go off with a real bang here. And, as Cantara said, what is a celebration without a few fireworks?

"They are up ahead," Angel informed his companions. "The way is clear."

"Heavens knocking," Cantara grinned, "and it's time let the hell in."

"You'll never make it as an action hero," Alvaro complained, ducking a thrown dagger. "your catch phrases just suck."

He picked it up and returned it to her, "and you keep losing your weapons. Bad form that."

"Just terrible," Angel agreed.

Creeping slowly forward, slowly because the wheels of the handcart tended to squeak, Cantara and her companions moved up the thoroughfare towards the waiting vampyres. They were of course looking in the opposite direction. After all, who would be coming from the city, except other vampyres. And us, Cantara thought as the wheel made an ungodly loud screech. Trust Alvaro to find the one cart in all of Upyr whose axle sounded like two cats mating in a heating duct.

Well, she had wanted to get a little closer. She guessed you couldn't always get what you wanted. At a nod, Angel lit the fuse. Seconds could just crawl by in moments like this. Cantara felt like she was waiting in line at a bank just behind some old fart who was trying to pay a bill from nineteen seventy three, and she was already twenty minutes late for work.

The explosion, when it came, was a little disappointing. The result as satisfying as she could hope. Twenty pieces of rebar leapt into the chamber like thrown spears. Those hiding in the darkness below were pierced, thrown against the walls or into the tunnel adits. Seconds after, before they had any time to do more than turn towards their attackers, a burning cart thundered into their ranks. It rocketed down the slope like a juggernaut, catching air at the bottom and exploding into the wall with a shower of flames and splinters. And then the six specialists were amidst them, swords and rosaries, claws and teeth flying.

Okay, Cantara thought, not exactly the date most girls dream about, but you just got to love the sound of steel on steel, the smell of sweat and blood, the cries of ecstasy when your blade found that sweet spot...... Okay, she was taking it a little too far, and the big brute in front of her had just messed up her make-up with one of his blades. No blush for her for the next few weeks, and the oozing cut on her cheek was probably going to leave a scar. And she had no intention of turning the other cheek.

Steel rang on steel as they came together again. For an Empusae he was pretty good. His one blade just missed trimming her love handles as Cantara turned sideways, his second blade almost piercing her lip as she ducked backwards beneath his thrust. Her blade took his wrist as she raised it and a cocky eyebrow simultaneously. Straightening, she pushed him away as the three blades met hilt to hilt. He leapt backwards to gain space but she followed. His blade met the first blow, and he caught the second on his wrist guard. The third sweep of her blade took off his knees, and then the big finish. Cantara spun about like a ballerina, taking his head in one smooth motion. Coming to a halt, she took a bow.

Her five companions clapped.

"Bravo, encore," Alvaro teased. "A little slow on the finish, but I would still give it a seven."

"Oh no," Angel disagreed. "No more than a six. I'm afraid

I couldn't dance to it."

"If you two clowns are ready to give up your day jobs," Cantara retorted, "I know of a darling empty crate right near an all you could eat dumpster. Meanwhile, the rest of us professionals have some work to do that way."

"Uhm," Alvaro interrupted. "I believe you mean this way."

"That's what I said, wasn't it?" Cantara appealed to the others. "Did anyone hear me say any different? I think not."

The last ambush they needed to defuse was the most important one. At a narrow footpath with a canal on either side that spanned two hundred feet the vampyres had set up two squads. Anyone wandering into the ambush would be caught in a deadly crossfire, and humans, unlike vampyres, were not immune to cross bolts. They could take out those on the near end, but then they would face a deadly barrage from those waiting on the other side. There was just too much open ground to cross, and no cover to hide their approach.

"Have I ever shown you the trick I used as a girl to check out naked boys?" Cantara asked with a mischievous smile.

She removed the pendant she always wore, and poof, she disappeared in a puff of smoke.

"I'm afraid there's no hope for her Angel," Alvaro shook his head in mock despair.

"And a peeping-Mary at that," Angel replied. "I'm afraid you'll never make a lady out of her, my friend."

"Whatever should we tell The Wandering Jew?"

Cantara's voice came from somewhere to his left, soft and seductive. "I still have my knives, and mama taught me how to deal with boys who are not behaving. Give me two minutes, and then take out this bunch. Make as much noise as you can."

It had been ages since she had done this, and she couldn't resist. And Alvaro offered such a tempting target, too bad his mouth was at the other end. He sensed her as he jumped into the shadows. She wasn't really invisible. Djinn lived in another dimension, and had the ability to cross from one to the other. When one of her kind spent too long on Earth they could no longer cross all the way over to their home dimension, and found themselves in a kind of limbo region that was neither here nor there. No matter that she could no longer go home. That was a choice she made long ago.

Besides, the ones who killed her family lived here, in this dimension. And it was time for a little pay back. On tiptoes, she ran across the narrow path, leaving a trail of slime footprints behind. In the dark she doubted anyone would notice, and she just didn't have time for a shower between gigs. Her services were that much in demand now.

Angel nodded to his companions. They had given the djinn enough time to cross several football fields, and if she was late for her date, she would just have to learn better time management in the future. The only one it would hurt was, well, them when they tried to cross the bridge with no one there to distract the now alerted guards. If noise was what she wanted, that's what she was getting. His blade missed the target, a chunk of rock exploding from the wall beneath the impact. A second blade materialized in his other hand, bursting through the torso of the vampyre he was fighting.

On the far side of the tunnel, Cantara stood next to her first chosen victim, waiting for the noise from the other side of the tunnel to distract him. Slipping on her pendant, she tapped him on the shoulder. And shoved her blade through his face. She caught his body, lowering it gently to the ground. Silently, she leapt across the adit, taking another's head as she landed. There was no catching that one. Her moment of surprise was over. Three daggers left her hand in the blink of an eye. Three equally quick targets leapt and dodged out of the way. As her last target flipped over the third knife, a fourth caught him in the eye.

Across the bridge Alvaro and Angel led the dash to come to her relief. Even in the split second it would take to cross that distance, the vampyres at the other end could fire off three bolts. With each step they waited for death to find them. And then they were through, and jumping into the fray.

Cantara was backed against the wall by three vampyres. Her companions took out their opponents, and stood leaning on their blades or against the wall, watching. She dodged one blow, caught a second on her blade, and kicked the third in the chest before he could strike. A quick glance at her companions, and a rather dirty look, and she was back at it, steel ringing on steel. Running up the side of the wall to escape a thrust, she took the head off its wielder as she flipped over his falling body.

Two left. "Well, are you going to help, or what?"

Alvaro took a flask out of his waistcoat and handed it to Angel. "Try not to get killed."

"Getting killed is definitely bad," Angel replied, accepting the flask. "And oh, try to stick that big steel thing into that one."

The both leapt in at her. Rolling, she cleft one of the two up to his chest as she slid beneath him. Coming to her feet, she spun, taking his head in such a way it sailed off towards Alvaro and Angel. Dodging her gruesome missile, the two laughed at her like school boys.

"I'm trading you two in for a Chihuahua and an old guy in a walker," Cantara commented, wiping her blade clean on Alvaro's pant leg.

"Wait," Angel held up his hand, stopping their play. "Someone just used Wiccan powers in a rather odd way. We are not the only ones down here anymore."

"And do you want to bet none of them are over twenty," Alvaro frowned. He really didn't like complications.

"I thought we had a union rule: no one under three hundred is allowed to charge into a vampyre's lair," Cantara asked, her face creasing with a frown.

"And what was your excuse again?" Alvaro asked.

"I got a letter of permission from your mother," Cantara stuck her tongue out at him. "And by the way, she wants you to come straight home. You are late for your piano lessons."

"So?" Angel asked. "Shall we go rescue our rescuers, or do you two still need a little play time?"

Chapter 34

Gabriel moved into the church, where April and Jean-Claude were attending a Vincent de Paul society meeting. Anticipating Jean-Claude's orders, he had already sent word to the Choir to muster in full combat gear at the subway entrance nearest the brownstone. The plan was in place. It had been for over a month now, since shortly after he and his team had arrived in the city.

Bending down between them, Gabriel whispered, "Crystal has been grabbed by the vampyre."

"Execute Operation Archangel immediately." Jean-Claude snapped, still whispering. "I must return home. April?"

"I too need to return home," April replied, her gaze steel. "My covens and I will be joining the Choirs."

"April," Jean-Claude pleaded.

"I have my orders too, Jean-Claude."

He nodded, accepting. He also knew teenage girls, and if he knew nothing else he knew Crystal would have left the house without the rosary he had given her, and asked for her to carry with her at all times. He would need it now. Jean-Claude took April's hand, and together they sprinted towards the brownstone. Both wore sensible shoes, although tonight Jean-Claude would slip into the running shoes he always wore when coaching basketball. He would need the traction down in the sewers, and the shoes he wore, while comfortable for driving, had all the traction of a bald tire on ice.

At the brownstone he raced upstairs, while April returned to her apartment. Jean-Claude stopped in his room first, quickly changing his shoes, and then checked Crystal's room. His Apotropaic was exactly where he thought it would be. Downstairs, he took one look at April and knew that something else was wrong.

"What is it, ma couer?" He asked,

"I found this note," April held a piece of wrinkled paper with an illegible scrawl scribbled across it. "Gwen and the kids have gone after her."

"Merd!" Jean-Claude swore. "Come!"

Down in the subway the first squad was forming with Gabriel at its head. The local transit cops had been diverted through a combination of a pre-arranged diversion, and a little in-house sleight-of-hand.

"The kids have gone on ahead of us," Jean-Claude spoke rapidly as he briefed Gabriel. "I know which way they must have gone, and will go head them off, no?"

"What is April and the Wiccan doing here?" Gabriel asked.

"This," April replied, drawing out an even larger version of the metal cathode Gwen had taken. It was hidden beneath the lining of the same box, where her girl would never thing to look. "Is a Wiccan Apotropaic. Much stronger than the ones you wield. When used by three full covens-." Thirty-eight women moved to form a wedge behind her, crystals held in hand. "Almost nothing born in hell can stand before it."

Both her babies were now in mortal danger, but at least they had some protection with them. If these two men thought she was not going down there to bring them safely home, they were bound for a life of disappointment.

"Bon," Jean-Claude replied, nodding. "You two follow the plan. I will go now and try to stop those silly little girls and their silly little boys."

And he was off.

Gabriel turned to begin marshalling his troops. He would send the Wiccans down with the first group – a little bit of shock and awe was always a good way to begin an assault against overwhelming numbers. He would send two full squads in the advance force, then every other wave in squad strength. They were no longer wearing the brown robes of monks, but the combat boots and full body armour worn by most elite combat troops. Only their weapons were different.

A full Choir had access to more advanced weaponry. All members of the Brotherhood carried the rosaries, but they also carried vials of holy water, the relics of saints, and items from the world over. Fire and smoke bombs worked well in the narrow confines of the underworld, and while not as effective against vampyres, it was a good method for screening troop movements and providing cover for retreat. No-one carried firearms down into the world below the cities, and no-one used explosives in an environment where a cave-in could destroy both sides. That kind of pyrrhic victory served nothing.

Shadow had returned to the surface by the quickest route. He had no desire to be in the city for the ritual slaying, and wished to use the diversion it caused for his own purpose. The church was already moving against Upyr by the time he reached the city. In the two hours it had taken him to reach it fighting had already taken place in the tunnels, and would not be long before it reached the city itself. It was not his business. This was not his clan or his people, and he had no intention of dying to protect them. His task was done here, and he had one last piece of business to attend to before he returned home to Japan.

On his long climb back to the surface his thoughts returned to his daughter. After all these years she had proven a disappointment, and now four of his sons had also died completing this mission. Perhaps in time he would find others to call his family, but for now he thought he might spend time in the long sleep, a time of suspended animation all vampyres sought for time to time to extend their lives. Shadow had no desire to see this drama play out. He felt tired, more tired than he had felt in many decades. And now, the one ray of sunlight in his life would have to come to an end, and the clouds of grief were beginning to gather in his heart.

The street about the brownstone was a sea of activity as the invasion of Upyr got underway. Shadow took up position on a rooftop directly across the street from his target. Settling into the darkness, a darker shade in a pool of black, he waited for the activity to die down. He was in no hurry. The neighbourhood would be in turmoil well into the next day, and while the coming of dawn would force him to leave, he would be done with his business and on a plane to Japan before the sun rose.

Crossing over to the brownstone's roof was an easy leap for a vampyre. Shadow waited for a moment when the street was clear, spanning the distance between the two roofs with a standing jump. Gaining access to the inside from here wasn't difficult. The old lady who rented the top floor apartment had a habit of leaving her windows open. She was deaf and nearly blind, and did not even stir in the chair she dozed in as Shadow crept behind her and out her door.

Out in the corridor he paused, listening to the quiet. The building seemed empty, but someone could still be around. He suspected the specialists were staying here, and he had no way of verifying their location, or even their numbers. Satisfied, Shadow continued his journey down to the second floor, where he paused at the landing. The door to the apartment was open, and he stood there staring, listening for any sound that would tell him someone was still home. And hearing nothing, he continued down to the first floor, and the last apartment in the building. This door was closed and locked.

A second door on the far wall led down into the basement. There was no hesitation now. The main room of the basement was a communal kitchen/living room with bedrooms leading off from it. Down a short hallway where Shadow expected to find bathrooms, he found his daughter. When he switched on the light he could see Aiko in a small cell through a two-way mirror, sitting on a cot staring off at the far wall, but not meditating. In fact, she seemed to be doing nothing more than waiting.

"My daughter," Shadow called out.

"Come no further," she warned, turning to look at him, although he sensed she knew he was there long since. "It is a trap."

Shadow dematerialized. No room was completely airproof, no room meant to house any living being at least.

"You will not get in," Aiko warned. "And if they have made it so you may enter, you will not get out. It is a trap sealed and warded by powerful apotropaics."

She was right. He sensed what she had warned him about as he neared the cell. Rematerializing, he stood looking in at his daughter.

"You have dishonoured our clan." He spoke calmly. Anger was wasted effort with no true rewards. "Why have you not atoned for your disgrace?"

"I would if I could," Aiko shrugged, holding out the chains that bound her to the wall. "They have taken even this from me. But live or die, my dishonour is nothing compared to the dishonour you and Yoshio Kagawa brought to our people."

"What is this you say?" Shadow hissed.

"The man you brought to Upyr intends to betray Vlad." Aiko laughed bitterly. "I heard our enemy talking. He intends to let the Succubus feed there amongst the two hundred thousand. And the concentration of pranic energy in one individual will shatter the Seven Seals."

"He is but a mortal," Shadow scoffed.

"I have long been faster and stronger than you," Aiko answered sharply, "and it was a mortal who trapped me in here."

"That is a petty boast, my child," Shadow barked. "If you were truly faster and stronger and more skilled than I, you would have replaced me long since."

"You are the only father I have known," Aiko bowed, touching her forehead to the floor. "I was not yet ready to give you up."

"Emotion in a warrior is weakness," Shadow scolded, wondering if her skill was truly greater than his own. Surely

Aiko had been his best student in centuries.

"And now I must pay for it with the loss of my honour," Aiko replied, "at least until the demons come to flay my flesh from my bones."

"I must -."

"Return home and warn Kagawa and our people."

Chapter 35

The scent of incense and candle wax hung heavy in the air. The constant susurrations of tens of thousands of vampyres, crowded on eight tiers rising up into the darkness, the chanting children playing, and smell of blood was everywhere. Slaves moved about delivering fresh bottles and other delicacies, rising in a constant chain from pits beneath the central square, where the victims for the day's feasting were held like livestock. Life blood, blood taken at the moment of a victim's death, was selling at a premium today,. Many spent their savings to treat their families on this monumental day, caught up in the festival atmosphere that had gripped the whole city.

Watching from the balcony of his office, Vlad was pleased with the turnout. Almost the entire population of Upyr was down below, waiting to congratulate him on his triumph, to share his joy and give him their adulation. His triumph would be complete with the death of the girl, and what better gift to his people than to share this day with them.

Looking down onto the courtyard floor, he studied the diagrams sketched out on its surface with sands of a dozen colours. From here there was no mistaking it for the circle and triangle of the Grimorium Verum, the diagrams used for centuries by wizards and others to summon demons. This mortal would take careful watching, very careful watching indeed. That is why ten of his most trusted guards would be part of the ceremony, his eyes and the swift swords of his justice should the ceremony deviate one iota from that Vlad had contracted for. And he would not take his eyes off the odious mortal, not even to blink.

The Church would try to rescue the girl. That was a given, and one that Vlad was prepared for, having set up dozens of ambushes throughout the city. And if they managed to fight their way through that, he had even more surprises in store for them here at the square. Nothing would interfere with the ceremony. His triumph would be complete, and the death of most of one of the Church's elite troops would be his reward. A wheel within a wheel, with dozens of objectives, no one depending on the other to achieve victory, but all interlinked at dozens of levels.

Already the son he did not want was gone, a dangerous enemy in council was exposed, and disposed of, and Kagawa had lost serious face on the Grand council. Even his Hand had been weakened in bringing the girl here. There was a lesson to learn from that. As the moment to start the ritual drew near, as the planets approached conjunction, and the moon moved towards eclipse, Vlad reviewed his plans. Every choke point in the city was heavily manned, tunnels were set to collapse should it become necessary, and every citizen was armed and ready to defend the square should it become necessary. And should every precaution fail, he was prepared to kill the girl and deny the church her services for another twelve years.

It was time. Vlad nodded to his guards, accepting his ceremonial cape from his valet before exiting his office. He waited as his honour guard formed, marching in perfect step out the door and down into the square. As he paused at the top of the long ramp leading down to the square, a roar rose from the crowd. A sibilant hiss that rose and fell in waves, rising to fill the dome roof of the chamber, and echoing down the tiers to reverberate off the floor. Vlad raised his arms, clasping his hands above his head and shaking them to acknowledge the adulation of his people.

"The moment of our triumph is at hand!"

The hiss of the crowd rose in volume, thundering down from the rafters.

"My people!" Vlad yelled above the noise. "It has been a long hard struggle. Our tribulations have been many, our sacrifices numerous and heartrending. Our kind has hidden in darkness and in fear for centuries while our enemy grew fat on our blood until we had the courage and the conviction to take a stand."

"Tonight!" Vlad spread his arms wide as if to embrace his people. "All those long years of suffering end. Tonight we claim our birthright!"

Vlad stood, watching the sea of pale faces, his eyes rising into the rafters to study the expectation and bloodlust he saw reflected back at him. Is this what his people had become? Is this what he had led them to? He knew they could be so much more, knew there was a better destiny for them than cowering in the sewers of some human habitation, waiting for the darkness to rise to the world that should have been theirs but for an accident of birth.

He nodded.

Twin doors on a side wall were thrown open. Guards led the defrocked priest into the central square. Even through the hood of his cowl, Vlad could see the man still wore the same insipid smile. There was no doubt that this Xavier was insane, and insanity was unpredictable at best. But Vlad could only work with the tools at hand, no matter how broken, and could only hope the precautions he had put in place were enough to prevent any unseen damage. He wore a black velour cloak – black to hide the blood his work created – it was covered with mystical symbols, many of them offensive to the audience. The insult was deliberate, and Vlad was of half a mind to feed him to that same crowd when his work was done, and probably would have if that was not exactly what his wife wanted in retribution for the damage Xavier had done to her handmaiden.

It was time to reward his people. Vlad gave another nod.

A larger set of doors in the opposite wall swung open. Four guards marched out, clearing a path towards the centre of the square, a path that had been roped off and cleared hours ago. And then two of his largest, deadliest guards stepped out, dragging a girl between them.

Crystal wore a white acolytes robe, her feet bare beneath its hem. So groggy she could barely stand, she stared up at a sea of pale, hostile faces that swam like a kaleidoscope before her eyes. She was having those dreams about vampyres again. Why was she still in the hospital, and who were all these people? Why couldn't see just wake up? She stumbled, and the strange orderlies did not wait for her to regain her feet, just dragging her forward towards what her confused thoughts took to be a hospital bed. It swam in and out of her vision. What was wrong with her eyes? She thought she had called out to Jean-Claude, but there was something wrong with her voice.

The two orderlies brought her up to the bed and threw her onto its hard stone surface. Crystal's confused thoughts couldn't sort the inconsistencies out – which was part of her dream, and which were real. A third man in a monks cloak approached, reaching to strap her down with metal bands, but the orderlies pushed him away. Crystal was glad. That man scared her. He did not look anything like Doctor Gilmore. Where was Doctor Gilmore? She wanted April. Why was she not here? Why didn't anything make sense? Someone poured some more of that foul tasting medicine down her throat, and she heard the doctor complaining about it, but again the orderlies slapped him aside.

Chapter 36

Gwen was worried. She wasn't really sure if it was more about her fear as they moved into passageways that showed recent use, or for Crystal, who had seemed to be missing for days. Brendan was leading them into the outskirts of Upyr itself, the boonies where most of the citizens came from the lower castes, and the caverns and chambers they lived in were hovels. If anyone was around to discover their presence, this would be the area they would be – too poor, or too damaged to be of service during the celebrations. Where their loyalty lay was a question of what was stronger, their hatred for the upper castes or their fear of reprisals.

Gwen's palms were sweaty where she gripped the metal rod so tightly her knuckles were white. Okay, this was not exactly what she had been training for all her life. Wiccans were healers and councillors, not warrior princesses. The last fight she had been in involved ice cream and cake, and she had whipped Jean-Claude's butt big time. The victory had been sweet right until her mother had grounded them both, putting an end to her fourth birthday party.

'Come on now,' she thought as they entered a long curving corridor. 'Bring it, you vampyre scuzzies!' And then she dropped her cathode, and went scrambling after it on her hands and knees. It came to a halt at a set of booted feet. Grasping it and looking up at the same time, Gwen found herself staring into the blood red eyes of a very large vampyre.

"Shazam!" She cried, raising the Wiccan Apotropaic. Powered only by her crystal, it did not have quite the kick as it did the first time she had used it. It was still enough to throw the vampyre off his feet and back into his companions, allowing Gwen to slip back behind Drake and his Goths as they came charging past. The curving walls of the tunnel kept either side from coming at each other in any numbers, and Gwen and the girls forming a wedge behind her could not fire a shot without endangering Drake or Brendan as they battled with the vampyre.

"Well," Jade complained, "do something!"

Shrugging, Gwen dropped to the floor, sending a blast through Drake's legs, taking the feet out from under two of the vampyres.

"Watch that!" Drake complained, back-flipping beneath the thrust of another vampyre's blade. "I felt that!"

"Nothing there anyone's going to miss," Morgana teased, clipping a vampyre off the side of the head with a vial of holy water, "and I should know."

"Just for that," Drake grunted out a reply, arm and arm with one of the vampyres, "you're staying a virgin until your ninety."

"What would you know about pleasing a woman?" His opponent taunted.

"At least I have one," Drake smiled in reply. "Not like this sausage fest we found you with."

His opponent hissed, throwing Drake back into his companions. Vampyres were faster and stronger than humans, and soon enough this one would tire. He leapt towards the fallen human and was caught in a blast from Gwen's silver rod.

"Don't you be pointing your metal rod at me," a voice from beyond the battling teens broke out. "Gwen Moonshadow!"

"Cantara!" Gwen called out. "Is Jean-Claude and mom with you?"

"There coming," Cantara called back. "Let's finish up here and then we'll all have a nice long talk."

Angel flew through the air just above the heads of the eight vampyres that blocked the corridor. He landed before the children, twin blades in each hand as he prepared to hold them off as his companions made their push from behind. He took out the first to press forward with his left-hand blade, punching it through with such authority that the others backed off a step. And found themselves pressed back by the others from behind as Cantara and Alvaro swept into their ranks, blades flashing and boots kicking. Pressed in both directions, it was a quick, nasty bit of business that was over in a matter of minutes.

Cantara moved through the clouds of rising dust from the disintegrating bodies of their victims and wove a path up to Gwen.

Gwen hugged her and stopped suddenly, her nose wrinkling in disgust. "What in God's name are you covered in?"

"Demon guts," Cantara replied, her nose rising in disgust. "And you?"

"Vampyre poop," Gwen shrugged.

"And that's the winner," Alvaro pronounced.

"I still get the shower first when this is over," Cantara warned, "I'm bigger and older than she is."

"That's okay," Gwen frowned, "I'll be a wrinkly old prune before I wash this smell away."

"What, if I may ask, is that suppose to be?" She asked in way of greeting, pointing to the shining rod in Gwen's hand.

"Oh," Gwen replied casually, "that's my vampyre zinger. I zing vampyres with it."

"Zing?"

"Sure, like this," Gwen replied, pointing to the wall and firing.

A chunk of brick exploded from the wall, showering them all with chips and fragments.

"No more zinging unless I say so," Cantara warned, smiling. "Now what are all you doing here?"

"Rescuing Crystal of course," Gwen replied, rolling her eyes. Sometimes she thought adults would just never get it. Something must happen with their brains when they got older, like they atrophied or something.

"I see," Alvaro interjected. "Twenty of you against, what, two hundred thousand vampyre. Oh yes, I forgot, you have your vampyre zinger. So what does that make the odds, four trillion to one?"

"Well, I wouldn't give the vampyres that much of a chance. We got this far, didn't we?" Gwen defended. "And I'm sure we'll think of something when we got there. It's not like we have to kill them all or something."

"Or something," Cantara replied sarcastically. "And where were you planning to go from here. Hmmm. Perhaps you planned to stroll right down the main avenue."

"I know a way," Brendan came to Gwen's rescue. "It leads right through Vlad's private office and into the main square. No one knows about it."

"Well then," Angel replied suggestively. "It seems their plan has a few more attractive features than our own. I always thought Cantara was a rather dull girl myself."

"I couldn't agree more," Alvaro teased. "And all we were going to do was climb into the upper chambers and toss a few vampyres off a balcony. Coming in behind them and zinging them sound much more exciting. It just has - a certain flair."

"And I think I can help give this thing a little more kick," Angel suggested, taking it from Gwen's hand to study it.

"Okay," Cantara replied. "You stay with us and you do as you're told. We'll take a look at this passage of yours and see what we shall see. I think something that involves Angel and Alvaro sacrificing their lives to rescue my pet toad...."

Once beyond the passageway where they had met, Brendan led them into the smaller tunnels used by the slaves during their daily travels. The wider, more ornate passages were for the upper castes, vampyres who did not want to see those who laboured for them as they grunted and sweated through their daily chores. It was why these parallel tunnels were built. They led everywhere, into every upscale home, and into the various malls and markets. It was a honeycomb of twisting passages and mazes that only those who worked and travelled them daily could navigate. Brendan had spent two hundred years of his life in these passageways, and still travelled them in his nightmares every night.

The first section was as deserted as the main corridors. Almost the entire population was in the city centre, and they had taken their servants with them. Which pleased Cantara to no end as she escorted twenty mortal children through the lion's den, wondering what she had done in her life to deserve this? So far Brendan was proving an asset. When he finished his training at the Academy he would make a fine addition to the specialists, and with their loses during this fiasco, they could use the help. Their kind was a dying breed in this world, and as it opened up with new technology like the internet and air travel, the places they could live were dwindling.

The closer they came to the central square the more traffic they encountered along their way. At Cantara's nod, Brendan led them into an empty chamber, the home of a minor city official who was currently in the central square to watch the festivities.

"We won't be able to use those passages any longer." Cantara suggested, frowning.

"There's another way," Brendan hedged. "Only-."

"Only?" Cantara prompted.

"Well," Brendan admitted, hesitantly. "The first part takes us through the guards' barracks, and…"

"And?" Angel complained. "How come there's always an and?"

"I think it's because they've been spending too much time with Cantara," Alvaro answered. "She really is a bad influence. I think when this is over we should sit down with April and Jean-Claude and have a serious discussion."

"For their own good, of course," Angel finished.

"Ignore these two," Cantara suggested. "They haven't been the same since the last time I dumped them on their heads."

"At their age," Gwen threw in, "it's probably just senility setting in. Although with adults it's so hard to tell."

"Oh burn," Morgana laugh. "Fist bump."

"Hey," Gwen apologized. "We girls have to stick together."

"I'm still waiting on the and," Drake pointed out. "This isn't exactly a Sunday social."

"Well," Brendan hedged again. "Most of them are rather small, and they're not all venomous."

"Most of what?" Gwen demanded. "Not spiders?"

"No, snakes," Brendan ended lamely. "Some of the guards like to race them. It's a vampyre thing."

"Eeeew!" Gwen squealed. "I hate creepy crawlies. How many snakes?"

"Just a couple....hundred...or so." Brendan concluded.

"But they're like in cages and everything," Gwen asked hopefully, "like Morgana's ball python?"

"No."

Gwen stood staring at the floor unmoving for a long moment. Then she sighed and looked up.

"I have two plans." She announced. "The first is that the boys go ahead and put all those nasty snakes into cages."

"That would take too long," Cantara suggested kindly. She would let the girl work out her own fear.

"Okay," Gwen said. "Remember that creature we saw in the tunnels? You know, the one that screamed at us."

"You mean the rat-eater," Brendan replied. "And that was you who screamed."

"Details! Details!" Gwen waved him off. "Go get that thing, and bring it here."

"What are you thinking?" Alvaro prompted, laying an arm across her shoulder.

"That the snakes won't bite me if they're too busy running for their lives," Gwen suggested, smiling weakly. "And that thing was ugly enough to scare away its own mother."

Cantara nodded, and sent two of the specialists with

Brendan to fetch the small Eater of the Dead they had run into in the tunnels. It had been gnawing on the corpse of a rat when they had come across it, and would not wander far from its meal. For a human girl, Gwen had a lot of moxie, and a good head on her shoulders. If they came out of this alive she would make a good squad leader in the Choirs – it was too bad the Wiccan council already had a claim on her. She had gotten a troop of raw recruits deep into the lair of the largest vampyre population in the world, and even if most of that population were already pre-occupied with the ritual that would kill the girl they had come to rescue, it was still an impressive feat. Gwen had used the resources at hand, including Brendan's knowledge of the city, and even had the makings of a half decent plan for the actual rescue attempt.

It wouldn't work, of course, Cantara realized. But it would make quite a diversion to buy time until the real troops arrive. Especially if the council chambers in Upyr were as heavily fortified as those in the other vampyre cities she had visited during her long career with the Church.

Brendan and the two specialists returned, dragging a hissing and spitting creature that looked like a cross between Gollum from the Lord of the Rings and a hairless Chihuahua. Smaller Eaters of the Dead like this were often kept in a vampyre city to help deal with vermin, although Nosferatu and others of their caste usually did a pretty good job of it themselves, kept on a starvation diet as they were, and dependant on any extra nourishment they could come by.

"Okay," Cantara instructed. "Lead on, but stay close to Angel."

Brendan nodded, and led the way out into the main corridor. The first stretch was out in the open, and the most dangerous portion of their trip. Even if the tunnels were completely black, vampyres could see them in the darkness as clearly as if it had been broad daylight. And no matter how often the instructors at the academy hammered this point home, humans still felt safe and hidden in the shadows that haunted these tunnels. Cantara kept this well in mind as her and her reinforced squad of sappers infiltrated deeper into the city's core. As soon as he could, she had Brendan lead them off the main path and into the back corridors.

The corridor he led them onto grew progressively narrower as they neared the barracks chambers. Both the narrowing of the passage and the frequent gates were defensive measures, and Cantara and her crew took advantage of these as they progressed down the corridor, barring each gate from the inside to prevent anyone from coming up behind them. Re-opening thee gates might slow them down on the way out, but the bars could also be used as wedges on the opposite side, creating barriers for those following. Not that Cantara really considered that they would have a chance to rescue Crystal and make a run for it. No, there little excursion would be along the lines of a major distraction, maybe enough to disrupt their little party long enough to make a difference.

The barracks were like any other barracks the world over. Two rows of bunks with a footlocker at the foot of each bed, racks spaced out at intervals to hold either crossbows or spears, and a table at either end. They were empty, as Cantara suspected they would be, with the entire guard stationed at various points of the city to intercept any rescue attempts. The main force would be in the central square, right where they were heading, but she did not want to scare the kids any more than they already were. Even Jean-Claude's plan had very little chance of succeeding, and that involved hundreds of more troops than her own motley crew.

"Okay," Brendan said, coming to a halt before what looked like a solid wall. "The snakes are behind here."

"We could still go with my original plan," Gwen offered hopefully. "Guys? Guys?"

Brendan touched several stones on the wall, and a section of it moved in and out to the side. Snake racing was illegal in Upyr, not for any ethical or moral reason, but for the same reason such pets were regulated on the surface – the critters tended to escape. Betting on the snake races, as with the gladiator games that pitted lower caste vampyres against some of the more gruesome Eaters of the dead, was big business. And, as everywhere unregulated gambling existed, unpaid debts tended to lead to violence. And so a large underground network had developed from an offshoot of the city's black market, and hidden chambers and passages like this existed everywhere.

The elaborate means used to hide the snake pit were simple compared to some secret lairs that existed in the city. A sibilant hissing rose from the base of the stairs that led down into the darkness. Angel and Alvaro threw the rat-eater down into the snake pit, then stepped back to wait. While Eaters of the Dead preferred non-living meals, they were not above helping their victims into their grave. Cold-blooded and sluggish in the cool, damp cellar, the pit full of snakes was like an all-you-can-eat buffet to the ravenous creature.

The sounds of his killing spree drifted up to the waiting rescue party. It would be days before it would return to eat what it killed, and in the meantime its hunt would keep the snakes preoccupied.

"You can hold my hand if you're feeling scared, Cantara," Gwen offered in a quavering voice, but still she was the first one on the stairs. It had been her plan after all. She should be the first one the snakes ate if it failed.

Shooting a warning look at Alvaro and Angel, Cantara followed directly behind her, placing a hand on the girl's shoulder. The two specialists knew that look, and remained silent. It had taken Alvaro two years to grow back the ear he had lost the one and only time he had ignored such a warning. As sweet as their little princess was, Cantara had the temper of a she-bear with a bad tooth and a pot full of honey.

One by one the others followed behind. Gwen's planned seemed to be working. They could hear rustling in the deeper darkness, and knew some snakes still survived, but saw nothing. Not that Gwen could see much in the heavy gloom. Every time she stepped on something, or barked her shin, she jumped, convinced some gianormous serpent was about to have her for lunch. Every time it was always only a pipe or a stone, but she knew those snakes had been talking to the spiders.

On the far end of the snake pit, a statue of Medusa pivoted to reveal a narrow passageway that ran off in either direction. Brendan explained that it gave access to every councillor's office, and led down to the market and the arena, where quasi-legal games were held for the upper castes' amusement. Brendan's desperate escape from that same arena had led to his discovery of these tunnels, and now he was using them to help extract his revenge on his tormentors. The thought gave him a warm fuzzy feeling inside. It was always nice to see someone's pride and arrogance turned against them, hoisting them by their own petard, as the saying went.

The tunnel was lined with solid cherry wood panelling, and well lit with old fashioned oil lamps, paved in polished Italian marble. It was the epitome of comfort and elegance, underscoring the disparity in a society where no expense was spared even in a simple access tunnel while others went hungry, and lived in mere cubby holes cut into the raw rock. It ended in a blank wall covered with a mural of the final battle of the thirteenth century Vampyre uprising, depicting the death of Vlad's father as its central image, and vignettes of the Diaspora around the perimeter. The trigger to open the door into Vlad's personal office was the pendant hanging around his throat, and Brendan depressed this, and then stood aside to let Alvaro and Cantara through to check out the office.

A minute later they gave the all clear sign, and the others moved into the chamber, barring the main door and blocking the one into the tunnel with Vlad's massive desk. Gwen crawled out to join Cantara on the balcony that overlooked the central square. The ceremony was reaching its climax. With a dagger held above his head, Xavier stood above Crystal's supine form.

"He's going to kill Crystal!" Gwen screamed.

Chapter 37

After leaving April and Gabriel, Jean-Claude sprinted down the subway tunnel to a utility door covered in graffiti. That it was in Latin, and the main phrase translated to 'God is Death' never seemed to register on the general populace, but for someone in Jean-Claude's line of work it was as clear as a neon sign saying: This Way. Picking the lock was easy, a few twists with his snake rake and half-diamond, and he was on his way down into the utility tunnels. Without stopping to inspect his surroundings, he turned left and sprinted down the passageway, off in the direction the kids had followed forty minutes earlier.

Half a mile down the hall, he dashed down a second set of stairs. He hadn't turned on the lantern on his helmet yet, the utility tunnel supplied with the illumination from single bulbs set in cages every forty yards or so. The tunnel down below had even fewer lights, but still he hesitated. He would need the light deeper into his climb down into Upyr, and batteries did not last forever. And what lights still worked down here, even if they were spread out sporadically with as much as a thousand yards between them, gave him milestones to aim for in the darkness that surrounded him.

Coming out of one of these long tunnels of darkness, Jean-Claude passed a large graffiti mural marking the beginning of the Dead Bang Boys territory. One of the marginal gangs who had taken to the subways and lower tunnels to avoid the larger, more organized gangs, they caused havoc on the transit lines and kept the police busy with a list of minor crimes like mugging, dealing and purse-snatching. The Brotherhood seldom had dealings with them or any other of the marginal gangs, although occasionally one of their members would fall prey to the predations of a vampyre raid.

They and the homeless who made their homes in these tunnels, those living on the margin of society where few kept track of their comings and goings, and fewer would miss them when they disappeared, were a main staple for the vampyre.

"What is this?" Lobos complained. "Grand Central Station or something. No one passes through our turf without paying a toll!"

"Silly little boys," Jean-Claude shook his head in disappointment. "I have no time to play with you today, no?"

"Si, hijo de puta!" Lobos screamed, "we will play, but you are not going to like it!"

"Silly boy," Jean-Claude clucked, "put away your knife and go shoot some hoops. Go, enjoy the sunshine."

"It's night, baboso," Lobos laughed, harshly. "I think maybe this one is a little loose in the screws."

His friends laughed, circling around to surround the lone monk.

Jean-Claude sighed. He had been practicing such things since he was nine, was a graduate of the Academy, but had never thought such skills had any use in the real world. Unfortunately, his real world was inside the covers of books, written in ink. Many who knew him would be surprised that he owned half a dozen black belts that had little to do with libraries and research.

Lobos lunged, blade first. Jean-Claude snapped his wrist with a quick twist. His snap kick was a little low. His up and down were not what they had been when he was eighteen. And still, he met the next gang member with a perfectly executed roundhouse kick – not a move best executed while wearing jeans. He kept his next two kicks low, wincing in pain despite never having been struck by any of the gang members.

Jean-Claude limped away, still complaining to himself about the truculence of youth. Not a lick of training in the bunch. You think at least one of them would have watched Ultimate Fighting, or a Bruce Lee movie or three. Back when he was a kid, Bruce Lee was the bomb, and every boy over the age of six could execute a reasonable drop kick. Today, it was cap this and blast that, nothing but guns and knives and sucking on razor blades. Where was the skill in that?

Further along the passage the skull of a crow sat in an innocent looking crack above a black shadow. Hidden in the deeper gloom the black of the tunnel, a second passageway gaped. Few humans would have seen the adit was there, and would have passed it by, unless, like Jean-Claude, you knew to look for it. He turned, picking his way forward. Perhaps now was a good time to use his light. He reached up and switched on his lantern, jumping back as its beam illuminated the desiccated remains of an alligator. Perhaps some urban legends were true, he thought as he made his way past his gruesome discovery, or was it only a college stunt gone horribly wrong.

This next leg of his journey was the one he hated the most. The broken, the dispossessed, and the crazy – everyone thrown away by society, or who had turned their back on their fellow man – living far beneath the ground, sleeping in mounds of rubbish. Like the vampyres he sought, they only rose to the surface to feed their hunger or their habits. And always there was trouble.

"Hey mister," a shape stumbled out of the darkness towards him. "That's my hat!'

He smelled of aftershave and cheap wine, and was obviously four sheets to the wind, and still Jean-Claude could not shake him.

"Silly drunk," Jean-Claude pushed him away gently. "I am not wearing a hat."

"I'll trade for my-hic – last swallow of wine," the drunk insisted.

He smelled of piss and body odour, and Jean-Claude nearly gagged as he stumbled against him a second time.

"I need my light for my work," Jean-Claude insisted, but he had attracted others with all his commotion.

A woman leapt out of another mound of refuge and grabbed his arm insistently. "Beware of the monsters lurking in the dark! It is the end times and the CIA is working with the devil. All Catholics will be dragged to hell, because President Kennedy is a liar, and he is in league with Nixon!"

She was still babbling on as he walked past her, preaching her delusions to a crowd of homeless, all long due for their medication, and many self medicating on booze and drugs. Not everything she was saying was delusions. There were monsters lurking in the dark down here, and if he did not find his way through all this and reach Upyr in time, all good Protestants, Moslems and Jews would find themselves dragged into hell along with his fellow Catholics. Either way this scenario played out, he thought, looking for a way to escape this shantytown, it would be hell on earth. But there was a third way for this to end, if he reached the city in time.

Climbing up to a narrow catwalk, he bypassed any further delays and sprinted off towards a distant ladder of steel rungs embedded into the concrete. It was a bit of a leap, and in his younger days he would not have given it a second thought, but he was pushing fifty and had shed a lot of weight over the past decades, most of it muscle. Four decades of jump shots came in handy, but even still, he almost missed the ladder altogether. Maybe it was time to get the prescription on the glasses checked, he frowned wryly as he managed to snag a rung with his left hand. Three inches further to the right and he would have made it down the three levels faster than he had hoped.

It felt like he had torn something in his chest. He definitely was getting too old for this. He was in better shape back in the day after he had graduated from the Academy and went off to university on a basketball scholarship. But not by much, he remembered. The only time his team had won a game was by default, when a freak snow storm had stranded the other team on the highway. It was a bloody long way down. And so dark he could not see the bottom, or not even mark his progress. Was he half way down? He couldn't even see the catwalk anymore, so maybe he was.

At the bottom of the ladder Jean-Claude found himself in a narrow passage barely wider than both his arms extended. Built of old yellowing brick, covered with white lime deposits and stalagmites, it might have been part of the old sewer works, or some remains of a defensive tunnel. He followed its westward arm, letting his light illuminate the puddles and pock marks on its floor. This deep into the tunnels there was the odd chance he could run into an Eater of the Dead, although he did not think he had climbed that far into the tunnels yet.

The passage ended in a large chamber that smelled like a charnel house. The beam of his light picked out the shattered remains of a large lime deposit, and the walls and floor were covered in a thick, black ichor. Something nasty had died in here, and judging by the score marks on the wall – marks that could only have come from Angel's sword – his specialists had been through here recently. Smiling, Jean-Claude turned towards a smaller, grated passage perpendicular to the one his friends had followed.

It was small, and cramped and slimy. Crawling through this with his knees was a personal hell in and of itself. By the time he had crawled twenty feet Jean-Claude was convinced he would never stand up again. And he still had eighty feet to go. How did Vlad expect to do it, the monk thought miserably, he's at least four hundred times my age? And twice my size, he thought bitterly for good measure.

Crawling out of the narrow pipe and standing upright nearly killed him. Jean-Claude used some words he hadn't voiced since he was a young man, and limped off down another tunnel. He was two levels below the vampyre city and almost there. So far he had seen no sign of the children, which was both good and bad. He regretted every lecture on the undercity and its geography he had ever given, every extra assignment he had assigned to a lax student. Jean-

Claude wished they were only lost somewhere in the miles of tunnels beneath New York City, but knew that they had Brendan with them, and he had spent centuries living down here. The way this day was going, they were already bearding Vlad in his den.

Two levels up he ran into the first signs of someone having travelled these corridors – footprints in the dust. For a short time his path would follow them, and then he would return to the secret pathway only Vlad and his family should know about. A little further along he came upon an area where the jumble of footprints and scuff marks told a tale of a struggle, but the lack of blood spoke of no mortal casualties. He frowned, relieved and concerned all in the same moment. If the kids had made it this far, with their lead on him they were probably already at the square. Hopefully they had met up with the specialists, and hopefully he would arrive in time to make a difference.

Chapter 38

"In nomine magni dei nostri Satanas, introibo ad altare Domini Inferi" Xavier chanted, opening with the lines of the traditional Black Mass, and then deviating from that point. He began speaking in Latin, backwards – a kind of pig latin that sounded like a foreign language.

"We gather today to offer the soul of this virgin child to the Great One, true creator of the Heavens and the Earth. May he return to his rightful throne. We offer up our prayers to you. Lord Hsatan hear our prayer."

"Lord Hsatan hear our prayers," the congregation intoned.

Xavier walked to the side of the altar and picked up a thurible. From a black candle burning beside Crystal's right ear, he lit the incense inside. He started at her head, swinging the thurible back and forth as he purified her with the smoke.

"With thine holy brimstone I do purify this offering. Lord Hsatan hear our prayer."

"Lord Hsatan hear our prayers."

Chanting Hsatan backwards and forwards, he swung the thruible back and forth, walking a slow circle around the altar where Crystal lay held down by two vampyres. Through a haze of smoke she watched the scene around her bend and stretch until it lost all sense of reality. She was confused again. Mama Flo had said vampyres weren't real, so she obviously was dreaming. But she wanted to wake up from this nightmare and go home to Jean-Claude. Where was Jean-Claude?

Xavier moved away from the girl. He stopped first at each of the four stars he had drawn within the main circle of the diagram. He waved the thurible over each of the four stars, calling on the names of the four Horsemen of the Apocalypse: in the East he called on Pestilence, the North he sanctified to

War, the Western star was dedicated to Famine, and the South to Death. At each he took a powder from the pouches hanging from his belt, sprinkling sulphur on the star of the east, a little gold dust in the north, dried blood in the west, and bone dust in the south. When he was done, Xavier turned his congregation.

"I consecrate these stars to your four faithful servants, Oh Great Lord Hsatan," he cried, "Lord Hsatan hear our prayers."

"Lord Hsatan hear our prayers."

Next Xavier walked the circle on the perimeter of the diagram, sanctifying the Great Serpent to his master. When his circuit was complete, he moved back to the altar, where Crystal was mumbling something incomprehensible. `Soon, my sweet,' Xavier breathed just beneath his breath, `soon you and I will play. And when we are finished, I will release you to feast on the souls of your enemies.' He placed the thurible back under the altar and picked up the aspersory and aspergillum to replace it.

"With the waters of the River Styx, I purify this offering," Xavier intoned. "Lord Hsatan hear our prayers."

Crystal felt water falling on her face. She went to wipe it off but found she could not move her arms. Were they still in a cast? She could not remember. Now she felt water on her feet, and remembered she was taking a shower. But her arms wouldn't move. Oh, yes, she was dreaming again.

Xavier repeated the same pattern at each star with the water as he had done with the smoke. None of this was necessary, but the fool Vlad believed it. Xavier was only wasting time until the planets were aligned, when that moment of perfect conjunction happened, and the meteor showers would streak through the heavens. In the meantime he would put on the show for his vampyre hosts, and have his fun with the girl. Even damaged she could do what she was destined to do.

Xavier returned to the altar, taking up the thurible a second time. He moved to a table that held his instruments and the box containing Abraham's hallaf, swinging it over the assembled whole and chanting to himself. 'Soon my dear, oh so soon my sweet.'

Walking back to the altar he took up the water of the River Styx, and again blessed his instruments.

When he was finished, he opened the lid of the box and took up the knife. Holding it above his head for all to see, he walked a complete circle around the perimeter of the diagram. Smiling, Xavier licked his lips, and still holding the knife above his head he walked slowly towards the altar until he stood above Crystal's supine form.

"He's going to kill Crystal!" Gwen screamed.

On the balcony above the ceremony she raised her cathode and blasted Xavier off of his feet, throwing him back out of the diagram. Without thought she leapt down towards Crystal. It was a lot further than she had thought, but she remembered to leap up at the moment of impact and roll. Morgana, Jade and the other five girls followed her over, and once they had committed, the others followed suit.

Swearing, Cantara leapt to rescue the girl before the vampyres could regroup and counterattack. She, Angel and Alvaro had barely gained their feet when the precautions Vlad had set in place to counter any rescue attempt rolled into motion. From every door leading into the central square squads of vampyres stepped out, carrying swords and shields, marching in unison in tight packed phalanxes. Others dropped down from the higher tiers to form a ring of spears around the girl and the altar. Gwen zinged away with all her might, blasting away at their barrier, but the more she knocked away the more jumped from the tiers.

Angel came to stand with her wedge of Wiccans, and this time when she zinged the vampyres a full half of them flew away. Cantara and the specialists leapt forward to exploit the breech. Swords and daggers and fangs they leapt towards the altar, making it as far as the perimeter of the inner circle before the two converging units of vampyres forced them back. They had missed their chance to free Crystal and all the specialists knew it, but the kids were not ready to give up. For all Gwen and her Wiccans were breaking up the vampyre formations, they were fighting a defensive battle and being pushed back up the ramp towards the council chambers.

Gwen realized they were not going to make it to Crystal when she found herself looking out over Cantara's head. She took the crystal raven from around her neck and stared down at it. She looked up, staring across the sea of hostile faces at the girl who was her best friend, and who came to be like a sister to her. Gwen had been shooting hoops with Jean-Claude since the time she could stand up on her own two feet. The only hoop here was the neckline of the robe Crystal wore. Instinctively she knew it was the right thing to do.

Taking a deep breath, Gwen eyed her target across the hissing horde of vampyres. It was just like a free throw at the end of a big game, except here the guards from the other team were trying to stick her with spears. The bloody spiders probably put them up to it, she thought as she looked down at her feet. With her hands she made the motions as if she were dribbling. Okay, so more like a clutch three pointer. In her mind she heard Jean-Claude's voice as he talked her through her first jump shot – bend your knees, raise the ball, jump and flick your wrist in one smooth motion.

The crystal raven left Gwen's hand. As it flew threw the air, Cantara and the specialists pushed forward to distract the guards. A perfect three-pointer, square in the middle of the collar of Crystal's gown, where it came to rest out of sight just above her heart.

The push forward carried them away from the ramp, and allowed the vampyres to get in behind them and cut off their retreat. Trapped between the ramp and the altar, too far from either to reach them. Smiling, Xavier picked himself up and scrambled amongst the feet of the vampyre guards, looking for his dagger. Even with the fighting, he intended to carry on with his play. With Abraham's hallaf in hand, he cut his way through the mass of bodies and back to his little sweetheart. His smile deepened. Still gripped in the hands of the two vampyres, the girl lay with her head lolled to one side. At his nod, they tipped the altar, bringing Crystal upright.

Gwen watched as the odious little man raised the dagger again above his head. She waited until his arms were fully extended, then zinged him again. With Angel standing beside her, this one had enough kick to throw him across the room and into the far wall, where he slid down like a boneless doll.

Xavier took longer this time to gain his feet. While they were unable to free his sacrifice, the Brotherhood warriors were disrupting his ritual. Especially the blonde girl with her little silver wand. It was almost time to free the Succubus, and she was not yet bound to his master. He was afraid he must take matters into his own hands, but it would not be easy, not with those beasts that guarded her. The angel was perhaps the most dangerous, but it was hard to tell with these specialists.

He would need the help of some of his brothers. All was in readiness. It only needed a little blood spilled at the right places....

Vlad's blade was at his throat. "Don't even think about it, puny mortal."

"They are interrupting the ritual. I just thought to bring a little help to distract them," Xavier simpered.

"They are surrounded," Vlad grated. "My men have the situation well in control, despite this new weapon."

The new weapon was about the only thing keeping them alive right now, Cantara realized. While not always lethal, it broke up any vampyre formations before they could press, and they were still too close to the altar for the vampyres to risk using their own crossbows. One stray shaft hitting either Crystal or Xavier and this was all for nothing. Yet the girls were tiring, and their crystals were rapidly depleting. She suspected much of what they were seeing was coming directly from Angel, and in some strange way Gwen. It was like she could draw from the spiritual energy directly. Perhaps this is why she was so coveted by the Wiccan Grand Council. And still, even she was beginning to run down.

"We need to choose," Cantara suggested. "We need to either break towards the altar or the ramp, one last big push."

"The altar," Gwen said without a moment's hesitation. "We need to be as close to Crystal as we can when Jean-Claude and the others arrive. If Angel helps me, I think I can make it a little easier."

Gwen took a piece of chalk from her pocket, just an ordinary piece of sidewalk chalk. As she began to sketch a large circle in the middle of her friends, Jade reached down to stop her.

"Gwen!" Jade pleaded. "Not an energy circle. Not for this."

"It's the only way I can make a real big zing," Gwen replied confidently. "We can't keep this up much longer."

Jade nodded and stepped back. It was too much like 'black magic' for her to feel comfortable with it. Wiccan magic was for healing and to promote well-being. They were counsellors, and helpers and bringers of good luck. What Gwen proposed was to psychically push away those between them and the altar, and that was violence and causing harm. It went against the Three Fold Law, but if Crystal died even worse things would happen. It was a moral conundrum that they were probably all too young to unravel, or perhaps just a simple conflict between what was ethical and what was moral.

Gwen finished her circle and began issuing instructions. "Okay, I need you girls to stand at the four cardinal points I have scribed, facing outward. Angel, you need to stand here, holding the cathode with me. You guys in front are going to want to duck when I yell."

The vampyres were massing in front of them, and pressing from all sides. Quickly, they stepped into place. Gwen's hand touched Angel's as he gripped the wand. For a moment she felt every childhood fear at the moment it slipped away, soothed by her mother's gentle touch, or Jean-Claude's laughter. Taking a deep breath she yelled.

"Everyone suck floor!"

The concussion, when it came, swept the room in a wave. It knocked everyone on their feet back a good thirty feet, and almost peeled Crystal off the altar as her two vampyres holding her down fell away. It was a last gasp. The twenty six Brotherhood warriors swept forward, making their last stand four feet short of Crystal. Gwen had nothing left to give. She doubted she could raise as much as a zi, let alone a full zing. Tears of frustration stung her eyes. If Jean-Claude did not get here soon, Crystal would be dead – and maybe so would they.

Already the vampyres were massing for one final assault. For most of those waiting to repel it, it was their last moments....

Chapter 39

"Hold!"

The suddenness of Jean-Claude's order froze everyone.

"Gwen, you silly little girl," he scolded. "What are you doing here?"

"Rescuing Crystal, you silly little man." Now that Jean-Claude was here Gwen knew everything was going to be alright. And she couldn't help the single tear of relief that crept down her cheek.

"And Vlad," Jean-Claude turned, shaking his head in disappointment. He slowly walked down the stairs, towards the edge of the diagram crafted onto the floor. "You silly little vampyre. The Grimorium Verum. Surely with access to the Greater Key of Solomon you must have recognized this?"

"How did you know?" Vlad stammered.

"Come my old friend," Jean-Claude chided. "A society that has slaves has no secrets, no? Shall I tell you which three of your guards your wife is having an affair with? And Xavier. You silly little demon. We should have met long ago, no? Tell me, which one of Shax's silly little minions are you?"

"It is over Jean-Claude," Vlad warned. "Either way the girl dies and so do you!"

"There is a third way this scenario can end, no?" Jean-Claude smiled sadly. "Xavier never did plan to kill her. He meant only to enrage her into a feeding frenzy. Even now the Crystal Raven is cleaning the toxins from her blood. Soon she will sense the presence of her prey. The Greater Key of Solomon was never written by a mortal. You have been played for a fool Vlad, no?"

And he stepped into one of the stars within the circle.

Sensing his dream slipping from his hands, Vlad leapt. With his barred fangs he tore the throat from his victim. He began to drink. And a wisp of dust drifted across his line of vision. Startled, he dropped the lifeless body onto the floor. Looking down at his chest, he found the graven eyes of Jesus Christ staring back at him, the base of the cross embedded in his chest. And below this, his last sight in this life, Jean-Claude, smiling even in death.....

Crystal stood, watching in horror as Jean-Claude fell to the floor, bleeding from the neck. "NO!"

She watched, the confusion in her mind becoming a red volcano of hate and anger. "NO!"

The vampyre holding her left arm exploded into a cloud of dust. The one on the right simply disappeared like rice paper beneath a flame. With each feeding she grew stronger, her rage burning hotter. To her left, massing for the attack on Gwen and Cantara and their companions, she found the largest concentration of vampyres. She leapt. Ignoring their spears and shields and swords, she fell upon them like the meteor showers now bombarding the atmosphere miles above their heads. The cloud of dust that rose from her feeding nearly choked her friends who were even now moving to her aid.

The death of Vlad had silenced the crowd above. When they realized that the Succubus was free and now feeding, the panic set in. Leaderless, and terrified, the citizens of Upyr still had plenty of fight in them. At the moment much of that fight was directed at each other as they clawed and bit and slashed to get out of the central square. Mothers were separated from their children, husbands from wives as survival instincts took over. When the dust of Upyr cleared days later, the Church would inherit almost a hundred orphans - orphans who needed blood with their mother's milk.

Down below in the square Crystal raised her head and roared, a scream that came from her soul. Her eyes as red as the sun, she scanned the square for more victims. She leapt again, avoiding Cantara, Morgana and Gwen as they tried to reach her. The white acolyte robe she wore was now grey from the dust of her victims, and she was looking for fresh meat. As she hunted, tears streamed from her eyes, almost blinding her.

Xavier stood to one side watching. Dancing an insane jig, he giggled to himself, chanting yes yes yes over and over. He couldn't have asked for a better outcome, and was savouring his victory right up until Angel's sword burst through his chest, killing both human and demon inside.

Angel and Shax had a long history. It was because of Shax's deceptions that he found himself exiled on earth, having failed at his primary duties as a guardian angel. Nothing made him happier these days then to end the existence of one of his minions – both happiness and revenge alien to what he had been in the past. The more time he spent in the company of humans the more he became like them, and right now he felt a great emptiness in his gut. He would miss Jean-Claude. The least he could do for the man who had become his first human friend on earth was to prevent his body from being defiled in this place of blood and death.

In the upper tiers the crowds began to thin, and more and more of the panicked vampyres spilled out into the many avenues leading away from the square, until these in turn became clogged. Behind the stampede bodies slowly fell into dust, more killed here then down in the square.

Chapter 40

The press of panicked vampyres fleeing their worst nightmare that had suddenly materialized in their central square held April and Gabriel and the relief column back. They and the two squads of Choir hunters fought their way against the tide of vampyres pushing in the opposite direction and were getting nowhere. Frustrated, April raised her wand. Whoever said beware of a women scorned had never met a mother whose daughters were misbehaving and in danger. She put all her anger and fear into the blast, sending a psychic wind fuelled by thirty-nine Wiccans straight into the bodies blocking their way.

Vampyres flew backwards as if fighting against a hurricane. Panicked still, they scrambled and dove into any opening along their flight. April strode down the hall like the harbinger of death, firing whenever the concentration of bodies grew thick enough to choke the passage. At her side, Gabriel moved, protecting her from any accidental contact with the vampyres, who were attacking everything and anything that got in their path.

All they knew was that the succubus was feeding, and they needed to carry her way from here before she fed too much. Those were Jean-Claude's orders, and they would carry them out despite any obstacles.

April and Gabriel arrived at the square, pausing in the main doorway. One glance and Gabriel assessed the situation.

"You get Crystal and the children out of here. We'll form a rearguard and keep this mob contained as well as we can."

April nodded and walked into the fray, moving unperturbed towards the source of the riot. Crystal looked up at her approach, eyes red and face bloody like a feeding dragon from some fantasy movie. She hissed at the approaching woman.

"Crystal Raven," April scolded. "Don't you hiss at me girl!"

April continued forward until she was arms length from the enraged succubus. Grabbing her by the shoulders, April forced her to look into her eyes. "It's time to go home now, Crystal. It's a school night and you have homework. Help me get Gwen and the others home."

Her words were so commonplace and out of place and time that they made Crystal pause. She collapsed into the woman's arms and began to sob. A moment later, Gwen came running to her mother, staggering through her tears and exhaustion. April held out an arm for her daughter.

"They killed Jean-Claude mom!" Gwen cried. "They killed him."

"I know dear," April soothed. "We'll deal with it when we get home."

"Cantara!" April barked. "Let's get these children home. They've seen enough for one night."

"Yes ma'am"

April turned and led her daughters towards the door, her coven falling in around them to shield Crystal from the vampyres. Cantara moved ahead with Alvaro to guide their way, and Angel followed behind with the other specialists forming an honour guard for the fallen monk.

All the teens were either fighting back tears or openly weeping. Drake let Morgana lean on his shoulder, her tears soaking through his shirt. Crystal and Gwen looked broken. Crystal was safe, but at what price? Her face was as red as her eyes, and streams of tears washed down her cheeks like rivulets. Every few seconds sobs wracked her body until only April was holding her on her feet, half carrying her as they pressed on.

The danger was not over yet. Tens of thousands of fear-crazed vampyres still lurked in the corridors and tunnels of Upyr, and while Crystal's presence acted as a deterrent, her proximity to so many vampyres endangered them all. Amidst her grief, still locked in a feeding frenzy, she instinctively sought out the same vampyres they all wished to avoid. Already the pranic energy she had consumed crackled and sparked about her like a charge of static electricity. They needed to get her out of here, and it was a long two mile climb back to the surface.

Brendan wanted to go and comfort her, but dared not. He could come no closer than the ten bodies of Wiccan women who separated them. Even from here he could feel the pull of her hunger. How many vampyres had she slain and how much pranic energy had she consumed were questions that were impossible to answer in the chaos that had ensued. Already the walls of the tunnels shook with mild tremors, bits of concrete and dust raining down on them. Much more of this and the world would topple in on their heads, and they would be trapped beneath the mortal world forever.

No one knew how many vampyre deaths it would take before the concentration of pranic energy in a single individual shattered the Seven Seals, and the one man who could have made an educated guess was dead. Those following behind were still battling Vlad's Praetorian Guard, who had become suicidal with their leader's death. If these two forces met, Crystal and these juggernauts, no-one was likely to survive the collision – not those down here with her, not those on the surface, or anywhere else in the world. Armageddon.

"Brendan!" April called. "We need the quickest way out of here, and we need it now."

"There's an old tunnel," Brendan answered immediately, "it's the quickest way to the surface, but it's very unstable."

"Take us there," April decided.

Brendan led the way into the first cross corridor. He made so many turns and switch-backs that the others were soon confused, but at least they had lost contact with their pursuers. At a blank wall in a dead-end passage, Cantara and

Alvaro helped him pry up a large flat slab of flagstone. Beneath it a gaping hole waited, the sound of running water drifting back up to them.

"Are you sure about this boy?" Cantara hissed, "because if I am going to get slimed again today it better not be for nothing!"

"This is the way to the tunnel," Brendan snapped. "I can promise nothing else."

They dropped down into the cold, dark water, its surface rising midway up their chests. It smelled of pond scum and old garbage, and was oily to the touch. Sloshing their way through the tunnel led by the young vampyre, they tried hard not to imagine what made the water feel so thick and slimy, only wishing to be free of it as quickly as possible. As he moved along, Brendan stared up in the darkness as if he were searching for something. By this point April and the Wiccans were using his and Alvaro's presence to force Crystal forward, and the older vampyre had no wish to become her latest snack.

"Are you sure you know the way, Brendan?" Alvaro asked kindly.

"Yes," Brendan nodded. "There's a manhole and ladder that leads up to the tunnel we want. I just can't remember how far down the tunnel it is."

"I'll help you look then," Alvaro nodded. "The fewer delays, the more likely you and I will live to watch another sunset, eh?"

It was another twenty minutes before they found the manhole, and as wet and cold as they were, they were all glad not to have to backtrack. Some of the rungs embedded in its concrete had long since rusted away, so Alvaro climbed up with the spelunkers rope the Goths had carried down with them. It was a long, gruelling climb. Midway through he was convinced he was getting too old for this – just by a century or two. Perhaps he should have let the kid do this after all. And perhaps, when this was all over, Alvaro would settle down with the water nymph in a villa somewhere in Italy or Spain. He had certainly earned his retirement, and if not in his decades of service to the Church, certainly with this climb.

With the rope the climb was easier for those who followed. Angel would let no one else carry Jean-Claude's body, and since he could fly straight up the manhole, even burdened, it made perfect sense. The Brotherhood column was reassembling in an ancient tunnel that looked to have been hewn out of the bedrock, and so long ago it had to have been by tooth and claw. The floor was rough and littered with fallen debris, the roof and walls raw, scarred stone. At infrequent intervals timber support beams still stood in place, and everywhere there were signs of past cave-ins.

Brendan was right to call the tunnel unstable, but, April thought, sometimes you just had to trust your instinct and pray the Goddess protected fools. And sometimes, you just got lucky.

Three quarters of the way up to the surface they came to a cave-in that completely blocked the passage. April left Gwen and Crystal and moved to the front of the column.

"We need to backtrack," Cantara winced.

April lifted her head. "I feel fresh air. The collapse can't be too deep."

She spent a long moment studying the rock fall in her lamp's light. "Alvaro could you move that rock for me, please."

"This one?" And the whole pile shook and rumbled.

"No, silly man," April tssked. "You need to pay attention. If you don't move them in the right order you'll bring the whole roof down on us. Now move this one, please."

Like a giant game of pick up sticks, April pointed out rocks with her wand and Alvaro, Brendan and Cantara moved them. Once or twice the pile trembled, and the three ducked, waiting for their whole world to become rocks and pain. Ignoring its groaning and complaining, April studied the dwindling barrier, confidently tapping on rocks and poking at her unwilling labourers.

Crystal remembered little of the climb back to the surface. Between her inner demon and her unrelenting tears, she saw nothing but the lifeless body of Jean-Claude. She felt only an emptiness filled with endless pain, and a desire to kill and keep killing until the blood washed the dull ache from her soul. She was unaware that they had stopped, of the cold and the wet, or that Morgana and Gwen clung to her, shivering and sobbing. She could still feel them moving, her enemies, her prey, down in the darkness beneath her feet. And longed to destroy them.

The desire to hunt became an overpowering compulsion, and she turned to retrace her steps. Crystal frowned. Strong hands held her back. Many hands, but she sensed none of her enemy except a few insignificant morsels behind her. She would come back for them later, when her hunger was not so sharp...

"It's time to bring Jean-Claude home Crystal," Angel soothed, refusing to let go.

Crystal hissed her frustration.

"Come," he chided, "it's not polite to hiss at your friends."

"They killed Jean-Claude," Crystal mumbled, confused. "Please let me go. I am terribly hungry and must eat."

"April will make you breakfast when we get home," he urged.

"She'll make us some pancakes," Gwen sobbed, pulling her friend back into her embrace, "with blueberries. And she'll turn the bacon into smiley faces just the way you like."

"Jean-Claude is gone, Gwen," Crystal replied flatly.

"I know."

"Why does everyone I love have to leave me?"

Chapter 41

The Earthquake That Shook the World

The headline of the morning's New York Times proclaimed, staring up at Crystal as she sat over her uneaten breakfast. Scientists and other talking heads were claiming the event was caused by gravitational disturbances caused by yesterday's meteor shower, and were waiting anxiously for astronomers to confirm that a large body had passed close to the earth. Already conspiracy theorists were all over the internet, claiming that simultaneous testing of nuclear devices had caused the tremors reported on every continent, and people were walking the streets proclaiming the end of the world was at hand.

The article about Jean-Claude's death was on the front page of the Metro section. It was a beautiful piece. Pure fiction, of the type only Anastasia could produce, his name and the fact he was dead about its only truth. Crystal felt too lethargic and weighed down by grief and guilt to work up any real anger, and still couldn't bring herself to push the article aside, clinging to this last connection to Jean-Claude like a drowning swimmer to a life preserver.

Crystal turned over the bacon smile on her plate so it reflected her mood, poking at it with her fork. She wasn't hungry. She wasn't anything, but angry. She even resented the sunshine that flooded in through the window. Determined not to sigh, she picked up the newspaper to reread the article, and sighed.

Local Hero Dies in Gang Violence

Many New Yorkers may recognize the name Jean-Claude Beaucour. He came to our attention several months back when his quick actions saved the life of a young sixteen-year-old girl who had been beaten and left for dead. Last night, he again saved the life of the Jane Doe who came to be known as Crystal Raven.

This second act of heroism came to a tragic end, not only for him, but for Transit Patrol Officer Malcolm O'Reilly.

Jean-Claude was a transplant from Montreal, Quebec, one of the many volunteers who flooded into our city after the nine-eleven attack. Friends and family say he loved the city so much he decided to settle down here.

Throughout his life Jean-Claude worked with troubled children, teaching at two local schools, and volunteering at many facilities, such as the Saint Vincent de Paul Youth Centre. He served as an example to us all, both in life and in death

Private services for Jean-Claude will be held later this week at Saint Dismas Church. Family requests donations in his name be made to the Saint Vincent de Paul Youth centre.

Crystal looked up from her reading to watch a red-eyed Gwen stumble towards the table. She stared down at a plate of pancakes with no appetite. The two girls had not spoken since they had stumbled into the brownstone a few hours short of dawn, cried-out and exhausted. Crystal did not know what to say. First, because she was no longer sure what the other girl thought about her and her role in Jean-Claude's death, and secondly, because she knew if she said anything she would only set off another crying binge. Gwen felt much the same way, blaming herself for his death as much as Crystal did.

"I miss the way Jean-Claude would come down to breakfast and steal a piece of our bacon," Gwen said quietly, the tears beginning to roll down her cheek.

"Or the way he always made an extra piece of toast," Crystal replied, starting to cry herself.

"Just so I could steal a piece." Gwen replied, her voice

barely audible through her sobs.

April found them like that, drowning the breakfast she had made for them. She tried to work up a `silly girls' for her two babies, but didn't have the heart for it. She wrapped a comforting arm around Gwen, and held out her other arm for Crystal. They stayed there, wrapped in a group hug for a long moment while the girls tried to dry their tears for her sake. Their wounds were so fresh, sometimes it felt like they would never stop crying until they drowned the world with their sorrow.

"You two need to eat and keep your strength up," April soothed encouragingly.

"Why?" Crystal complained, "all I ever seem to do any more is cry."

"Me too." Gwen sniffled.

"Jean-Claude wouldn't want you to remember him this way," April rubbed their backs.

"I'm so sorry I got him killed," Crystal sobbed. "I wish I'd never been born so he would still be alive. He died because of me."

"And me," Gwen cried.

"Jean-Claude," April replied in a soft but firm voice, "lived for you. You were his life, both you girls. Jean-Claude always knew how and why he would die, just not when. He believed in you Crystal, and believed he had found a way to deliver you from your curse. Convincing the Brotherhood council of that was not only like moving a mountain, it was like teaching it to dance."

April paused for a full minute. "Come. I think it's time you girls saw this."

April shepherded the girls down into the basement like a mother goose with her goslings, directing them in the opposite direction of the specialists' barracks. The utility room she led them into looked like any other, and contained no great revelations or epiphanies that the girls could see. It was dusty and dirty, with bare concrete floors and walls, and wires and pipes in the ceiling. April stood before a metal bin and fished out a locket she wore around her neck, something that looked suspiciously like one of those half-hearts boys gave to their sweethearts. She took this and inserted it into the lock of the cabinet, pulling up on it sharply.

The cabinet slid away from the outside wall, the least likely to hide a secret passage, let alone a stairway leading further down beneath the building. April led the way inside, catching the light as she went. The stairs led into a climate controlled room entered through a pair of sealed doors, set parallel like an airlock. A large table dominated its centre, with a lectern standing at the head of the room, and free standing book shelves surrounding it. Hundreds of old tomes, scrolls, and books filled the shelves, labelled and catalogued to exacting detail.

A large series of shelves on the far wall immediately drew their eyes, and it was towards these that April led her charges. Seventy volumes, bound in black leather, filled these shelves, set apart from the others on a low dais. The last of these books lay open on the lectern.

"This is the Brotherhood's secret library," April explained, indicating the entire room with a sweep of her arms. "And this, this is Jean-Claude's life work."

"What is it?" Crystal breathed, afraid to hear the answer.

"It is the sum total of our knowledge of your past lives," April explain. "This is you Crystal. This is all you."

Afraid to touch anything or even breathe, Crystal grabbed Gwen's hand and dragged her up to the open book. Calligraphied with a beautiful script, the bold hand was inked upon thick velum, the rich texture of the paper evident even from where the two girls stood. Crystal reached out a hand to touch the paper, and felt as she was reaching out to Jean-Claude even beyond death. She could feel his presence here even more strongly than she could in the apartment they had shared during their brief time together, and felt tears well in her eyes.

"Don't cry," Gwen warned, her voice cracking, "you might smear the ink."

"I won't if you don't," Crystal challenged.

"I can't read it," Gwen complained, "my eyes are too teary. What does it say?"

"It's in Latin," Crystal replied, carefully smoothing out the page. "It's an inscription. It says: To my daughters I dedicate my life."

They were going to cry then, they just had to, and they stepped back from the lectern to avoid damaging the ink.

"It was his life's work. For thirty years he gathered every story about your past lives he could find," April continued to explain. "Some may not be true, and some may have parts missing, but he collected them all and set them into these volumes for you."

Later that night the girls lay side by side in Crystal's bed, staring up at the shadows on the ceiling. For a long time they were still, pretending to sleep and listening to the other's breathing, but neither able to rest in the long hours before Jean-Claude's funeral.

"Are you asleep?" Gwen asked.

"No." Crystal breathed a long sigh. "I'm too afraid to close my eyes."

"Me too." Gwen agreed, rolling over to face her friend and propping her head up on her hand.

"It's all like some bad nightmare," Crystal continued, "but I'm afraid if I wake up I'll be somewhere worse."

"Mom's been crying a lot," Gwen whispered. "Whenever she thinks we're not around, I hear her."

"Sometimes I'm jealous of you and your mother," Crystal replied, "all the time you had with Jean-Claude. I hardly got to know him."

"I think mom was very much in love with him," Gwen explained. "They met when mom was first pregnant with me. He was the only father I've ever known. My first teddy bear was a stuffed basketball."

Both girls laughed through their tears.

"What time is it?" Crystal wondered.

"Four: twenty-eight," Gwen replied, looking over Crystal at the alarm clock on the bedside table.

"We might as well get up and get dressed," Crystal grumbled. "The service is at eight."

She got up and turned on a light, glaring blearily at her reflection in the mirror. "My eyes are so red they look like their bleeding."

"Don't put on any mascara," Gwen warned. "You'll burn your eyes when we start crying again. I did that this morning."

"Thus speaks the voice of experience," Crystal teased, her attempt at humour falling flat as the other girl leaned on her shoulder, tears streaming down her cheeks.

The tiny church of Saint Dismas was packed, the crowds flowing out the door and onto the lawn, where a loud speaker had been set up. The Brotherhood Choir wore their ochre monks robe, making it look like the funeral of a medieval church potentate. On the left side of the church, in the pews directly across from Crystal and the Moonshadows, the Mayor sat with his wife and children, and at the front of the altar, the Bishop was celebrating the mass with eight other priests in attendance. And wherever city and church hierarchy assembled, a few members of the press were sure to follow, dancing attendance to Anastasia as she fed them the official version of the day's events.

Some of the specialists were not able to attend, those few like Brendan who could not tolerate the rays of the sun. They would say their goodbyes later that night in a private graveyard ceremony. Those who were there, like Cantara, sat at the front of the church in the pew reserved for the family. Crystal sat between Gwen and April, wearing one of the two veils that Cantara had lent the girls. Neither girl had the courage to ask where and when the Djinn needed a veil, let alone found enough occasions to have a small collection. They eyed the Wandering Jew suspiciously as he sat quietly on her far side, wondering if it would be safe to ask him, and if they really wanted to know the answer, or should just be satisfied that no-one could see them weeping.

The first three rows held a strong representation of students from the Academy and from the grade school Jean-Claude had taught in. Amongst them sat Mama Flo and Doctor Gilmore, and Crystal was glad to see them here, even if they would have little time for more than a quick hug.

A choir of local children sang Amazing Grace for the processional hymn, filling the small church with their sweet, sad notes. A priest carrying a cross led the way, followed by two altar boys with candles, and a second priest swinging the thurible. Behind these came the Bishop leading the coffin and its pallbearers, the six Choir members dressed in full combat gear as they slow marched up to the altar with their burden. The strange, hypnotic stutter-step attracted and held Crystal's eyes, helping her to avoid looking up at the coffin. As long as she did not look at the coffin, she kept telling herself, he wasn't really dead.

The service was not too long, following the traditional funeral mass. Gwen got up to read a poem she had written, and her mother gave a short eulogy. April spoke of how they had met shortly after the death of her husband, nearly seventeen years ago when she was attending college in Montreal. Unlike Jean-Claude, she was a native New Yorker, alone in a strange country with a child on the way. She told how their meeting, and how her and her daughter came to live with him, first at his house in Montreal, and then at the brownstone here in New York, exemplified Jean-Claude's charitable nature. How that personality trait had led him to help so many people in his life, and to come to New York to share the burden of the grief and suffering after the nine/eleven terrorist attack.

A soloist began to sing Ava Maria as the Bishop and his retinue lined up to escort the coffin out of the church. Crystal and Gwen, walking hand and hand, followed immediately behind Jean-Claude's body. Out in the parking lot there was the usual shaking out of the funeral procession, but the girls and their mother were safely beyond these minor details in the first limousine behind the hearse, accompanied only by Cantara. Behind this, Bishop O'Malley would follow in his own personal limousine, the last of the initial vehicles as the mayor had chosen not to attend the actual burial. Thirty other vehicles would make up the remainder of the procession, with many others having already started to make their way to the grave site.

At the graveyard Crystal and Gwen did not want to get out of the car, and they held up the ceremony as April talked with them briefly. They had done so well at Black Rose's funeral, but she understood that this death was so much more immediate and personal to them. Coming to the graveside would make it all seem too real, and whatever sense of denial they had been clinging to would disappear, but she knew the two girls needed the sense of closure and comfort the burial would give them as much as she did herself.

"Ashes to ashes," Bishop O'Malley prayed. "Dust to dust...."

First Crystal and the Moonshadows, and then a long line of mourners came to drop a handful of dirt on the lonely coffin. Standing at the graveside in a kind of reception line, accepting the condolences of friends and strangers alike, Crystal watched the coffin slowly disappear through increasingly bleary vision. Jean-Claude was gone and she would never see him again.....

Chapter 42

"Crystal, Gwen!" April stuck her head into the doorway at the top of the stairs. "The lawyer's here."

Crystal had been spending almost all her time down in the secret library, and Gwen had been her constant companion more so than usual since the funeral. One obsessed with reading every word Jean-Claude had ever wrote, the other afraid to be alone – April was not sure what to do with her two daughters. She was well aware of the seven stages of grief from her counselling, and April was willing to allow them to work through it themselves with only a little prodding. At the end of the week, when the Academy reopened, she was sending them back to school to immerse themselves in their regular routine.

Upstairs, Mr. Dumount, a long time friend and personal lawyer of Jean-Claude's, was waiting for them in the living room to read the will. From his briefcase he removed a number of papers and spread them out on the coffee table.

"For legal reasons," Mr. Dumount explained, "the will must be read in full. There is some paperwork to be signed, and then the will needs to be filed with the probate court. I will be looking after most of this, but as executor, April, I will need to consult you from time to time."

"Certainly," April cleared her throat, remembering long ago when her husband had died, and going through much of the same thing.

"I, Jean-Claude Philippe Beaucour, residing at New York City, New York, being of sound mind, do hereby make,
publish and declare this to be my Last Will and Testament and do revoke any and all other Wills and Codicils heretofore made by me.
Article 1.
1.1 - I direct payment of my debts, funeral expenses and

expenses for administration of my estate.
Article 2.
2.1 - I give the rest of my estate to my three silly girls...."

Crystal and Gwen were weeping again. In the preparation of his will, despite all the legal language, everyone in the room could hear his voice and the warmth of his personality in every word.

"The current value of this estate is roughly five point eight million dollars and two properties: this brownstone and a property in London, Ontario. I am instructed to tell you girls the house in London is reputedly haunted." Mr. Dumount smiled at this last bit of intelligence that was so much like Jean-Claude with his love of teasing. The girls were smiling through their tears, as he was sure his friend intended.

As soon as the lawyer took his leave, the girls escaped down into the basement and the Brotherhood library. Later that evening, when their schoolmates began to arrive, April sent them down. Let the church object. Those girls needed more companionship right now than those mouldy old books could offer.

Looking up from the book, Crystal announced, "I know what we have to do to end the war with the Vampyres. But it will not be sanctioned by the Vatican, and you're not going to like it Drake."

"Name it and it's yours," he replied.

"You will have to recruit the best Goths there are."

"Consider them yours."

"No Drake," she warned. "I'm not just talking about from our Academy, or even from just the other twelve academies. I'm talking the best in the world, no matter who they are with."

She turned to her best friend. "Gwen, you will have to form your own coven with the strongest Wiccan girls we can find."

"But I'm not twenty-one yet," Gwen complained. "And I know there's going to be spiders. There's always spiders."

"Nevertheless," Crystal replied, and turned to the sylph. "And Kristen, you will have to give up your boys."

"My pretties!"

"And replace them with twelve others," she pointed to the lone vampyre in their group. "You can start with Brendon."

"Him," Kristen sniffed, "he's barely acceptable."

"But worth twenty of your pretties for what we have to do," Crystal supplied.

"And then," Drake pressed.

"And then we train and study until we are the best of the best. Stronger, tougher, smarter than any who have come before us."

"And then," Drake continued, knowing he had not yet heard the part he would not like.

"And then we must kill my father."

"Your right, I don't like it," Drake swore without anger. "Your father has got to be at least a major Demon Lord."

"No Drake, he's something worse than any minion of hell."

And then she told them his name.

Epilogue

"Your life is mine, Aiko."

"Have you finally come to kill me then?" Aiko replied, hiding her fear in the shadows.

The girl's smile was chill and feral. She had changed since they last spoken, become more powerful like an elemental force of nature.

"Why destroy a perfectly good tool. You will be the instrument of my vengeance."

"I do not kill my own," Aiko hedged.

"Come, Aiko," the other taunted. "The lie does not become you. I know your name, Aiko, and your scent. There is no place in this world or the next you can hide from me."

"Hai."

"You will take a blood oath to obey me," the girl slit her hand and extended it. "Come Aiko, take the crystal raven. It's time for you to join the Ghost Sisterhood."

-30-

Chateau Clique

Available at Amazon September 2012

1

An unmarked car raced along Fanshawe Park Road. Its driver stared out of the windshield at a dawn touched with fog, at a lonely stretch of road with little or no traffic, at a perfect setting for a B movie or a life that had fallen into a rut. Bleary-eyed with exhaustion, Detective Sergeant Michael Harrow raised a mickey of vodka – a little hair of the bitch that was still riding him. He watched the highway dividers flash by like the chalk outlines that marked his profession. Fresh from a shower whose chill still gripped his bones, he sped towards another murder scene, another in a series of crimes that dominated his personal horizon and was creating a myopia that threatened to shut out the world.

He cruised through a tunnel formed by clouds and dirty snow. The landscape matched Harrow's mood – a little dirty, gritty, and ass-butt ugly. He should have stayed home last night, should have kept his drinking private and avoided both the dust up and what he suspected was either a case of the crabs or bed bugs. At one time the drive out to a crime scene would have sent his pulse racing with an excitement inspired by the Hardy Boy novels of his youth, and later nurtured by the stories of Agatha Christie and Arthur Conan Doyle. Today, he just wanted to pull over and puke.

His eyes returned to the hypnotic blur of the highway dividers. Reminiscent of the outlines of humanity's cruelty, the resonance of the moment shook loose a bitterness that settled into the pit of his stomach. Beneath his gaze a scowl touched his lips as he turned off the highway. The clothes that complimented these eyes, a battered fedora and a nondescript leather jacket, gave their owner a look somewhere between a Hollywood detective and a wino. Pale skin and dark hair framed his eyes and lent him a wraith-like appearance, completing a look better suited for the morgue than the city streets.

He tracked the commotion outside his vehicle as it pulled up behind a patrol car. Less than twenty minutes ago a call from dispatch had shot Harrow out to this concession road on the outskirts of London. Now he looked on at the charred remains of the city's most gruesome murder in twenty years. He paused, listening to his idling engine as he collected his initial impressions of the crime scene.

'Fuck am I hurting. And those twats give me a stranger on stranger murder,' he swore. Self-doubt ate at him like a parasite. He fit into the London Police Force like a nun in a whore house, and he knew if not for his record of solved cases the powers-that-be would have turfed him out years ago. He cursed his own failings for bringing him to this time and place, to the beginnings of a murder case that, without a break, would head straight to the Cold Squad. Yet his curses were half-hearted. He was only going through the motions, knowing that once the forensic anthropologist had identified their victims he and his partner would needlessly seek a motive amongst the friends and relatives of the dead. Needlessly, because his instincts and frustration screamed at him that he faced another Linda Shaw, another unsolved roadside slaying like the one that had broken when he had first joined the force.

Maybe, with good karma and a rabbit's foot he could catch a break, solve this case and not find himself tossed off the force without a pension. And maybe the Pope would get drunk on sacramental wine and declare him a saint. His pocket full of miracles had a hole in it, his bottle was empty, and he now faced a challenge that would test his mettle as a detective at a time when he felt he had reached the nadir of his career. 'Fuck it! This is hurt balls.' Harrow chucked the empty bottle into the back seat, searched the glove compartment for his emergency stash, then rifled through the empties in the back of his car looking for a swallow. Definitely hurt balls.

Amidst the budget cuts and political upheaval that currently rocked the force he found that he just didn't care anymore. His depression was one symptom of a growing morale problem amongst civic employees, who faced wage rollbacks and the layoff of twenty officers when the recent annexation of outlying areas had left the force severely short-handed. This wasn't fucking Mayberry, and he wasn't Andy Griffin. No-one said they had to like his ass to be a good cop. Nor had this job ever promised him a hard-on, or even a life – if he didn't find himself suspended, and had enough coin at the end of the week for a bottle, he figured he just about broke even.

Through the windshield he watched an uniformed officer struggling to hold back a crowd of reporters. Sheryl Frontinac stood in their midst like an apostle of the Apocalypse. A journalist from the local television station, Type-A personality, conspiracy theorist, and cold stone bitch, her presence typified his morning so far. His hangover had not even caught up with him yet, and now the nightmare with a microphone. He lacked the energy to face both her and a gristly murder scene. A somewhat reclusive individual, Detective Sergeant Harrow hated reporters even before the acrimonious debate over the cuts to the police budget had strained the relationship between the media and the police. Now his hatred was pathological.

'And they wonder why the sight of them makes me puke,'

he scowled angrily. 'Blackfriar and his rag empire led the smear campaign that gutted the department, and now we're suppose to kiss and make up? Fuck that noise!' Every officer on the force dreamed of finding some dirt on the local media mogul, and their rancour extended to his front line soldiers- the reporters, columnists, and editors of his newspaper, television and radio stations. Already miserable, Harrow watched the scene unfolding outside his car with growing irritation. His drunk was wearing thin, dozens of vehicles and feet had contaminated his crime scene, and the Chief wanted them to make nice with these vultures. Fuck!

He turned off his ignition with a grunt and opened his door. The acrid odour of raw gasoline and charred flesh tickled his nostrils. He fought the sensation struggling to overwhelm him, a volcanic eruption of memory dredged from the darkest corner of his own personal hell...

Wiccan Apotropaic

Available from Amazon November 2012

Chapter 1

"Scramble! Scramble! Scramble!"

Drake's bark sent them pelting off in a dozen directions. Crystal fled across the nightscape, her weight bowing a narrow board stretched across two rooftops. She raced through a surreal kaleidoscope of flashes of shadows, snatches of sound and fragments of smells. Footsteps echoed in the darkness, spurring her to speed. Senses stretched taut she felt the night, every second expecting a cry of discovery that would not come. Her pursuers would pounce in perfect silence.

It was called Death Tag and the Goths played it across the rooftops of New York City. Somewhere the chasers from Razor's pack were out there hunting. Speed and balance were all that mattered here in the night. That, and protecting your colours, a strip of rag attached to her back like the flag used in football. Only a fall here wasn't as pleasant as a tumble onto the soft grass of a field. Not by a long shot, Crystal thought as she leapt out into the darkness, praying the far roof was there to meet her.

"Watch out!" Gwen cried.

Crystal barely managed to roll out of the way before Gwen leapt across to her side.

"We're busted!" She squealed. "Cantara's after us!"

"Shit! Ollie! Ollie! Oxen Free!"

Far worse than meeting a vampyre when you were out two hours past curfew was a run in with Cantara. Especially when Crystal had dragged Aiko along with them. The vampyre was not Cantara's favourite person, although Crystal was rapidly replacing her on Cantara's list of people she would like to drop off a steep cliff. Her habit of breaking curfew in more imaginative ways was giving the djinn fits. Like now.

Simply splitting up was not as much of a tactic. Not in this game of cat and mouse, and not when their pursuer knew exactly where they were heading, and only needed to lurk in ambush at a position overlooking their few means of entrance – namely the back fire-escape. Unlike Aiko, Crystal and Gwen could not become a mist, and shamelessly pretend to have been asleep in their rooms after drifting unseen past their hunter. Sighing in resignation, Crystal accepted that getting caught was as much a part of the adventure as flinging yourself blindly off a roof. Sometimes you had to make a leap of faith, praying the far roof was there to meet you and not the long drop to the cement of the alley below.

Crystal was trapped and she knew it. Cantara was following her, but at a lazy pace that kept her between Crystal and the brownstone. Ever since waking up that night in Upyr - that night Jean-Claude had died - Crystal hated feeling helpless. She lost all reason, succumbing to blind panic that drove her into a rage. Anger lent her eyes a tinge of red and she hissed in frustration. Anger also brought the nightscape into sharper focus, her inner demon collating scents, sounds and sights at a faster rate, analyzing her various options in between heart beats. There was one way she could get behind

Cantara, but it was risky. She would need to make the leap of her life from one side of the street to the other, and then hide out in the shadows.

Biting her lip, Crystal moved to the edge of the building and looked down. It was a long bloody way down, and bloody and broken is the way she would end up if she missed. More and more she was testing herself lately, pushing the boundaries of her possible and stretching her abilities to new limits. It was like there were two of her – one an almost normal girl, and a second consumed by the pranic energies of more than two thousand vampyre with almost god-like powers. And there was just no way to control which of the two would show up tonight, at this moment when she most needed her inner demon.

She backed up a dozen steps and took a running start. 'Shit,' Crystal thought to herself as she leapt into the darkness, 'why the hell can't succubi fly.' She kept her eyes glued to the darker
blackness that she hoped was the far rooftop. The sensation of flight gave her a mild sense of exhilaration right until the rooftop rushed up and smacked her in the chin. As she hung half off and half on the far roof, the old adage about biting off more than you can chew transformed itself into something about leaping towards something further than you flew. Nervous laughter almost dislodged her from her perch.

"How do you like those apples?" She gloated as she clung to the safety of the rooftop. "You may be a djinn, Cantara, but I'm a full fledge succubus just coming into her power."

Scrambling with her feet, she managed to inch herself up over the rooftop just as Cantara came into sight. Lying perfectly still, Crystal watched as the djinn stopped on the far side of the street, looking in two directions. She turned left back towards the brownstone they shared, and Crystal knew the race was on. It all came down to who reached the rear window first, and Crystal had the advantage. She was on the right side of the street. Cantara would have to climb down and race for the door, and then up one flight of stairs. And she knew she was faster than her opponent. Okay, she wouldn't have time to change, and that would make it harder to fake that she was asleep, but she could put on her IPod and just pretend she had not heard Cantara calling.

Or she could climb up into the attic and hide out for the rest of her life. Only the brownstone did not have an attic. Friggin' lousy architects, she swore bitterly as she raced across the rooftops, imagine not anticipating a teenage girl's need to hide from her angry guardians. It was an outrage.

She arrived at the brownstone moments before Cantara. Damn that djinn was fast! Fortunately the race across the rooftops had given Gwen time to get home ahead of her. She could see the basement window was closed and locked. Slipping in through the second story window to her own bedroom, she closed and locked it, then opened one of her text books and slipped on her earphones. Seconds later, Cantara entered the room.

"Where have you been?"

"What?" Crystal replied, pretending she had not heard her and removing the buds from her earphones. "I've been here all night, studying."

"And do you always read Greek upside down?" Cantara asked sarcastically, turning the book right-side up.

Just then April came up with a sulking Gwen in tow.

"Sit there, both of you!" She instructed, pointing at the two girls and then the bed. "It's time we had a little discussion about your nocturnal activities."

Crystal had never seen April so angry. She didn't even try to deny that they had been out past curfew, and neither did Gwen.

"There are still thousands of vampyres lurking in and about New York," April sighed, exasperated. "It is still dangerous out there, and we cannot allow you and your friends to be running around half the night. What do you think you were up to?"

"That's why we need to train," Crystal tried to explain.

"And that's what the school is for," April countered. "And why you both should be in bed hours ago."

"It's not enough," Crystal muttered. 'Not for what we need to do,' she added to herself.

The fall of Upyr was not the strategic victory it had at first seemed. Vampyres, families and sometimes whole clans, were scattering across North America and down into Mexico. Tracking so many flights was not only difficult, it was impossible with the limited resources at hand. The Vatican had to recall the Choir and most of its specialists as the crisis spread from North America to the four other inhabited continents, leaving only Cantara and three other specialists behind to watch over Crystal.

"And speaking of sleeping," April decided to broach the subject tonight, dealing with all their problems in one talk. It was time for the girls to move on from their grieving. "It's time we allow Cantara to move into the second room."

"No!" Crystal whirled and threw her jacket off in a random direction. "That's Jean-Claude's room!"

"Crystal," April soothed, gently. The girls were still both struggling with the loss of Jean-Claude. "Cantara can't sleep on the couch forever."

"Whatever!" Crystal stormed, but she knew that April was right. It had been almost five months since Jean-Claude had died.

"We'll pack his stuff up this weekend," April offered, "Just Gwen, you and me."

"Cantara can help too I guess," Crystal countered in a voice that was a little too snotty even for her ears.

As long as the room was left the way it had been on the night Jean-Claude had died, it felt as if he were only out for the evening, as if he would be coming back at any moment. The moment they packed up his stuff Crystal knew she would have to face that he was never coming back. How many times had she gone through the various stages of grieving in her life? It never got any easier. She seemed to return to this world only to grieve over and over again for loved ones she would never see again. Crystal doubted there was enough pieces left of her heart to ever be touched by love again, but it would come like a thief in the night when her guard was down, and with it the pain would wash over her soul.

"It's late," April concluded, "we'll talk about this more tomorrow."

Their morning routine had expanded in the wake of the collapse of Upyr. Sleepy from their shortened nights, one of the two girls stumbled downstairs each morning to let Aiko out of her cell. Shortly after dressing, the vampyre would lead them on a grueling two mile run. Returning to the brownstone, they showered and headed out to the Academy, all before sunrise.

The pace was brutal, but Crystal was not willing to let up. Four or five hours of sleep a night, pushing herself and her friends both mentally and physically – punishing herself for the death of Jean-Claude. She wanted to move Aiko from the cell to the Academy, like Brendan, to free up more time for training and was annoyed by Gabriel and Cantara's interference. Strangely, Crystal did not blame the vampyre for her part in the battle of Upyr. She knew the fault lay with her, knew he had fallen victim to a personal feud that had been brewing for centuries before his birth. She and her lover, Vlad the Impaler, leaders of the Church resistance against the vampyres during the Long Night of the Vampyres, had crossed the Romanov's and earned their hatred and bitterness. Not even Vlad Romanovs death would end this blood feud.

Today's run took them down along the Hudson River. Crystal let her thoughts drift, keeping time with the thump of her running shoes on the tarmac, blocking out everything but the rhythm of her breathing and the ache in her legs. Sunrise was still two hours away, and her surroundings were a series of silhouettes against the lighter black of the fading night. She could feel her exhaustion pull at the edges of her awareness, and ignored it. Months with only a few hours sleep was beginning to take its toll. But she would not let up.

He was out there. The one responsible for all her suffering. And her final solution would end everything. The vampyres, him, and herself.

Catching her second wind, Crystal raced Gwen and Aiko back to the brownstone.

"Last one there does dishes for the next month!" Crystal cried, sprinting ahead of the other two.

"No fair!" Gwen complained.

For a human she was fast, but when those two got their inner demons going there was no catching them. Even full out, she would fall behind by a block or two.

"First one there has to kiss the Toad!" She cried in desperation, watching Aiko and Crystal disappear around the corner.

Crystal was making breakfast and Aiko was in the shower when Gwen caught up to them. The vampyre had a disconcerting habit of walking around nude –not so bad as it sounded in a household full of women, except for her perfect body. Talk about rubbing it in! Lithe and muscular, with full breaths and soft curves, not skinny and gawky like Gwen's figure. Still, Gwen hated to have to remind her to put on clothes before leaving the apartment and making her way down to the cell. There was two men in the building – Angel and Alvaro – and the outside door was not always locked.

Gwen began peeling off her sweats when she heard the shower stop. She had no intention of taking a shower last, when the hot water was iffy, and slipped into the bathroom while Aiko was still toweling herself off.

"Hey!" Crystal complained, good-naturedly.

"You snooze, you lose," Gwen giggled, stepping into the shower.

"Just for that I'm spitting in your coffee!" Crystal threatened.

"You do and I'll put itching powder in your bras!"

Aiko lifted her eyes in disgust. Such girlish banter had never been part of her life. It was too sweet for her temperament, and threats were a waste of breath. Much easier just to rip the other's throat out and be done with it. With a towel wrapped around her waist, and a second on her head, she walked out into the kitchen to accept a glass of blood from Crystal. Cantara had woken up, and was now stumbling around the kitchen, hunting for a cup of coffee. The two women eyed each other with distrust.

"Dress in Crystal's room today, would you?" She complained to Aiko. "You're giving Angel fits."

Aiko raised an eye and padded down the hall to the bedroom. These gaijin had strange hang-ups, and little honour.

"It would be better if you let her live at the school," Crystal suggested. "Or at least up here with us."

"And where would she sleep?" Cantara countered.

"On the couch, as soon as you move into the other room. Not that vampyres sleep anyway," Crystal replied. She wouldn't call it Jean-Claude's room, not when they were forcing her to give it to someone else.

"I don't see how you can trust her," Cantara commented, scowling down at her coffee.

"I know her true name," Crystal replied with her customary answer, and then thought better of it. "She has given me a blood oath on a Wiccan crystal."

"Crystal!" Cantara choked on her coffee.

"I need her," Crystal caught and held the djinn's eye, "and you know why."

Aiko emerged from the bedroom dressed in black leather pants, Doc Martins, and a black silk blouse. It was only thirty minutes until dawn, and she would remain at the Academy until sunset. While she read and wrote several languages, she had never received any formal education. She was not sure if she liked it.

"I must leave now," Aiko interrupted the other two.

"Gwen and I will be along in about an hour," Crystal replied. "We'll meet you in the library."

An hour later the Ghost Sisterhood met at the Academy's library, gathering around a set of tables in the back corner. Most of their actual research took place in the Brotherhood Archives hidden in the basement of the brownstone. These morning sessions were about sharing news, brainstorming, and gossip.

Morgana opened the meeting. "Drake has a line on a flight of vampyres. Eight to ten."

"Are they the ones who killed the two prostitutes?" Kristen asked, her face wrinkling in distaste. Despite the flock of boys she kept dangling on a string, she was rather prudish – much to the amusement of her friends.

"We think so," Morgana shrugged. Unless caught with their fangs in the neck, as saying went, there was no real way to know which vampyre had drained which victim.

"Any sign of Delph?" Crystal asked, hunger tingeing her
features.

It was scary, Gwen thought, how blood-thirsty her friend had become since the nightmare in Upyr. Although she was not sure if she blamed her. During the interim between Crystal's human incarnations, the vampyres of Upyr under Lord Vlad Blackheart Romanov had hunted down and slain all of her kind. Being the last Succubus in creation was like being an orphan. She had materialized to become the victim of a brutal attack that had left her broken and near death. Rescued by Jean-Claude, a monk from a secret order within the Catholic Church charged with tracking demon incursions on Earth, Crystal had recovered from her injuries. Through the efforts of this same monk she had enjoyed the first taste of childhood in her long life, making friends with a group of girls, her homies, and starting a romantic, although platonic relationship with a boy. She had even managed not to seduce and consume the soul of her rescuer.

And then one night that childhood had exploded. Lord Vlad and a demon, Shax, conspired to kill the last succubus. They had managed to kidnap and drag her deep under New York's streets to the secret vampyre enclave of Upyr. There her story would have ended except that Shax planned to double cross-his allies.

That night the whole world almost came to an end. If not for the sacrifice of Jean-Claude humanity would be months into the beginnings of Armageddon, and Crystal would have become the key to the gates of Hell. Her friend had become dark and cold since his death, Gwen mused, more the demon than the girl who had become like the sister Gwen had never had. She wondered what price Crystal's loss of humanity would demand of both their futures. More and more she was becoming a driven stranger who thought only in terms of revenge.

And could any of them really condone the genocide she was contemplating?

"Nothing." Morgana replied. "Not even a hint that he's still alive."

"Okay," Crystal decided. "We won't report this nest to the Brotherhood. It will be a good test of our training."

"Drake," Morgana started. She was going to suggest he would not like it, but that was the old Drake, the one who had died along with Jean-Claude so many months ago. The war was changing them all and she was no longer sure if she liked it.

"Can plan it out with Gwen," Crystal finished. "Only we better wait until the weekend."

"We were so busted last night," Gwen concluded, "that out great grandchildren will be up to their necks in it."

"It's getting pretty deep at my house too," Morgana complained. "Mom thinks I'm screwing around, and threatened to send me to the clinic for a pregnancy test."

"Well, aren't you?" Gwen teased, dodging a thrown

notebook.

"Only in my dreams," Morgana moaned, and the group broke up in a cloud of laughter.

Made in the USA
Charleston, SC
09 December 2012